Published by: OK

Copyright

GW01451659

Cover & Layout Designed by OK62 Publishing

Also available from the same Author:

Preface

All the characters detailed in this pulsating conclusion of 'Shug's story' have permitted me, once again, to record a variety of events which they were involved in, and for that I am eternally grateful.
Oh, and did I change their names for legal reasons?
of course I did.

◇◇◇◇◇◇◇

Acknowledgements
A debt of thanks is owed to my long-suffering wife, my family and my friends. Without you, I would never have written these books.

Respect x,

Ochil Kinnaird

Chapter 1

I counted more than fifty bikes as we poured out of the city and onto the motorway. Up ahead I could barely see Indie, he was driving like a madman, within minutes, we were all struggling to keep up.

After some real crazy riding, taking chance after chance, we arrived at the farm. I think this was the first time we had done it in less than 30 minutes. As I turned down the lane, I had a quick look ahead then behind me. There must have been at least a mile between Indie and the last bike to arrive, he hadn't half given it laldy all the way back.

Heading down the lane I got to the sharp corner where Rooster and I had crashed. I got a bit of a cold shiver, so I made sure I slowed down to take it, the last thing I wanted was a repeat performance. When I straightened up, I could see that Indie was off his bike and already making his way into the farm.

I stopped in front of the steps and parked up. Looking around I was surprised to see so few bikes, I kind of expected 'everybody and their Grannies' to be here, waiting on our arrival.

I went inside and could hear Indie roaring at the top of his voice. Angel was trying to calm him down but was having little success. I approached him and stupidly asked him if he was okay.

"Okay? O-fuckin'-k? Do I look like I'm o-fuckin'-k?" he screeched at me.

I held my hands up in front of me gesturing for him to back-off and said, "Hey listen, man, whatever the fuck's eating you - don't fuckin' take it out on me!

To which he replied, "Well, don't ask such a st fuckin' question then!"

He gave me a bit of a stare, shook his head, about turned then walked towards the office without saying another word. I watched as he entered and slammed the door behind him.

I looked at Angel and asked her what the fuck his problem was. She told me just to leave it and that she'd fill me in later. She grabbed my hand, gave it a bit of a squeeze, smiled then made her way to the office. Unlike Indie, she closed the door quietly behind herself.

I just shook my head as I started making my way towards the kitchen, mumbling and cursing Indie under my breath. As I walked in, I saw Rooster and straightaway I knew he had caught the tail end of my spat with Indie.

"What the fuck's going on, Shug?"

"Honestly, Rooster, I don't have a fuckin' clue. I saw Indie looking really pissed I asked him if he was ok and he blew a fuckin' gasket, started ranting and raving at me, then stormed off into the office and slammed the door."

"You think I should go and have a word with him, Shug?"

"Please your-fuckin'-self, Rooster. Do what the fuck you like. But me, I'm keeping well the fuck out of his way!" I told him.

I went back outside just in time to see the stragglers arrive. Cowboy and Flick were standing at the steps with DD, discussing the ride back. I lit up a smoke and joined them. The consensus was that Indie definitely had a death wish by the way he was riding.

We were laughing and joking about the dodgy moments we all had trying to keep up with him. We then started taking the piss out of the last two, who had arrived a good few minutes after everyone else.

As we shared our lighthearted banter, I told them about Indie having a go at me and this led to a lengthy discussion about what we all thought was up with him.

As we mulled it over another dozen bikes arrived. It was the rest of the Central guys who hadn't managed to come down south.

One of them was Scribe. I went over to catch up with him, hoping he might know a little bit more about what had happened up north. He pretty much told us the same as Indie. However, the one thing that he did tell me that I didn't know, was that Mark was now back with the Bats.

"Mark! You're talking about Mark, my neighbour Mark, Scooter's brother? Aye, gid yin, Scribe, you're takin' the pish now," I told him, as I started to laugh.

"No. Straight up, Shug. After he lost his kid, he went off the rails a bit and his Mrs. left him. The next thing he's in my shop getting another tat. Telling me he was back with the Bats and that this time it was for good."

"Holy shit, man. I can't believe it. Mark back with the Bats! I never thought in a million years that would happen. I think I only heard him talking about being in the Bats once or twice in all the time I've known him. The one thing I do remember him telling me though was that he never actually became a full patch member. Do you think that means he'll need to Prospect again?"

"Nah. No way, Shug. Mark was already offered his Colours. The only reason he didn't take them was because his burd was knocked up and he had some real serious family shit going on at the time. I'm pretty sure Indie will give them to him straightaway. You see, what happened back then Shug, was that Scooter and Mark were both Prospects at the same time and their father developed dementia. He quickly deteriorated and had started hitting their mother. He became very unpredictable, so someone needed to look out for her. Mark decided that it would be best if he did it. He was already in a relationship and planned to get married, so he felt it made sense for him to walk away from the club.

Provo told him at the time that he would always consider him a Bat. Anytime he felt he wanted to come back, he would welcome him with open arms. Mark's mum died shortly afterwards, and his dad's condition had deteriorated further. It became so bad he ended up getting sectioned and put into hospital. Mark then got married and decided he no longer wanted to be a Bat and well, you know the rest."

Fuck me, another one with a story to tell. The more I heard the more I thought to myself that the farm was just like one big fuckin' orphanage for adults.

"So, do you know where Mark is now, Scribe? Is he here?"

"Yep, he certainly is, Shug. Well, he was half an hour ago when I left to round up the troops ..." he said, pointing in the direction of the barn. "He was in there, fuckin' about with his bike. I'm guessing he'll still be there."

I shook hands with Scribe and thanked him for filling me in then made my way towards the barn. As I walked, I thought about all the times Mark told me to get out, or at least be really careful with what I got involved in, and here he was, doing the very same thing he tried to get me to avoid.

All I could think of was how really settled and happy Mark seemed to be with his life then bang, one thing happens to you and your life changes forever. It seemed that almost every one of the Bats had a similar tale to tell.

Then it dawned on me that Scribe had told me he was messing about with his bike. Fuck. In all the time I'd known him he never once mentioned that he still had a bike! It just shows you. You think you know someone pretty well, but actually you don't know jack-shit.

I went into the barn and saw him kneeling in front of a bike. I shouted over to him and he turned around to see me and gave me a bit of a nod.

"Hi. Mark. How's things, man?" I asked him, offering out my hand for him to shake.

"Ach, you know, Shug, getting there, man," he told me as we shook.

"Sorry I missed your kid's funeral, man. I would have been there if I'd known when it was," I explained to him.

"I know you would, Shug, but under the circumstances we just wanted it to be a really small thing, immediate family only. You know the script."

I could see the tears welling up in his eyes so thought it best to change the subject.

"Are you heading up north with us?" I asked.

"Sure am. Just need to finish changing the oil then I'll be ready to go," he told me, turning back to his bike.

He knelt back down and carried on 'spannering away'. I told him I was heading outside and would catch him later. He just gave me another bit of a nod as I left.

Rooster was still standing outside chatting with a few guys. I got hold of him and asked if he knew what was up with Indie. He told me he didn't, as he was still in the office, but that Jelly, Hotwire and Brutis were now in there with him.

"Not sure what's going on, Shug. I've spoken to some of the guys who've just arrived, and they said nothing's happened around here since we left. I reckon it must all be to do with the North Chapter."

I decided it would be best to hang around outside for bit and wait till someone came out to tell us what the fuck was going on. I noticed Cowboy and Flick were standing chatting with Gunner, DD and Freddie and remembered Cowboy still hadn't told me what Indie said to them after their spat.

I walked over to them making a mental note to ask him about it later.

Just as I approached them, the house door swung open and Indie shouted, "Everybody, barn, five minutes," then went back inside, slamming the door, nearly taking it off its hinges.

'Ah well, not long now till we find out what the fuck's going on,' I thought to myself, as I began making my way back to the barn.

Rooster caught up with me on the way and said, "Fuck me, Shug. He's still in one stinker of a fuckin' mood, is he not!"

"Aye, isn't he just. And you know as well as me, whenever he's got the hump, there's always fuckin' trouble brewing," I reminded him, which got me a nod of approval.

We went into the barn and straight over to Mark and saw he was just finishing up.

"Is that you good to go then, big fella?" I asked.

"Fuckin hope so, Shug, 'cause it looks like I don't have time to do anything else to it," he said, nodding in the direction of the door.

I turned around and saw Indie coming in with his posse in tow.

"I guess you're right," I agreed, "He looks like a man on a mission. Oh, by the way, any idea when you're likely to get your Colours?" I asked him, in a whispered tone.

"Not sure. Indie told me I'd get them when he came back from down south, but I don't think I'll bother asking him 'til we're done with all this shit."

I told him I thought that was a wise move and that I had always found it best to keep out of his way when he was in a mood like this.

Chapter 2

Indie jumped up onto some crates and roared at the top of his voice, "Right! Shut that fuckin' door and listen up! We have one major fuckin' problem on our hands and I need to speak to all the officers now. Just so you know, we won't be heading up north 'til first thing tomorrow morning - if you need to do anything, now's the time to do it. I want everyone back here by eight o'clock sharp and ready to go. Remember, there's no fuckin' excuses and no fuckin' exceptions."

With that, he jumped back down off the crates and shouted, "All Officers, Conservatory," then stormed out.

Gunner approached him as he headed to the door and asked him if he meant the South officers as well. Indie let rip at him.

"Jesus fuckin' Christ, Gunner! How many fuckin' times do I need to say things! Right, listen the fuck up, I'll say it again for the hard of fuckin' thinking.

"You're a fuckin' officer, aren't you?" he screeched at Gunner, who just nodded, looking decidedly uncomfortable.

"I did say all the fuckin' officers, didn't I? So, you tell me what bit of 'all the fuckin' officers' you didn't fuckin' understand."

Fuck. While he was ranting away, he was that close to Gunner I swear he could've bitten his nose off. When he'd finished his tirade, he just shook his head and mumbled under his breath as he made his way to the door.

After he'd left, Gunner tried to make light of it by saying, "Well, that's me put in my place. Best I get a fuckin' move on. Don't want him to have a heart attack shouting at me for being late as well."

Then he also headed out, making his way towards the house.

I was now in a bit of a quandary. I was going to ask Indie the same question, but now I had no fuckin' idea what to do. I didn't want to go in and be told to fuck off, but I also didn't want him to go off his nut because I didn't show. I decided the best course of action was to follow them. Try to get some eye contact from Indie so I could gauge his reaction at me being there. I approached the conservatory just behind Rooster and realised I was the last to enter.

Thankfully, I didn't actually need to say anything because Indie looked straight at me and said, "Well Shug, anytime you're ready, shut the fuckin' door." So, with a bit of relief, I did exactly that, thinking 'Thank fuck I never needed to ask him anything'.

"Right, guys, we have a major problem up north. The bastards have smashed up the clubhouse again and given our brothers a proper kicking. Four of them had to be treated in fuckin' hospital and apparently some of their injuries are pretty bad. The ones who're not in hospital aren't too fuckin' clever either. The bastards set Ammo on fire as revenge for what we did to their President. He's one of the four in hospital and the worst out of everyone. I don't really have much more to tell you. All I do know is that they've told us we better stay away or else they'll start a war, so if that's what the bastards really want then they're just about to fuckin' get it."

'Holy fuck! It just gets worse and worse' I thought to myself.

I was brought back from my thoughts with a nudge from Rooster. I realised Indie was focusing the discussion directly at us.

"Rooster, Shug, I want you to get around everybody and find out if anyone is missing and, if so, go fuckin' get them. Grab Flick and Cowboy and tell them to help."

He then started dishing out specific orders to the others and within five minutes, we were all leaving the conservatory and beginning to follow his instructions. The last thing he said was that Brutis was taking the rest of the North guys back up the road, straightaway. They would check out what the fuck was happening but wouldn't do anything until we all arrived the next day.

Rooster and I then caught up with Cowboy and Flick and between us we agreed how we would all do our bit. We split up, all heading towards different areas. I had the outside. Cowboy covered the Barn and the other two had inside the house. Looking around I saw there were a few pockets of people scattered about. Some seemed to be just chatting, others were farting about with bikes and the rest were getting ready to split. I spoke first of all to the guys who were just about to leave and asked them to wait a bit, until I touched base with the rest.

By the time I'd got around them all I had a good picture of who wasn't there. I arranged for the guys that were leaving to give them a chap on the way home. I reckoned, if we were lucky, there were only another four or five who needed to be chased up.

When the guys left, I stuck my head in the barn to see how Cowboy was getting on. He told me he was done so we made our way back to the house to hook up with the other two.

The first person we clocked was Flick. He was sitting at the kitchen table staring into space, nursing a beer.

"You done, man?" I asked him.

"Yep, sure am," he told me.

"Well come on then, spit it out. How many more have you got?" Cowboy asked him.

"Never got a single person, not fuckin' one. Seems everyone who's able is already here," he told him.

Just then, Rooster joined us and asked the same question we did. Turned out Rooster had only managed to identify two people who weren't here either. When he phoned them, he found out one was nursing a broken leg and the other was working away from home.

Cowboy said he had possibly got three and that a couple of the guys were going to chase them up. 'Fuck me!' I thought to myself. All we had managed to identify from everyone was seven extra people. Seven poxy fuckin' people, and who the fuck knew if any of them were actually able to come. So much for rounding up the reinforcements!

We then all agreed that it would be best if only one of us went to see Indie, considering the mood he was in. Much to his disappointment the three of us voted unanimously for that person to be Rooster. Judging by the look he gave us it was obvious he wasn't best pleased to be the nominated person.

"Ok, I'll do it, ya shower of shite bags. But remember, you all fuckin' owe me one," he moaned.

We all just laughed while nodding in agreement as he turned tail and made his way to the conservatory.

Chapter 3

The three of us tried to work out how many guys we would actually have for the run but couldn't really agree. We reckoned it would be anything from forty to sixty

When Rooster came back and told us that Indie was still behaving like a madman it didn't really surprise me. He said that Indie was still well pissed and after he told him about the numbers we were looking at, he was even more fucked off.

He said that all the time they spoke he was pacing the floor, inhaling really deeply on his cigarette and looked like he was going to spontaneously combust if he didn't calm the fuck down.

At that point we actually burst out laughing even though we knew how serious the situation was. Eventually we all agreed the laughter was much more to do with how Rooster told us rather than what he actually said.

The worrying thing for me though was that I always thought Indie was very good at keeping his emotions in check. Now, seeing him like this, I had real concerns that he was going to have us all doing something really fuckin' mental. That wasn't something I was looking forward to.

Indie summoned all the officers back to the conservatory, but this time he included Rooster and excluded me. Initially I was a bit miffed I wasn't invited, but deep down I was pretty relieved.

He had them in for around an hour or so before the doors opened again. After his talk with the officers he went straight into the office, closed the door and apparently never left there the whole night.

What he did have though was his officers running around like headless chickens for fuck knows what.

Some of the guys were probing the officers trying to find out what was going on, but none of them would crack a light. Cowboy, Flick and I all had a go at getting Rooster to spill the beans, but he said it was more than his life was worth to say anything.

The rest of the night was pretty quiet. All the guys who stayed were just mulling around having a beer and talking about what they thought would happen the next day.

I spent a bit of time chatting with some of the South guys during the evening and it was pretty clear to me that most of them were shitting themselves. I think if they had known that they would end up getting involved in this type of shit so soon, they would have run a mile.

I eventually decided to dip out and crashed on one of the couches around midnight.

Next morning, I was up just after seven and by then the biggest majority of people were already getting organised for our trip. For the next half hour or so there was a steady stream of bikes arriving.

I grabbed myself a cup of tea and went out to see who was there. Just as I opened the door, I was a bit surprised to see Indie arriving on his bike.

I was sure that when I went to sleep the night before I noticed that he was still in the office. I had no idea if he had left late last night or early this morning, but either way, he was still looking like a man with the weight of the world on his shoulders.

He parked up his bike and made his way towards the door, as he brushed past me, he said, "Shug, Tell everybody I want them in the barn in the next five minutes, ok?" then headed inside.

I stood where I was and shouted to anyone that was listening.

"Hey, guys, Indie wants everybody in the barn in the next five minutes."

Then I made my way inside repeating the message in every room. Cowboy got hold of me as I was going back out and asked me if I had been told anything, but I assured him I knew no more than he did.

We went into the barn and I noticed it was filling up pretty sharpish, there was a kind of buzz about the place - which was probably caused by the amount of whispering going on.

By the time Indie and the officers came in, the place was bursting at the seams.

I was standing pretty close to the South guys and I could see that the biggest majority of them were really agitated and still shitting themselves waiting to find out what the fuck they were going to be doing. I kind of remembered that feeling, in fact I still got it at times like this, so I could sympathise with their plight.

Indie jumped up onto the crates and brought everybody to order.

"Right, guys, here's the fuckin' script. We'll be leaving in five minutes or so and I want you all to make sure you're tooled up before we leave. Anybody who needs anything - see Jelly and he'll sort you out.

"We're going to stop off at the North clubhouse first and see what the state of play is there. Then I'll fill you in with what's next. We'll stop at the first garage on the motorway and fuel up. Then no more stops 'til we get there.

"Oh, and if anybody tries to break our ranks on the way up, make sure you fuckin' waste them, ok?"

He then jumped down and headed out.

At that point, the rest of us made our way to our bikes and began tying our sleeping bags on and looking for the best places to attach our chibs.

My bike was sandwiched between Cowboy and Rooster's so, as we were getting sorted, I asked Rooster if there was anything he could tell us, but all he said was that we should make sure we take some decent weapons with us.

With all the bikes being fired up, you could hardly hear yourself think. I looked at Cowboy and asked him what he thought about Rooster's advice, but he just shrugged his shoulders.

By now, we were all ready and Indie led the procession up the lane. I was around about the middle of the pack - with DD next to me. Cowboy and Flick were just behind us, and Rooster was riding up front with the officers.

Chapter 4

This was by far the biggest turnout for a run I had ever been involved in, and to say it was a fearsome sight was an understatement. Just looking at the faces of the guys, you knew this was no jolly. I never saw a single smile from anyone the whole journey.

Indie pulled into the garage as promised and nearly everyone had to fill up. It must've taken a good 30 minutes for all of us to get done. Some people paid, others didn't, and a few guys helped themselves to stuff from the shop.

When we finally made our way out, you could actually see the relief on the two attendants faces. I don't think they really cared about who had and who hadn't paid for their fuel, they were just so glad to be rid of us.

Indie was sitting at the front of the slip road - waiting 'til we were all ready. Before he moved any further, he got a couple of guys to park themselves across the inside lane, allowing us all to get onto the motorway unimpeded. By the time I got onto the motorway, I noticed the cars in the other two lanes had stopped as well. Once we were all on, and the outriders had joined us, Indie moved into the middle lane and we all followed suit. It was a pretty strange ride, we were cruising around 70mph for most of the way, and at no time did anyone try to overtake us.

We turned off the motorway around twelve miles from our destination and as Indie slowed, heading up the slip road, the outriders he'd selected made their way past him up to the roundabout.

Two of them went on to the roundabout and stopped the oncoming traffic. The others sat in front of all the junctions to make sure we all stayed together and, again, there were absolutely no protests from any of the other road users.

As I entered the roundabout, I laughed away to myself thinking about what we were doing. We'd just stopped all the traffic in all directions. I don't know why, but this was something that always made me smile, even on such a shitty day as this.

Just knowing that we could do almost anything when we all rode together gave me a real sense of power and presence, like no other feeling I have ever experienced.

As we drew closer to the clubhouse, Indie turned off the road and headed in the opposite direction. I had no idea where he was going but guessed it must be part of his plan.

We ended up in a car park at the side of a loch and by the time we all parked up there was hardly a space to be seen. Three of the North chapter guys were waiting to greet us and immediately surrounded Indie as he got off his bike.

When we got there, there were a few cars in the car park and some people mulling around. Within minutes of our arrival they all moved on.

After his quick chat with the North guys, Indie got hold of the officers and started dishing out orders to them, sending them amongst us to pass on his instructions.

Rooster, and one of the North guys called Crookie, came over to the group I was with and explained what the script was for us.

"Right, guys, we've stopped here because Indie's had word that the clubhouse is being watched and he only wants a few of us to be seen arriving there. Your group is going to make their way to the clubhouse and everybody else is heading up north to wipe out the Cannibals."

Straightaway, DD questioned Rooster, asking him why the fuck he had to stay put instead of going with everyone else? Rooster drew him a right stare, telling him it was Indie's instructions, and if he wasn't happy about it then he should take it up with him, but that if he wasn't prepared to do that, then he should shut the fuck up. DD didn't even reply.

Rooster then sarcastically asked DD if it was all right to continue then started to tell us how we were going to play it.

"We know who, where and roughly how many are watching the clubhouse. When we get there, we'll make a bit of noise just to make sure they know we've arrived. We want to look like we're in party mode and hopefully we'll catch them off-guard. Crookie has already organised for some chicks and locals to arrive just after us, which should confirm our intentions to them. Once we get the call from Indie that they're at the Cannibals' clubhouse, we'll then set about the cunts who're watching us. Okay? Good. Let's get moving then."

Rooster then turned to Indie, giving him the thumbs up and Indie nodded back in his direction. I kicked my bike into life and instead of the usual disappointment I felt when I missed out on something all I felt this time was relief.

Indie's instruction to Rooster was for him to select ten of us to head to the clubhouse and I was glad he had picked me and the three guys I was most comfortable with.

Chapter 5

Rooster, Tosh and Scribe were in front, followed by Flick, Cowboy and me. Mark and Scooter were next, with Freddie and DD taking up the rear. As we made our way out to the road everybody exchanged nods with the guys who were left.

We then turned back on the main road and began making our way to the clubhouse. We were about two miles away from the clubhouse when we noticed four guys on bikes coming towards us and it was obvious that they were members of the Cannibals.

Rooster slowed us down a bit and as we passed them, we all exchanged stares and hand gestures. The four guys were smiling and laughing and looking pretty happy with themselves. We, on the other hand, remained stern faced and determined.

DD drew up beside me and started roaring, asking why we weren't going after them right now and I explained to him that we needed to stick to Indie's plan.

"Well, I think we should get the bastards right now," he moaned, still shouting.

I yelled back at him telling him to take it easy as he would get his hands on them soon enough, he just shook his head and slowed back to re-join Freddie.

I started thinking about DD for a bit and replayed in my mind how he reacted in certain circumstances and the more I thought about it the more I could see how similar he was to Malky.

It made me feel kind of sad, but also made me smile, all his impetuousness and impulsive behaviour and his 'couldn't give two fucks' attitude was exactly how Malky rolled with it.

When we arrived at the clubhouse, DD was off his bike like a shot. He made a beeline for Rooster, demanding that he explain why we hadn't attacked the Cannibals. Instead of explaining anything to him, Rooster just told him to shut the fuck up and get inside.

I could see DD was pissed with the answer he got. So before he said anything else, and with the help of Freddie, I dragged him away 'til Rooster disappeared.

"Fuck's sake, DD. I told you to let it go, man! What the fuck are you doing?"

"Listen, Shug, we should've grabbed the bastards and booted their cunts in there and then. But, oh no, instead, we let them waltz right past us, laughing away, giving us the bird. What kind of fuckin' pish is that?" he demanded me to tell him.

"Listen, DD, it's the kind of pish we were told to do, and you better start getting fuckin' used to it 'cause let me tell you: Indie isn't someone you want to argue with! Oh and, by the way, neither the fuck is Rooster, so come on, man, get a fuckin' grip of yourself, and chill out a bit.

"You'll get your chance to burst them soon enough, make no mistake about that, but for now you need to trust Indie, he's always spot-on when it comes to all this shit."

I put my arm around his shoulder and tried to get him to relax a bit.

"C'mon, man, take it easy, let's just go in and see the guys."

Freddie piped up, trying to lighten the mood even more.

"Hey, Shug, you know what his problem is don't you? He's tense as fuck because he needs a good shag

- but with a face like that there isn't a cunt anywhere I know that would let him, ha ha."

Still laughing, he put his arm around him and kissed him on the cheek, which made DD push him away, telling him to shut the fuck up. Then DD burst out laughing himself.

They then did the man / hug thing and DD suggested it was actually Freddie who couldn't get the chicks.

We all went into the Clubhouse, still laughing and joking, but very quickly stopped as the mood inside was anything but jovial. There was a real undercurrent of anger about the place and all the guys were looking pretty bashed up and very serious.

Rooster pulled DD aside and told him never to question him again in front of anybody or he would wipe him out, to which DD just nodded and mumbled an apology.

Rooster then headed over to where Brutis and a guy called Axe were standing and immediately got involved in discussions with them. Axe seemed to be doing a fair bit of the talking and I kind of guessed they were sharing the info they had on the Cannibals.

As I watched, I caught Brutis' eye and gave him a bit of a nod. He came over to us as we made our way to the bar and asked how we were doing. We exchanged some pleasantries for a couple of minutes, and I asked him who Axe was?

He told me he was one of the older members who'd been in jail for a while, but that he was now out and back in the fold.

"Axe was our VP before he went inside but decided to give up his post because of the length of his sentence."

He then quickly explained that the both of them were running things together until they sorted out the rest of the jail stuff.

DD asked him if he knew how many Cannibals were watching the clubhouse and he told him that they thought there were around ten of them scattered about.

Then he explained that over the last couple of days they had also noticed some other guys, without Colours, fucking about on bikes, who they knew were definitely not local and guessed they must be with them.

He then excused himself and made his way back to Rooster and Axe, telling us he'd catch us later. We got some drinks in and grabbed a seat. I looked around the clubhouse and I noticed that instead of there being a bunch of guys all getting it together as normal it seemed that most were just hanging in two's and three's. I think the biggest group around any table or standing together were the four of us.

Straightaway, DD started banging on about Brutis not telling us anything and said he was going to try and find out from someone else what the fuck was going on. Because no-one answered him, he turned his attention to me.

"Come on, Shug, you've been doing this shit for a while, tell me why we're not just going out there right now and wasting the fuckers!"

Just as I went to offer him my opinion, the rest of the guys who rode with us started grabbing chairs from various places and sat at the table beside us.

Once everyone was seated, I then started to explain to DD that I wasn't really sure how it would play out., that I was confident there would be some kind of plan being hatched to get the bastards, and reminded him that we were waiting for Indie to call.

Just as we all began to debate it, the clubhouse door opened, and a mixture of guys and chicks came pouring in. They were all giggling and laughing as they entered and definitely gave the impression they were here to party.

Somebody then cranked up the music. Brutis, Rooster and Axe told us all to gather around with the exception of the 'party people'. They were dancing away and trying to have a good time, completely unaware that we were up for something much more serious.

Axe then told us he had just spoken with Indie and began to explain what the plan was - much to DD's delight. He then kept elbowing me in the ribs whispering that this was much more like it.

I actually had to tell him to shut the fuck up as I was struggling to hear what Axe was telling us because of his incessant fuckin' yapping.

A combination of Rooster, Axe and Brutis all gave us bits of info which we took on board. It wasn't exactly a war strategy or battle plan, but the gist of it was for us to go and get them, give them a proper doing, then bring them back to the clubhouse.

We were all organised and ready to go within ten minutes and Axe was at the door ushering us out in two's and three's. Some of the guys made their way to their bikes looking like they were heading off somewhere, another couple jumped into a motor and me, Mark, Scooter, DD and one of the Prospects left on foot.

Chapter 6

We left the Clubhouse, all with a chick in tow, laughing and joking as if we were drunk. Our target was the three guys who had been seen closest to the clubhouse.

Within a couple of minutes of getting outside we were on them and caught them well by surprise, two of them were leaning against a building having a smoke and the other was sitting on his bike.

As we passed them, cuddling our chicks and talking a lot of shite, DD commented to the guy sitting on his bike that he thought it was cool, but the guy never responded.

At that point, the girls moved sharply away, and Mark scudded the guy sitting on the bike, knocking both him and the bike to the ground.

Scooter started ladling into one of the guys who had been standing at the wall and DD punched the other one who seemed to buckle way too easily.

I was left standing with the Prospect, almost wondering what to do. The three of them already seemed to be in full control of the situation. That was until the guy who Mark dropped got back up and started swinging his helmet trying to hit him.

I was behind him at this point and caught him a beauty on the side of his head, which pretty much knocked the stuffing out of him, but just for good measure, as he was falling, Mark caught him on the chin with his boot, rendering him unconscious.

The other two were now both on the ground and no longer in any condition to put up any resistance so we grabbed them, pulled them up on to their feet, and hauled them back to the clubhouse. As previously agreed, we tied their hands and feet together then sat them at the front of the clubhouse strapped to the fence. When we left them to go inside, they were all conscious, but looked pretty groggy.

Within 15 minutes or so the others were back, and like us, they all had people in tow. They followed our lead by tying them to the fence then came inside.

Inside the clubhouse the guys were buzzing and all eager to tell their story about how they had got on and how easy it was to take them down. I on the other hand, began to wonder what Indie had in mind for them as no-one had actually told us.

There were ten of them altogether and I was pretty sure he wasn't going to bump them off or anything, but I also knew that there was no chance of him letting them off scot free.

DD had got us some drinks from the bar and placed them on the table then shouted over to us to join him, which we did.

"That was way too fuckin' easy, guys," he remarked, as he lifted the drinks from the tray. "Would someone like to tell me what the fuck happens now?" he asked, directing his question towards me.

"Not sure, DD, but I'm guessing that Brutis, Axe or Rooster will be letting us know pretty soon."

Sure enough, within five minutes of sitting down, Axe brought us all to order.

"Right, guys, here's the heads up. Indie wants us to keep the pricks tied up here as a sort of insurance 'til they've sorted out the rest of them up the road. Once they're sorted, he'll give us a bell and tell us what he wants done with them."

We all sat speculating about how we thought things were going with Indie. The overall mood started to become a little lighter with most of the guys getting back to their normal selves.

DD, as usual, was really talkative, but most of what he said was a lot of shite, and everyone around the table let him know it by winding him up at every opportunity.

I kind of drifted away, turning my thoughts to Julie and hoped that she was ok.

I then began to wonder if Mrs. Boardman would still offer me the job when I got back. However, what was really concerning me the most was what Indie had in store for the Cannibals tied up outside and I didn't need to wait long to find out.

About ten minutes later we heard the roar of the bikes coming towards the clubhouse and we all went out, thinking it was more Cannibals, but thankfully it was Indie and the rest of the guys who had headed up north.

As the bikes started piling in, we all started to mingle, greeting them like long lost family, but we were all as curious as each other wondering why the fuck they were back so quickly. We had been waiting, expecting to get a call from Indie, but instead here he was with everyone else, and not an injury to be had between them.

I thought, that after they had wasted the Cannibals, that he would've left some of the guys up there for a bit, to make sure everybody got the message that the Bats were now in control, but watching them arrive I was pretty sure that everybody had come back together.

Chapter 7

Indie jumped off his bike and went straight to the first guy who was tied to the fence. He knelt down in front of him, grabbed him by the throat, took his knife out and directed it at the guys face, then started talking.

It was impossible to hear what he was saying over the noise of the bikes, but it looked like he was going to cut the guy up.

Axe went over to him and stood beside him and some of us followed suit hoping to hear what he was saying.

"Right, dickhead, this is a onetime offer and I'm only going to fuckin' ask you once so best you listen up. If you don't tell me what I want to know you're a dead man, then I'll continue up the line till one of your shitebag brothers spill the beans. Got it! Here's the deal, if you tell me, I'll let you all go, and that'll be an end to it, okay?"

At that point, the guy just stared at him and never said a word.

"Right, what I want you to do is tell me what the fuck's going on with you and your arsehole brothers and where the fuck the rest of your wee fuckin' gang are hiding out?"

He then placed the point of his blade on the guy's cheek. The guy, to his credit, however foolish, continued looking Indie straight in the eye and told him to go fuck himself then spat on him.

Indie wiped the spit off his chin and said, "Wrong answer, prick," then pushed his blade slowly through his cheek until it went into his mouth.

As the guy began screaming in pain, Indie pulled it back out then stabbed him in the thigh, pushing the whole of the blade in right up to the hilt.

The guy let out an even louder scream which I'm sure could have been heard on the other side of the country. Indie smiled at him then told him he'd be back in a minute to get his answer.

He then knelt down in from of the next guy who by this time was already shitting himself. Indie then did the same thing to him, placing his now bloodstained blade on to his cheek.

"Ok. What about you? Have you got anything to tell me?" he asked him.

The guy started speaking straight away, telling him that he had no idea where the rest of the guys were. He explained that he had been down here for over a week keeping an eye on the clubhouse and that was all he knew.

"Ok, now we're getting somewhere, that's good," he told him.

Just then, the first guy looked at his brother and told him to shut the fuck up.

Indie turned and looked at him then stuck his knife back into the wound in his thigh, this time twisting the blade a bit, reminding him he'd had his chance to talk.

"Listen, dick, I wanted you to speak earlier and you chose not to, so I don't want to hear another fuckin' word from you, okay?"

Again, the guy let out a loud scream, but this time he was calling Indie all the names under the sun.

While Indie was torturing the Cannibals, Gunner and Ludo came over to us both, shaking their heads and looking strangely confused. Straight away, DD was right in there demanding them to tell him what the fuck had happened up north.

Gunner told him to relax and let him try to explain.

"Tell you what, guys, you'll never fuckin' believe it, fuck, I don't believe it myself and I was fuckin' there!

"When we got there, we stopped just short of the Cannibal's clubhouse and parked up, knowing that by now they would have heard us arriving. Indie had explained that there was no plan. He just wanted us all to steam in, waste everybody and make sure that there wasn't a single man of theirs left standing when we were finished. We all got tooled up ready to go and Indie led the charge towards the Clubhouse.

"We expected to be met by them outside, but strangely there was no one there, Indie booted the door in and we all poured in, swinging our bats and chains, but to say we were stunned was an understatement. Most of us were now inside, but none of us could believe it, there wasn't a single cunt there. It was the weirdest thing - the place was totally deserted.

"We all looked around at each other, wondering what the fuck had just happened. Straight away, Indie ran back outside with some of us following, half expecting them to be waiting on us, but there wasn't a single soul to be seen anywhere.

"Indie stood still, scanning the place with a real worried look on his face. You could see, like the rest of us, he had no idea what the fuck was going on and it appeared, for a split second, he had no idea what the fuck to do next.

"By this time, we were all standing outside, our eyes firmly fixed on Indie, waiting for him to decide what was going to happen next. Jelly and Hotwire were now standing beside him and Jelly asked him what he thought was going on.

33

"Fuck knows, man, but this is the last thing I fuckin' expected, the bastards must be up to something! You and Hotwire go back in and see if there are any signs of where they might have gone or if they are planning to come back.

"Check everywhere, there must be some kind of fuckin' clue as to where the fuck they are!"

"They both just nodded then headed back inside. The rest of us just stood looking around, everyone as bewildered as Indie. Within five minutes, the two of them came back out and were again speaking with Indie.

"We were all silent, trying to listen to what was being said and heard Jelly explain that he thought they were not planning to come back.

"The place is empty, man, there's no sign of any personal belongings or shit anywhere, it looks to me like they've split, with no intention of coming back."

"Indie then took a minute to process what he had just heard and told the rest of us to gather around.

"I think the dirty bastards have set us up, we need to get back to the North's clubhouse fuckin' sharpish, I'm sure the bastards are there!"

"He then ran towards his bike while roaring at us, "Don't wait on anyone, just get on your bikes and ride like fuck, 'cause if the bastards are there, our brothers are in a shit load of trouble."

"We all then ran back to the car park to get our bikes as fast as we could, fired them up then shot off.

"All the way back, it was a free for all, with lots of dangerous overtaking. For me, it seemed like the guys had turned it into a race.

"Indie and Jelly were last to leave, but within about ten minutes, Indie had already emerged as the front runner and seemed to be pulling away from the pack with every turn of his wheels.

We all ended up taking a few chances as we wanted to make sure we got back here as fast as we could."

As Gunner finished filling us in, I was watching Indie, who was now getting some more info from the second guy. The next thing that happened caught us all totally by surprise.

It was the Cannibals, they descended on us like a swarm of bees, they had obviously been waiting for the right time to charge us, and with everyone watching Indie, no-one was really ready.

They came at us, all tooled up waving chains, baseball bats and all sorts of weird and wonderful weapons.

As they made their way towards us, they kicked over some of our bikes, which, in hindsight, was actually a good thing, as it gave us a bit of time to process what was going on.

Within seconds, it was a full-scale battle and people from both sides were dropping like flies. There must have been at least thirty of them, not counting the guys who were tied up, but with the element of surprise they initially seemed to be getting the better of us.

As we all piled into them, we were picking up weapons that people had dropped, and we seemed to be getting the upper hand. I was having a right tussle with one of them and was just starting to get the better of him when somebody stabbed me in the side.

As I turned to see who it was, I got a smack on the head with a piece of wood which knocked me out cold. The last thing I saw before I fell, was one of our

Prospects standing behind me with his knife covered in my blood.

From that point on, I never saw another thing. I was told afterwards that the fight had lasted about half an hour and that we'd eventually came out on top.

When I awoke, the first thing I saw was Rooster leaning over me and asking if I was ok. I could see the ceiling lights shining behind him and wasn't sure where the fuck I was. My initial thought was that maybe I was in a fuckin' hospital somewhere. I asked him where the fuck I was and what the fuck had happened.

He told me that I was in the clubhouse and that I had been out for about an hour. He then explained that one of the guys had checked me over, given me some medicine, stitched up my wound and put me in the recovery position. The guy had said I was fine and suggested that I was left to sleep it off.

I went to sit up and realised I had a proper burning sensation in my side and my head was hurting like hell so I stayed put.

I was trying to remember the last thing that happened and then it came to me - The fuckin' Prospect! - that was it! That fucking idiot had stabbed me. I demanded Rooster tell me where the fuck he was, but he told me to settle the fuck down and explained that it was an accident.

"Listen, man, it was like a fuckin' war zone out there for a while and he's really upset about it, so you need to cut him a bit of slack. Anyway, I'm pretty sure you're not the only one to have got melted by one of our own. Look around, man," he told me, "You're one of the lucky ones, some of the guys here are way worse than you."

At that point, and with a little help from Rooster, I managed to sit up a bit and noticed that there were a lot of faces I didn't recognise.

I rested my back against the wall and had a good look around the room, Rooster was right, loads of the guys did have much more serious injuries than I had. I then asked him what the fuck was going on and who the fuck all the strangers were?

"Listen, Shug, the Cannibals are no more," he told me.

To which I replied, "Thank fuck for that! I'm glad we got the bastards, so seeing as though I missed half of it, gonnae tell me how the fuck it all played out?"

"Whoa, man, shut the fuck up and listen, I need to give you a wee heads up here, be careful what you say about them, all the strangers you see are Cannibals, so just sit quietly and let me explain."

I went to start on another rant, but he put his hand over my mouth. With his other hand, he put his finger to his mouth, gesturing for me to say nothing. I was so curious that I nodded in agreement as, by now, I was completely baffled.

"OK, Shug, listen up, here goes: it was the strangest fuckin' thing I've ever seen, just as we were starting to get the better of them and we could see them retreating a bit, their President called out Indie.

"So, right in the middle of us knocking fuck out of each other, both Presidents stood face to face and were shouting for us all to back-off, the fighting just sort of stopped, we pushed each other away and all ended up standing about three feet apart, staring at each other.

"It was so surreal it actually reminded me of a war film where the two generals meet in the middle of the battlefield to discuss terms! Honestly, man, it was the most fuckin' bizarre thing I'd ever witnessed.

"In the end it came down to Indie and their President standing talking. The rest of us, at this point, were helping the guys like you who were injured into the clubhouse and the Cannibals were also moving their injured guys back out of harm's way.

"Apparently their Prez told Indie, right in the middle of the scrapping, that he wanted to give up his Colours and join the Bats.

"By the time we'd all split up and got our injured out of the way, I could see they were still talking. I watched them as closely as I could from where I was, and the first thing I noticed was that they were no longer standing toe to toe, their Prez had taken a couple of steps back.

"I was able to hear most of what was said and Indie, straight away, made it very clear to him that whatever he hoped to gain from the chat he should know that he would not be backing down and that his only interest was in totally wiping out the Cannibals. He then told him that he wouldn't stop 'til it was done.

"Talk about an opening fuckin' gambit! He made it well clear that there was no leeway whatsoever for discussion if he didn't agree. I wondered what the fuck their Prez could come back with.

"When he started talking you could see that Indie was listening intently without taking his eyes off him. I then heard the full discussion. Their Prez then said, 'Look, Indie, we knew that you had much more strength than us and that you were thinking of patching over a club up here the same way that you had already done in the south.

'We didn't really want to take out the Devils, but we felt we had no choice, what we really wanted was to be left alone up north to continue as we were, but when we heard the Devils were thinking about patching over we made them an offer to become Cannibals - which they declined. We reckoned that if we wiped them out and got some of them on board it would give us enough strength to keep you from coming up here. We know now we made a big mistake trying to take over the Devils, but we didn't realise until it was too late that they'd already agreed to patch over as Bats.'

"Indie continued to stare him straight in the eye then let rip, 'Okay, so give me one good fuckin' reason why I should believe any of that shite you just spewed out? You knew fine well we were patching over - it wasn't like it was a fuckin' secret! Tell me this, if you really wanted to be left alone, why the fuck are we here knocking ten bales of shite out of each other?

'Let me tell you what I think. I think that this was you playing 'last chance saloon' and attempting to try and wipe us out, but now, because you couldn't, you want to get into bed with us – well, I don't fuckin' think so!

'Oh, and by the way, you'll only be left alone if you drop the Colours and become an MCC or go back to just being a bunch of fuckin' fuds farting about with no Colours.'

"He then replied saying, 'Indie, you don't need to worry about any of that. As I told you, the Cannibals are now no more and most of us want to become Bats.'

"At that point, Indie kind of walked around in a small circle with his head down, pulling back his hair from his face with one of his hands and lighting up a smoke with the other. He looked like a man deep in thought and we were all watching him - wondering what the fuck was coming next?

"He stopped walking about and went back to his original position, and to say he surprised us with what came next was a fucking understatement if ever I heard one! He began, 'Right, here's what's going to happen, if anybody wants to join us, excluding the officers, they'll do so as Prospects.

'The only way they'll patch up is by our officers giving a unanimous vote at our table when we think they are worthy of it.

'The officers will patch up straight away but will be on probation for three months. I need to make sure you're very fuckin' clear on this because there will be no fuckin' patch over! From now, as far as I'm concerned, your club no longer exists.

'Now get you and your guys away to fuck out of here and tell anyone who agrees to my terms that they can come back and see me here tomorrow at twelve, okay? Oh, and by the way, this is a onetime offer, it expires at Noon tomorrow.'

"Indie then turned to make his way towards the Clubhouse, raising his arm, gesturing for the rest of us to do the same. Their Prez then asked him to wait as he had something to say. Indie turned back around, not looking best pleased, and said, 'Okay, talk!' he told him, 'and make it fucking quick!'

Their Prez then cleared his throat before saying, 'Listen, Indie, we don't have to wait 'til tomorrow, we've already discussed our plans as a club and we all agreed that if we lost today we would disband our club altogether and, if you were agreeable, we could either be a new Bats Chapter up here or we could patch over and join your new North Chapter.'

"I swear tae fuck, I saw Indie foaming at the mouth, his face went fuckin' scarlet, and he was physically shaking. I'm not sure I'd ever seen him so angry - and that's saying something!

"You know the saying 'steam coming out of your ears'? Well, looking at him, I'm sure I saw it there and then for the first time.

"Indie stared at him for a bit before letting rip again, 'You know what? You're all a shower of fuckin' arseholes - the fuckin' lot of you! And you! You're the fuckin' worst! You come down here, armed to the teeth, ready for a rumble, get your arses kicked, then you tell me you want to join us!

'Don't you fuckin' think it would have been much easier if you'd just arranged a fuckin' meet? Fuck's sake! There are guys lying around totally fucked because of this and you're telling me now that you wanted to fuckin' join us anyway?

'Go on then, fuckin' humour me!' he suggested then fired into him again, 'Ok, tell me why the fuck you think that after all this that I'd want any of you cunts as Bats?'

"Again, he cleared his throat before speaking, which I thought was a kind of nervous thing, then said, 'Well, the thing is, Indie, before you arrived, we had a meeting and decided we were going to dissolve the Cannibals.

'Most of the guys were disappointed, as they didn't want the club to fold, but deep down, everyone knew it would come down to this.

'Most felt that they still wanted to be part of a Club, but knew you were much stronger than us and our days were pretty much numbered.

'We all agreed the best thing to do was to face up to you and let you see what we were made of then you could decide for yourself if you thought we were worthy of becoming the next Bats' Chapter.'

41

"Indie then stared at him, with a look of disbelief, before almost roaring at him. 'Holy fuck! What a shower of fuckin' bampots you are! I can't believe what I'm fuckin' hearing. Fuck's sake, you lot really aren't right in the fuckin' napper!'

"He made it clear that he was well pissed, and it didn't go down too well with the Prez or some of his guys. Looking around, I thought they were going to kick off again, but then the Prez said, 'Listen, Indie, man, we're bikers, what the fuck else would you expect from us?'

"Indie stood for a minute or two, shaking his head, then burst out laughing. He took a step closer to their Prez and gave him a bit of a man / hug, he was whispering in his ear, but no-one heard what he said.

"Their Prez smiled and nodded at Indie then went over and released his guys that were tied to the fence and they all then joined the rest of the Cannibals.

"Once Indie saw they were all together, he turned to the rest of us and motioned again for us to follow him, so we all headed back into the Clubhouse. As I went in, I had a quick look back and saw the Cannibals all gathering together in a bit of a huddle.

"When we were all inside, the first thing Indie did was send the Prospects out to pick up the bikes and check for any damage. Then he announced to everyone that the Cannibals would be joining us, which caused a bit of a rowdy and lively debate to say the least!

"He then told us all to shut the fuck up and listen, then went on to explain that the patch members and Prospects would come on board as Prospects and the five officers would be patched up straight away, but the whole lot of them would be on a three month probation.

"Then someone asked, 'What about their fuckin' Prez?'

"Indie didn't sound too pleased about the question but fired back saying that their Prez and VP will become officers straight away, but with the same conditions as the rest. He then went on to tell us that he wanted us all to give them a warm welcome when they came in.

"One of the North guy's then shouted, 'Fuck's sake, Indie, surely you're havin' a fuckin' laugh here, man? We've just spent the last half hour knocking fuck out of them - look at the injuries some of our brothers have - and now you want us to make them welcome in our Clubhouse? I say fuck them!'

"After he spoke, there were a few shouts of 'here, here' and shit like that, but it was very much from a minority. The minute the shouts ceased, I think the guy wished he could take back his rant as Indie was staring straight at him.

"If ever there was a time someone wished they'd shut their fuckin' mouth then this was definitely it.

"Indie stormed over to him, pushing people out of the way as he went. He stood facing him with about two inches separating them, then let rip.

'Do I look like I'm having a fuckin' laugh? Eh, well, do I?' he roared at him before turning away. He then went back to where he was originally standing, shaking his head a bit before talking to us again. 'Right, everybody, listen up and listen fuckin' good! Regardless of what anyone thinks about it, this is happening.

'I've already discussed this, and some of the other scenarios that I thought might have come about, with the officers from all of our three Chapters before we came up here.

43

'We decided on a few options - however this played out, and agreed if they wanted to join us, this is how it would work – okay? Now is there any more stupid fuckin' questions?'

"We all kind of looked around at each other, there was a lot of shoulder shrugging and whispering, and the guys who hadn't heard the conversation outside were staring at each other with blank expressions - wondering if they'd heard right.

"No-one else actually said anything, but you could see they were all thinking the same thing.

"One of the guys, who'd been standing at the window, then suggested we take a look outside. Within seconds, there were dozens of us peering out the two windows that faced the front of the building.

"It seemed like the Cannibals were all having a bit of an argument and then some of them left with their Colours on, shouting and finger pointing at the rest.

"I counted about six or maybe seven of them leaving, but from where I was watching, and with the darkness descending, it was difficult to tell exactly how many.

"The guys who stayed then began taking their Colours off and chucking them on the ground on top of each other - their Prez was last to remove his. After he did, he knelt down, got his zippo out and set them all alight.

"As the fire gathered momentum, they all stood back a bit from it, but I could still see from their faces shining in the glow of the fire that they were certainly not a bunch of happy bunnies.

"After about ten minutes, the fire started to die down and they all made their way into the Clubhouse. Indie went to the door and as they entered, he shook every one of them by the hand, welcomed them in, and directed them straight to the bar.

"As they continued to pile in, most of them had a good look around, some nodded a bit to the guys they got eye contact from - some of us did the same back, others gave them a cold stare.

Chapter 8

"Once they were all inside, Indie spoke to their President for a minute or two then stood on a chair and asked us for a bit of hush, saying, 'Right, everybody, shut the fuck up and listen! As from now, all the ex-Cannibals in the clubhouse are our brothers and I want you to treat them as such.

'I want you all to get to know each other over the next half hour or so and, just to make it very clear, if there is any animosity between you then I'll take it as a personal insult and deal with it in the usual way. I want all officers in the back room now.'

"He then jumped off the chair, grabbed a pint from the bar, and headed through to the back room. And, hey ho, here you are, now wakened and up to speed. Oh, and by the way, they're all still fuckin' through there."

"Holy fuck! That's some fuckin' shit I missed out on," I told him.

"Hey, look around you, there are still a few people out cold. In fact, you're the first of the guys who were KO'd to waken up!"

I then had a thought which I shared, "Hey, Rooster, why are you not through the back with the rest of the officers?"

"I would've been, but Indie wanted me, Gunner and Brutis to stay here and make sure there were no more spats."

He then helped me up and sat me on a chair.

"Right, now I know you're ok, I need to go and mingle a bit, 'cause I'm such a nice guy. I'll get you a couple of beers first. Oh, and no more fighting 'cause you're fuckin' pish at it, ha ha ha!" he told me as he made his way through the crowd, laughing like a fuckin' madman.

I just shouted back at him, "Fuck you, ya prick!" and he gave me the bird as he forced his way towards the bar.

I had another look around the room and noticed that most of the Bats and ex-Cannibals were drinking and having a bit of a laugh with each other - which I couldn't get my head around.

I kept thinking that less than an hour ago we were all knocking fuck out of each other and now here we all are drinking and laughing together - it just didn't seem right.

By now, I was deep in thought, trying to understand how in fuck's name it was possible for people who were sworn enemies an hour ago to now be standing drinking with each other, having a laugh and looking like best buds? If it was the other way around, I don't think I could've done it.

I was jolted out of my daydream by the Prospect who stabbed me. He pulled a chair over and sat next to me.

"Eh, Hi, Shug, is it ok if I join you for a minute?" he asked.

I gave him a bit of a stare and decided to have a bit of a laugh with him.

"Are you not the fuckin' Prospect prick that fuckin' stabbed me?" I said, staring straight at him. "Why the fuck do you think I'd want you to sit here?" I then asked him, sounding as aggressive as I could.

"Look, Shug, I'm really, really sorry, man, it was a pure accident and…"

I interrupted him.

"You could have seriously fuckin' injured me or even fuckin' killed me, ya fuckin' idiot, and you say you're fuckin' sorry! You stabbed me from behind, ya fuckin' balloon. Tell me something, how in fuck's name did you not see my Colours, eh?"

By this time, I noticed he'd turned a funny shade of grey and decided I'd wound him up enough. Just as I was about to tell him I was fucking with him, Rooster appeared back with my beer.

"Thought I best get you two, didn't think you'd be able to get to the bar without hurting yourself - you being a pussy an' that," he said, as he placed them on the table.

He then gave me a bit of a wink and turned his attention to the Prospect.

"Well, well, Shug," he started, "What the fuck have we got here? Isn't this the little cunt that stabbed you in the back during the scrap?" he said, staring him straight in the eye.

Fuck, I swear to God I could smell the shit running down the poor cunt's leg.

I was about to tell him he was being wound up when Rooster started again. He turned to look at me and I could see he was dying to laugh, but he carried on with his wind-up.

"What do you think we should do with this treacherous little bastard, Shug?" he said, removing his knife from its sheath.

We both stared at him at the same time and I said,

"You know what, Rooster? Considering the damage he's done to me, I think it's only fair we give him something to remind him of his mistake."

Rooster, at this point, was running the knife up and down his open hand and staring at it while moving his head from side to side like a fucking madman.

I began talking again with both of us still looking straight at the Prospect.

"You fuckin' ready for this?" I asked him, to which he could only manage a very nervous nod.

I pushed one of the beers in front of him and told him he better drink it in a oner or I'd let Rooster loose with his knife.

He looked so upset and worried that I thought he might have a heart attack. He tried to start talking again, this time leading with an apology, but we couldn't hold it in any longer and both burst out laughing.

Rooster put his knife away and patted him on the back.

"Come on, man, get that pint down your neck. I'm sure you're needing it by now," he said, still laughing.

I held my hand out for him to shake, telling him to relax, that we were only winding him up. As he put his hand out, I could see it was visibly shaking.

As we shook hands, I could actually feel the sense of relief pass through him.

"Come on, grab your beer, man, time for you to chill," I told him, releasing his hand from my grip.

He grabbed his pint and took a large swig, trying his best to finish it, without success. He then placed the glass back on the table, let out a huge sigh of relief then began talking.

"Fuck's sake, Shug, you really had me there! I thought I was up for a stabbing or at least a severe kicking. When Rooster brought out his knife and started rubbing his hand up and down it, I thought I was going to shit myself.

"I reckon if you'd kept it going much longer that I would've keeled over and landed on the floor."

"Well, maybe it'll help you remember the next time you're wielding a knife about that you're meant to stick it into the cunts you're fighting and not one of your own."

"I'm pretty sure I'll never ever do that again. I've been shitting myself to come and see you since it happened. I'd been watching you for what seemed like a fuckin' eternity, waiting for you coming around."

I could see he was still a bit on edge, so I said to him,

"Look, shit happens, don't worry about it, you know we're good so just relax, finish your beer then grab me another and we'll call it quits."

He finished his drink sharply, got up, and made his way to the bar. Rooster and I burst out laughing, feeling pretty good about our wind-up. I, however, had to keep a bit of pressure on my side with my hand as it hurt like hell when I laughed.

"Do you know how it's going through the back, Rooster?"

"No, not sure, Shug, but I'll tell you what, it seems to be going pretty well out here, I've not even seen one bit of aggro - which has surprised the hell out of me.

"I thought after a few beers it would've been a bloodbath, but it's turned into a, 'I'll show you my scar if you show me yours' kind of night.

"There are still a few from both sides that are pretty quiet, but they don't look like they want to start anything."

The Prospect then arrived back at the table with my beer and Rooster stood up, ready to leave.

"Right, Shug, I need to mingle a bit, I'll catch up with you later on."

Before he left, he had a final crack at the Prospect. He put both hands on his shoulders and leaned over to whisper in his ear,

"Now, remember, the next time you play with your little fuckin' knife, make sure you know what the fuck you're doing with it! Ha ha ha."

He then did that fuckin' thing I hate to the Prospect, putting his arm around his neck, grabbing his head and rubbing his hair with his knuckles. Fuck, I hate it when he does that to me.

He smiled and nodded to me, roaring and laughing as he went.

"Hey, Shug, by the way, don't you think that that means you're off the hook, I'll be back to do you later," he said, as he disappeared out of sight.

I sat and had a bit of a chat with the Prospect for a while. I found out he was called Alistair Watson, but everybody called him 'Winker'. He was an only child and told me he didn't even know who his was father and wasn't sure if his mother did either.

Winker had just turned eighteen and was about ten months younger than me. He, however, looked his age, whereas I looked, and felt, fuckin' ancient.

He seemed a pretty sound wee guy, was right into bikes and the Bats in a big way and was hitting me with a barrage of questions about everything all at once.

After answering a few of his questions, I told him enough was enough and offered him the same bit of advice that Rooster had offered Malky and I when we became Prospects. I told him the best thing to do is look, listen, speak when you're spoken to, and do what's asked of you and you'll do fine.

I then burst out laughing, thinking about the advice I'd just passed on, and started to remember Malky and the fact that he never took a single bit of Rooster's advice onboard and did the exact opposite of what he was told.

Winker then asked me what I was laughing at, but I told him I was just thinking about someone I used to know and how he'd coped with the same advice.

He went to start talking again and I told him to stay quiet as I noticed Indie and the guys were coming back into the bar. Just then, Rooster, Cowboy and Flick came and joined us.

There weren't enough chairs at the table, so Flick told the Prospect to get up, which he did, then Flick plunked his arse on his chair and Winker was left standing like a spare prick looking at Flick who then said,

"What?"

Winker then about turned, shaking his head, and disappeared into the crowd.

"That's fuckin' shite, Flick, by the way, there was no need to do that to him, he's a sound wee guy and I was speaking to him."

"Shug, get a fuckin' grip, man - he's a fuckin' Prospect. It's his fuckin' job to be miserable and do what the fuck we tell him, you know that, so what's the big fuckin' deal - you shaggin' him or something?"

Before I could get into it with him, Indie sat up on the bar and was joined by the ex-Prez of the Cannibals who was called Truck.

Chapter 9

Indie banged a glass on the bar and shouted for everybody to shut up.

"Right, guys, here's the script. Truck and his guys will stay at their clubhouse in the meantime. Nothing much will change for them - except some of our guys from the North and Central Chapters will be moving up there for a bit ... to keep them right on the way we do business.

"They are now all Bats or Prospects and will receive their cuts before they leave. They'll not be a separate Chapter and will have North on their patch - the same as Ammo and Axe's guys.

"However, one thing we need to deal with fairly quickly is the guys who decided to leave rather than join us.

"I need to know they're not running around with Colours on and Truck has given me his assurance that he'll deal with it whenever he gets back up the road.

"There are some other issues we need to resolve, but we've organised another meet to do that and maybe we'll turn it into a run if we can.

"Ok, guys, that's all for now. I'm sure you have loads of questions for us, but there's no point in us trying to answer them just now, we don't have all the answers yet.

"So let's just get to know each other, and remember, everyone here is now part of the only MC in Scotland."

People started to cheer, but Indie held up his hand and the place fell silent again.

"Before we start the celebrations and continue to get to know each other, I want us to welcome our new brothers to the North Chapter. Three cheers to our new brothers!"

We then raised our glasses and did the whole 'hip, hip, hooray' thing. Most of the guys who were next to a newbie either shook hands or did the man / hug bit with them.

We, however, all just sat back down. I asked Rooster if he knew who was going up north and he told me he had no idea, but that he would find out from Indie later on.

Cowboy then told us he was really on edge about the whole thing and reckoned that Indie may have bitten off a bit more than he could chew.

When Rooster asked him why he thought that, Cowboy explained that he didn't think it was a good idea for them to have two different Clubhouses for one Chapter.

"He didn't let them do it down south so I reckon he may end up getting some flak from the South guys. If it was me, I'd be well pissed as it looks like he has one rule for some and one rule for the others."

I commented that I thought he raised a good point but was shot down straightaway by Rooster.

"Listen, guys, its two completely different situations.

"Down south, the guys were all within a three-mile radius so there was no need for more than one. Here, it's not as easy as there is about twenty-five to thirty miles of a difference between them. Anyway, we have no idea what actually went on in there and I'm sure Indie must have some sort of plan - he always does.

"Hey, here's a novel thing, guys. Why don't we just wait and give him the benefit of the doubt before making any fuckin' assumptions?

"Just because he didn't mention the clubhouse situation doesn't mean he hasn't decided what to do about it.

"Okay, girls, I'm going to leave now and let you get back to your knitting patterns. Guess I should go and speak to the real men - not the fuckin' worry warts."

With that, he stood up, laughing away to himself as he disappeared into the crowd.

"You know what, guys? Rooster's right," I told them. "Come on, let's just fuck the speculation and mingle, have a few beers, and get to know our new brothers."

I then stood up, followed Rooster's lead, and headed towards the bar, although I did it at a much slower pace than him, holding my side as I went. I pushed my way through what seemed like a wall of people, nodding and smiling as I went.

Eventually, I found myself standing beside Scribe, who was also trying to get a drink.

"Hi, man, how's tricks?" I asked him.

"Things are good, Shug, but they'd be so much fuckin' better if I could get a fuckin' drink," he said, smiling, then totally changed the subject. "What did you think of Indie's speech?"

"I think he only gave us a bit of what's to come. I'm more concerned with what he didn't tell us than what he did. I thought he was a bit guarded with what he told us," I said, shouting back over the noise.

"Listen, Shug, I've known Indie a long, long, time. He's always been a pretty deep guy, but very rarely has he been wrong. I've always trusted his judgement and you should do the same, you can bet your life that he's already three steps ahead of the rest of us.

Whatever he's got planned, its good enough for me," he roared back.

Just then, the drinks arrived. Scribe picked up his, raised it aloft in my direction, nodded his head then began navigating the way back to his table. I smiled and nodded back then turned towards the bar, leaning my arms on the counter.

Very quickly, I was deep in thought. I could see Indie, Truck and the rest of the officers in the back room through the bar hatch but couldn't hear anything. They were all sitting at a table talking and my mind was racing a mile a minute - wondering what the fuck they were saying?

The rest of the night played out as expected. Although there were a few skirmishes, nothing serious went down. And by the time we all started to crash, everybody was best buds.

Chapter 10

As usual, I woke up pretty early the next morning, and the minute I moved, I realised I was in agony with my side. It had seemed ok the night before, but I'm guessing that was because I was full of drink and drugs.

I got to my feet and made my way to the door, being careful not to stand on anyone as I went. As I walked, I could feel the burning pain in my side and noticed the pad I had covering it was stained with blood.

I went outside and tried looking around, but the sun was blinding me. Even with both hands on my forehead trying to block it out, I could still hardly see a thing.

I sat down on the steps and lit up a smoke and it was only then that I realised someone else was there. A guy was sitting on the bottom step and he turned towards me, offering me his hand at the same time as introducing himself, telling me his name was Guppy.

Again, I had to cover my eyes with my hand to see him. I shook his hand and told him who I was and straight away he began chatting.

"What do you think of this whole patch over thing? Do you think it'll work out?"

I couldn't believe he'd just asked me that and decided it best to play my cards real close to my chest.

"What do you mean?" I asked him.

"Well, one minute we're all knocking fuck out of each other and the next we're bosom buddies getting pished and having a laugh together.

"You know, some of the guys were pretty pissed off that we patched over. In fact, half a dozen or so left with their patches on and said they'd never be

Bats and that they were going to keep the clubhouse and do a bit of recruiting when they went back up the road.

"They're parting shot was to tell us that they wouldn't let us wear our new patches in front of them and that they would fight us to the death."

"That all sounds a bit dramatic," I suggested to him, "I thought your Prez said everyone had agreed to patch over?"

"Aye, that's what he said, but he knew some of the guys were dead against it," he told me.

"So why were they here fighting if they knew they were going to be expected to patch over?"

"The guys that left were pretty confident that we would beat you and that there would be no patch over."

"What did you think about it?" I asked him.

"Me? I wasn't giving two fucks either way. I've only had my patch for six months. I just want to ride my bike, get pissed, do some shagging, have a laugh and get involved in the occasional rumble. Wearing a patch, whatever it is, allows me to do that," he explained.

I wasn't exactly sure how to respond to that, but he actually summed up everything I thought about how it should be, being part of a club.

"Do you think they'll put up much resistance when you go back up the road?"

"Not sure, it all depends on Wolfie. He was the SAA and was dead against the whole thing from the start but couldn't get any of the other officers to vote with him.

"After the spat we had, he was the one who was trying to talk everyone out of the patch over, but again, lost on the vote.

"The guys who left with him are the ones he's really tight with so now he's kind of leading them and I reckon if he can drum up enough support, he'll put up a hell of a fight.

"He's been a Cannibal for over ten years, and I think it means more to him than even our Prez. What about your man, Indie? Do you reckon he's a good Prez?"

"I think he is, he's been a member a long, long time and knows his way around the Club. He became Prez when Provo was killed, and he has one hundred percent backing from everyone.

"It was a really, really hard time for him to take over as the club was on its knees and he got us all back on track. If there was anyone I would totally trust to run the Bats it would be him. There's no bullshit, everything's black and white and you know exactly where you stand with him," I told him.

"Well that's some recommendation. I'm not sure any of our guys would have said the same about Truck."

"Why's that?" I queried.

"Well, Truck's a good guy an' that, but he's one of these folk that if he likes you, you're in, but if he doesn't then he just kind of puts up with you. It pisses people off because he tends to give the guys he's not fussed about all the shit jobs, you know the script," he told me.

"Well, I can assure you that's not something that will happen with Indie. He doesn't give a fuck who you are as long as you're doing your bit for the Club. I'm not even sure he has what you could call a 'best mate'.

"The two people he was really tight with were Provo and Stiff. One's gone and the other is no longer part of the club so there's none of that kind of shit you described with him."

He then stood up, thanked me for the info, and told me if what I said was true then he was well happy to have joined the Bats.

I assured him it was and if he needed anything else to give me a shout. We shook hands again then he went inside. When the door opened, I heard a bit of noise and gathered that everyone was beginning to stir. I finished my smoke then, still holding my side, I wandered over to my bike to see if there was any damage to it.

I had a good look around it and all I could see was a very small dent in the tank, a couple of scratches on the side panel and a broken rear indicator. When I looked around at the other bikes, I realised that I was pretty fortunate as some of them had way much more damage than mine.

I started it up and gave it a couple of revs before moving it away from the rest of the bikes. I parked it beside the clubhouse, gave it another couple of revs and checked to see if there were any leaks. When I couldn't see any, I switched it off feeling comforted that it would get me home.

I sat on the ground, laid my back against my bike and lit up another smoke.

By now there was a fair bit of activity outside, with guys all moving their bikes about to get a better look at them checking for any damage.

From what I could see most of the damage was superficial, but it was still enough to make some of the guys pretty pissed off. I wondered if it would be enough for some of them to have a go at the ex-Cannibal guys who had kicked them over the previous day?

When Indie came out, he also made his way towards the bikes. A couple of the guys were shouting for him to go and see the damage done to their bikes, but he ignored them and went straight to his own.

I watched him as he circled his bike. He placed his hand on the handlebars and knelt down to get a closer look, then got up and did the same at the other side. He sat on, fired it up, and moved it over beside mine.

As he got off, he said, "How's the side, Shug?"

"It's ok, Indie, thanks," I told him, lying through my teeth.

He just nodded to me then went to see the guys who were doing the moaning earlier about their bikes.

I looked at his bike and noticed he also had a broken rear indicator and his back light was busted as well, there were some scratches on one of the back shocks and a rip in the seat, but I wasn't sure if it was like that before he came?

I hadn't noticed Rooster coming out, but when I heard another bike starting up, I knew it was his.

I lifted my hand above my eyes, again to deflect the sun, and saw him and Mark standing together, both checking for any signs of damage. Cowboy came out and sat beside me, lit up a smoke and pointed towards the bikes.

"You see much damage to any of them, Shug?"

"Nah, not so far, I think most of it is superficial, nobody's bike has failed to start, it's more indicators and shit than engine damage.

"I think we may be ready to head shortly. Indie was telling some of the guys that he wanted to get back pretty sharpish so I wouldn't be surprised if we left within the next half hour."

"So what's with Smudger and DD then? They seem to be having a bit of a go at Indie about something."

"I think they're pissed about the damage to their bikes and want Indie to do something about it. From what I can see he's having none of it. You know what DD's like, he just can't let it go, but I think Indie's made it very clear to him that he better not keep going on about it."

Cowboy then stood up and told me he was going to have a look at his bike. I told him I'd seen it and it didn't look like there was any damage done.

"Fingers crossed then, Shug. I could do with a bit of luck," he told me, as he wandered away.

Indie was heading back into the clubhouse and summoned for everyone else to do the same. Cowboy came back over and asked me what I thought he wanted us in for and I told him I reckoned he would be giving us an update on what's coming next.

Just as I got to my feet, our van arrived and it was being driven by Angel. Fiona was in the passenger seat and I went straight over to them to find out why they were here.

"Well, girls? Aren't you a sight for sore eyes! What brings you up here?" I asked them.

"We just came up to see you, Shug. We were missing you so much, isn't that right, Fi?" she announced.

"Absolutely, Angel, we just couldn't wait on you coming back so we drove all the way up here just to be with you," she said, smiling at me.

"Ok, girls. Cut the crap, what the fuck are you doing here?" I asked them again.

"There's a box in the back. Can you take it in and give it to Indie?" Angel asked.

I smiled and told her, "No probs, sexy, anything for you," before going around to the back of the van.

I opened the doors and there was a large box. I shouted to the girls, asking them what was in it, and Angel shouted back telling me it was none of my business.

I lifted it out and realised that it was pretty heavy. I was finding it hard because my side was giving me jip so I shouted on Cowboy to give me a hand.

As he walked towards me, he called me a pussy and a wimp, slagging me off because I needed a hand, so I shouted back at him to come over and lift it his-fuckin'-self.

"No probs, Shug. Put it down and leave it to a real fuckin' man. Oh, you could open the clubhouse door for me if it isn't too hard for you?" he said, laughing away.

I watched as he lifted the box and saw he was struggling a bit to keep a good grip on it.

"Too heavy for you, old man? You want a hand?" I asked him sarcastically.

"Don't be such a prick, Shug, even if I did need a hand, I'd get one of the girls to help me before I asked you," he told me.

I opened the door and he went in and placed the box on the bar. I looked at him and saw he was panting a bit.

"You want me to get you a chair and a glass of water, auld yin? You look done in," I asked him, laughing away to myself.

"I'll do you in, ya wee fud, if I get any more of your fuckin' 'auld yin' wisecracks so hold your fuckin' tongue or I'll poke you in the side," he said, grabbing hold of me and wrestling me to the ground.

I burst out laughing and he gave me a bit of a playful slap then helped me up.

63

"Lucky for you I'm in a good mood or I would've laid you out," he said, smiling.

"So what's in the box then, Shug?" Cowboy asked, thinking that the girls had told me.

"I've no idea, Cowboy, but it must be something Indie needs 'cause he wouldn't have had the girls drive all the way up here for fuck all!" I suggested.

Indie came and told us to get the rest of the guys back inside ASAP and to tell the girls to head off. He then went over and lifted the box off the bar and placed it on a table.

When we were all in, he opened the box and lifted out a cut-off and held it up.

"Right, guys, I have the cuts for our new Brothers and I want you to officially welcome then to the club."

Everybody began clapping and cheering as Indie summoned Truck first. He put on his cut-off, Indie shook his hand then they hugged each other.

Indie then held up his hand asking for a bit of hush.

"Right, listen up a minute, folks, Truck will now give his guys their new Colours and when they're patched, I want you all to welcome them as brothers."

Indie then began lifting the cut-offs from the box and handing them to Truck. Truck pointed to the guys who were officers and they all went forward one at a time. He gave them their Colours, shook their hands then did the man / hug thing.

Indie then gave them something and did the same. All the rest were given Prospect cuts and were welcomed in the same manner as the ex-officers were.

As the guys came back among us, everybody either shook their hands or gave them a pat on the back. I watched them as they mixed with the rest of us and thought they all seemed genuinely happy to be Bats.

I asked the first guy who got his Colours what Indie had gave him and he told me it was a name tag with 'North' on it.

It took around half an hour for everybody to get their Colours and when Truck was finished, Indie held up his hand again.

"I've given all the guys a tag for the front of their cut-offs with 'North' on it and I have tags for everyone back at the farm with 'Central' and 'South' on them. When you get back, see Angel and she'll give you yours.

"Right, guys, now that's done, I need all the officers in the back room, ASAP."

As they headed through, I saw Truck summoning one of his guys and realised it was his ex-VP and he followed him through.

I'd seen him the night before and he struck me as a bit of an oddity. He was small and chunky, reminded me of a prop forward in a rugby team, and looked like he could handle himself. I didn't know his name, but I was sure I'd find out soon enough.

At that point, I was feeling pretty rough and decided I needed a hair of the dog to sort me out. While I waited at the bar on my pint getting poured, I watched through the hatch and saw the officers all gathering around the big table.

Everyone was sitting except Indie and Truck and I watched Indie talking and pointing but couldn't hear a word he was saying. I picked up my pint and after a few sips I began to wonder what the fuck he was plotting now?

There seemed to be a couple of heated exchanges going on and it was driving me mental that I could see them but couldn't hear a fuckin' thing. Eventually, they all stood up and made their way back into the bar.

65

Once they were all in, Indie shouted for a bit of order and everyone quietened down. I think most people were having the same thoughts as me.

"Right. We've agreed that all the North guys will be heading back up the road to sort out the shit with the wankers who still want to keep the Cannibals thing going.

"I want Scribe, Mark and Smudger to head up with them. They'll stay there until everything is sorted then they'll come back and let us know how things have panned out.

"The rest of us will head back down south and pick up where we left off. I want to make sure that nobody has decided to keep wearing Colours. We'll be stopping at the farm on the way, be ready to leave within the next half hour."

There was a bit of a mumble and a few moans from some of the Central guys as we all headed outside, but I think it was mainly because they had to go down south.

I guessed a few of them had things they wanted to do which they now have to put on the back burner. However, nobody mentioned anything to Indie as they knew it wouldn't do the slightest bit of good.

The North guys were first to leave - with Truck, Ammo and Axe leading the way. It was about another ten minutes or so before we were ready to go.

Rooster wandered over to me for a bit of a chat before we left, and I mentioned to him that I was going to head straight to the hospital.

"Funny, that's exactly what I was going to say to you," he told me. "I just spoke with Indie and told him the script and he's cool with it, but want's us back down south tonight."

Well, that was enough for me to go on a rant.

"Fuck's sake, man, who the fuck does he think he is? Telling us where we can and can't go and what time to be in, he's no oor fuckin' faither!

"See, Rooster. That's what I hate about this fuckin' shit! There's always some cunt telling you what's next - like you don't have a mind of your fuckin' own."

"Shug, fuck's sake, man, listen to yourself, you need to shut the fuck up and get a fuckin' grip, here's not the time or the place for a fuckin' rant like that, keep it in 'til we get to the hospital, for fuck's sake, will you?

"It's a good job everybody's firing up their bikes and no cunt can hear you!" he said, shaking his head in my direction.

I never said anything else, but I was fuckin' raging inside. As usual, I began to internalize, and that only made me feel worse. I was glad when we got going as it gave me something else to focus on.

Chapter 11

It was a glorious day, and that feeling I got every time we rode in a big pack was now overpowering the shit about Indie and I was enjoying the ride in the sun.

We were about forty-five minutes into the run when we came to the motorway turn-off. As most of the guys filtered onto the slow lane, making their way to the slip-road, Rooster and I drew out onto the outside lane. As we passed Indie, we both gave him a nod which he returned.

We'd already decided not to stop 'til we got to the hospital. By the time we arrived, we were both tired, hungry and pretty cold - not to mention still a bit bashed up looking.

We parked up and I suggested we head to the toilets and give ourselves a bit of a clean up, but Rooster was having none of it, he'd already decided he was heading straight to the ward.

We began our walk through the hospital, neither of us saying a word. I guessed we were both thinking about how we thought Julie would be.

It had been five days since we were last here to see her and as we got closer to the ward my mind was working overtime. I began to wonder if she might be under some kind of suicide watch or if maybe she was better and now discharged?

I wasn't really sure which one I would have preferred, but they were the only two scenarios occupying my head.

When we got to the door, Rooster stopped and turned to me with a worried look in his eye. This was a look I'd only seen from him on the odd occasion. His eyes were already a bit glazed from the long journey to get here, but I'm sure some of it was also down to tears.

"Shug, what if she's fucked, man? Or even dead and it's all my fault? What the fuck will I do then?" he asked.

"Listen, Rooster, she'll be fine. It was probably just a blip for her. Fuck, we've all had them from time to time, I'm sure she's realised by now that what she did was a complete mistake.

"C'mon, let's get in and see how she's doing," I suggested, patting him on the back.

Even though I seemed to have perked him up a bit I was way less sure about my words to him than I let him know. I was not only screwed up inside about her attempt to kill herself, but also fully guilt-ridden about what Julie and I had been up to, prior to Rooster coming down.

I began to wonder if she would be conscious, and if so, what her state of mind would be like. I wasn't sure if she would mention anything about us to Rooster.

By now, the washing machine in my stomach was working at fast forward as we approached the nurses' station.

A young student nurse came out from the office, asking if she could help us. Rooster explained that we were here to see Julie Richards and she headed back into the office asking us to give her a minute to check.

We stood looking at each other for what seemed like an age, although it was probably just a couple of minutes, until the nurse came back out.

"Hi, sorry to keep you, I was just checking with the Ward Sister," she told us, then went on to explain that Julie Richards had been discharged the previous day.

"That's great news," I told her, thanking her for her time, then went to leave.

As I turned to head out, Rooster asked her if she knew where she was discharged to.

"I'm sorry, I'm not sure. I'm guessing it would be back to her home address. Give me a minute and I'll check with Sister."

"Why did you need to ask her that, man?" I wanted him to tell me. "Fuck, Rooster, she can only be one of two places. I know where she lives in the nurses' home and you know where her folks live. We just need to split up and check them both out."

"Shug, I've got no idea where the fuck they live. In all the time we went together, I was never once at their house. She stayed in a flat in town with some other nurses, remember?" he told me.

Fuck, I couldn't believe it. In all the time they were together, he never even bothered asking her where the fuck she lived!

I was just about to say something to him about it when we were interrupted by the Sister. She directed her questions at Rooster.

"I believe you're looking for the home address of a Miss Julie Richards, is that correct?" she asked him.

"Yep, that's exactly what I'm looking for," he told her, in as polite a way as Rooster could manage.

"Well, I'm sorry, but it's not hospital policy to give out such information. I suggest you contact a relative or friend of hers, they may be able to help you. So, if there's nothing else, we have work to do," she told him, raising her hand in the direction of the door.

I knew exactly what was coming next, so I started to make my way out.

"Hey, Sister, thanks for nothing, ya fat jumped up poxy bastard! I hope your next shite's a fuckin' hedgehog, fuckin' boot," he let rip, before leaving.

I was now laughing away under my breath. I just knew the way he was feeling that he couldn't leave without paying her a compliment or two.

As I held the door open for him, I watched her scurry up the ward, not best pleased. I had a glance at the nurses in the office and noticed they were all trying very, very hard not to laugh.

"Feel better now, man?" I asked him, as we made our way along the corridor.

"No. Do I fuck, Shug. That jumped-up fuckin' boot needs a good slap - cheeky fuckin' cow! Anyway, how the fuck are we going to find Julie now, if she's not staying at the hospital? I'm guessing that's us fucked!" he ranted.

"Hey, it's no probs, big fella. Someone at the nurses' home will have her address and if not, I'm sure I can get it from Mrs Boardman," I suggested, which seemed to relax him a bit.

We agreed to head straight to the nurses' home, grab a bite to eat then suss out how to get her address.

When I sat back down on my bike, I could feel the bottom of my back and my arse throbbing. It was the pain you only get after you've ridden a fair old distance. When I grabbed hold of my handlebars, I could feel the rest of my muscles were also aching. I wasn't really sure if it was due to the long ride here or the fact that I was still a bit sore from our scrap with the Cannibals, or just the fact I was getting a bit agitated about Julie? All of a sudden, I felt totally fucked.

I took the lead and Rooster followed as we drew out of the car park onto the main road. All the way back to the other hospital I was checking my mirror to make sure I could see Rooster. He was on my tail all the way, never less than a couple of feet behind me.

We entered the hospital via the back gate and went straight to the nurses' home. When we'd parked up, I decided I should have a word with him about the mood he was in earlier, just in case he was still pissed and ended up going off on one again.

I wanted to tell him about the warden and shit before we went in as I was a bit concerned that he might have a go at someone for no real reason. I knew that if he did, it would end up impacting on me and my job.

"Hey, Rooster, when we go in, please let me do the talking, man? I know a few people here and I'll probably have a better chance of getting some info. I don't want you pissing off anyone else in case it fucks up my job and shit."

He drew me the dirtiest look he could then went on a major rant.

"Whoa, whoa, just hang on a fuckin' minute, Shug. When the fuck did this all become all about you? I thought we were here to find Julie? Not for you to suck up to all your new fuckin' bum-chums ... you really are a selfish bastard sometimes, aren't you?"

"Hey, come on, Rooster, play the fuckin' game, man. There's no need for that pish," I roared back at him. "You're bang out of order saying that. You know this has fuck all to do with me. This is all about Julie, but if you go in there 'all guns blazing' you'll get the same response we got at the other hospital and we'll be no further fuckin' forward, so best you wind your fuckin' neck in."

Thankfully Rooster then kind of backed off.

"Ok, Shug, sorry, man, you're right. I'm just well agitated about Julie. I need to know that she's alright and all this jumping about getting nowhere is driving me fuckin' mental."

72

"Hey, come on, you're not alone on that, I feel exactly the same, but we'll get there. C'mon, let's go in and see if anybody knows where she is."

We went in and, as usual, there was nobody about. We headed straight up the stairs and along the corridor to her room.

I gave her door a gentle tap and called her name, but there was no reply. I tried knocking again, this time a little harder – again, no response. I told Rooster the best thing we could do was head to Lisa's room because she was one of Julie's mates.

I knocked on Lisa's door, but again, there was no answer. By this time, Rooster was well agitated and was for kicking down all the doors in the corridor 'til he found her. I persuaded him the best move would be to go to the dining room and see if I recognised anyone there who I thought might know Julie. Thankfully, he agreed.

The dining room was pretty busy, but I noticed Calum and Becky sitting together and made a beeline for them. When we approached them, they both seemed genuinely happy to see me. Becky saw me first and gave Calum a bit of a dunt and nodded in my direction.

When he looked up, he seemed nervous for some reason then began speaking,

"Eh, hi, Shug, nice to see you again! How are you doing, mate?"

"I'm ok, Calum, thanks," I told him, trying to sound as relaxed as possible. "I've just been to the hospital looking for Julie, but they told us she was discharged yesterday, any idea where she is now?"

Calum didn't say anything back, he just turned his head towards Becky and they both stared at each other for a minute or so.

I was quite happy to wait for them to do whatever the fuck it was they were doing, but Rooster had other ideas.

"Right, you two. Fuck this pish! Tell me where the fuck Julie is now or I'll have the fuckin' both of you!" he demanded.

Calum then broke his gaze from Becky and turned, looking towards Rooster, then began talking.

"Listen, guys, I'm really sorry, but I can't tell you where she is. She made us promise that if you came here looking for her that we'd keep it to ourselves. She told us to tell you that she didn't want to see either of you ever again."

Rooster then leaned over the table, almost to the point where he was touching noses with Calum, and very quietly told him that if he didn't tell him where she was he would stab him in the eye, rip out his fuckin' tongue and shove it up his fuckin' arse. Calum, at that point, got up and told Rooster to back-off.

Before Rooster replied and all hell broke loose, I got between them and tried to defuse the situation. I suggested that we should all sit down and discuss it rather than rolling about the floor knocking fuck out of each other.

I was well aware that Rooster could scrap, but I remembered Calum telling me about his karate exploits and wasn't sure if Rooster would've been able to take him.

I knew if that was the case then I would have to back him up and that would definitely be an end to me having any chance of working here.

Thankfully, after a couple of minutes of me speaking about us all overreacting and them eyeballing each other, I managed to persuade them both to sit down.

Firstly, I asked Calum if he could tell us how she was and what she was up to rather than where she was. He told us that, thankfully, she now seemed better and much more like her old self.

I wondered then if she would want to go back to work in a mental hospital after having a bit of a breakdown herself and asked him if she'd said anything about it.

He told me that he'd only had a brief conversation with her, but that her plan was to return as soon as she could. However, the doctor had signed her off for three months and that during her time off she had to attend a series of counselling sessions before he would declare her fit for work.

I had a quick glance at Rooster as I was conscious that he'd never taken his eyes off Calum during our conversation.

He remained silent, but I was also aware that he seemed a bit shell-shocked with what Calum had said.

"You okay, Rooster?" I asked him.

"Shug, don't be so fuckin' stupid, of course I'm not okay. I'm anything but o-fuckin-k. I need to know why the fuck she doesn't want to see us? Do you reckon she thinks that we've caused her breakdown or something?"

Calum then interrupted and began speaking, this time directly to Rooster, trying to offer him some kind of reassurance. He told him that what had happened to her could not be attributed to any one person or thing and that situations like this are more likely to be brought on by a whole series of circumstances.

"Sometimes, when you make too many changes in your lifestyle at the same time, your coping mechanism struggles to keep up and your brain ends up a bit fried which causes you to flip a bit. In most cases it's a temporary thing and once you identify the triggers you can reset yourself," he told him.

"Well, thanks for the lesson in psychobabble fuckin' bullshit! That makes me feel oh so much fuckin' better, NOT," Rooster replied sarcastically, "However, that still doesn't tell me where she is or how I can get in touch with her. So, what about spilling the beans and let us get the fuck out of this shithole?"

Calum then stood up, telling us he needed to go as he was working. Rooster was having none of it and also stood up, telling him he was going nowhere until he told us where Julie was.

Calum looked at Rooster and said he was not prepared to tell him anything else and that if he really did love her then he should respect her decision. He then started making his way out of the dining room.

I was waiting on Rooster going off on one, but instead, he sat back down and held his head in his hands. I gave him a bit of a pat on the back telling him it was the right thing to do and reassured him that I would find out where she was staying.

"Shug, I know you mean well, but how the fuck will you find that out if no cunt's talking?"

"Remember, Rooster, I've got to meet the nursing officer about my job. I'll get her to give me her home address and we'll take it from there. C'mon, let's grab something to eat then I'll go see her."

We grabbed a couple of rolls and some juice from the counter. I paid for them and suggested to Rooster that we should take them outside to eat which, thankfully, he agreed would be the best idea.

We made our way to the front of the building, sat on the steps outside, and began munching away. Neither of us uttered a sound between the time we sat down and the time we finished eating.

I told Rooster that I was going to Mrs Boardman's office to see if I could get some info on Julie and suggested that he head into town or at least get out of the hospital for a bit and clear his head.

We arranged to meet at the pub after I had seen her and then we could decide what to do next. Rooster jumped on his bike, gave me a bit of a nod, then left. I thought it best to wait 'til Rooster had gone before I started up my bike. I didn't want both of us roaring our bikes up towards the main building at the same time.

Before he left, I'd given him directions to the pub, but he obviously wasn't paying any attention because, instead of heading out the back entrance, like I'd told him, he ended up going through the hospital on his way to the main gate.

As I started my bike up, I just shook my head and smiled, wondering if he would encounter any patients like I did or if he would get lost on the way to the pub?

I rode to the car park in front of the main building and parked up. I went into the waiting room and spoke to the strange wee dude on the switchboard that I'd met when I was in for my interview. I asked him if I could speak to Mrs Boardman.

He never said a word, just pointed to his ear and mouthpiece, then to one of the chairs and raised his two fingers signaling he would get to me shortly.

I sat staring out of the window and began to play back some of what had went on in the last week or so.

I wondered how the fuck it was possible for me to get involved in the amount of shit I did.

I was away in a world of my own when the guy slid open the window and asked me what I wanted. I explained that I was hoping to speak to Mrs Boardman and asked if he could find out if she was available.

He replied really abruptly,

"Down the corridor, second on the left, knock before you go in," then closed the window back over.

I thought to myself 'What a pig ignorant little cunt he was and if things fucked up here then he was going to be the first prick I would lay out'.

I headed to her office, knocked on the door, but suddenly remembered I was still wearing my Colours and originals. Fuck! Just as I thought about removing them, I heard her shouting, "Come in," and I had no time to do it.

'Ah well, fuck it', I thought to myself. She'll just need to take me as I am. When I entered, she looked a bit surprised to see me and said so, while offering me a seat. I thanked her, nodded, then sat in the chair directly opposite her desk.

"Are you feeling up to starting yet?" she asked.

I told her I was and apologised about taking so long to get back in touch. I started to give her a 'cock & bull' story about why, but she interrupted me.

"Listen, Ochil, it's fine. Remember, I did tell you it was ok to take all the time you needed. I knew you would want to make sure Julie was on the mend before you started and, with her now back home at her mum's, I kind of expected to see you sometime this week."

I thanked her for being so understanding then asked her what happens now?

She said, "We'll get your medical done then give you a start date and that's it. I can get your medical done later today if you'd like? There are another couple of new starts being done, so I can fit you in with them. It does mean, however, that you'll need to come back here around four-thirty, if that's ok?"

"Yes, that's great. Thanks very much. I'll make sure I'm here," I told her.

Mrs Boardman then stood up and made her way to the door, opened it, and gestured for me to leave.

"Go to reception when you arrive and they'll tell you where to go," she said, smiling as I walked towards her.

I thanked her again then remembered about Julie.

"Oh, Mrs Boardman, I don't know if you can help us. We all had a bit of a whip-round and got Julie some flowers and stuff, but none of us know her mum and dad's address?

"I knew her old one, but they moved a couple of months ago. I never thought to ask her where because, with her staying in the nurses' home, I never gave it a thought that I'd need it.

"Would it be possible for you to give me it so I can get them delivered?"

"Yes, of course, no problem, just give me a minute, her file is on my desk."

As she walked back towards her desk, she then said something that made me feel really guilty and embarrassed, all at the same time.

"What a lovely thought that is. I'm sure she'll be delighted to get something from her friends. I'm sure it will raise her spirits knowing everybody is thinking about her."

Fuck. I didn't know where to look when she handed me a piece of paper with the address. I could actually feel myself blushing from the inside out.

"Give her my regards and let her know we're all thinking about her, and I'll see you at four-thirty."

I smiled, thanked her, then scurried out of the office as quickly as I could. When I got outside, I felt the need to inhale large breaths of air to try and stop myself from hyperventilating.

I got my breathing back to normal, jumped on my bike, and made my way to the pub to catch up with Rooster. As I turned into the car park, I was glad to see his bike. I thought that he might have got lost when he went out the wrong gate, but, thankfully, he made it. I parked my bike alongside his and went straight inside.

He was sitting in the corner staring out the window like he was in a trance or something. He never even noticed me coming in, which I thought was really weird. I went to the bar, got a couple of beers, and made my way to his table.

"Penny for them, big fella?" I asked him, as I placed the drinks on the table and sat down.

"Oh, Hi, Shug, sorry, man, I was miles away," he told me, like I hadn't noticed. "Well? Did you get it then?" he asked.

"Yep, sure did," I told him, letting him see the piece of paper from Mrs. Boardman.

"How far away from here is it?" he asked.

I told him I wasn't sure, but having been through the town a couple of times, I thought it would take less than half an hour to get there.

"Come on then. Let's get a fuckin' move on," he said, standing up and finishing his drink.

"Fuck's sake, Rooster, gonnae gimme a minute, man? I've just got a round in. Let me at least get a fuckin' drink before we go? Anyway, we need to talk about what we're going to do when we get there."

"See! There you go again, Shug. You're always the fuckin' same. Overthinking shit every fuckin' time. It's dead simple. We knock on the door, ask to see her, check she's ok, have a bit of a chat and that's that. Why the fuck would we need to think about it?" he told me.

"Listen, Rooster, it isn't that simple, man. She's already made it very clear that she doesn't want to see us. I don't think her parents will exactly welcome us turning up at their door."

"Shug, you listen to me, I don't give two flying fucks about her parents. I only want to see she's ok and talk to her for a few minutes to straighten things out."

"Fuck's sake, Rooster. If you go in there 'all guns blazing' her dad will call the cops. Fuck, he's already told us that.

"I think we need to find a better way of catching up with her than caving her old boy's fuckin' heid in," I suggested, but, Rooster being Rooster, he was having none of it.

"Ok then, Mr brain of fuckin' Britain, you tell me how the fuck you think it's going to work then?" he said, really sarcastically.

"I've no idea, Rooster, but what I'm sure of is, if we do it your way, it'll only end in tears. Maybe I could pick up some flowers and take them to the door? If her father lets me speak to her, I could then give you the nod, and you could come to the door as well. What do you think?"

"What do I think? I think you're a fuckin' idiot! How in fuck's name do you think turning up at her door with a bunch of fuckin' flowers is going to clinch the deal? Anyway, just say that it does, what if he invites you in? Where the fuck does that leave me?" he demanded to know.

"Look, if I get in, I'll explain to her that you're here and want five minutes with her. I'm sure she'll go for that."

"Fuck's sake, Shug, your head's full of fuckin' mince, but I don't have a better plan, so I suppose I'm just going to need to roll with it. But just so you know, if it doesn't work, I'm going in there to speak to her one way or another."

"Ok, let's do it," I agreed, telling him I wasn't going to have any part in his plan if mine didn't work.

He just nodded and started to make his way to the door. I stood up, had a drink of my beer then followed him out.

Chapter 12

As we drove through the town, I remembered I'd seen a florist the last time I was here. I turned off the main street and drew up beside it. I went in and bought a nice bunch of flowers. When I came back out, I sat on my bike then wondered how the fuck I was going to get them to her without damaging them?

I looked at Rooster and he was laughing like a fuckin' madman at me.

"This I must fuckin' see," he said, still laughing away.

I got back off, lifted up my seat and got a couple of bungee straps out. I laid the flowers on the pillion seat and wrapped a bungee around them.

I took off my jacket, hung it on the sissy bar to cover the flowers and wrapped the other bungee around it to hold everything in place.

Feeling pleased with myself, I looked at Rooster.

"Well? What about that for a piece of clever thinking!" I told him.

"You're no right in the fuckin' bap!" he told me, shaking his head as he drove off.

Ignoring his comment and thinking about how clever my idea was, I blasted off too. I caught up with him just as he turned off the main street and onto the dual carriageway.

I didn't realise how cold it was, but riding without my jacket, I was shivering like anything. By the time we turned off the dual carriageway, I swear to fuck I was purple with the cold.

I stopped at the first layby, signaling for Rooster to do the same. He drew in and I told him I reckoned Julie's street was only a couple of hundred yards from where we were.

I suggested that when I turn into her street, he should hang back a bit, and once I'd found which house was Julie's, I'd give him a wave and he could park up where he could see the house, but wouldn't be seen by her parents.

I'd then speak to Julie and give him the nod if she wanted to see him.

"Listen, Shug, I'm cool with that, but even if she doesn't want to see me, I'll still be having my five minutes with her and her parents can go fuck themselves if they think they're going to stop me - so make sure you tell her that!"

I just nodded and moved back onto the road. After a couple of wrong turnings and getting directions from an old lady, I was turning into her street. I looked back and pointed towards the side of the road, hoping Rooster would stop and, thankfully, he did.

The street was a dead end with a big turning circle at the bottom of it. All the houses were detached, and I got the impression this was definitely the posh side of town.

I counted the numbers as I headed to the turning circle, clocked Julie's number and drew up in front of her drive.

I got off my bike, put on my jacket, checked the flowers and felt pretty chuffed that they were still in pretty good nick. I picked them up, tried to kind of sort them, then turned around facing towards her house.

Before I even got the gate open, Julie's father was out, telling me to go away. He stood behind the gate like it was a fuckin' barrier, holding on to it with both hands, then said that I'd better leave as his wife had already called the police.

I asked him why they'd done that? And he told me it was because they blamed Rooster and me for Julie's 'accident' - and now that she was feeling much better, they were not prepared to let us anywhere near her.

I was fuckin' fuming but decided to play the game and let him think I had accepted his wishes.

"Ok, I understand how you must feel about me, but trust me, you're barking up the wrong tree," I explained.

"I know you're not going to let me see her, but can you at least give her these flowers? They're not just from me, but also her workmates, and please, tell her I'm sorry. I'd be really grateful if you could let her know that I won't be taking the job, so she won't need to worry about seeing either me or Rooster ever again."

I offered him the flowers and asked if he would give them to her with our best wishes. He initially refused to accept them. However, he decided better of it when I told him that I would stand there all day until he did. I offered them again and this time he took them from me, about turned without saying anything, and headed back inside the house.

I got on my bike and made my way out of the street. As I passed Rooster, I gave him a nod and pointed towards the layby on the main road then made my way there to wait on him.

As I drew to a stop, I heard him fire up his bike and rev the arse out of it. He hadn't even bothered to put his helmet on. He quickly drew up alongside me then jumped off his bike and demanded to know what the fuck had happened.

I lit up two smokes, plunked myself down on the grass verge, inhaled deeply on both then handed one to him which he grudgingly accepted.

"Whit the fuck's going on, man? Why the fuck did you leave without speaking to her? What did that old cunt say to you?"

Rooster was now in my face and looking dead aggressive.

Suddenly, I could hear police sirens and pointed in the direction of the sound.

"The dirty old bastard called the pigs on us," I told him.

"Fuck's sake, Shug. What the fuck did you say that made him call the police?" he asked, demanding I explain.

Rooster was now venting his anger towards Julie's dad rather than at me but was still expecting me to tell him what I had said to upset him. I gestured for him to sit on the grass, which he did. As the sound of the siren became louder and louder, I told him everything that was said which made him curse the old cunt even more.

Just then, the cop car passed us and turned into the street. I suggested to Rooster that we should make tracks, but he was having none of it.

"Shug, you please your-fuckin'-self, mate, but me, I'm going fuckin' nowhere. The minute the pigs leave, I'm right in there. Fuck the old cunt and his threats! I came here to see Julie and I'm not leaving until I do," he told me, as he lay down on the grass, smoking away at his cigarette.

I sat watching as the two policemen got out of the car and began chatting to Julie's dad, who was again standing behind his gate. He continually pointed in our direction as he spoke and, on a couple of occasions, the policemen turned to look at us. One of them was taking notes and I guessed the old cunt was painting as black a picture of us as he could.

I looked at Rooster lying back, smoking and staring at the sky, he looked like he didn't have a care in the world - which really pissed me off because I was well agitated.

"Fuck's sake, Rooster, let's get to fuck. Don't you think there's enough shit going on right now without us creating anymore? The pigs will be coming to see us shortly and I can't afford to end up in the nick. C'mon, man, let's just get the fuck away from here."

Without even looking at me, and in a completely relaxed manner, he spoke quietly, "Shug, you please yourself what you do, mate, but me, I'm not fucking moving until they fuck off and I get a chance to speak to Julie."

This agitated me even more. Just looking at him lying there was driving me nuts.

"Mon tae fuck, Rooster, you know there's only going to be one outcome here and it's not you and Julie kissing and making up. We both know that if you stay here the only thing you're going to see today is the inside of a fuckin' prison cell and you fuckin' know it."

Again, really calmly, but this time looking straight at me, he said, "Well, bud, you know the script ... what will be will be," then laid back and closed his eyes.

"Shug, you should go now. I don't want you to get involved in this. It's my spat, not yours. I'll deal with these two cunts if they come over."

Every time he spoke, he made me madder and madder. I actually felt like I wanted to hit him over the fuckin' head with my helmet or something - to see if I could knock some fuckin' sense into him.

"Rooster, don't give me any of that pish. You know fine well that won't happen. I won't be leaving here without you and you know it. So cut the fuckin' crap!"

I then decided to follow his lead and lay back on the grass, staring at the sky. As I inhaled deeply on my cigarette, I expected him to go off on one, but was really surprised that he never said a single word. As I lay there staring up at the sky, I was wondering to myself what the fuck was coming next, even though, in my heart of hearts, I knew exactly what would happen.

Bang on cue, and with their siren still wailing away, the cop car drew up alongside our bikes and the two officers got out.

"Which one of you is called 'Shug'?" one of the officers asked us.

And, almost in unison, looking like it was rehearsed, Rooster and I lifted our heads at the same time, looked at them, then at each other, shrugged our shoulders, then lay back down.

Rooster then began his reply,

"Officer, my friend and I know no-one of that name so I'm guessing that you're currently speaking to the wrong people. If there's nothing else we can help you with this fine day then you should be on your way," he said really sarcastically, in his best posh voice.

At that point, I couldn't contain myself and burst out laughing. When Rooster heard me, he looked at me and ended up doing the same and it didn't half infuriate the two cops. Almost instantly, the older of the two stood at Roosters feet, completely blocking the sun from him, and gave the sole of his boot a bit of kick then began,

"Right you, ya little prick. Listen here and listen fuckin' good! You can either fuck off now, and stay away and we'll call it quits, or you can act like an arsehole and stay where you are. However, if you decide on the latter, then we'll have ourselves a big fuckin' problem, okay?"

He then went down on his hunkers and stared straight at Rooster.

"Now, here's the way I see it: I could lift you right now for threatening behaviour and harassment, keep you in jail overnight, with a visit to the Judge in the morning OR I could go the full hog and also add assaulting a police officer and resisting arrest to it if you like.

"By my reckoning, I guess that'll get you both at least six months. That's assuming, of course, that you have no previous, but by the look of you, I'm pretty confident you're no strangers to the inside of a prison cell.

"I'm sure the Judge will take all your previous antics into account and maybe add a bit more time to your sentence. So I'm asking you again, for the last time, why don't you just be nice little boys, get on your little toys, and fuck off!"

I looked at Rooster again, wondering if I should maybe say something to try and defuse the situation, but before I got a chance, Rooster sat up and started,

"First of all, I want an apology from you for kicking me," he said, pointing to the officer directly in front of him. "Second, I want you both to get in your little panda car and fuck off. When, and only when you've done that, we'll be on our way. Now, how does that sound to you?" he asked, smiling.

I could see the officers were seething and knew, at that point, we were going to be boxing. So, still lying down, I stretched my arm out and grabbed hold of my helmet - just in case - and thought to myself 'Ah well, fuck it! There goes the job for real so let's just fuckin' do it'.

As I stood up, the officer did the same, and told me to stay where I was then asked his colleague to call for backup.

"Make your fuckin' mind up! One minute, you're telling us to fuck off and the next, you're telling us not to move. So, which is it?" I asked him, equally as sarcastically as Rooster had done earlier.

"You've had your chance to go, dickhead. You, and your arsehole buddy here, have made it perfectly clear that you'd rather stay here and 'come the cunt'. So sit on your fuckin' arse and wait until I tell you it's ok to move."

Rooster then jumped up, and as he did, the cop stepped back. Rooster then squared up to him and I thought 'hey ho, here we go' and decided it best to keep an eye on the other officer who was on the radio.

Rooster looked like he was going to headbutt him and I could see the officer was ready for it. He already had his hand on his truncheon. Rooster took that step closer, the one where you know you've crossed the line and invaded the person's personal space, but instead of hitting him, he just laughed, which threw me a bit.

Then he started talking, this time, though, he sounded much more serious.

"You know what? You're not fuckin' worth it! You're just another fuckin' shite bag hiding behind a shiny fuckin' badge. So, now, either arrest me or get the fuck out of my fuckin' way!" he told him, as he brushed past him, dunting him with his shoulder.

I couldn't fuckin' believe it. The cop just stood back and gesticulated to his colleague to put down the radio. Without looking back, Rooster walked to his bike sat on it, put his helmet on, fired it into life, then fucked off. I thought I'd best do the same in case the cop decided to do me instead so very quickly I jumped on my bike and chased after him with no idea where the fuck he was going.

I looked back and saw both the cops were already in their car and following us up the road. I drew up alongside Rooster and pointed to my tank, letting him know I needed to stop at the next petrol station, and he gave me the thumbs up. We'd only ridden about three miles when we saw a petrol station and drew in.

We got off our bikes at a pump and as we filled up, we both watched the road for 'Hoddit & Doddit' passing, but they never did.

"Guess you've frightened them off!" I shouted over to Rooster, laughing away.

"I knew from the minute he came over, Shug, that he was a fuckin' shite bag," he roared back, also laughing.

Next to the garage there was a 'Little Chef' and I suggested grabbing a bite to eat. Rooster agreed, saying he could do with a bit of a munch. After we paid for our fuel, we drove around the back of the garage and into the car park. As we walked towards the restaurant, I asked Rooster what he thought we should do about Julie. His response kind of threw me a bit – well, in actual fact, it literally took the feet from me.

"You know what, Shug? Fuck her! Fuck her father! And fuck every other cunt that she knows! She's made it very clear that she doesn't want to see or hear what I have to say. So, fuck it, I'm done. It's time for me to move on and forget all about her. Right, let's get some grub …" he suggested, pointing towards the door.

He then put his arm around my shoulder and said, "By the way, Shug, it's your treat," and continued laughing away to himself as we entered the restaurant.

This time, I definitely couldn't work him out. I was sure we were going to be heading back to Julie's and then ending up in some serious shit.

I wasn't sure if I should be worried or relaxed about the sudden change in his behaviour. Knowing him as well as I did, I would never have expected him to walk away like this. I thought maybe I should chat to him about it, but then decided I should probably leave it well alone until we were away from here and back amongst more familiar surroundings.

"So what are you eating, Rooster?" I asked him, pointing to the menu.

"You know what, Shug? I think I'm going to give it a miss, man. I'd rather head down to the clubhouse and see what's happening there. Hopefully, there'll be a bit of a party going on and I can get fuckin' laid and totally off my face."

"Could you hang around for a bit, Rooster? I've got my medical at the hospital at half-four."

"Fuck's sake, Shug. You're not still going on about that fuckin' job thing? Jesus fuck, man! Why in fuck's name are you bothering your arse with it? You'll end up in that fuckin' nurses' home with all the cunts that are Julie's mates and you do know they'll give you the bums rush."

He then leaned over the table until his head was about six inches from mine.

"Listen, Shug, I really don't think you've thought this through very well. You need to get your fuckin' brain into gear, man. Think about it: what if you do decide to move here? I'm guessing you'll need to give up your flat, yeah?"

I just nodded and let him continue talking.

"So tell me what happens when we're done with the South Chapter and head back home - what then? Where the fuck will you live? In the fuckin' barn? I can't see that happening, can you?"

I was going to interrupt at that point, but he put his finger to his mouth and told me to shut the fuck up 'til he was finished, which I did.

"Ok, Shug, let's just say you decide to move here and stay with the South Chapter. Do you think for one minute you'll still be able to keep up as an active Brother in the club whilst living here and working all sorts of fuckin' shifts? Another thing, what if Julie comes back to work and is living a couple of doors away from you, what then?" he asked, as he moved back to his original position.

"Rooster, I won't be on my fuckin' todd," I told him, "You'll be here, and I'll be running with the South Chapter, so I'll have plenty mates less than fifteen minutes away. C'mon, man, don't give me this guilt trip bullshit, you know I really need to do this. I need to get away from the toon for a bit and get my shit together."

Rooster stared at me for what seemed like an age. I really didn't have anything to add so we had one of those uncomfortable silent moments where we just eyeballed each other, but then, thankfully, he started talking again.

"Ok, Shug, fine, I get it. I know where you're coming from. I understand your need to get away, but here? Why the fuck here? I'm telling you, man, if you stay down here, you'll regret it.

"I need you to know I think if you do, you'll be making the biggest mistake of your life. You're going on about needing to get away, so tell me how the fuck this is going to be any better?

"Fuck, Shug. Think about it, man! You'll be living in a place that's full of Julie's mates who won't fuckin' talk to you. I'm telling you, man, it's a frying pan and fire fuckin' scenario. Don't do it, mate, you'll fuckin' regret it.

"Right, man, you get yourself fed. I'm going to hit the road. My advice, for what it's worth, take a bit of time to clear your head, even think about moving to the North Chapter. That'll give you a bit of breathing space and a totally new beginning 'cause you won't know any cunt up there.

"All I'm saying is weigh up the pros and cons, bud, before you decide what to do. Right, I'm off. I'll see you back at the clubhouse later. Remember, Indie wants you back tonight. Ok, take it easy, man."

We both stood up, shook hands and slapped each other on the back.

"Take care, man," Rooster told me, and I replied, telling him to do the same.

Chapter 13

I sat back down and watched him ride off. My head was now so full of shit that I felt like it was going to blow off my shoulders. I had no idea what the fuck I should do. Before I had spoken to Rooster, I thought I had it all worked out, but now he'd put all this other shit in my head I had no fuckin' idea what to do.

'Thanks for fuck all, Rooster,' I thought to myself.

Just then, the waitress put my food in front of me and I thanked her - even though I no longer wanted it. I nibbled away at it, but my mind was racing, trying to process everything.

My big brainwave was to visit Julie again. If she would speak to me then I knew I'd be ok here. If she didn't, I'd take Rooster's advice and fuck off back home and give the job a miss.

I looked down at my plate and realised I had finished my food – I guess I must've been hungrier than I thought. I checked the clock and it was just after 2 p.m. I reckoned a couple of hours would give me enough time to get back to Julie's, talk things through with her and still get to the hospital by the back of four.

If Julie gave me a bummer then the medical would be a waste of time and I would just fuck off. I paid the waitress then headed out. The rain had started just as I left the car park and I thought to myself, 'Fuckin typical. That's all I fuckin' need now. By the time I get to Julie's, I'll be like a drowned fuckin' rat!'. I cursed my luck all the way there and drew into the layby Rooster and I had been in earlier. Thankfully, by this time, the rain had reduced to a spit.

I switched off my bike and lit up a smoke. I tried to think of something tangible that I could use for my opening gambit because, as sure as fuck, I'd need something to get passed her prick of a father. I couldn't really come up with anything, so I decided to leave my bike in the layby and walk to her house.

I thought it might give me the element of surprise and it may even be Julie that answers the door. I walked down the street on her side of the road knowing that no-one in her house would be able to see me until I was at the door. I got to her house and went around the back without being detected, or at least so I thought.

Just as I went to knock on the door, it opened, and Julie was standing right in front of me. I kind of gaped at her with my mouth open. Now I was facing her, I had no idea what the fuck to say.

"Shug! What the fuck do you want?" she asked.

I then blurted out that it was good to see her and that she was looking well.

"Have you been hiding somewhere, waiting on my parents to leave?" she asked.

"No, Julie, I didn't know they'd left," I told her. "Look, Julie, I don't mean to bug you. I just wanted to see if you were ok and have a quick chat if you were up for it."

She then repeated her question, but this time with real venom in her voice.

"Shug, what the fuck do you REALLY want?"

"Well, Julie, what I didn't want was to upset you and I can clearly see that you are, so I'll make it quick. Then I'll split and leave you be."

I took a breath, had a bit of a cough, and started again,

"Nobody I asked would tell me anything about how you were. I've been going out of my mind worrying about you and thinking all sorts of shit. I needed to come and see how you were for myself. When your mum called the cops, I was pretty sure I wouldn't see you again which screwed me right up.

"I gave your dad some flowers from Rooster and me and asked him to pass a message on to you. He said he would, but I'm guessing by the look on your face that he didn't."

When I looked at her, she lowered her brow and shook her head.

'I fuckin' knew it,' I thought to myself, 'what a little cunt he was,' but I did my best not to show Julie what I was thinking.

"Look, Julie, I only wanted to see that you were ok. I'm guessing now, after seeing you, that you're on the mend so I'll head off. I'm really sorry for bothering you," I told her, as I turned to walk away.

"Shug, wait, don't go," she shouted after me, which in a sick kind of way made me smile.

Before I turned back around, I made sure I had turned my smile into a look of sympathy. Julie sat on the kitchen floor, with her feet on the step, and I walked back towards her.

"Look, Julie, for what it's worth, I'm really sorry about what has happened and if I could turn back the clock I would. I never meant to do anything that would hurt you. I hope you know that.

"Calum told me you were hoping to return to work soon, so I just want you to know that you don't need to worry about seeing Rooster or me again. He's decided not to try to contact you anymore and I'm going to give the job a miss and return home. I really hope everything works out for you and that you keep well."

I leaned over her, kissed her on the forehead, and said, "Take care of yourself, Julie."

I then turned and started making my way up the path for a second time. This time, however, I didn't get a shout from Julie.

Instead, she grabbed hold of my arm and pulled me around, giving me a huge big cuddle, squeezing me as hard as she could. She nestled her mouth in my neck, just below my ear, and began to whisper,

"Shug, what I did had nothing to do with you or, for that matter, Rooster. You see, what actually happened was, well, eh…"

Suddenly, she stopped talking and pulled away from me. She took hold of my hand and made her way back into the house, dragging me with her.

When we went in, she led me straight into the living room and sat me on the couch. She pulled the coffee table towards me, sat on it, faced directly opposite me, then continued from where she had left off.

"Shug, when I had the abortion and moved down here, I thought I had coped with it and moved on. I convinced myself at the time that it was the best thing to do under the circumstances. Strangely enough, I was more worried about my parents finding out than anything else and was really glad I had managed to hide it from them.

"The night I cut myself I had agreed to go to a party in the common room. Lisa had arranged it as a surprise for her pal's birthday and I was looking forward to it, but when I awoke that morning, for some reason, I felt really really low. I lay in bed most of the day and all the feelings of guilt about aborting our baby seemed to overwhelm me to the point I was crying and crying and just couldn't stop.

"After her shift, Lisa came back with some food and stuff for our lunch and was all excited about the party. When she saw the state of me, she knew something was up and I ended up telling her everything then we both ended up crying.

"I told her that there was no way I could go to the party the way I was feeling and that she should just go herself. But you know what she's like and how she can go on, so I ended up agreeing to go for an hour or so.

"Anyway, we had something to eat then Lisa left, telling me she would give me a shout later. I lay back down and ended up sleeping for the rest afternoon. I woke around tea-time went and had a shower, which seemed to brighten me up a bit, got dressed then went to the dining room for something to eat.

"It was pretty busy and lots of people were rushing in and out picking up food and heading back to their wards. All the people I knew either waved over to me or gave me a nod on their way out which I was glad about as I didn't want to talk to anyone.

"Lisa came in just as I was leaving and tried to talk me into staying with her while she ate. Stupidly, I told her I needed to head back to my room to get ready for the party.

"It was the only thing I could think of saying which would allow me to leave. She then said 'Great. I'll give you a shout later' smiled at me then began eating her meal. I quickly made my way back to my room, wishing I'd never went out. I lay on my bed wondering how I was going to get out of attending the stupid party.

"I then, for some reason, started thinking about the abortion again and it was really, really upsetting me. I started crying uncontrollably for what seemed like an age. Anyway, I must have dozed off and was wakened by the door being banged. I looked at the clock and it

99

was after eight. I couldn't decide if it was morning or evening and it took me a few minutes to come to.

"I opened the door and Lisa and Calum were standing there, all dressed up and smiling away. Lisa barged in and wanted to know why I wasn't ready. I told her I didn't feel like it, but she was having none of it and again she went on and on until I ended up agreeing to go for an hour or so just to shut her up.

"When I was there, all I could think about was how to get out of staying, but Calum and Lisa were equally determined that I didn't leave. I'd been there for over an hour and although I still wanted to leave, I was feeling reasonably ok. Someone came in and told me there was a phone call for me and, as I felt I was ready to leave, the call couldn't have come at a better time.

"I excused myself, telling Lisa and Calum that I would only be a minute, even though I had no intention of returning. When I got to the phone it was Rooster. He kept on telling me how much he loved me and how sorry he was about making me get rid of the baby.

"He then went into great detail about how he was really sorry for putting the Bats before me and kept apologising about it saying that if I went back with him that things would change.

"He said that he should never have treated me the way that he did and that he was an idiot for doing so. He made it clear that, from that point on, I would always be his first priority and the Bats his second if I agreed to go back out with him.

"All the stuff he told me was all the stuff I'd wanted to hear him say before we split, and I ended up agreeing to meet with him. After the call, I made my way back up to my room. As I walked, I began to feel almost numb and my mood became very flat. All I could think was why didn't he tell me all this when I was pregnant. If he had, things could have been so different.

"When I got back to my room, I grabbed the vodka from the table, sat on my bed, opened it, threw the lid on the floor and began drinking straight from the bottle. The more I drank, the more I cursed him, the more I cursed him, the more I thought about our baby and the sadder I got. Then I noticed the sleeping pills I was given from the doctor.

"One minute they were on the table, the next, I was ramming them into my mouth and washing them down with large swigs of vodka. I looked at the pill bottle and realised that it was empty then began to wonder what the hell I was doing.

"I'd drank more than three quarters of the vodka, took God knows how many pills, and was feeling totally numb. At that point, I just burst out crying and felt like I had the weight of the world on my shoulders.

"For some strange reason, still unknown to me, I grabbed hold of the sharp knife I kept for cutting bread and slashed my wrists with it. I then slumped on the floor not really knowing what I'd just done. I rested my back against the bed and watched the blood flow out onto my hands down onto my legs and then eventually onto the floor.

"Next thing I know, I'm waking up in hospital with my parents sitting at either side of my bed."

"Holy fuck, Julie, that's some fuckin' shit. No wonder your mum and dad don't want you anywhere near Rooster or me."

"Shug, the reason they don't want any of you near me is because you told them about the phone call.

They blame Rooster for me cutting myself so, by association, they don't want you here either.

"I tried to tell them that it was nothing to do with him and that I had been a bit depressed for a while. That it had only happened because I was drunk and took too many sleeping tablets. I told them that I knew straightaway it was a mistake, then made up some bullshit story about being lonely and of course they blamed that on Rooster as well."

"Fuck me, Julie. You don't half know how to fuck things up. I think we must be kindred spirits or something. It sounds exactly the type of thing I would do."

We both began to laugh and again ended up cuddling. Julie moved off the coffee table and onto my lap. She wrapped her arms around me and was again snuggling her face into my neck.

I held her close and rubbed her back gently.

"Shug, please tell me you're joking," she said, sitting up a bit so she could see my face.

"What?" I asked her, knowing exactly what she was talking about.

"Jesus fuck, Shug. You've got a fuckin' hard-on, haven't you?" she yelled, moving off my lap and on to the couch beside me. "You just couldn't make it up, Shug, could you? Here I am, pouring my heart out to you, and you're getting a fuckin' stiffy. Un-fuckin-believable," she said, shaking her head.

"Come on, Julie. Be fair. It's not my fault. It just happens. You know that. I've told you umpteen times before. Every time I'm with you, no matter what the occasion, I get one. It doesn't mean I'm hoping for a shag or anything."

She just shook her head, smiled, then burst out laughing. As she cuddled in, I lifted her back onto my lap. This time, however, instead of sitting still, she was squirming around, teasing the fuck out of me.

"You can be one cock-teasing bastard when you want to be and don't you fuckin' know it!" I told her.

She then whispered in my ear, "Who's teasing?" then started kissing my neck.

"This better not be another fuckin' wind-up, Julie!" I said, as I placed my hand on her tit.

The next minute, she's bucking away and got her tongue down my throat, fumbling about trying to unzip my jacket.

"Whoa, whoa, slow down a bit here, Julie," I said, as I pushed her back a bit, "Let's take a breath here. Half an hour ago, I was public enemy number one. Now we're back where we were a week ago. Are you sure about this?" I asked her.

"Fuck, Shug. Sometimes you can be pretty slow, I love you, I need you, and, fuck, I want you right now. What the fuck else do you want me to say?" she told me, as she continued to remove my jacket.

"Julie, I love you too, but this is fuckin' crazy. What about your folks? Where the fuck are they? What if they come back and we're lying bollock naked on their couch? I can't imagine that going down too well!"

"Shug, you worry too much. Do you think for a minute that I'd do this if there was any chance of them coming in and catching us? They're away for a long weekend to my auntie and uncle's caravan, it's sixty miles away, so I think we're pretty safe," she told me.

Well, that was enough for me. I didn't even bother unbuttoning her blouse. I just ripped it open, unhooked her bra, lifted her tits out, clasped them in my hands and began tweaking and biting away. Julie was moaning then let out a bit of a groan as she pulled

103

my shirt over my head and started to undo my belt. I stood up and she wrapped her arms and legs around me, holding tight, as I laid her on the floor.

Within what seemed like a nanosecond, we were both naked, kissing and touching each other like a couple of frenzied animals - until I eventually entered her. Julie wrapped her legs around my lower back and dug her nails into my shoulders. I got myself into a bit of a slow rhythm, trying really hard not to cum, which was almost impossible the way Julie was bucking underneath me.

As she bucked and panted, she dug her nails even further into my back. She was telling me to fuck her harder and harder. Well, at that point, I was gone, and within two seconds, I shot my load right into her. I swear to God if I hadn't come when I did, she'd have ripped my back to shreds.

I slumped on top of her, seriously out of breath, and feeling really weak. It took me all of my time not to land my full weight on her as my arms were shaking. I can't remember the last time I had such an intense orgasm. I leaned down towards her head to give her a kiss, but she was having none of it. Instead of kissing me, she grabbed hold of my head and directed it towards her pussy.

I was more than happy to oblige, licking pussy was one of my favourite things. However, just as I got in position and my tongue touched her clit, she grabbed my hair with one hand pushing my head beyond her clit and right into her hole then she started rubbing her clit with her other hand.

She was so frantic that I felt like she was trying to suffocate me by pushing my head deep inside her. By now she had her four fingers rubbing and pulling at her clit as she tried to bring herself to an orgasm. I swear to God I felt like my full face was inside her pussy and she was still pushing my head trying to get me deeper and deeper inside her.

At this point, I was hoping and praying she'd shoot her load pretty sharpish. I was struggling to breathe, and her nails were digging right into my head. Almost within seconds of me starting to worry, she let out a scream as she brought herself to an orgasm, rubbing and pulling on her clit as hard and as fast as she possibly could.

She then pushed my head away and began shaking and jerking before going limp, breathing like she'd just ran a marathon. I got myself up onto my knees, taking in some deep breaths, trying to refill my lungs with air, my face covered in her cum and blood trickling down the side of my head.

"Fuck me, Julie. I think I might need fuckin' stitches now," I told her, referring to the deep scratches she'd left in my head and back.

She just ignored my rant and curled herself up into a ball on the rug. I noticed that she was shivering so I lay down beside her and cuddled in. She had her eyes closed and there were tears rolling down her face. She tried to cover them with her hand, but I lifted it from her face and gave her a kiss.

She then began to cry as we cuddled, and I held her for about ten minutes as she continued to sob without saying a word. Her shivering seemed to be getting worse and I could feel myself getting cold, so I asked her if she wanted me to get her a cover or her clothes and she just nodded.

I got up, stuck on my jeans and T-shirt, then lifted the blanket from the sofa. I helped her up and wrapped the blanket around her then sat her back on the chair. She seemed to be staring into space and I had to ask

105

her three times if she was ok before it even registered with her that I was talking.

"Sorry, Shug, what did you say?" she asked, looking right through me.

"I was just asking if you were ok and if you were warm enough?" I told her, and again, all she offered was a blank expression.

I started to wonder if she was still a bit loopy and had no idea what the fuck else I should say to her. I just gave her a cuddle for a bit then suggested she put her clothes back on.

"Why do I need to put my clothes on, Shug?"

"Because you're cold and you don't want to be sitting about undressed," I told her.

"Ok, Shug, I'll put them on," she said, getting up from the chair, but still staring into space.

I gathered her clothes up and laid them on the chair. She looked at me, then at the clothes for a bit, before starting to put them on.

I watched her closely as she dressed. She actually looked like she was a fuckin' Zombie. She never said a single word, and when I asked her if she was feeling any better, she asked me why I wanted to know?

"You were a bit emotional earlier. I just wondered if you still were, that's all," I replied.

"I don't feel emotional. I feel fine," she told me. "I'm going to make a cup of tea. Do you want one?" she asked me as she finished dressing.

"What about your top, Julie? Don't you think you should change it? There's only one button left on it," I told her.

"Oh, I never noticed. I'll just go and get another one from my room," she said as she made her way out the living room and up the stairs.

I lit up a smoke and started pacing the floor a bit. I had no idea what the fuck to do. She was clearly still out of her box and I wondered if I should call somebody. In my mind I started to question her so-called caring parents. I couldn't believe that they'd left her on her own. They must have known she wasn't right.

Fuck. It was hardly a week since she tried to top herself and there they were swanning off to a fuckin' caravan. I still wasn't sure what I should do, if anything. First thing I thought about was calling the nurses' home to see if I could get hold of Lisa or Calum but wasn't sure if I was just panicking over nothing. I sat down on the chair and tried to clear my head.

When I thought about it, Julie seemed like her old self when I'd got there, so maybe she had convinced her parents that she was ok. She came back downstairs and into the room. She'd changed into a pair of trackies and a sweatshirt and sat on the sofa.

"You feeling okay now, Julie?" I asked her.

"Yeah, I'm okay, sorry about earlier. I just felt a bit emotional and having sex seemed to release all sorts of shitty endorphins making me feel a bit crazy. You don't have to worry, Shug, I'm not going to grab a kitchen knife and stab you in the head or anything, if that's what you're worried about?"

"Ha, ha, don't be daft. I never thought anything like that. I was just a bit worried when you went all starry-eyed and quiet. You just seemed to zone out. You never even heard me talking and I was worried something was up," I told her.

Fuck. I hadn't thought about her wanting to hurt me until she mentioned it. Just listening to her say the words, I wondered if she was actually capable of it?

"Sorry about your head. I never realised I was hurting you," she said, pointing to the blood on the side of my face, "Let me get some stuff from the kitchen and I'll get you cleaned up."

She then got up and made her way to the kitchen. By this time, I'd got myself so worked up. I had no idea what she would come back with. In my head I pictured her running at me with the bread knife and trying to stick it in my heart.

'Fuck's sake, Shug. Come on. Get a grip of yourself, man!' I thought. Julie came back in with a bowl of water, a towel and some cotton wool - I breathed a huge sigh of relief.

Julie clocked me and said,

"Shug, Are you for real? Surely you didn't think … no, really … tell me you didn't think I could …, Fuck, even you think I'm fuckin' mental. Jeez 'o. You're the last person I thought would treat me like this!"

"Whoa. Hang on, Julie. What the fuck are you on about? You'll need to rewind a bit. I've no fuckin' idea what the fuck you're talking about?"

She then put the bowl on the table, threw the cotton wool and the towel on the couch, then told me to fuck off. I tried to protest, but she was having none of it. She started screaming at me telling me to fuck off or she would call the cops and tell them that I had broken in.

"Come on, Julie. You're being a bit over fuckin' dramatic here. Why don't you sit your arse on the chair and we can chat about it?"

"How many fuckin' times have I to tell you?" she said, picking up my jacket and boots, then storming back through to the kitchen.

The next thing I hear is the back door opening then her shouting again for me to fuck off. I got up and thought 'Fuck this for a game of soldiers!' and headed into the kitchen and let out a rant of my own.

"You know what, Julie? I can well do without this pish. I came here because I care for you and was worried about you. And you know what? I was right to worry, 'cause you're fuckin' mental. The quicker you phone your doctor the better, if you ask me," I yelled at her, as I went outside, picking up my boots and jacket.

"Well, I'm not asking you, so you won't have to worry. Oh, and by the way, don't ever come back here again coz you won't be welcome, ya fuckin' prick!"

Before I could reply, she slammed the door and I heard her turning the lock as she ranted away. I sat on the step and put my boots on, thinking to myself 'What a fuckin' cow she was' and began to wish I'd done the same as Rooster and kept well the fuck away.

Chapter 14

I stood up, put my jacket on, fumbled about for my cigarettes and lighter, lit up a smoke then headed back to my bike. I unhooked my helmet, fired up my bike and headed back to the hospital, still cursing her under my breath. I had no idea what time it was and really didn't care whether I made it in time or not.

I entered the hospital by the main gate and as I turned towards the admin block, I saw the clock showing twenty-past-four. I parked up and went into the reception. There were three people sitting there when I went in, one guy and two girls.

I tapped on the window and it was the same little fucker I'd spoken to before who answered. He just pointed over to where the others were sitting then turned away from me. Not sure why, but I tapped the window again and gestured for him to open it. He swirled around in his chair, slid it open, covered the mouthpiece on his headset and gave me a right aggressive look and said, "What?" in a very hostile and demeaning tone.

I stuck my head in the window and very quietly told him if he was ever rude to me again that I would drag him out of his fuckin' goldfish bowl, punch his cunt in, then ram his headset right up his fuckin' arse. He sat there, momentarily stunned. He seemed to be totally shocked by my comments which I found really hard to believe.

There was no way he hadn't been spoken to like that before. An ignorant little cunt like him must have been told that ten times a day.

I snapped my fingers at him and said, "I'm here to see Mrs Boardman. Can you please call her and tell her I've arrived?"

He then snapped out of his trance and said, "Certainly, Sir," closed the window slowly then turned back to his switchboard.

I turned around to find Mrs Boardman standing directly behind me and thought 'Holy fuck, Shug! That's you! You've definitely blown it this time. Agghh. Fuck. I couldn't believe I'd done it again'. I noticed out of the corner of my eye that the three others sitting in the room were all sniggering. When I looked at Mrs Boardman, I swear she was sniggering as well, even though she was trying her best to hide it.

"Hi, Ochil, sorry I'm late. Just head along to my office and I'll meet you there …" she said in a stern voice, pointing towards the door.

As I made my way out, I heard her speak to the others and guessed they were there for a medical as well. I went into her office and sat on one of the chairs that were along the wall behind the door. I looked around the room and out the window.

I wondered where the fuck she was, she seemed to be taking ages. Of course, the longer I sat there on my own, the more I began to think. I wondered if she had actually heard me saying anything to the little prick and guessed she must have or she would have brought us all along to the office at the same time. I thought about telling her how Julie was, to see if she could offer me some advice, but wasn't sure if it was a good idea.

I thought about the job. Did I really want it? Could I even work with lunatics? Could I stay here after all the shit that had gone on? Fuck. So many questions. Just then, she came into the office and closed the door. I kind of wondered where the others had gone, but not really enough to mention it. Mrs Boardman never even looked at me when she entered. She went straight over behind her desk and stared out of the window.

I was kind of taken aback by this and wanted to ask her if she was ok, but decided it was best to keep schtum and let her go first. She turned back around, pulled her chair out from behind her desk then sat down. She lifted her head and looked at me.

"What am I going to do with you, Ochil?" she said, staring at me.

"What do you mean?" I asked her, shifting forward in my chair, trying to process what she had just said.

"Well, Ochil. I want to be brutally honest with you, so forgive me if I say anything that upsets you, but I'm beginning to wonder if offering you the job is going to the best thing for either of us?"

I went to reply, but she held up her hand and asked me not to interrupt.

"Please let me finish. I need you to hear this," she told me, "Initially, when we met, I thought you were like a breath of fresh air. Someone different from the normal type of person we hire. I saw a bit of a glint in your eye and felt that you would have a lot of empathy with our patients. I thought you'd bring a bit of drive and energy that I hadn't seen in anyone for a long time. I was sure you would fit in well and be a good addition to our staff. Now, however, I'm not so sure. I need you to explain a few things to me before we go any further and I need you to be honest with me."

I told her to just go for it and ask me anything she liked.

"See. That's what I mean, Ochil. With you it's a case of what you see is what you get, and you always want to cut to the chase," she said, smiling.

"Well, as far as I'm concerned, there's not much point in beating around the bush," I told her, "Good or

112

bad, I'd much rather people say it how it is and be done with it."

"You know that's a rare quality these days, Ochil, but you have to understand, working in a Psychiatric Hospital … it's full of grey areas. Nothing is ever just black or white as most of the patients here have a distorted sense of reality. A lot of them will say things that can hurt or upset you without them even knowing it. I fear you may not have the temperament required to cope with it."

By this time, I was starting to become well pissed off from listening to all her psychobabble bullshit and felt like she was trying to fuckin' psychoanalyze me so I interrupted her again.

"Look, I'm sorry to interrupt you again, Mrs Boardman, but I have no idea where all this has come from. As far as I'm concerned, nothing has changed for me since I was offered the job. The thing is, Mrs Boardman, I really wanted this job and I reckoned, given time, I would have been very good at it.

"But I guess, with what you're saying, that you've decided you no longer want to give it to me. If that's the case, then just tell me and I'll be on my way. In fact, you know what? I'll save you the bother!"

I stood up and made my way to the door, thinking I should never have come here in the first place. Now I just wanted to leave and forget about the whole sorry fuckin' episode. Waiting around to be let down gently wasn't really my thing, especially with all the other shit I had going on. Deep down, in my heart of hearts, I knew it was probably for the best anyway. Just as I put my hand on the doorknob, Mrs Boardman called to me.

"Please, Ochil. Don't leave like this. Just give me five minutes of your time. Surely that's not too much to ask?"

I lifted my hand off the doorknob, turned back around, looked at her, and said, "Listen, Mrs Boardman, I appreciate the offer and I know you now wish you hadn't made it so I'll make it easy for both of us and head off. There's no need to let me down gently. I'm a big boy. I'm well used to this kind of shit."

"Ochil, please close the door. I really don't think you understand. I don't want to withdraw the offer. I want to talk to you about which ward I want you to work in: to find out if you would be comfortable with it. Please have a seat and let me explain."

I was kind of speechless. I thought she was building up to tell me to 'sling my hook' and now she's telling me she wants to discuss where she wants me to work.

I made my way back to the chair and sat down. She came around to the front of her desk and eased herself onto it, leaving her legs dangling. Looking straight at me from her slightly elevated position I had no idea why, but I started to feel a bit intimidated. When she started talking, it didn't make me feel any less uncomfortable.

"Ochil, why would you think I didn't want you to take the job?" she asked.

It took me a few seconds to get my head together before I eventually answered.

"I'm not really sure. I just had a gut feeling about it. Then, when you heard me threatening the telephone dude, I thought that was that."

She burst out laughing and said quietly, "If there was ever a reason for giving someone a job in the hospital then being abusive to Larry would certainly do it."

I just smiled and suggested that I couldn't have been the first person to have words with him. She told me I wasn't, but that she hadn't heard anyone being just as descriptive about their intentions as I had.

She then changed the subject and started to tell me where she wanted me to work.

"I'm not sure how much you know about the hospital, but most of the patients we have here are either geriatrics or long-term. All with some kind of mental health issue.

"We also have two types of admission wards in the hospital, one for acute patients and the other for non-acute. The acute ward is a locked ward and most of the patients who are housed there are considered a danger to either themselves or to others. I wanted to know how you would feel if I was to put you in there?

"Normally we would start new nursing assistants in either the long-term or geriatric wards until they were familiar with the role. However, one of the nursing assistants who worked there has just left to start his training and rather than move someone in from another ward I thought it would be ideal to put you in there. What're your thoughts on it?"

I was having trouble processing what she had told me. I'd gone from thinking I was getting the 'heave ho' to being asked to go straight into what seemed like a pretty dangerous environment. I really wasn't sure what I said, and I think I just blurted out something about being happy to be given the opportunity or something like that.

Then I remembered about the medical and asked her if I was still getting one? She told me not to worry about the medical and asked if I could start the following Monday, to which I agreed.

We spoke about me getting a room at the nurses' home and I gave her my measurements for my uniform. She went on to explain that I'd have an induction before I started and that she would arrange for me to get my medical as well.

She then told me she had some stuff to do and that I should head off. I thanked her and made my way towards the door again. As I was leaving, she called me back again.

"Oh, Ochil. I forgot to ask you, how's Julie? Have you seen her lately?"

I about shat myself where I stood, she must have seen the blood draining from me 'cause I sure as fuck felt it. I really wasn't sure what to tell her, so I decided to keep it superficial and avoid any details.

"Yes, I was with her just before I came over today and we had a bit of chat. She was quite bright when I arrived, but before I left, she was feeling pretty tired. She was well chuffed with the flowers and stuff too, which was nice," I lied to her. "I gave her your regards and told her that everyone here was thinking about her which really perked her up."

"That's good, because everyone here is wishing her well and looking forward to her return."

She then excused herself, telling me she was late for a meeting.

"I'll see you next Monday, Ochil. Now remember, nine o'clock and don't be late," she said, as she smiled, then pointed towards the door.

I took that as my cue to split.

"See you then," I told her, smiling back, then made my way out.

I walked up the corridor, opened the outside door, took a huge gulp of air then slowly exhaled.

I seemed to be doing this way too often recently for my liking. After another big breath I made my way to my bike then began to wonder what the fuck I'd done. Then it hit me like a sledgehammer, bang, right on the fuckin' napper. I must be off my fuckin' trolley. I'd just signed up to work in a fuckin' loonie bin! Fuck. I couldn't even help Julie … somebody I cared deeply for. How in fuck's name was I ever going to be able to look after cunts I didn't know?

Immediately my thoughts turned to Julie. I knew before I left her that she was having some real trouble, but did I care? Did I fuck. I just left her anyway. And why the fuck did I leave her to her own devices? So I could come here for a poxy fuckin' medical which I didn't even end up getting. Some friend I was! What a fuckin'wanker.

I sat on my bike staring into space. Trying to make some sense of why I would leave her for this? The only thing I could come up with was that I was a self-centered prick who really only gave a fuck about himself. By now I was sweating, and I thought my heart was going to burst out my chest, it was beating that fast.

I'm not sure if it was guilt, worry or fear, but I had an overwhelming feeling that I needed to get back to Julie's as quickly as possible. I fired up my bike and blasted out the hospital, hit the main road and sped all way back to Julie's. All the way there, all I could think about was why had I left her on her own. I was petrified at the thought of her alone and doing something stupid again.

I knew she was a bit of an emotional wreck, but because she threw a strop I just fucked off and left her when I really should have tried to help her. I kept replaying our argument over and over again, trying to figure out the main reason she'd kicked off. My best guess was that it was because we had shagged and afterwards she'd freaked, knowing it was the wrong thing to do.

I turned into her street, my heart still pounding like anything. I slammed on the brakes right at her gate, jumped off, left my bike running and still with my helmet on, raced to the back door. I banged on it really loudly and was shouting her name. When no-one answered, I tried the door and it was locked. I banged it another couple of times, still shouting her name, but after a few minutes I thought 'Fuck this!' and booted the door in. As it swung open, it hit one of the wall units and one of the glass panels shattered, leaving glass all over the kitchen floor. I just ran over the top of it and made my way straight into the living room.

There was no-one there, but the telly was on. I stuck my head into the dining room and the downstairs bedroom, but again, no-one. I ran up the stairs and by this time I was totally shitting myself about what I might find.

I looked in both bedrooms, again nothing. The only room left to check was the bathroom. I stood in front of the door knowing it was the only place she could be.

In my head I had visions of her blood splattered body lying in the bath. I stood still for a minute, almost frozen to the spot, then I put my ear to the door. I could hear music, but nothing else.

I took a deep breath and tried the handle, it wouldn't turn. 'Fuck!' I thought to myself. If I wanted in, I knew I'd need to burst it open. I decided I had no choice, so I barged it with my shoulder and burst my way in. As I entered, I heard an almighty scream. It was Julie. She was having a shower with the radio on. When she saw me, she thought I was a burglar or something.

At the same time as she let out her scream, she lost her footing and slipped in the bath. She grabbed hold of the shower curtain which then came away from the rail and she ended up falling directly towards me. I managed to grab hold of her just before she hit the ground.

Almost immediately, we both ended up on the floor. Me first, then Julie on top of me. I started laughing almost involuntarily, which I guess was probably some kind of relief mechanism on my part. Unfortunately, as far as Julie was concerned, it was definitely the wrong thing to be doing. She certainly didn't seem to find it in the least bit funny.

"What the fuck are you doing, Shug? Have you lost your fuckin' mind?" she began screeching at me as she lifted herself to her feet, grabbing a towel in the process, "I should phone the cops and get you arrested for this. You're a fuckin' nutter! Right, Shug, you've got two seconds to tell me what the fuck this is all about or I swear to God I'll call the cops!"

"Whoa, Julie. Hang on a fuckin' second, will you?" I roared back at her, "It's not what you think. Fuck me! I'm only here because I was fuckin' worried about you."

"Worried? Fuckin' worried about me? Oh, right. So because you're worried about me you break into my fuckin' house, burst open my bathroom door, scare the livin' shit out of me - all because you're supposed to be worried about me? Do me a fuckin' favour!" she ranted, still screeching at the top of her voice.

I tried lowering my voice in the hope she would calm down a bit.

"Julie, look, I'm really sorry. Please just let me explain."

"No, Shug. I don't want to hear any more of your bullshit stories. I've heard enough. I just want you to get the fuck out of my house right now," she told me, although this time she was no longer roaring at me and seemed like she had calmed down a fair bit.

I tried again to get her to let me explain, but she just turned and headed to her bedroom.

I picked myself up off the floor and followed her along the landing like a fuckin' puppy dog pleading with her again to let me explain. When she got to her bedroom door, she turned around, stared straight at me, and repeated her earlier threat about calling the cops. That was enough for me. I kind of lost it at that point as I knew I was on a hiding to nothing.

"You know what, Julie? Fine. You win. I'll go. Just so you know, the reason I came back here in the first place was because I care about you. When I left earlier, I couldn't get you out of my mind and I just needed to see you were okay. I was worried that you weren't doing so good. With your parents away I thought you might be lonely and that you could've done with a bit of company, but hey, bigger the fool me!"

Half-way through my rant she'd gone into her room and closed the door. I continued talking until I had said my bit then shouted to her that I was leaving. I went back downstairs and headed for the kitchen. As I entered, I saw all the glass. Fuck! I'd forgotten all about that and for some reason, when I saw the mess I'd made, I felt compelled to clean it up. I opened the walk-in cupboard and found a dustpan and brush. I swept up the glass and put it in the outside bin then removed all the shards from the cupboard door.

Before I left, I made sure there were no traces of glass anywhere and tried to fix the lock on the back door. I only managed to get it to open and close, but the actual locking mechanism was bust. All the time I was there I kept thinking that Julie would come down the stairs to see what I was up to, but she never did. I checked my pockets for cash, but all I had was twenty quid so I left ten on the worktop to go towards repairing the damage I'd done.

I went out to my bike and smiled. It had been idling away all the time I'd been in the house and I hadn't even heard it. I looked for my helmet then realised I still had the fucker on - which made me go from a smile to a laugh. I just shook my head, got on my bike and wondered once again how in fuck's name I kept getting myself involved in shit like this.

Chapter 15

I rode out of her street and onto the main road, not really sure where the fuck I was going. I rode for a few miles then stopped at a layby, got off and sat on the wall. I lit up a smoke and tried to figure out what best to do next.

I knew Indie was expecting me at the clubhouse before dark, but I wasn't sure I really wanted to be there. My preferred choice would've been to head back to my flat, shut the door, have a few cans and just chill for a couple of days, but I knew if I did it would give me a whole lot of other problems when he next caught up with me.

The other thing was Rooster, the next time I see him I know the first things he'll want to know are: Did I take the job? And had I see Julie? I jumped off the wall and paced up and down for a bit, trying to figure out what to tell him about her. It was a racing certainty that if I told him the truth that he'd flip his fuckin' lid.

Deep down, I knew I had to go to the clubhouse and that I had to face Rooster. The problem I had was what to tell him? I knew he would be on my case about her the minute he saw me. As much as I didn't want to lie to him, I felt I had no choice.

I decided the best thing for me would be to tell him that I hadn't seen her. I knew he wasn't going to see her again so I reckoned telling him that I hadn't seen her would be the best way of avoiding an interrogation. I got back on my bike and headed down to the clubhouse.

All the way there, my mind was running on overtime. The closer I got, the more my thoughts turned to Indie and the Bats. I had no idea what the fuck would be going on. I hoped that all the shit that happened before we left would be behind us and that there'd be no more fuckin' aggravation.

I turned off the main road and immediately saw all the bikes in the pub car park. I found myself a space and killed my engine. I got off feeling really weary and a bit downtrodden. I hadn't realised just how much the last twenty-four hours or so had done me in. It was like someone had just pulled out my plug and drained away all my energy.

I leaned up against the wall, lit up a smoke and looked around at all the bikes. I could hear music coming from inside and guessed there was a bit of a party going on. It kind of pissed me off because I really couldn't be arsed being sociable.

On the plus side, however, it gave me a sense of relief because I knew there was no way Indie would let the guy's party if there were still things that needed sorted, or so I thought. I made my way inside, and to say the place was rocking was an understatement. Fuck! I opened the door and was instantly hit by a wall of sound. There were half-naked girls dancing on tables, people sprawled about on the floor and the place looked like a bomb had gone off in it.

I must have spent a good ten minutes trying to make my way from the door to the bar. I chatted to some of the guys as I went, all the time looking to see if I could spot Rooster or Cowboy. When I eventually got to the bar, I met DD, Freddie and Gunner. After exchanging pleasantries with DD and Freddie, I turned to speak to Gunner and noticed he was pretty well bashed up.

"Holy fuck, man! What happened to you?" I asked him.

"Remember the spat I had with Cowboy before we went up North?" he told me, to which I just nodded.

"Well, when we got back, he was being a dick so I called him out. We started a bit of a ruck in here which was broken up really quickly so Indie told us to follow him into the other room. He wanted us to settle it with a handshake, but we wouldn't do it, so he called a 'Bat battle' and … well, I'm sure you can guess who came off worse."

"Fuck's sake, Gunner! I thought you'd both put all that shit behind you. I knew you'd never be best mates or anything, but you looked like you were at least getting on, or that's what it seemed like to me," I suggested.

"Well, it's sorted now so there'll be no more animosity between us."

"Where's Cowboy anyway? Do you know if he's still here?"

"He's over in the corner with his mates, probably bragging about beating me."

"Hey, he's not like that, Gunner. He'll be just like you, glad it's over and ready to move on. I'm sure of it," I told him.

I shook his hand, gave him a bit of a slap on the back, nodded to DD and Freddie then left them to it.

I made my way toward Cowboy's table, pushing past people and trying my best not to spill my beer. I got to the table and sat down on what was probably the only spare chair left in the whole room.

"Fuck me, Cowboy. You look in a bit of a state, man," I told him.

"Shug, I might be a bit of a mess, but that cunt is worse, believe you me," he said, smiling and raising his glass.

"I know he is, I just spoke to him at the bar. You're some man, sir. You just couldn't leave it, could you?"

"Nope, and I had no intention of either. I just needed to wait for the right time to get it sorted. I knew he was a prick and I needed to let him know I could burst him. So now he knows and I'm happy about that," he told me with a smile.

"Well, it looks like he gave a good account of himself - judging by your dish," I suggested.

"Only superficial, ma man, only superficial," he replied, still smiling away.

"Ok, so what else did I miss then, guys?" I said, looking at Flick and Rooster.

"You didn't really miss anything, Shug, we've been partying since we got here. Indie's been milling about a bit, chatting to a load of the South guys and there are four new club Prospects," Rooster told me.

"How about you? What's the script with the job?" he asked.

"Supposed to start a week on Monday, but still not sure if I want it," I told him.

"Did you get a chance to catch up with Julie?"

Fuck! I knew that would be the next thing he wanted to know. I braced myself before starting with my lies and told him I hadn't.

"I went to her house and knocked on the door a few times. Either she wasn't in or she was ignoring me, I'm not sure what. I didn't see her old man's car there, my guess is they've fucked off somewhere, taken her with them to make sure we can't contact her."

"Aye, you're probably right, Shug," he agreed, "I'd have done the same if she was my daughter. The last thing I would've wanted was a couple of pricks like us hanging around her," he told me, laughing away to himself.

Flick then interrupted us, "Any chance you two could talk about something else? All this fuckin' 'chick shit' is getting right on my fuckin' nerves."

He'd hardly finished talking when Rooster went right on the defensive and challenged him in a really aggressive manner.

"Ok, Flick, let's change the fuckin' subject then, why don't we talk about 'Arseholes'? Then you can tell me how you always manage to be the number one in that department."

Fuck! Straightaway, Cowboy and I looked at each other, then at Flick, then Rooster and then back at each other. We both knew exactly where this was going. It took a second or two for Flick to register exactly what Rooster had said. He then let rip with a verbal volley of his own.

"You've got some fuckin' cheek calling me an arsehole, Rooster! When you're the cunt who's spouting off about some fuckin' chick who blew you off. From where I'm sitting it's you that's the fuckin' arsehole, boy. If I were you, I'd check the next mirror I pass - if it's a big arsehole you're looking for - that's exactly where you'll find it."

Just as Flick finished talking, Rooster jumped up and made a lunge over the table to get at him. As he did, Flick made a similar lunge towards him.

I grabbed hold of Rooster and Cowboy grabbed Flick. We both tried our best to wrestle them away from each other, but Rooster had a hold of Flick's jacket and Flick had a hold off Rooster's hair. When we tried to pull them apart, all that happened was the four of us landed on the floor and the table of drinks landed on top of us.

As we fell, everyone in close proximity to us just moved a bit until they were out of our way. The funny thing was, very few of them even bothered to watch what was going on. At this point, I was on top of Rooster and Cowboy was on top of Flick. We were both trying to talk some sense into them.

I have to say, Cowboy was having way much more success than me. Flick seemed to be quite happy to let it go, but Rooster, as usual, wanted to take it all the way. When I pointed out that I thought it was him, and not Flick, who was out of order, I thought he was going to burst a fuckin' blood vessel. Next thing, Indie and Hotwire were standing over us and Indie was demanding to know what the fuck was going on?

I'll tell you what, I was never so relieved to see the big man as I was beginning to lose my grip on Rooster and knew he would not think twice about laying me out if it meant he could get at Flick.

When Indie grabbed me and pulled me away, all I could think was 'Thank fuck he'd done it'. Rooster quickly jumped to his feet and told Indie to move as he was having Flick. Flick, by this time, was well out of the way after being dragged off by Cowboy.

Indie stood toe to toe with Rooster and told him to back off, reminding him that they were Brothers and told him he better sort it out asap.

Rooster told Indie the only way he was sorting it out was by punching Flick's cunt in. Indie replied, "Listen to me, Rooster. You'll be punching fuck all cunt in. You get this shit sorted out without a fuckin' blow being struck 'comprendé'? Flick's not only your Brother, but he's one of your best mates. So get a fuckin' grip of yourself."

Indie then looked at me and told me to take Rooster outside until he'd cooled down. Rooster about turned and headed for the door, with me following on behind. He was fuckin' raging at Indie and for a minute or so I thought he was going to have a go at him – thankfully, he thought better of it.

When we got outside, he started pacing about, still ranting on about Flick. I gave him a smoke and asked him to calm the fuck down a bit, but he was having none of it. As far as he was concerned, it was all Flick's fault and if he didn't apologise then he was getting wasted, and if Indie tried to stop him again then he was getting it as well.

He eventually sat on the steps beside me. He was by now no means calm, but he was certainly much less psychotic than he had been minutes earlier.

"Do you think I was in the wrong, Shug?" he asked me.

Before I got a chance to answer, he started again.

"What would you have done if it was you, Shug? I bet you would have wanted to punch his cunt in, wouldn't you?"

I knew for a fact I would have reacted in a completely different manner. However, if I'd told him that then he would have gone off on one again, so I avoided answering any of his questions.

"Look, man, the four of us have been mates for a long time and we've all had our differences along the way, especially you and me, and we're still mates. I think you could both have handled it better. You should get your heads banged together and both agree that you made a 'mountain out of a fuckin' molehill'. The bottom line is Flick touched a raw nerve. If it had been about anybody else other than Julie then you wouldn't have given two fucks and you'd just have laughed it off."

"That's not the point, Shug. He called me a fuckin' arsehole. You heard him."

"Hey, hang on a second, Rooster," I interrupted him, "It was you that started the whole arsehole thing remember, not him."

"See! I fuckin' knew you'd stick up for him, Shug. I fuckin' knew it," he said, as he stood back up.

"Come on, Rooster, get a fuckin' grip of yourself, man," I roared back at him, feeling pretty pissed that he'd even thought that of me.

I then went on a rant of my own,

"Now I know you're havin' a fuckin' laugh. You better not believe that for one fuckin' minute. You know I'll always have your back. Don't start your fuckin' pish with me," I told him.

"Well, that's how it fuckin' feels from where I'm standing," he roared back, before turning and walking away towards the car park.

I knew that he was upset. I could hear it in his voice. I got the feeling that he was close to tears. I guess this thing with Julie was really taking its toll on him. I followed and saw him standing facing the wall, his head resting on his raised arm. I put my hand on his back and asked him if he wanted to talk about it, but he just shook his head.

"Come on, man. I understand how you feel. I was the same with Lorraine, but it does get easier, I promise."

"Lorraine never tried to fuckin' kill herself because of you, did she? No. So how the fuck can you say you fuckin' understand? You've got no fuckin' idea how much it's eating me up."

By this time, he was in floods of tears and I had no idea what the fuck I should do.

When this had happened to me in the past, I never had a fuckin' clue what I was supposed to do or say. So, now, seeing Rooster like this, I was totally fucked.

I knew he was right about me not understanding - even though I was trying my best.

"Listen, man. It wasn't you're fault she did that. There were loads of factors which contributed to it that you don't know about. She knows it was a mistake and she said if she hadn't been drinking it would never have happened."

Rooster then lifted his head away from his hand and looked at me. I thought he was going to thank me for supporting him - how fuckin' wrong was I!

"How the fuck do you know all that?" he asked me, starting to square up to me.

Jeezus fuck. I about shat my pants. Fuck. Come on, Shug. Think. Say something for fuck's sake!

I was trying to force myself to talk, but just couldn't think of single thing to say. He then moved even closer to me and asked me again.

"Well, Shug? I'm waiting!"

I turned away from him, planning to walk in the other direction, to give myself some thinking time, but he grabbed my arm.

"Shug, talk to me, talk to me fuckin' now, Bro," he demanded.

"Okay, Rooster, take it easy, man. I'll tell you, but you can't let anyone know or I could end up losing my job," I told him, as I turned back to face him.

"See this fuckin' job. You just keep going on about it, Shug. It's the bain of my fuckin' life. You know what? I couldn't give a rat's fuckin' arse about it. Just tell me how the fuck you know all this about Julie?"

"You know what, Rooster? You can be one selfish cunt as well when you get started," I told him.

"Shug, right now I really don't give two fucks what you think of me. I just want you to spit it out."

I sat down, leaning my back against the wall. By this time I'd got my shit together and was ready to talk.

"Okay, Rooster, fine, I'll tell you what I know, but you have to promise me that you'll keep it to yourself?" I said, looking at him.

He never moved his eyes from my stare, just nodded in my direction. I took the gesture as a sign he'd keep it to himself.

"Do you remember when I spoke with Mrs Boardman about getting Julie's address? She told me the script then but warned me that it was confidential information that she'd received from the doctor who treated Julie in hospital and that I couldn't tell anyone else. I promised that I'd keep anything she said to me in the strictest confidence, and here I am blurting it all out the first time I'm asked about it!"

"Fuck's sake, Shug. Who the fuck am I going to tell? There's not another cunt in the slightest bit interested other than us. So come on, keep talking."

I knew Rooster wouldn't say anything, but that wasn't what I was worried about. My concern was when he knew all the facts - what the fuck would he do then?

I decided I would just tell him everything and let him do what the fuck he wanted with it. I was past caring about what he would do. If truth be told, I was so fuckin' tired of everything that I couldn't give two fucks about the outcome, so I started to fill him in.

"She told me that when Julie was in hospital one of the shrinks visited her and had a session with her. When he was done, he reported back to Mrs Boardman. He recommended that Julie should have a course of counselling as soon as she was physically strong enough.

131

"The gist of what he'd found out was that she was so drunk that she didn't realise how many tablets she'd taken and couldn't even remember slashing her wrists. Apparently, that's quite a common thing.

"Anyway, when he dug a bit deeper with her she told him that the last thing she remembered was thinking about her father and how he continued to force her to do as he expected. She said that both her and her mother were shit scared of him and that he was a total control freak. She then went into great details about her life with him when she was growing up.

"She said her mother called him an 'outside angel and a fireside devil' because everyone thought that he was such a nice, kind, sincere man who would help anyone. Nobody would ever believe what he was really like. She said they were constantly bullied to the point that neither of them had any self-worth or confidence left and that it was her mother who suggested nursing, as she knew Julie would need to move away if she got the job.

"She told him that it was only when she left home that she actually realised they were both bullied. She just took it for granted that everyone else's life was just like hers. When she was home, she always tried to talk her mum into leaving him. She actually thought she'd convinced her to do it, but on her last visit her father found out and went ballistic at both of them.

"He gave his Mrs a bit of a tanking and grabbed Julie by the throat, threatening her, that if she ever spoke to her mum again about leaving, that he would kill them both. He then took her back to the nurses' home and chatted away in the car like everything was okay. When Julie got back to the hospital, her head was all over the place and then - well, you know the rest."

"That dirty little fuckin' bastard. I'll do time for that little cunt, you see if I don't! I knew he was a little fuckwit. How in fuck's name could that little prick bully any cunt?" he ranted.

It was no more than I expected. I knew that this was exactly how he'd react. Even listening to him, knowing that he'd go and fuckin' blooter her father to within an inch of his life, I really didn't give two fucks.

"I'm going to get that fuckin' little prick right now. Are you coming?" he asked me.

"Not me, Rooster. I'm taking fuck all to do with it, but you do what you have to do," I told him.

"Why aren't you coming? Lost your fuckin' bottle or something?"

"No, I haven't lost fuck all, Rooster. I just think that wasting him is only going to make it worse for Julie and her mum."

"How in fuck's name do you work that out, Shug?" he demanded me to tell him.

"Well, I reckon you're only going to kick his cunt in to make you feel better, it's got fuck all to do with Julie and her mum.

"Anyway, five minutes ago it was Flick or Indie who was getting it, you're all over the fuckin' place, man. If you want my advice you should jump on your bike and go for a run, clear your fuckin' head before doing anything."

"I'll go for a run all right. Straight to that little prick's house. That'll be the best way to clear my fuckin' head."

He then jumped on his bike and fucked off. Just as he shot off, Cowboy came out.

133

"Where the fuck's he off to in such a hurry, Shug?"

"It's a long story, Cowboy, and you really don't want to know, but you can be rest assured that he'll be spending the night, and maybe longer, in the fuckin' cells - that's a racing certainty!"

"Shouldn't we go with him and help him out?"

"No fuckin' way, man. The only reason I'd go after him would be to try and stop him, but I know if I do then me and him'll end up getting into it. You know me, Cowboy, I've done that way too many times already and every single time I've ended up with my cunt kicked, so I won't be doing it again."

Even though I knew Rooster wouldn't get the old cunt as he was away to the caravan, I was still worried about how Julie would react. I couldn't decide if she'd call the cops, invite him in or if she'd end up trying to stab him or some shit like that.

"You think I should go after him then, Shug?"

"Please yourself, Cowboy, it's your call."

He then asked me to tell him what it was all about?

I gave him a short version of what Rooster was up to then gave him Julie's address. Just then, Flick came out and joined us and asked all the same questions that Cowboy had asked. All Cowboy told him was that he needed to go after Rooster to stop him getting into bother. Flick then told Cowboy he was going with him and made his way to his bike. I watched them shoot off and immediately I felt myself having severe pangs of guilt.

Aghh! Fuck's sake! I knew I had to follow them. I would never forgive myself if Rooster ended up getting into bother and I wasn't there to at least try and prevent it. I ran to my bike, jumped on, and sped after them.

I'd just about caught up with them when I realised that I had no helmet on, but there was no turning back now. As we got to the end of town, I jumped a couple of sets of lights and passed Cowboy and Flick, pointing to the next left turn. I headed down the road and the next thing they were beside me, having also jumped the last set of lights.

I thought Rooster would be okay, knowing that Julie's cunt of a dad was away. When he couldn't get his hands on him, I thought he'd calm down, but I was still worried about what Julie might tell him about us.

We drew into the cul-de-sac and I cursed when I saw Rooster's bike already sitting at the front of the house. I started worrying like fuck that Julie would spill the beans and he would end up taking his rage out on me.

I stopped my bike and jumped off, closely followed by Flick and Cowboy. I went around the side of the house and my heart missed a beat when I thought I saw the old cunt's car in the drive. Thank fuck it was the neighbours as him being here was probably the worst thing I could have possibly imagined.

The back door was lying open. As I entered, all I could hear was Julie crying. My first thought was that he'd given her a slap or something. I ran through the kitchen and into the living room only to see him sitting cuddling Julie on the couch. She was snuggled into his chest and breaking her heart. The tears were rolling down her cheeks and her eyes were all red and puffy.

"Rooster, what the fuck have you done, man?" I roared at him, demanding an answer.

But before he could speak, Julie looked up and asked me what I was talking about? Just then, Flick and Cowboy came bursting into the room, both, like myself, wondering what the fuck he'd done.

I stared at her for a minute or so with an almost apologetic look on my face before my focus turned back to Rooster.

"Everything ok here, man?" I asked him.

"Shug, everything's fine here now. Why don't you fuck off and take that pair of cunts with you? Can't you see I'm busy?"

Julie then sat up, wiping the tears from her eyes, and asked, "What's going on, Shug? What are you all doing here?"

Cowboy then blurted out, "Where's your dad, Julie? Is he here?"

"Eh, no, do you think I'd be sitting here with Rooster if he was? He's at the caravan with my mother. Why does everybody want to know where my dad is?" she asked.

Rooster then piped up, "Julie, the fuckin' morons standing in front of you thought I was coming here to beat up your dad. My guess is that they came here to stop me," he then turned back to us and said, "Okay, guys, it's time for you to split."

As he looked at us, he nodded towards the door, as if to reinforce his words. The three of us looked at each other. I think we were all feeling a little bit fuckin' stupid as we about turned, making our way to the kitchen and out the back door.

We'd just got outside when Rooster came to the door and gestured for us to wait.

"Hey, guys, listen, thanks for coming after me. I know you meant well, but I'm cool. Nothing's going to happen. Anyway, I can't do anything to her old man, he's 60 fuckin' miles away. So you can all relax."

Flick then offered his hand to Rooster, apologising to him for earlier. Rooster took his hand then said,

"Listen, Flick, it's me who should be apologising to you, man. I was well out of order. I just snapped. You know what it's like," he told him.

They both then hugged, and Cowboy looked at me, sticking his fingers in his mouth as if to indicate he was going to throw up - which made me laugh. Rooster then gave me and Cowboy a bit of a hug as well.

"Fuck's sake, Rooster, get a grip, man! You'll have us all blubbering like fuckin' Julie if you don't stop all this soppy pish," I told him.

Rooster's reaction was to grab me around the neck and rub my fuckin' head with the knuckles of his other hand. I tried to grab him and push him away, telling him he was a prick and to stop fuckin' doing it before I gave him a good slap. All I succeeded in doing was crashing us both into Cowboy and Flick, knocking the four of us to the ground for the second time today.

As we landed, we all burst out laughing. I was so glad that we were all together and sharing a light-hearted moment - it had been such a long time since we all laughed together. We rolled about, slapping each other and calling each other names then we were stopped in our tracks when a car turned into the drive.

As I looked up, the first thing I saw was Julie standing on the back steps, smiling away as she watched us. Within an instant, her expression changed to that of fear.

I turned around to see what was causing her such concern and realised it was because her dad was getting out of his car.

"What the bloody hell's going on here?" he roared at us.

137

The minute I heard his shout, I knew I'd need to keep hold of Rooster and so did Cowboy and Flick.

As he roared at us our mood changed, in the same way Julie's had. We went from laughing and joking around back to a state of anger and aggression in an instant. This was a feeling that had been far too prevalent for us all over the last few months.

The minute Rooster realised what was happening, he demanded we get off him, but we all held on to him to prevent him from moving. I was trying to reason with him, hoping to get him to see sense and let it go, but he was having none of it. Her father approached us. As soon as he saw we had a good hold of Rooster, he shouted to Julie to call the cops.

He then started ranting at Rooster about how he blamed him for Julie turning out the way she did. Fuck! At that point, I thought Rooster was going to blow a gasket. Even the three of us were now struggling to hold him back. The next thing that happened took us all by surprise. Julie marched over to her dad then told us to let Rooster up. I personally didn't think this was the best idea she'd ever had.

She then slapped her father on the face and told him the reason she was so fucked up was not because of Rooster, but because of him, then said to him he was no longer welcome in the house. He stood gaping at her with his mouth wide open looking totally stunned.

Julie then got hold of her mother, who by this time was trying to act as a barrier between father and daughter, pulled her to the side then told him that they both wanted no more to do with him and that it was time for him to fuck off.

He looked like he was raging and flipped big time, he stepped forward, pushed his wife out of the way then made a grab for Julie, getting hold of her hair. As Julie's mum fell to the ground, she started screaming at him to let Julie go.

We were all getting to our feet just as her dad slapped Julie right across the face, telling her she would live to regret her actions. The next thing I know, Rooster's hooked him, knocking him to the ground. He then jumped on top of him and started punching the living daylights out of him.

I went to grab him, but Cowboy stood in front of me, suggesting I give Rooster another couple of minutes. I decided he was right and that the bastard deserved a good fuckin' doing. I helped Julie's mother to her feet and stood with her and Julie.

By this time, the old cunt was well out of it so the three of us tried to pull Rooster off him. As we struggled with him, I told him that he really needed to stop before he killed him.

"That's what the bastard deserves," he screamed at me, as he tried to give him another boot.

"I know, Rooster. But anymore and you'll end up inside for murder," I roared at him.

"Like I give a fuck about that!" he roared back.

"Come on, man. Think about it, for fuck's sake. If you're banged up - what about Julie? Who the fuck's going to look after her then?"

I wasn't sure if I'd managed to strike a chord with him or if he was just knackered, but he started to calm down a bit.

He then turned his attention to Julie, apologising to her for what he'd done to her father, but also reminding her that he deserved it. As they moved towards each other and cuddled, I heard her telling him that she was glad he did it as the bastard did deserve it after the way he'd treated her and her mum and that she was glad he'd beat him up.

Julie's mum, on the other hand, was frantic. She was on her knees trying to talk to her husband and at the same time screaming at Rooster for what he'd done. Then, right on cue, we heard the sirens in the distance, and I suggested we should split pretty sharpish. Cowboy and Flick both agreed, but Rooster was having none of it. I tried to coax him to come, but he made it perfectly clear he was going nowhere.

"Guys, this is my bag, get the fuck out of here. I'll deal with this shit on my own," he told us.

Flick then said to him, "No way, man. You stay, we stay. That's how it rolls, you know that." then opened his cigarette packet and passed some smokes around.

By the time the two cop cars arrived, Julie's mum had brought out a bowl of water and some towels and was trying to clean up her unconscious husband's face. Julie was screaming at her to leave him the fuck alone. Rooster was telling Julie to let her mother do what she wanted.

In amongst all this chaos, the three of us - well, we just shrugged at each other and planked our arses on the path with our backs against the wall of the house, having a smoke, waiting for the pigs to lift us.

I counted six cops, three in each car, as they jumped out, batons in hand, ready to take on all comers. We sat watching them, smiling away to ourselves as they approached us. I recognised the first one as the older guy who'd tried to give it tight to Rooster and me the last time we were here.

"Well, well, well! If it isn't the little fuckwit back again," he said, as he stood over me.

I knew we were heading for the cells anyway, so I was just as sarcastic back to him.

"Should you not have said hello, hello, hello, instead of well, well, well, ya fuckin' dick?" which brought a ripple of laughter from Cowboy and Flick, much to the plods displeasure.

Before he had a chance to say anything else, I carried on.

"Well, if it isn't the fat old fucker back again! And guess what, guys? This time he's brought his fuckin' pals with him. Oh, and they've all got little sticks with them," I said, smiling at him.

Cowboy and Flick continued laughing out loud which made him as angry as fuck.

Just then, the ambulance arrived, and the two medics made their way over to Julie's dad. The cop then told a couple of his guys to keep an eye on us and that if we moved to 'scud' us, then went over to speak to the medics. By this time, I think everybody in the street was out, trying to see what the fuck was going on.

Rooster suggested to Julie that she should help her mum up and take her into the house, which she did. The fat cop followed them inside. I guessed he wanted them to tell him what the fuck had happened. I suggested that one of us should maybe go in too, just in case Rooster ended up blootering fat boy, but I was told sharply from one of the cops standing over us, that none of us would be going anywhere.

The three of us looked at each other and burst out laughing again. I could see the two of them were beginning to feel a tad uncomfortable and unsure what to do next. Cowboy stood up with Flick then I followed suit.

"If I decide I want to go into the house are any of you planning to stop me?" Cowboy asked them.

One of the cops then said, "You sit the fuck back down, ya mouthy git. You're going nowhere near the fuckin' house and neither the fuck are your poncey pals, ok?"

The other guy, at this point, looked decidedly worried and shouted to the other two cops, who were with the medics, to join him. Then he nodded to the one who was trying to keep the people away from the scene. Cowboy then started to wind them up. He suggested they should call for more officers if they wanted a scrap as the four of them wouldn't be enough to lift us.

As the tension between us started to rise, we watched the ambulance speed away. Just then, Julie's mum came running out the house, screaming for the ambulance to stop. One of the officers, who was standing in front of us, got hold of her and told her that she should go back inside and that he'd take her to the hospital within the next fifteen minutes.

Julie, who had come running out behind her mum trying to stop her, managed, with the help of the cop, to usher her back inside. Cowboy then started with the wind up again.

"And then there were three," he said, staring at them, before turning to Flick. "What do you think their odds are now, Bro?" he asked him.

"Pretty shit would be my guess, Bro," he replied.

Cowboy then turned to the cops and said, "So what do you reckon then, guys? Do you think you'd win three on three?"

The cop who'd been doing all the talking earlier then spoke again, "Just shut the fuck up right now, cunt. I'm telling you, if you or any of your fuckin' cronies takes one step then I'll lay you out."

Cowboy then leaned forward and smiled at him, "You know what? I'd really love to kick your cunt in, boy. So why don't you try and hit me with your poxy little fuckin' stick? Then we'll see how fuckin' hard you are!

"Come on, there's plenty people watching, let's put on a show for them."

I knew Cowboy was winding him right up, trying to get him to strike the first blow and the cop knew it as well. To his credit, he also leaned forward until he was right in Cowboy's face, then said,

"You must think I'm as stupid as you fuckin' look. Make no mistake, I will strike the first fuckin' blow, old man. But it won't be here, it'll be back at the station, unless of course you give me good cause to do it here!"

Cowboy took a step back, realising that his best attempts to wind him up had failed. He turned to us and said, "Come on, guys. I've had enough of this fuckin' shite. Let's get tae fuck out of here."

He then turned back to the cop and asked him, "Are we under arrest then?"

To which he replied, "No, but you'll stay where you are. Right now, you're suspects in a crime, and we're within our rights to detain you for questioning. However, if you try to leave, which, by the way, would be my preferred option, we'll see it as you trying to flee the scene and arrest you all immediately."

Flick then grabbed Cowboy's arm and pointed to the corner of the house. We all looked around, including the cops, and saw Rooster and the old cop coming towards us. He looked at the cop who was doing all the mouthing at us and said, "Let them go."

143

The young cop took a minute to register what he'd been told and could only muster one word to the sergeant,

"What?"

"Let them go. That's a fuckin' order," he repeated.

"But, Sarge, I ..." and before he could say anything else he was interrupted.

"Just do what the fuck you're told. Let them go and get back in the cars - NOW!" he said, raising his voice.

To say we were all dumbfounded was the understatement of the year. We all looked around again, including the cops, wondering what the fuck had happened? To confuse things even more, the Sergeant then turned to Rooster, shook his hand, thanked him then made his way to his car.

As the police cars drove off, the three of us turned and looked at Rooster. He was lighting up a smoke and smiling, like the cat that got the cream, as he watched the cop cars head off out the cul-de-sac. I tried to attract his attention, but he seemed to be miles away.

"Rooster, what the fuck just happened, man? You going to tell us what the fuck that was all about?" I asked him.

He turned and smiled at us then said,

"Well, guys. You know what? That was one of the best things that ever happened to me in my whole life."

He nodded in our direction then started walking back up the path towards the back door.

I went and caught up with him, grabbing hold of his arm, turning him back around to face me.

"Eh, I don't fuckin' think so, Rooster. You're going fuckin' nowhere until you tell us what the fuck went on in the house!"

He put his hand on mine and lifted it from his arm.

"Listen, Shug, I'll tell you all about it back at the pub in about half an hour or so. Right now, I need to go inside," he then nodded and told me to trust him.

"Trust you? Fuck's sake, man! You can't just fuck off and not fill us in," I told him.

"Look, Shug, there's something I need to do first so please cut me some slack, shoot off just now, stick a pint in the tap for me, and I'll explain everything when I get back."

He then gave me a hug, slapping me on the back a couple of times.

He told me to take it easy then about turned and disappeared back into the house. I turned back towards Flick and Cowboy. They still looked as totally confused as I did.

"What the fuck's going on?" Cowboy asked, more making a statement than actually talking to either of us. "Is it just me or was that the weirdest fuckin' thing ever?" he asked, again not talking to anyone in particular.

"Well I don't know about you two," Flick blurted out, "but me, I haven't got a fuckin' clue about anything that just happened and I'm not going to stand around here trying to second guess Rooster, I need a fuckin' beer!"

I agreed with Flick and suggested we do as Rooster asked and head back to the pub. After a bit of head shaking, nodding and mumbling between us, we got back on our bikes and made our way through the village towards the pub. I knew the two of them would be trying like fuck to work out why things turned out

145

the way they did, bursting to come up with a plausible explanation by the time we arrived.

Me, on the other hand, I knew exactly what had happened. The only thing bothering me now was what the fuck Rooster and Julie were getting up to. I tried to tell myself that nothing would be happening between them and I nearly managed to convince myself until I thought about their history and the emotional state Julie was in. I knew she would definitely need a shoulder to cry on and hey, ho, who would be there for her? Fuckin' Rooster! I then tried to convince myself that if anything did happen it would have no effect on me and that I didn't give a fuck about her. Deep down, though, I was so hoping she wouldn't take him back.

Chapter 16

When we arrived back and parked up, Cowboy told us that he reckoned Julie's dad was some kind of criminal, as when the pigs went into the house they'd found incriminating evidence and that was the reason why they didn't charge Rooster for booting the fuck out of him.

Flick and I looked at each other then started laughing.

"Fuck, Cowboy! You've got some fuckin' imagination, I'll give you that!" Flick told him.

As we continued to laugh, he started to get the hump.

"Ok then, ya couple of smart arses, you tell me why the fuck the cop would shake Rooster's fuckin' hand then?"

By this time, we were almost pissing ourselves laughing and unable to answer him. I could see that Cowboy was getting well pissed at us, so I tried to lighten the mood a bit for him.

"Maybe they're both in the fuckin' Masons and have to shake hands when they meet or some shit like that?" I blurted out, which didn't help one fuckin' bit as it just made Flick laugh even louder.

Well, that was enough for Cowboy and he stormed off towards the pub door, calling us a couple of pricks, which made us laugh even more. It took us a couple of minutes to stop laughing. We thought we better get it all out of our system before we went in.

We knew if we went in, still laughing, that he'd really take the hump. We got to the bar and I apologised to Cowboy for taking the piss and he told me it was cool and handed me a pint. Flick then hugged him and gave him a few pats on the back. Cowboy handed him a pint as well.

Just as Cowboy picked up his pint, Indie appeared in front of us, demanding to know where the fuck we'd been and why Rooster wasn't with us. I told him the whole story and I could see from his face that he wasn't sure whether to believe me or not.

"Honest, Indie, that's exactly what happened," I told him, trying to convince him that I was telling the truth.

He then looked at Flick.

"You and Rooster sorted then?"

"Yep, we're good, man," he replied.

"Well where the fuck is he then?" Indie challenged him.

"No fuckin' idea, man. He was still with Julie when we left."

"Okay. Tell him when he comes in that I need to see him right away."

He then walked away, shaking his head. The three of us looked at each other.

"He didn't believe a fuckin' word I told him, did he?" I suggested, looking at both of them.

"Nope, not a fuckin' word, Shug," Cowboy agreed.

"Ah well, fuck him! Rooster will sort it when he gets back," I suggested, before ordering up some more beers.

We picked them up and made our way over to one of the tables. As we sat down Flick said,

"Is this not just one of the weirdest days ever? Fuck, I'm knackered. Another couple of these …" he said, pointing to the pints on the table, "and I'll be snoring."

"Aye, it's certainly not been the best one I've ever had," Cowboy agreed.

Just then, one of the Prospects came walking past our table and Flick shouted for him to stop.

"Hey, Prospect, what's your name?" he asked him.

"Am Spooky," he told him.

"Spooky? What kind of fuckin' name's that?" Flick enquired.

"Had it for years, can't even remember why, but it just stuck," he told him.

Flick handed him a fiver and sent him to the bar for another three beers. He then looked at us and said,

"Spooky? What the fuck!" and burst out laughing.

We both joined in, even though it wasn't really that funny. I think the laughter was more in relief - knowing we were back in the clubhouse rather than spending the night in the cells. Spooky came back, dumped the drinks on the table then left, telling us he had to go and pick up empty glasses.

We'd been sitting blethering for about ten minutes when Cowboy asked Flick if the Prospect had given him his change.

"Did he fuck. The little cunt fucked off with it in his pocket. I'll boot his fuckin' arse when I get a hold of him!"

I started laughing. I raised my glass at Flick and suggested to him that maybe Spooky was saving up for something.

"I'll 'fuckin saving up for something' him when I get a hold of the little cunt," he moaned, as he scanned the room looking for him.

"Fuck's sake, Flick. Settle your knickers down, man, for all it is," Cowboy told him.

"It's not the money, it's the principal of the fuckin' thing. If he does that with every cunt in here then he'll be on a fortune. I'll turn the cunt upside down when I see him!"

149

While Flick was ranting away, Cowboy nudged me under the table and nodded towards the door. It was Rooster. The minute I saw him coming in, all smiles, my heart sank. All I could think was 'that'll be me and Julie well and truly fucked'.

I watched him as he made his way to the bar, laughing, joking, patting guys on the back and shaking hands - it was the happiest I'd seen him looking in a long time and all I could think was 'what a cunt'.

I didn't even need to speak to him to know that Julie and him were back on, seeing the way he was acting was enough. As I continued to watch him, all I could think about was how I could fuck off without giving Indie the hump?

Rooster picked up the pint I'd left in the tap for him, scanned the room until he clocked us, then made his way to our table.

"Alright, girls, what's happening?" he asked, still fuckin' smiling away.

"Fuck all, Rooster," Cowboy replied, "but you need to sit your arse down and tell us what the fuck happened back at the house!"

He pulled a chair over and went to sit down.

"Rooster, don't sit down, you need to catch up with Indie first. He said he wanted to see you the minute you got back," I told him.

"All in good time, Shug," he replied as he sat. "I'm sure another five minutes won't make any difference."

"Well, on your fuckin' head be it, as long as he knows I told you. I don't want him over here moaning the fuck at me."

"Fuck's sake, Shug. Take a breath, man. I get the message. Has some cunt stole yir scone or something?"

The smile drifted from his face and he stared at me with a much more menacing look.

"What the fuck's eating you?" he demanded me to tell him.

I think I realised at that point that I was way overreacting, but I couldn't help it. I was raging with him. I so wanted to tell him about Julie and me, just to piss him off, but I knew that would be absolute madness. I then reverted to 'plan-B', the safe option.

"Sorry, man. I've just had a really shit day and I'm still kind of wound up about it. I just didn't want you to get any aggro from Indie."

"Hey, Shug, that's cool, man, we all have shit days!"

I leaned over the table and offered him my hand and we shook and I thought 'Thank fuck! Normal service resumed'. However, inside, I was kicking myself for letting them see how I was feeling.

Flick then started getting into Rooster about him not telling us what happened.

"Okay, okay, gimme a fuckin' minute and I'll fill you in," he told us as he stood up and took his jacket off.

"Right, where the fuck do I start, guys?"

"Fuck, Rooster! Stop pissing about and just tell us, for fuck's sake!" Cowboy demanded, sounding very irate.

He sat back down and eventually began.

"Here goes then, guys. Julie's father's a fuckin' bully and the old cop's Mrs was a friend of her mother's, okay?"

Cowboy and Flick stared at each other in disbelief, but I never took my eyes off Rooster.

"When we all went inside, Julie started to have a go at her mother because she wanted to go back out and help her father. She then asked her why the fuck she wanted to help him after all the years of abuse he had forced upon them.

"That was when the cop took over and asked her mother if it was true? She eventually admitted it was and shared a few of things he'd done to Julie and her over the years. The cop then said that he'd already had an inkling about it as his wife had suspected it for years. Me? I was well shocked - I had no fuckin' idea – as all the time I was with Julie, she never mentioned a fuckin' thing.

"The cop then turned to me and said that he was happy to overlook what I'd done, that I needed to be aware, that if her father wanted to press charges, then I'd need to take my chances in court. He then said that neither he, nor any of his colleagues, would be able to verify any claims that he made because the altercation was over before they'd arrived. He then nodded and that was when we all came out."

"Un-fuckin'-believable! Who the fuck would have thought it? That little cunt was a fuckin' bully. I hate that fuckin' shite, man. We should all have kicked his cunt in, the little fuckin' wanker," Cowboy ranted.

Then Flick piped up, "Just fuckin' shows you, man! You never know what any cunt's capable of, do you?"

"What the fuck are you talking about?" a voice said from behind us.

I turned around to see who it was? It was Indie and he was standing directly behind me. He then spoke again, but this time with a bit more aggression in his tone.

"Is some cunt going to tell me what the fuck's going on?" he demanded to know.

He then looked at Rooster.

"Why the fuck didn't you come and see me whenever you came in?"

Rooster looked at him for a bit then said, "It's cool, Indie. Everything's sorted. Sorry I didn't come over straightaway, but I needed to fill the guys in first."

"That's not what I fuckin' asked, Rooster. I want to know why the fuck you didn't come back with the '3 fuckin' Amigos'?"

"I had a bit of personal business to attend to," he told him.

"Personal business? You had personal fuckin' business? Fuck's sake, Rooster. We're right in the middle of a pile of shite and you fuck off to help out some fuckin' burd! C'mon, man, you need to get your fuckin' priorities right!"

At that point, Rooster's whole demeanour changed, and he interrupted him,

"Right, Indie, you've had your say. Now it's my fuckin' turn. Firstly, for your information, Julie is not just some fuckin' burd. Secondly, there was fuck all happening here when I left. Julie's my old lady and she was in trouble so I weighed up my priorities: 1) Do I sit here getting pished? or 2) Do I go and help her? For me, it's a no fuckin' brainer."

This time it was Indie who did the interrupting.

"Just you hold it a fuckin' minute, Rooster! You're way off the mark here and you fuckin' know it! If you're telling me that she's your old lady and that she was in some sort of bother then you know you should've come to me about it.

"We'd all have gone with you to sort it out, not just 'Hughie, Dewey and fuckin' Louie' here. So tell me, why didn't you come to me with this?" he said, staring at Rooster, waiting on his response.

"Look, Indie, you know I would've come to you, but I didn't really have time. To be honest, I wasn't really sure if there was anything going down or not. I thought it best to go on my own to suss it out before mentioning it to you. As for the guys, they followed me, I never asked them to come," he told him.

"Well, from what I'm hearing, you did way more than suss it out. You could've ended up in the fuckin' nick and more than likely the 'three fuckin' amigos' here would have joined you! Anyway, that's not important right now, I need you to come with me. We're having a meet and you need to be there."

Indie then walked away.

Rooster looked at us as he stood up. He put his hands on the table and leant into us, "This isn't over, by the way. I'll be having words with that cunt when we're done. He's not telling me who the fuck I can and cannot see or when I can see them!" he said, giving us a bit of a nod before he left.

None of us said a word until he was out of earshot. The first to speak was Cowboy.

"Holy fuck, guys, this isn't good. What the fuck do you reckon he'll do? Do you think he'll dig him up right enough?" he asked us.

I went to reply, but Flick beat me to it.

"Come on, Cowboy. You know fine well he'll have a go at him, he wouldn't have mentioned it otherwise. Depending on how he approaches it will determine what comes next."

I couldn't wait and butted in with my own concerns.

"Hughie, Dewey and fuckin' Louie! The three fuckin' Amigos! Who the fuck does he think he is calling us that? Fuckin' prick! Anyway, think about this: What if he does challenge Indie and Indie calls him out? Where the fuck does that leave us?" I asked them.

"What do you mean?" Cowboy asked curiously.

"Well, the way I see it is there's a couple of scenarios: Firstly, if they end up boxing and Indie gives him a licking, should we break it up to help Rooster or leave him to get his cunt kicked in? Secondly, if it's the other way around and Rooster's winning and somebody jumps in to help Indie, do we jump in as well?"

"Never thought about it like that. I just assumed that if anything came out of it there would be a 'Bat battle'?" Flick suggested.

"Yep, that's my opinion too," Cowboy concurred.

"Well, I hope to fuck you're right, 'cause if it goes any other way then it could fuck the Bats right up!" I told them.

"Hey, Shug, I really think you're being way over dramatic as usual," Cowboy told me.

"Well, I hope for everybody's sake that I am!"

The next thing, Flick jumps up and quickly grabbed someone who was passing the table and hauled him over.

"Well, well, if it isn't the fuckin' Spook boy! Where the fuck's my change, ya little cunt?" he demanded to know.

The Prospect stared at him for a bit, as if he was sizing him up, then lifted Flick's hand off his shoulder.

"Don't ever grab me like that again or I'll punch your cunt in!" he told him.

To say Flick was flabbergasted was an understatement. It took a second or two for him to process what had just happened then he ripped into him,

"I think you're getting your ambitions and your capabilities mixed up a bit here, 'boy-o'. The quicker you apologise, give me my change back and fuck off, the better - before I rip your fuckin' head off," Flick growled, squaring up to him.

To his credit, however ill-fated it was, Spooky never backed down and let rip back at Flick.

"Listen, I'm well happy to go outside with you right now 'cause I can fight like fuck and you don't fuckin' phase me one bit. As for your change, you're getting fuck all back. I don't do change. Anything over goes right into the club's coffers. And as for an apology, you can fuckin' swing for that too - I don't do apologies either."

By this time, Flick was absolutely fuckin' raging and grabbed him by the throat, telling him to get his arse outside for a square go. Surprisingly, Spooky didn't even blink, he just said, "Cool," pushed Flick's hand away, then about turned and headed for the door. Flick went to follow him, but Cowboy must've been thinking exactly the same as I was. We both jumped up and grabbed hold of him at the same time.

"Come on, Flick, think about it, man! You really don't want to do this? It can't work out well for you. Take a breath, man. Sit back down and I'll go and see the little cunt, find out what his fuckin' problem is," I suggested.

"Like fuck I'll sit down! I'm having the little cunt right now and so should you be, by the way. So the both of you better move out of the fucking way, or come with me if you want, either way, I don't give a flying fuck 'cause I'm fuckin' havin' the little cunt right now."

Cowboy looked at me then relaxed his grip, giving me the nod and a shrug of his shoulders.

"Fuck it, Shug! He's right, man. We'd both do the same so best we let him go."

I knew he was right, so I let him go as well. He immediately made his way to the door, pushed it open then hurried outside - with Cowboy and myself chasing behind him.

As we stepped outside, we were just in time to see the first punch. Flick never even spoke a word. He just hit him flush in the face with a beauty of a right hook. Spooky staggered back slightly, but never even looked like he'd go down.

"I'll give you that," he told Flick, "I deserved it for taking the piss, but if you hit me again then we'll be boxing."

He hardly had the words out his mouth when Flick hit him with another beauty and this time he did go down. He staggered a bit as he got back to his feet and made a bit of a lunge at Flick. At that point, Cowboy joined in. Giving Spooky a few digs about the head and back, reminding him that he was a fuckin' Prospect and that he should never challenge a 'Full Patch' Brother.

I didn't really want to join in, but felt I'd need to. I gave him a few boots whilst calling him a fuckin' idiot. Spooky fell to the ground, assuming the foetal position as we continued to leather into him. Next thing, Indie, Rooster, and a few of the Brothers who had come out to see what was going on, started getting in amongst us and pulling us apart.

Rooster and Indie pulled up Flick and stood directly in front of him while another few of the Brothers did the same with Cowboy and me. Indie then lifted up Spooky, who was looking a bit worse for wear, and had him by the throat, demanding he spill the beans. You could see that he was pretty well bashed up. Funnily enough, though, he didn't really look like he was done in.

Indie stared at Spooky, waiting for an answer, still holding him by the throat.

"Well, Prospect, spit it out!"

Spooky obviously thought he was doing the right thing by telling Indie that it was Flick's fault.

He said, "I never did a thing, Indie. It was all Flick's fault, man. He asked me outside and I wasn't going to back down," he told him.

Indie blew up at him again, reminding him that he was only a fuckin' Prospect, and told him that if a 'Full Patch' Brother asked him to lick the shit off his boot then he'd expect him to do it. He then told him that he should apologise to us and if he ever did anything like this again, he'd be out. Everyone would then take great pleasure in give him the kicking of his life.

"Now best you apologise and ask Flick to forgive you because if he doesn't, you're out. So when you say it you better make sure you fuckin' mean it."

He then hooked him right in the mouth, dropping him to his knees, then pulled him back up and pushed him towards Flick, who by this time, looked like he'd calmed down, or so I'd thought.

With everybody watching, Spooky stood in front of Flick. But before he could apologise, Flick also hit him a drive in the face, knocking him back to the ground. Spooky took a bit of time to pick himself up and now looked like he was pretty fucked. It was clear to see that he was fuckin' raging with Flick. He looked at him as if he wanted to kill him. He looked at Indie, who just stared back at him, then looked back at Flick.

Spooky swallowed hard and apologised to him in front of everybody, but the way he said it you just knew he didn't mean a fuckin' word of it. Flick then, being a bit of a smart arse said to him,

"What did you say, prick? You'll need to speak up. I never heard you."

Spooky took a deep breath then said it again, this time much louder. Indie then decided that that was enough, told them to shake hands and let it go. They shook hands, but it was clear that they both thought there was still some unfinished business.

Indie directed everyone back inside and told the two of them to get to the bar, have a beer together, and sort out their shit.

We all wandered towards the door and Cowboy asked me if I fancied going to the bar and winding up Spooky for a bit of a laugh. I told him he was being a dick if he did wind him up 'cause there was nothing surer, he would end up boxing again and there was a good chance Indie would horse him out. Not for the first time, Cowboy told me I was being a fuckin' 'drama queen'.

Our conversation was broken up by Rooster wanting to know what the fight was all about? I suggested to him we should hang about until everyone else had gone back inside then I'd fill him in with the gory details. After I'd got him up to speed, we both agreed that Spooky had shown a right pair of balls to do what he did. We also agreed it was probably the stupidest thing any of us had ever seen from a Prospect since Malky.

We then went back inside. Rooster nudged me, nodding towards the bar. I turned to see what he was looking at and saw Flick and Spooky standing with their arms on each other's shoulders, drinking and laughing away like long lost buddies. Cowboy was standing beside them and was also laughing away.

159

"Fuck me, Rooster! That's a turn up for the books if ever I saw one," I suggested.

"Isnae fuckin' half, Shug. I never thought for one fuckin' minute that Flick would even talk to the cunt again."

"You want to go over and see them?" I asked him.

"Nah. Let's grab a seat. I want to fill you in on a couple of things anyway. You grab some beers and I'll find us a seat," he told me, as he headed for an empty table in the corner.

Chapter 17

I made my way towards the bar, wondering what the fuck he was going to say? As usual, my mind was racing at a hundred miles an hour. I was pretty sure he was going to tell me he'd squared things up with Julie and that really worried me as I had no idea how I would react to it.

I guessed that he'd expect me to be happy about it, even though I felt the exact opposite - I knew I'd need to do my best to fake it. I then turned my thoughts to Julie and wondered if she had mentioned anything about us to him? Oh fuck! What if she's told him everything! He's going to go off his fuckin' nut!

I tried to reassure myself that she hadn't. Knowing him as I did, I knew he'd have already challenged me about it. That's of course unless Julie made him promise to keep quiet about it. Holy shit, that would be the worst thing ever. I'd think he knew, he WOULD know, and want to kick ten bales of shite out of me, but couldn't because Julie would chuck him. To make matters worse, we'd be in each other's company every single day knowing what we knew and at some point, it would have to come to a head. Agghhhh, Fuck me! What a fuckin' nightmare!

I picked up the beers and made my way to the table, doing my best to try and empty my head. By the time I'd reached the table, I was relatively calm on the outside, even though my guts were in washing machine mode.

I placed the drinks on the beer mats and sat down.

"So what's up then, Rooster? What have you got to tell me?" I asked him, trying to sound dead nonchalant.

Before saying anything, he took a swig out his pint, placed it back on the mat then began,

"I just had a chat with Indie. Well, actually, he had a chat with me. It seems that Gunner no longer wants to be the VP. Him and the other South guys who were going to be Officers had a chat with Indie at the farm and told him they would be much happier just being Bats or lower ranking Officers with much less responsibility.

"Indie said that after the ruck up north they thought it would be best if others from either the Central or North chapters with some experience took up the senior positions. So guess what, Shug?"

Fuck! I didn't know whether to laugh or fuckin' cry. All that panicking and it was for fuck all. It was nothing to do with Julie!

"Shug, eh, hello? Are you with us?" Rooster snapped his fingers in front of my face, which made me jump.

"Shug, what the fuck's wrong with you, man? Snap out of it, for fuck's sake. Did you even hear a word I fuckin' told you?"

He jolted me out of my wee trance and my focus returned back to him.

"Yep, I heard you, sorry, man, I must have drifted off. Been getting that a lot lately, fuck knows what it is," I lied to him. "Sorry, you were saying that Gunner and his guys don't want to be Officers. Why the fuck not?"

"Who the fuck cares why not? Maybe they've just shat out of it or maybe they don't feel up to it. Either way, I couldn't give a flying fuck."

"So why are you telling me all this, Rooster?" I asked him, feeling slightly confused about it.

"Fuck's sake, Shug. Sometimes you're slower than a week in the fuckin' jail, man! Why the fuck do you think I'm telling you? Indie wants me to be the VP and you to be the SAA. He also wants Cowboy and Flick to be Secretary and Treasurer. How cool's that: the four of us down here and all Officers?"

He was now staring at me with the biggest stupidest grin I'd ever seen, waiting on me to say something. However, I don't think my reply was exactly what he was expecting.

"How come he's offering me the SAA gig and not Flick or Cowboy?" I asked him.

"Jesus fuck, Shug, are you for real, man? Honest tae fuck, I don't think I'll ever understand you. I'm convinced you're not right in the fuckin' heid. How the fuck should I know why he offered it to you instead of them? Fuck me, man, I thought you'd be over the fuckin' moon. But oh no, as usual, you go and do all that over thinking pish that you always do. So do you want it or what?" he demanded to know.

"Fuck, Rooster, of course I want it. I just can't believe he's offered it to me, that's all. I had no idea what you wanted to talk to me about, but I never expected this!"

I lifted my glass in the air and Rooster followed suit. We clinked our glasses together and both nodded to each other. By now, I was smiling like a Cheshire cat as well - some of it was with the news Rooster had just shared, but mostly because he hadn't mentioned anything about Julie.

"Shug, you need to keep this to yourself for a bit. Indie and Brutis are going to see us later on today before they tell everyone about the changes, okay?"

"Yep, no probs, mate," I told him.

"What's the big excitement then, guys? Come on, spill the beans."

Cowboy, Flick and Spooky had made their way to the table and must have seen us with our glasses in the air.

As quick as you like, Rooster told them that we were celebrating the fact that Julie was doing okay, and her prick of a father was locked up. Cowboy raised his glass and made a toast,

"Amen to that. To Julie, and also to the good old pigs - who've actually done something right for a fuckin' change."

We all laughed as we clinked glasses and the three of them grabbed chairs and joined us at the table. As they were settling down, Rooster leaned over to me and whispered in my ear to remind him later to fill me in about Julie. Ach, I fuckin' knew it. Just when I thought he had nothing to say about Julie, bang, there he goes and drops the fuckin' bombshell. I wanted to ask the fucker straight away to tell me what it was about, but I knew he'd wonder why I was so keen to find out so I just nodded and he nodded back.

Rooster then changed the subject completely and asked Flick and Spooky what the script was with them? Flick put his arm around Spooky then said,

"We had a bit of a disagreement, as you know, but we're sound now coz he knows his fuckin' place!" then they both burst out laughing.

Spooky then added that he realised he was out of order having a go at Flick while he was just a Prospect and knew now that he'd have to wait 'til he was a 'Full patch' member before having a go at anybody. They then raised their glasses again, looking like they were best buds. I looked at Spooky as they jollied it up and I knew, reading between the lines, he was talking about having a go at Flick and not just 'anybody'. I made a mental note to get to know him a bit better and suss out what kind of guy he was.

We were all sitting blethering and having a laugh when Brutis came over. He was a man of few words and, true to his style, he proved this again.

"Indie wants to see you all in the back room, now," he told us.

We all stood up and he then said, "Except you, Prospect. You get the empties gathered in and collect another fiver from everybody."

With that, he turned and made his way towards the back room.

The four of us looked at each other, all apparently wondering what was up, doing the shoulder shrugging and frowned forehead stuff. Although Rooster and I already knew, we played along.

"Bet this is about earlier!" Cowboy announced, "I knew he was well pissed with us."

Flick then added, "Can't decide if it's about the shit with Julie or Spooky, but you can guarantee it'll be about one of them, that's a cert."

Rooster then piped up, "Look, let's just wait and see and we can take it from there."

Brutis was standing at the door, holding it open and gestured for us to get a move on. When we went in, I was surprised to see it was only Indie who was there. I'd just assumed there would be a few Officers in there with him. He then pointed to the chairs, making it clear he wanted us to sit. Brutis closed the door and sat down next to Indie.

The room was quite big. It looked like it was a function suite or something like that. Indie had positioned the table with two chairs at one side and four at the other. Once we were all seated, he began,

"Right, guys, I need to talk to you about something. Before I do, I need your word that you won't do anything as fuckin' stupid as you did tonight with Rooster's chick's father, okay?"

It seemed like the four of us had nodded in unison and that seemed to satisfy him.

"Right, onto the main thing I want to talk about: Brutis and I have been chatting with Gunner and the other Officers in the South chapter and they've told us they no longer wish to have key roles. They'd be happy enough to be Officers, but with a less prominent profile. So we've decided that we want to offer you four the positions they've vacated. We'll review it after six months.

"My plan is that you stay longer and make this your Mother chapter. Rooster, I want you to be Brutis's VP. Shug, I want you to be his SAA. Cowboy, I want you to be Secretary and Flick, I want you to be Treasurer. Brutis and I are now going to leave you for a bit, so you can have a chat. When we come back, you can let us know what you think."

They both then got up and headed out.

I'm not really sure what happened next, but there seemed to be a bit of an eerie silence for a good five minutes or so before Rooster spoke,

"Fuck me, guys, there's a turn up for the books, any thoughts?"

I piped up with, "Wonder why the South guys really turned down the gigs? I can't fuckin' believe he's offered me the SAA - I don't even know what one's supposed to fuckin' do!"

Rooster then spoke again, this time directly to me,

"Shug, you're perfect for that gig, man. All that over thinking shit you do will make sure you cover all the bases before making any decisions."

He then offered out his hand and congratulated me. At the same time, Flick and Cowboy were giving me pats on the back whilst also offering me their congratulations. They then did the same with Rooster and of course, by this time, we're all congratulating each other like we had been given the Prime Minister's job or some shit like that. When we all sat back down, reality hit home for us all.

Rooster reminded us that it was only for six months to see if we could hack it.

"We'd all better be sure we want to do it before Indie and Brutis came back. What about you, Shug? You sure want to do this?" he asked me.

"I definitely want to, Rooster, but I'm not sure what the fuck I'm supposed to do?"

"Don't worry. You'll be fine. As long as you want to do it, I'll keep you right," he reassured me.

"Okay then, fuck it, I'm in!" I told him.

Rooster then asked Cowboy and Flick about their positions and they both agreed they were happy to take them on. But, like me, they really weren't sure about what they actually had to do.

I was about to tell them that I wasn't sure why I'd been offered the SAA post and that I would have expected one of them to be offered it before me, but Indie and Brutis came back in before I got a chance.

"Well? Are we all sorted then?" Indie asked, directing his question at Rooster as he sat back down.

"Yep, we're good to go here," Rooster told him.

"That's good, because I've just told everybody out there that you're all now Officers."

He then reached into his pocket and threw four name patches on the table.

"Get them stitched on as quick as. Right, now I need to head out on a bit of business but won't be long. We'll be having a meeting with all the South Officers in about two hours. Make sure you have them on your cuts before then, okay?"

He then left with Brutis, leaving us all looking at each other again.

Rooster picked up the patches and handed us ours. He then said he was going out to catch one of the chicks or a Prospect to stitch his on. We all agreed we should do the same and made our way back into the bar. Rooster had already identified the chick he wanted and made a beeline to her the minute he saw her. Flick went looking for Spooky. 'No surprise there' I thought to myself, sniggering a bit.

I spoke to a couple of girls at the bar and one of them agreed to do mine if I licked out her pal. 'Fuck me. What an odd thing to ask' I thought but agreed straight away so the deal was done. I gave her my cut-off then took her pal through to the back room eagerly anticipating my task. I knew she was pretty pished by the way she was talking.

When we got inside the room, she told me she wanted me to fuck her and cum inside her first, then lick her out. I started laughing and told her there was no fuckin' way I'd be doing that, and it was either a lick out then a shag or fuck all. She just laughed back and said, "Ach well, it was worth a try." That was one thing I just couldn't do. The very thought of my own spunk in my mouth or even near it was enough to make me want to boak.

She sat on one of the tables, attempting to lower herself back, but her arms gave way and all she ended up doing was falling right back and banging her head. I started laughing just thinking about the whole situation. As I watched her rubbing her head and moaning away about how sore it was, I laughed even harder.

Looking at the state of her, I was surprised she could feel anything. With a little help from me, she lifted her legs up and opened them as wide as she could. The bang on the head must have sobered her up a bit as she closed them again and grabbed hold of her skirt, trying to pull it down. It was a denim one which, when she was standing, sat just above her knees.

She couldn't seem to pull it down, so she decided to yank it up the way. She pulled and tugged away at it until she finally got it up past her arse. She then opened her legs again telling me to lick her out. I put my hands under her arse and yanked down her tights and knickers and threw them on the floor. She then started laughing, telling me she forgot she had tights and knickers on in the first place. I looked at her for a minute and thought 'What a fuckin' boot!'. I was getting pretty well pissed off with her to the extent that I almost went and sewed on my own fuckin' badge!

Anyway, I put my head between her legs, and I have to say, it was the worst looking pussy I'd come across AND stinkin'! Fuck me, honestly, it smelled of dead rats!

I'd expected it to be a bit minging, but fuck me, nothing like that. After looking at it for a minute or so, I pulled her pish flaps apart and decided there was no way I was sticking my tongue anywhere near it so I rammed three fingers in instead - I think she was that drunk she couldn't tell the difference anyway.

By now she was lying flat on the table, wriggling and moaning away. Within a matter of minutes, she was screaming and groaning her way to an orgasm. All I could think was 'Thank Fuck!'.

169

I pulled my fingers out and they were soaking, so I wiped them dry on her skirt and she never even fuckin' noticed.

She was now urging me to fuck her, but again, there was no way I was putting my dick anywhere near her. I told her that I had kept my end of the bargain and that I was off to see if her pal had finished with my cut-off.

The next thing I see is she's lifted her legs up into the air and started playing with herself. I just shook my head and left, thinking to myself 'What a dirty fuckin' cow she was!'.

When I went back into the bar, I saw a couple of the Prospects standing talking and told them to get their arses into the back room as there was a chick playing with herself and gagging for some cock.

Let me tell you, they didn't need to be told twice, they were off like rats up a drainpipe. I laughed at the speed with which they both disappeared, thinking back to me and Malky's first experience with the club.

I then spoke to the chick who was sewing on my patch and she looked like she was almost finished.

"That you just about done then?" I asked her, quickly realising how stupid a question it was, considering I could see she had almost finished.

"Yep, that's me," she told me, handing my cut-off back.

"Did you keep your part of the bargain?" she asked.

"Well, kind of," I told her.

"What's that supposed to mean?" she asked, changing her tone a bit and sounding pretty forceful.

"Look, she was well pished. To be honest, I didn't really fancy it, but I did finger her off and she seemed happy with that. I left her playing with herself and the two Prospects are away through to give her all she

170

wants," I explained. "Can I ask you, is she always like this?"

"Only when she's drunk, which, by the way, is nearly every weekend now that her and her man are not seeing eye to eye."

"She's fuckin' married? Tell me you're having a fuckin' laugh! Fuck me, I know that she's your friend and all that, but she's a fuckin' boot," I told her, which didn't seem to go down to well.

I sat on the bar stool next to her, got her a drink from the bar and apologised for my outburst. I gave her the drink, told her my name and she nodded telling me that she was called Karen.

"So how did you end up here then?" I asked her politely.

But instead of answering, she fired a question right back.

"Why the fuck would you ask me that?" she replied, almost demanding an answer.

"Well, I've been to a few of these things," I told her, "and most of the chicks that come are more like your pal through the back than you. I just didn't think you seemed the type I'd expect to see here, that's all."

"And what fuckin' type would that be then?" she asked, again with aggression in her voice.

"Look, there's a certain expectation about the chicks who come to these things. Your chum - she's all that and a bag of chips for them. All I'm saying about you is you don't strike me as the type to get bollock naked and fuck everything that moves. I just didn't think that it would be your idea of fun, that's all."

"Oh, so you can tell all that just by having a two second conversation with me! What are you? Some kind of fuckin' psychologist or something?"

171

Well, that was enough for me. I'd already had my fill of lunatic women and the last thing I needed was to get involved with any more.

The alarm bells started ringing loud and clear and that was my cue to split. I stood up, thanked her for doing my cut-off, put it on and told her I wasn't interested in playing any of her stupid fuckin' mind games.

I suggested she grab her pal and fuck off before somebody tried to fuck her on the bar. As I walked away, she shouted,

"Maybe that's exactly what I want! Obviously, you're not the man to do it so I guess I'll just need to find someone else."

I stopped for second and thought about what she said but knew it would be a stupid idea to get involved with her, so I turned and let rip.

"Hey, listen, if that's what you're here for then I'm sure you'll have no problem getting someone to fuck you. You could even start by joining your pal through the back. I'm sure the Prospects would welcome another fuckin' boot to hump. As for me, I couldn't give two fucks what you do," I told her then I headed over to the table to join the guys.

"What's the script with her, Shug?" Cowboy asked, as I sat down.

"Fuck knows? I think she's fuckin' mental, a real fuckin' bunny boiler. If you want my advice – you'll stay well clear."

"Not sure I can, Shug. She's heading straight towards us," Cowboy told me.

I turned around just as she approached the table. I was going to tell her to fuck off, but she started yapping before I got a chance.

She stood between Cowboy and Flick, putting her arms around both.

"You two fancy a bit of fun?" she asked them, giving them both a kiss on the cheek.

Cowboy and Flick looked at each other then at me. Cowboy told her to get her kit off and he would fuck her right here on the table which seemed to startle her a bit. Flick stuck his hand between her legs and gave her a bit of a rub.

"Come on then, bitch, let's do it, get your fuckin' kit off," he told her.

The minute Flick grabbed her pussy, she jumped back then started to splutter a bit.

"Whoa, guys. Hold your Horses! Can we not go through the back room beside my mate before we get into it?" she suggested.

I looked at her and had no idea why she was doing this. She was absolutely petrified. I think if Cowboy and Flick had stood up, she would have bolted. Cowboy just drew her a look and said,

"You know what, hen? You're in the wrong fuckin' movie here. So the quicker you fuck off, the better, before we drag your sorry arse onto the table and fuck you sideways."

That seemed to do it for her. She gave me a bit of a stare then turned and hightailed it through the back room to get her pal.

The four of us looked at each other and burst out laughing. We were still laughing and hi-fiving when Brutis came over.

"Back room, now, guys," was all he said.

We all stood up, lifting our drinks, and made our way to the door. Before we reached the door, we saw the two Prospects coming out of the back room. They were half dressed and carrying the rest of their clothes in their hands.

The next thing, we see is Indie, shoving a naked girl out at the back of them. We watched as she toppled straight onto the floor in front of us. Indie went back in shaking his head. He then came out again, this time dragging the mad bitch by the hair and throwing her on top of her pal.

She was screaming at the top of her voice, but Indie ignored her and went back in again. This time he returned with a pile of clothes and threw them on top of the two girls. He shouted to the Prospects, who by this time were fully dressed, and told them 'to get the two chicks away to fuck out of here' then turned and headed back into the room for the umpteenth time.

The four of us were next in, with the rest of the Officers following behind us. Indie told us to push some of the tables together and grab a chair, which we did. Indie nodded for Brutis to sit at the head of the table then, pointing to the chair on his right, gestured for Rooster to sit. He then did the same to me with the one on his left. He told everyone else to grab a chair and he sat at the top of the table beside Brutis.

I had a quick squatch around the room counting the bodies, there were the four of us plus Brutis, Indie, Gunner, Freddie and Ludo. Indie brought us all to order and explained that, as from now, the group in the room would constitute the Officers of the new South chapter and that Brutis would be taking the lead from here on in.

He spent about ten minutes explaining what he expected from us and told us that he'd be down once a week on our meeting night for the first few weeks, to see how we were getting on. He then got up, wished us luck, shook Brutis' hand and told us he was off for a beer.

I was thinking to myself, 'meeting night?' Fuck! I didn't even know we had meetings once a week. Just shows you I've been hanging about with the Bats for years and always thought they just had meetings when something was up.

Brutis sat back down then began explaining what he wanted. The first thing he told us was that all the officers had to report directly to Rooster on any matters that arose between meetings. He said we should only come to him first if Rooster was unavailable. Any other time Rooster would decide if they're needed to be any action taken.

He then went on to tell us that Rooster and him would meet every morning. If they needed anything done that day Rooster would speak to the officer concerned to get him to carry out the action. Lastly, he explained what he expected from the rest of us. When he came to me, I began to wonder what the fuck I'd gotten myself into! He went on about weapons, strategies for dealing with situations and shit like that.

It's not until you hear it all explained that you actually realise how much shit goes on behind the scenes to keep a club running. I always thought that the likes of Provo, Stiff and Indie had the easy end of it, telling everybody what to do, like fuck they had. As usual, my mind began to wander, and I was back thinking about my job.

I wasn't even sure if I'd have time for a job with all the fuckin' stuff Brutis was expecting me to do. Fuck, I didn't think I'd even have time to go for a shite. I was snapped back to reality by a dunt in the ribs from Rooster. I looked at him wondering why he had done it, but he just nodded towards Brutis. I looked at him and noticed he was staring directly at me.

Fuck! I hadn't heard a thing and I was pretty sure I was supposed to respond to something.

"Well, Shug? Are you okay with it or not?" he asked me.

"Yep, I'm cool with that," I could hear myself saying, even though I had no fuckin' idea what I'd just agreed to.

"Right, unless there's anything else, the meeting's now closed."

"Hang on a second, Brutis, I've got a quick question," Freddie piped up.

"Okay, Freddie, shoot! What is it?" Brutis replied.

"Well, what I want to know is if me and Gunner have to point out the dealers to Shug, why can't we just tell them the script right away? Why do we have to come back here and have a meet about it?"

Brutis then looked at me and said, "Well, Shug?"

All I could think was, 'Well, Shug, what?' I had no fuckin' idea what any of them were talking about. I swear to God I thought I had missed a few seconds of the chat, but 'fuck a duck', it was obvious I'd missed a whole fuckin' conversation.

With no idea what to say and the sweat running down the shuck of my arse, I blurted out something about planning a strategy and making sure we were prepared before going to see them, just to make sure we got the right people first time and I then spieled some other shit that popped into my head.

I must have sounded reasonably convincing because Brutis then told the three of us and Rooster to stay back and discuss it. He then got up along with the others and left.

Freddie and Gunner suggested they'd go and grab some beers for us. I told them that was a great idea and the minute they left, I was about to get Rooster to fill me in on what I'd missed – however, he spoke first.

"Shug, what the fuck is wrong with you, man? This is probably the most important meeting you've ever been at and you're miles away! It's like you're in some kind of cloud fuckin' cuckoo land.

"You better get a grip, man, or you're fucked. I'm not sure Brutis clocked it. But me, Flick and Cowboy knew you were talking a lot of pish there. I'm telling you, Shug, you better wise the fuck up and pretty fuckin' sharpish too or you'll be fucked. Brutis won't stand for any shite from anybody, especially not from his Officers. He's under pressure from Indie to make sure he takes control down here so you better wise up."

I interrupted him before he said any more as he was getting on my tits with all his fuckin' moaning.

"Look, man, I'm sorry, but it's not really my fault," I lied to him. "Remember I told you that I was having blackouts? Well, I think I've just had another one! I missed the whole conversation, but I couldn't tell Brutis that in case he thought I wasn't interested. Come on, man, for fuck's sake, fill me in before they all come back?" I heard myself almost pleading with him.

He stood up and started walking about the room, sweeping back his hair with his hands and giving his head a bit of a rub.

"Fuck's sake, Shug, yir some man. Right, pin yir fuckin' lugs back and listen: Brutis wants us to find out who the main drug dealers are and tell them we're taking a slice of the action. Freddie and Gunner are going to point out to you who the runners are and then we … well, YOU … will come up with a plan about how to take over their areas.

"That's the short version, but at least when they come back you'll have an idea about what the fuck they're talking about. Oh, and by the way, see instead of going to work in a fuckin' hospital, maybe you'd be better visiting a fucking doctor in one!"

Before I got a chance to reply, the two of them came back with our drinks and we got down to discussing how we were going to go about our business. We agreed that the four of us would hit the town the following night and Freddie and Gunner would show us the lay of the land.

By the time we'd finished, my brain was mush. I looked up at the clock and saw it was only ten-to-twelve, but for me it seemed like it was so much later. I'd just had yet another one of those days that I thought was never going to end.

Rooster was for grabbing another few drinks, but I told him I needed to crash as I was totally fucked. As usual, he called me a lightweight, but at that point I really didn't give two monkey's fucks. I gave him a pat on the back and told him I'd catch up with him in the morning. I went in search of Gunner to see if he still had the keys for the house.

When I got hold of him, he told me that there were already some people over there, and the door would be open. I headed outside and made my way towards the house.

As I walked, I thought about the meeting and started to feel really uncomfortable again about the whole Bats thing. I knew the next day that I'd need to be the SAA for real. I decided the best thing to do was to put it to the back of my mind and try and get some sleep.

I walked up the path and I could have just about turned and headed home. The music was fuckin' blaring and I could see through the window that there was a rake of bodies all in party mode.

I knew I needed to stay, but I also knew I needed a good night's kip. I wasn't sure what would be best, the pub or the house, but seeing as the house had beds, I decided to plumb for that.

When I went in, I was hit with a wall of sound and enough smoke to get wasted without putting a spliff anywhere near my mouth. I just nodded and smiled as I squeezed and pushed my way through the downstairs rooms and out into the hall. I headed upstairs and stuck my head into the first two bedrooms only to see they were occupied by naked bodies giving it laldy.

Thankfully, the other bedroom, which was a small single room with a bed settee, was empty. I went in and jammed a chair under the handle of the door, pulled out the bed and plunked myself on top of it. As I began to relax, I replayed the day in my mind.

I was thinking about all the heavy shit that had went down, but in the forefront of my thoughts was my new role. Fuck! I was now the SAA in the South chapter of the Black Bats. As I said it over and over again, I still couldn't get it to sink in. I could actually feel my entire body trembling at the thought of it.

I wondered what Malky would have thought of it and laughed away to myself thinking of how he would have reacted. I reckoned that if he'd still been with us, he would've been an Officer by now anyway. He would've expected not only to be an Officer, but to be at least the VP, if I was the SAA. There was no way he'd have accepted anything less. I must have dosed off, still smiling away to myself, thinking about him and all the what ifs?

I woke up with a bit of a start. I could hear shouting and it sounded like it was right outside the bedroom door. I jumped up, noticing I still had all my clothes on, kicked away the chair then yanked open the door to see what all the fuss was about. Fuck! I couldn't believe it. There were bodies everywhere, cunts with baseball bats and pieces of wood - and loads of screaming and shouting. I had no idea what the fuck was going on but decided I should get right into the mix.

The guys with the bats and sticks all seemed pretty well dressed, which for some reason reassured me as I knew that they were not members of another bike gang. There were four guys from our chapter standing at the top of the stairs, in various states of undress, kicking and punching the blokes on the stair.

From where I was standing, I could see the bottom of the stairs and it was almost a replica of the top - with our guys trying to get at them as they swung their weapons about.

A quick assessment of the situation made me wonder if the blokes on the stairs had even thought about what they were going to do. They were trapped in between us, with no hope of winning.

As the SAA it should have been my responsibility to guide the rest of the guys and make sure we came out on top, but I had no idea what the fuck I was meant to do. I just let out a roar then jumped over the balustrade and landed on top of a few guys.

My momentum, and the speed of what could only be described as my fall, took them by surprise and about half of them, including myself, ended up at the bottom of the stairs.

This gave our guys a chance to relieve our unwanted guests of their weapons and duly set about them, giving them a kicking they'd never forget.

The guys upstairs were now either backing off or being kicked down the stairs, and within a matter of minutes, they were all on the floor at the bottom, getting ten bales of shite kicked out of them.

I still had no idea what the fuck was going on or why the cunts had turned up at the door, but I'll tell you what, I bet they wished they'd never came fuckin' near! When I realised that they'd had enough, I shouted at our guys to stop and get them all outside.

Thankfully, they took heed of my instructions and started horsing them out of the door, just in time to be greeted by plod turning up in a couple of Panda cars. As they made their way up the path, all they could see was bodies being either thrown or kicked out of the house.

Thinking it should probably be me who went and greeted them, I pushed myself out the door and went to the first officer I saw. Brazen as fuck, I walked up to him and said, "I hope you're here to lift these cunts …" pointing in the direction of the guys on the ground, who by this time were starting to lick their wounds a bit, "I want the whole fuckin' lot of them charged," I told him.

"Listen, boy, just back off right now or it'll be you who'll be getting arrested, okay?" he growled at me.

"Look, they just barged into our house waving weapons all over the place. If that's not enough for you to fuckin' charge them then tell me what the fuck is?" I roared back at him.

"One more word from you and you'll be the first to get lifted. Now back the fuck off and let me do my job," he shouted back.

I just shook my head at him and made my way back to the door, staring at the guys who were now ringed off by the rest of the cops.

I was just about to go back in when I heard some shouting and turned around just in time to see about thirty guys running down towards the house. I clocked it was our guys and raced out to stop them. As I made my way around the cops and the injured, I could see the colour drain from all of their faces.

They must have been really shitting themselves as it looked a real fearful sight. Fuck! I was worried and I was with them!

I managed to catch them before they came into the garden, and when Indie held up his hand, most of the guys stopped. Just as I began to tell them what the script was, I noticed DD continue his run. I tried to grab hold of him, but he side-stepped me, like a rugby player avoiding a tackle.

He managed to land a few punches on a couple of guys who'd just got back on their feet before I eventually got hold of him. At this point, some of our unwanted visitors saw this as an opportunity to start scrapping again and directed their blows at both DD and myself.

The minute they started laying into us, the rest of our guys began weighing into them, and before the cops could restore order, they were well and truly fucked for a second time.

By now, another three cop cars and two ambulance crews had arrived. The cops had ushered everyone either back into the house or a bit up the road towards the pub. This allowed the ambulance men to deal with the injured. DD and I were handcuffed and put into the back of one of the cars.

I kind of accepted it and never put up any real resistance, knowing it would be a waste of time. However, DD was kicking and screaming for all he was worth and calling them every name under the sun. I thought it was pointless - he was still going to end up sitting in the back alongside me just the same.

Chapter 18

When they eventually got him in the van, he smiled at me and said, "Ah well, Shug, at least I made them work for their money tonight."

I just burst out laughing and so did he.

DD obviously thought I was laughing at his gag, but I was really laughing because I was thinking about Malky again. I knew for a fact that he'd have done exactly the same as DD. He'd have seen us sitting in the back of a pig's van as some kind of successful end to the night.

By the time we'd stopped laughing, we were well on our way to the station, with the old blue lights flashing away.

DD asked me what the fuck had happened and why the guys had attacked us? I told him I had no idea and gave him a quick version of what I knew. For some reason, he burst out laughing again. When I stared at him and asked him what the fuck he was laughing about, he never said a word, he just laughed even louder.

The cops in the front must've thought we were barking mad.

"What?" I asked him, giving him a bit of eye.

By this time, he'd managed to get his laughing in check.

"Sorry, Shug, but I just had a picture of you jumping off the landing onto the guys on the stairs. Tell you what, I'd have paid good money to see that. I just wish to fuck I'd been there to watch it live," then burst out laughing again.

The cop in the passenger seat turned around. He fixed his eyes on DD and said, "Shut the fuck up! You've got nothing to be laughing about."

DD replied, "Fuck you, pig!" and carried on laughing.

When we arrived at the station, they booked us in and marched us to the cells. On the way there, I asked them what we were being charged with and was promptly told to shut my mouth.

When they opened the cell door, I was un-handcuffed and pushed in. However, when DD's handcuffs were removed, he was punched and kicked by one of the officers who'd lifted us, before being shoved in beside me.

As they closed the door, DD got up and lifted the viewing flap and spat out some of the blood in his mouth, hoping to catch one of them with it. He then began shouting obscenities through it, calling anybody who could hear him all sorts of shit. I sat down on one of the beds and suggested he do the same, but it fell on deaf ears. Still ranting away, he began pacing the floor which was really getting on my tits.

"For fuck's sake, DD! Will you shut the fuck up and sit on your fuckin' arse, man? You're dain ma fuckin' heid in," I roared at him.

"Sorry, man. I just can't believe we've ended up in here. The wankers lifted the wrong people. We should never have got canned for this. We did fuck all."

"DD, would you just listen to yourself for one fuckin' minute. Fuck's sake, man! You're the reason we're in here! What was all that about anyway?" I let rip at him, "Everything was sorted and none of us were going to get done. But, oh no, you just had to get a few digs in! Now look at us! If I get charged for this then I'm holding you responsible," I began telling him, but he interrupted me asking what the fuck I meant by that, so I sarcastically said it again,

"Okay, DD, pin your ears back and listen, I'll repeat it again for the hard of thinking: If I get done, I'm going to boot fuck out of you! Is that clear enough?"

I seemed to take the wind out his sails for a minute and he stopped pacing the floor and sat down on the other bed. He lifted his head and gave me a bit of a look. By this time, I was lying on the bed and thought it best to sit up, just in case he wanted to start something.

He continued to stare at me, so I stared back at him, waiting on him saying or doing something. But he didn't look like he was ready to move or going to say anything. I was getting pissed with him, so I spoke first.

"What?" was all I said, hoping to trigger a response from him.

"Well, Shug, I'll tell you what?' I'm not best pleased with you threatening me - especially now you're the SAA. If you weren't, we'd be boxing!" he told me.

I was already well pissed off with him for getting me canned. As far as I was concerned, his comments were the final straw. I stood up, removed my cut-off and threw it on the floor.

"Stand up, ya fuckin' prick, and listen good! As far as I'm concerned, there's no fuckin' rank in here, so if you want it then lets fuckin' do it!" I told him.

The bastard then lunged at me, pushing me back onto the bed and caught me with a couple of digs in the guts. I could feel my wound burning like fuck and I was worried that it had burst. I managed to push him over me, and he smacked his head on the wall, which gave me enough time to spin him around and get on top of him.

I laid into him with both hands, catching him mainly on the face, but I missed with one of my punches and hit him in the throat. That punch seemed to do more damage than any of the others that I'd caught him with. He went a bit limp and started holding his throat with both hands before dropping them to his side - it looked like he wasn't breathing.

I got up and stood back, looking at him and wondering what the fuck was going on? His face was bright red and his eyes were closed. At that point, I realised that three cops had come into the cell, one of them grabbed me, pushed me into the corner out of the way and stood directly in front of me.

The other two were at DD and I couldn't really see what they were doing because of the guy standing in front of me. A few seconds later, I heard DD coughing and spluttering. Within a matter of minutes, they had him sitting up. One of them got him a glass of water, which he drank really quickly.

They then helped him up and escorted him from the cell, leaving me on my own. I was going to ask them where they were taking him but knew there was no point - they wouldn't have told me fuck all anyway, so I never said a word.

I lit up a smoke, closed my eyes and inhaled deeply. As I blew out the smoke, I started to think about what just happened. I was sure he'd stopped breathing and wondered what would have happened if the officers hadn't come as I would've had no fuckin' idea what to do?

About half an hour later, one of the cops came back, swung the door open and told me I was free to go. The first thing I asked was how DD was? He told me he was fine, but that I was one lucky little git.

"If one of the officers hadn't had medical training, your buddy would've died, and you'd be facing a murder charge instead of being released!"

I then asked him what had happened to DD? He explained that the punch to the neck I'd given him had compressed his esophagus and prevented him from breathing. If the officer hadn't given him mouth to mouth, then he'd have died.

Fuckin hell! I couldn't believe what he'd just told me. I felt a shiver down my spine like no other I'd felt before. I could feel my legs buckle under me as I walked along the corridor to the main door.

My head was spinning, and I felt like I was steaming drunk. As I walked, I tried to get my shit together and composed myself enough to ask him where DD was now?

"He's been checked by our doctor and was let out about ten minutes ago. The doc recommended that he should go to hospital overnight as a precaution, but he was having none of it."

I never said another word. I'm sure he said something about the guys who'd gate crashed our party also being lifted, but I wasn't really taking incoming calls - all I could think about was what if DD had died!

When I got out of the cop shop, I lit up another smoke and looked around. I had no idea where the fuck I was or how to get back to the house. I half expected that someone would have been there, waiting to pick me up, but there was not a single person in sight.

I decided to walk towards the lights, guessing it was the main street, as I knew how to get to the house from there. As I walked, I wondered if someone had come to pick us up and if they had, had they picked up

DD? Did he tell them what happened? Had they fucked off without me? What would be waiting for me when I got back? What about the fight at the house, what the fuck was that all about? How was it resolved? Fuck! So many questions and not a single fuckin' answer! I spied a bench and decided to plank my arse on it for a bit to try and get my bearings. As I sat, I looked up at the sky, watching as the darkness of the night began slowly breaking into the brightness of dawn. I had no idea what time it was, but I knew it must have been getting close to morning.

I was snapped out of my daydream by someone shouting my name. I turned and looked in the direction of the shout and noticed it was DD, Rooster and Cowboy.

'Ah well, here goes!' I thought to myself as I stood up. I faced them as they walked towards me, bracing myself for who knows what? As they came closer to me, DD picked up the pace and was a few steps ahead of the other two.

I began to wonder what the fuck he'd told them and if it would be just me and him, or if Rooster and Cowboy would get involved as well. Surely to fuck the history we had together would mean something and that they would stay out of it?

The first to speak was DD, which didn't surprise me, although what he said kind of knocked me for six. He was about six feet away from me when he began talking.

"Shug, please accept my apologies, man. I was way out of order tonight," he told me, holding his hands up in a sort of surrender pose.

I was dumbfounded. I'd nearly killed the cunt and here he was apologising to me. I had no idea what to say, but thankfully, I didn't need to talk as DD kept yapping away.

As he approached me, he put his arms around me. He then gave me a hug, continually saying sorry, and asking me if I could forgive him. My arms were trapped by my sides and I could see Rooster and Cowboy over his shoulder. I screwed up my eyebrows in their direction only to see them smile back at me. I was standing there thinking 'what in fuck's name is going on?'.

Sometimes you can find yourself in a position where things don't make sense or you don't understand the whole picture, but at this time, I was standing there like a polar bear dumped in a fuckin' desert. I didn't have a clue as to what the fuck was happening.

"Whoa, whoa, that's enough. Just hold it a fuckin' minute," I said, moving back from him. "What the fuck are you playing at? I nearly fuckin' killed you tonight and you're asking me to forgive you? What the fuck am I missing here? Would someone care to explain?" I said, hoping one of them would.

DD then started, "Look, man, I was bang out of order a few times tonight. I know all you did was try to protect me. The thing in the jail - well, if I hadn't provoked you, there would never have been a fight. I just want to say sorry, Shug, and hope we can get back on track?"

He then held his hand out for me to shake, which I did. However, even after his explanation, I still felt I was none the wiser, but decided not to dwell on it.

I thought it best to change the subject, so I patted him on the shoulder and gave him a bit of a nod and told him we were cool.

"Anybody know what time it is?" I asked, hoping someone had a watch on.

"Twenty-to-four," Cowboy piped up.

"Fuck me, man, I've almost been awake for twenty-four hours - no wonder I feel fucked!" I told them.

Rooster then said to me that he was wiped out as well.

"Come on, let's get back to the pub. We've got a busy day tomorrow as well," Rooster reminded me.

Chapter 19

Cowboy and DD were walking in front of me and Rooster. After a few steps, I grabbed hold of his arm and gestured for him to slow down a bit, which he did.

I got out my cigarettes and handed one to Rooster. He stopped and lit up then waited 'til I'd lit mine. I looked ahead and saw that Cowboy and DD were a good few feet in front of us and guessed they were out of earshot. When I was sure, I asked Rooster what the fuck that was all about? He told me that Indie had gone through DD like a dose of salts.

"What happened was, Freddie picked up DD from the jail and brought him back to the pub. When they arrived, Indie was in the middle of trying to find out who the guys were that'd crashed the house. When he saw them, he asked DD where you were?

"When DD said he wasn't sure, but thought that you might still be in jail, Indie blew a fuckin' gasket. He laid into DD big time, telling him the whole sorry episode was all his fault. He said that if you end up getting charged, he would boot him out of the Bats and take great pleasure in giving him a kicking like no other he'd had before.

"Freddie interrupted, telling Indie that he was out of order, so Indie had a go at him as well. He finished up by reminding them both that you're an Officer and that whatever you tell them to do, they're expected to do it, end of discussion.

"DD then started to plead his case, telling him that he nearly died because of you. But Indie let rip again, reminding him that if he'd done what you'd told him to do, he'd never had been in that position in the first place and that the next time he sees you he'd better apologise to you, and better fuckin' mean it.

"He then told Freddie to sit on his arse and sent me, Cowboy and DD to the jail to see what was going on with you - and hey, ho, here we are."

"Fuck me, nae wonder he was all over me like a rash! I thought he seemed genuine enough as well, but now I'm not sure if he was just acting like that because Indie forced him to?"

"Nah, Shug, we spoke to him on the way over and he seemed pretty upset about the whole thing. He hoped that you both could get back to being mates."

"Well, I've no problems with that, Rooster, but I'll make sure I keep an eye on him for a while."

"I agree, Shug, me too, and I'll also watch that cunt Freddie like a hawk - I'm not sure about him either."

Rooster then gave me a pat on the back, and we picked up the pace to catch up with them.

As we walked, the topic of conversation was the scrap in the house. We tried to make sense of it, but none of us could come up with anything tangible.

When we arrived back at the pub, most of the guys seemed to have crashed out, except Indie, Brutis and Gunner. They were sitting at a table having a smoke, so we went over and joined them. We all nodded and said our hello's - except Indie. The first thing he said was, "Are you two sorted yet?" looking between DD and myself.

"We're both good, Indie," I told him, which seemed to satisfy him.

Rooster asked him if they'd sussed out who the guys were and why they had barged into the house. Indie told us that they now knew exactly who they were and why they did it and that we would be giving them all an early morning wake-up call.

When he said that, all I could think was 'Fuck! Here we go again!' - I thought I was coming back to

193

get some zeds, but guessed that was out of the question now. Having done wake-up calls before I knew we would be on it by 6 a.m. I glanced at the clock and it was now half-four. Only an hour and a half before we were back out, so I knew a sleep would need to wait.

"So who the fuck were they then?" Rooster asked Indie again.

"Do you remember the little stuck up cow with the long black hair at the bar?" he asked him, then looked at me.

"Shug, you were sitting talking to her at one point?" to which I just nodded, "Well, see the other bint that ended up getting fucked by the Prospects? Apparently, she was married. When she went home and her man saw the state of her, he demanded she tell him where she'd been and what she'd been up to. She told him that we'd forced drink down her neck and tried to rape her. He went off his nut, rounded up some of his mates and well, you know the rest."

"What a dirty, lying little fuckin' cow! She wanted me to lick her out and fuck her, but I thought she was a right minger. I told her to fuck off and sent the Prospects in. They told me she was gagging for it and that she couldn't get enough!" I explained.

"Well, it seems like 'hubby boy' believed her story. Apparently, he has a bit of a rep around here as a hard nut and was looking for blood. It might be a good thing this has happened, though. It'll give us a good excuse to establish ourselves quickly down here, or should I say, yourselves. Wipe this cunt out and you'll probably have a free run I reckon."

Indie looked straight at me. I knew he was looking for me to come up with something, so I asked him who got the info. Indie pointed at Freddie, so I asked him how many were involved. He told me there were eight there last night, but that Rocko, the boot's husband, could probably get a crew together about treble that.

Indie then interrupted telling us he was going to have an hour's kip and wanted wakened at quarter-to-six. He then got up and left us to it. Brutis then spoke up.

"Ok, Shug, how'd you want to play this then?" he asked me.

What a fuckin' nightmare! Talk about getting put on the spot! Five minutes in the fuckin' job and already I've got to come up with something to get this cunt and his team.

I knew I needed a bit of thinking time, so I told DD to get a hold of Flick and Freddie to grab Ludo. While they were away, I went to the loo and gave my face a bit of a slunge and tried to plan what I was going to say.

I tried to recall some of the stuff I'd heard Stiff and Provo talk about when they were planning shit. Thankfully, I came up with what I thought would be a good strategy. When I went back in, everyone was sitting around the table, but no-one was speaking. I sat down on the only vacant chair and began,

"Right, guys, here's what we're going to do: there's eight of us around the table. I want each of us to grab three guys. Gunner, you get the addresses written down where these 'Rocko fuckers' live and pass them around.

"Make sure each group has someone local, so they know where these addresses are. We'll all leave here at 6 a.m. sharp. Make sure everyone is tooled up and, for fuck's sake, make sure you get the right people!

"I don't want anyone beaten to death, but I want enough damage done to them so that they know not to fuck with us again. Anyone that isn't hospitalised will get the same treatment again tomorrow, okay? Any questions?" I asked.

"Just one," Rooster said, "Any thoughts on what we should do if he manages to get the rest of his team together?"

"Yep, we'll do exactly the same to them. From today, we make sure everyone knows we're here. After we do them, I want groups of six riding around the city all day - it's time to make our presence felt."

"Gunner, when we get back, I want us to meet to discuss the drug stuff, okay?"

Gunner gave me a bit of a nod then spoke up,

"Shug, you'll probably kill two birds with one stone here because Rocko is the guy we used to get our drugs from. He's one of the main dealers about here."

"Okay, that's excellent," I told him. "Right, let's get our groups sorted and grab any weapons we need. Gunner, give me a shout when you've got those addresses written out! Brutis, can I have a word?" I asked the big man.

"Sure, Shug, what is it?" he asked.

"Needs to be private, if that's okay?"

"Yep, no probs," he told me, so we sat back down and waited until everyone had split.

As Rooster went to leave, Brutis grabbed his arm. "No, man, you wait," he told him, then turned to me and said, "Okay, Shug, let's hear it?"

"Well, I just wanted to see if you thought what I was doing was the right thing? This is the first time I've had to organise anything like this and I'm a bit concerned that I may have missed something or that I am doing something that may not work?"

"Listen, Shug, there's no right way or wrong way in these situations. If it works - it's right, if not - it's shite. The main thing is, that if it does go tits up, then you've got a plan-B to fall back on. Tell me what your plan-B is and I'll let you know how I feel about it."

Fuck me, I hardly had a plan-A! Now he wanted me to give him something else. I kind of stuttered my way through it, telling him some kind of shit about regrouping, taking stock then trying it another way. To this day I've no idea what I said, but he seemed satisfied enough to tell me he was happy with my plan.

I made my way to the door for a bit of air and was glad no-one followed me. I sat on one of the chairs, which was wet with condensation, and I was now officially shitting myself. All I could think of was, what if this didn't work? What if they were all at one address and the four who went to that house got a licking and we weren't there to help them? What if they were still in the nick and we barged into family homes with wives or kids and our targets weren't there?

Again, so many questions – again, no way to answer them! I was deep in thought when Rooster gave me a dunt.

"You okay, man? You seem like you're miles away."

"That's coz I am, man, I've no fuckin' idea if this is going to work. There are way too many variables and I'm worried as fuck something will go wrong and some of our guys get fucked."

"Shug, you're going to need to calm your jets a bit, man, you'll give yourself a fuckin' heart attack! For what it's worth, I'd have done it exactly the same way," he told me.

I looked at him with a bit of a wry smile.

"Tell me this, Rooster … when we were back at the farm and there was some shit going on, was it not Stiff and Provo that organised this kind of stuff?"

"When they were running the show, it was mainly Indie who sorted it all out. What you never saw was the meetings, like the one we've just had with Brutis, most of the time Provo, Stiff and Indie would meet like that, then either Provo or Stiff would pass it on to the guys."

When I started thinking back, I managed to recall a few occasions that I'd looked around for Indie and wondered why he wasn't there when the big man was telling us the script, but never really thought too much about it.

I remembered asking Stiff about him once and he told me he was already out and about doing one of his 'reckies' to make sure he'd covered all the bases. I mind Stiff laughed a bit, telling me Indie wasn't too big on the talking stakes, but shit hot on getting things like this done with the minimum of fuss.

I tried to recall some of the meetings from back then, but to be honest, my memory of it all was pretty fuzzy. You always just thought that everyone was there when Provo was having one of his gatherings. Rooster then suggested we head back in and make sure everyone was ready to go. By this time, most of the guys were armed and pretty well up for it. Gunner gave me the addresses and I called the Officers to gather around for a final bit of prep.

I handed out all the addresses, made sure everyone knew where they were going and told them all to make sure they knew where everyone else would be. I also explained to them that if they crashed any of the houses and none of the fuckers were there, then they should get to the closest house on the list, ASAP, to help out - in case there were more dudes there than expected.

I finished by asking if anyone had any questions. Other than people mumbling to each other, everyone said they were good to go.

"Okay, let's do this. Let's get the bastards," I said then we all made our way to the door.

Just as I got outside, Indie pulled me to one side and said,

"Good stuff, Shug. You did well in there. Let's hope everybody listened to you."

"Cheers, Indie, I wasn't too sure if I'd done things right, but I guess we'll soon find out," I told him.

"It'll work well, Shug. I'll tag along with your group, if that's okay?"

I almost burst out laughing - Indie asking *me* if it was okay! Oh, and like I had a fuckin' choice! What if I'd said, 'Indie, you just sit your arse here until we get back. We don't fuckin' need you.' - can you imagine what he'd say to that! 'Aye, nae bother, Shug. Hope it all goes well for you pal,' - aye, like fuck that would happen!

I must have been sniggering a bit as Indie asked me what I was laughing about. I told him I was just thinking about how weird it would be on the bikes with him at the back. His facial expression then changed to a very serious look.

"Who the fuck said I would be at the back?" he growled, in a dead aggressive tone.

I then apologised and tried to tell him what I thought, but he told me to 'Shut the fuck up' as he was

199

just shitting with me. He then gave me a bit of a soft slap on the cheek.

"You need to relax, man, you'll give yourself a fuckin' stroke!" he told me as he made his way towards his bike, leaving me with my thoughts.

I looked around - everyone was now on their bikes and stuffing their weapons anywhere they wouldn't fall off. I jumped on my bike, stuffed my baseball bat down the back of my jacket then kicked my bike into life. I had DD, Ludo, Spooky and Indie with me. I'd decided to take Rocko's house, not because I really wanted to, but because I felt I should.

Everybody waited 'til I drove out the car park with my group, they then followed behind, turning off at various junctions. I followed DD as he turned off the main road and into a housing scheme. After a few right and left turns, he drew into the side of the road and pointed to a house, right on the corner of the next junction.

We all parked up then had a quick pow-wow about how we were going to play it. I wanted them all to be sure they knew who the targets were and who to leave out of it. All agreed, we charged up the pavement and down the path.

DD was in front and didn't even change his stride as he approached the door, he just jumped up and booted it in. DD and Ludo ran up the stairs as agreed and myself, Spooky and Indie took the downstairs. We went into the living room and saw there were four guys. They looked like they'd been sleeping soundly right up until their door getting booted in.

There was absolutely no resistance whatsoever, none of them even looked like they knew what was going on. The whole thing was over in a matter of minutes. A few blasts with our bats and they were all out cold. Their initial reaction when they saw us was pure fear.

I got the impression that they were all shite bags. Two of them were sobbing before they even got hit. I could hear a bit of noise from upstairs, so I thought I better investigate. As I went to go back out to the staircase, Indie must have had the same thought and was halfway up before I even reached the bottom stair. I followed him up and into the main room where there was still a bit of a struggle going on.

One guy was KO'd and another two were having a bit of a scrap with DD and Ludo. I entered the room just in time to see Indie smack Rocko on the side of his head with the base of his bat and watched as he collapsed onto the floor. The other guy wasn't doing anything other than holding on to Ludo's bat to prevent him from hitting him with it. Indie hit him a couple of digs in the ribs until he let it go. Ludo then booted him, and he landed on the bed.

DD and I went and checked the other two rooms, but there was no-one else there, so we went back into the room. We watched as Indie slapped Rocko in the pus, trying to get him to come round. All of a sudden, Indie took control of the situation and told us to grab the other two and take them downstairs.

DD grabbed the guy on the bed by his hair and told him to move his arse, which he did. All I could hear, as he dragged him down the stairs, was him squealing at DD telling him the raid on the Bats the previous evening had nothing to do with him.

The dude on the floor was now moaning and, like Rocko, was starting to come too a bit. I followed DD's lead and grabbed him by the hair, pulling him towards the stairs as well.

In the midst of trying to behave like the proverbial hard man, I nearly burst out laughing. Watching him crawl on his hands and knees in only a pair of scants was hilarious. I dragged him down the stairs and into the living room then gave him a boot, forcing him into the corner where Spook had laid out the other guys. I've no idea what Indie was doing upstairs, but I could hear Rocko screaming. I thought I'd better go back up and see what was going on. Knowing Indie, there was a good chance he could end up killing him and that was the last thing any of us fuckin' needed.

When I made my way up the stairs, Ludo was standing on the top landing. He signalled to me by moving his hand from one side of his neck to the other as if to suggest Indie was killing him.

I moved a bit quicker, making my way towards the room, not really sure what I was going to find - all I could hope for was that he was still living and, thankfully, he was. Indie had lifted him up, leant his back against the bed and was kneeling in front of him with a knife in his hand. To my surprise, they actually looked like they were having a conversation.

When I entered, they both looked up at me and the relief I got in seeing Rocko covered in blood but still alive was almost overwhelming. I had visions of needing to dispose of a body or some shit like that. More and more, I felt like I was becoming mentally unstable and the thought of someone else dying would probably have been enough to send me right over the edge.

I knelt down beside Indie and we nodded to each other.

He then said, "Shug, Mr Rocko here is telling me that there's enough business in the city for both of us and that he's happy to split it with us fifty-fifty. Why do you think he wants to do that?" he asked me, not really looking for an answer, but I gave him one anyway.

"Not sure, Indie, maybe he should explain it to us?" I replied.

Indie then looked at him and said,

"Well? Come on then, cunt, let's hear it!"

Rocko began speaking, but I don't think Indie was even listening. I was, though. Just as he began talking, we heard a few bikes come to a halt outside and Indie interrupted him.

"I think that's some reinforcements arrived, Shug. Do you think we'll need them?" he asked me.

"Don't think so, Indie. I think we're covered here. What do you reckon, Rocko?" I asked him.

"Guys, look, you won't need anybody else. Can we not just make a deal right here, right now?" he suggested.

All the time we were kneeling in front of Rocko, Indie kept twirling his blade and rubbing his finger up and down it. This was not only making Rocko uncomfortable, but me as well.

Some of the guys who'd just arrived bundled into the room to see what was going on. One of them was Cowboy so I stood up to talk to him. I asked him how his group had got on and he told me everything was cool. Indie then explained to Rocko what we'd done, and I swear I saw a tear in his eye.

It was at that point that I realised he'd been shitting us before about the deal. He was only telling us what he thought we wanted to hear so he could get out and re-group. As usual, Indie was right on top of it, whereas I would've tried to strike a deal and more than probably ended up with egg on my face. Indie then took his knife and held it under Rocko's chin and started speaking to him.

"Right, Rocko, this is what we're going to do, so best you listen good to this bit," he then pressed on the blade a bit more, which made Rocko lift his head up a bit while nodding.

"You're now going to tell me where you get your gear then you're going to take me and introduce me to them. I'll decide what I'm going to do with you after that, okay?"

Again, Rocko just nodded.

"If I can strike a deal then maybe you'll get lucky and I'll let you live. So come on then, spill the beans," he told him.

I got up and left at that point: 1) because I didn't want to see what came next and 2) because I wanted to find out how everyone else had got on.

Cowboy followed me out and asked how I was doing. I told him I was fine, even though I was far from it. If I thought I could've gotten away with it, I would've ran down the stairs, jumped on my bike and kept driving until I ran out of fuel. Instead, I went outside with Cowboy and watched as even more of the guys arrived.

Cowboy told me that the house he'd gone to belonged to the parents of one of the guys who'd been involved in the raid. When they booted in the door, the guy rushed from the living room, knife in hand, as if he was going to have a go at someone. The minute he saw them, he'd tried to make his way out the back, but was caught in the kitchen, pushed outside and given a pretty good beating.

His father had then come rushing out, wielding a baseball bat, telling the Bats to leave his son alone and so they'd ended up having to do him as well, then told him the reason why his son had got a doing.

"Not sure he believed us, but hey, who gives a fuck?" he said as he finished off.

I then spoke to some of the others who all had fairly similar stories to tell, except for Flick, who explained his story in detail from the time that he arrived at the house until the time he was done.

He said, "We booted the door in, only to find a young girl sitting in the kitchen, breast feeding. The guys who'd ran up the stairs barged into the two rooms, found one empty and one with a youngster of around five or six, screaming his head off. The girl told me that her boyfriend had abandoned her and the kids and gave me the address where he'd moved to. I apologised to her for the intrusion and got one of the guys to hang back and fix the door for her.

"We then went to the other house and gave the little cunt the beating of his life. I had to physically stop the guys wiring in to him - another couple of blows and he could've drawn his last. You want to have seen the nick of the girlfriend when we left! She was going fuckin' mental, throwing things at us and screaming like a fuckin' banshee."

"Flick, just tell me he's not going to pop his fuckin' clogs - that's all I want to know?"

Then, not for the first time that night, I was told to chill before I had a stroke. I must've been looking pretty stressed when people were all dishing out advice to me about my health. All I really wanted was to get back to the pub or the house and crash out. Maybe the fact that I'd had no sleep in the last twenty-four hours was why people thought I looked hellish and were so eager to give me health advice.

Indie came outside with a bit of a smile on his face, which worried me way more than seeing his normal grumpy puss.

"What's the script, Indie?" I asked him.

"All in good time, Shug, all in good time," was all he said then suggested that we all head back to the pub.

By the time we were leaving, most of the guys were gathered at Rocko's house. The drive back was awesome. The sun was shining it was about seven in the morning, everyone revving the cunt out of their bikes and, if I say so myself, a successful raid to boot.

I actually thought to myself on the way back that Indie was bound to have been impressed with the organisation and planning for my first forage out as the South chapter's SAA.

I braced myself for plenty back slapping when we hit the pub. As we drew into the car park, I felt for the first time in over twenty-four hours that I wasn't tired. I guessed that the buzz from our success was keeping me going. When we went in, I asked Indie what the script was with Rocko and what our next move would be?

He pulled me into the small room, telling me he needed a private chat with me. I couldn't believe his reply, it nearly fuckin' floored me. There I was, waiting for all the adulation and plaudits that could be bestowed on me, and what did I get? Indie's fuckin' wrath, both fuckin' barrels, right on the nose!

"Well, see if you'd waited with me in the room instead of fucking off, you'd already know what the fuckin' script was! Don't you ever leave a Brother on his fuckin' own again - no matter what's happening elsewhere, ok?"

I tried to interrupt so I could get my tuppence worth in but was quickly told to shut the fuck up and listen.

"You know what, Shug? Sometimes I think you're quite a clever cunt and other times, like tonight, I think you're as thick as fuck. You couldn't wait to get out and see what was going on elsewhere when you should've stayed and listened to what was happening inside. You're a fuckin' Officer now and this was your fuckin' raid, not mine."

I then butted in, thinking 'fuck you, Indie!'.

"I'm not listening to anymore of your fuckin' pish, Indie. You can do what the fuck you like afterwards, but I'm having my fuckin' say!

"Aye, Indie, this was my fuckin' raid, or at least so I thought, until you decided to take over. I was handling everything well enough, but oh no, you just had to fire right in there and undermine me.

"All the info you got from Rocko, I would've got just as easily, and it would've let the guys know that I was on the ball. Now they'll be thinking that I needed you to give me a dig out. Surely to fuck you must see that?" I ranted.

I watched him as he stared straight at me. I knew by his reaction that I'd over-stepped the mark, but instead of the major rant and shouting I expected from him, he turned away, sat down and gestured with his hand for me to sit as well.

I sat down directly opposite him and waited for him to speak.

"Shug, you know what? If anybody else had spoken to me like that I would have buried them, but I guess you've got a point. I'm not saying you're right, but I agree that perhaps, maybe, I should've let you have a go at Rocko.

"What you need to understand, Shug, is I've been running the whole fuckin' shooting match since we lost Provo and Stiff and I just deal with things as they come up. Tonight was one of these things. I'll let you take the lead on this as long as Brutis and Rooster are happy with it. Go and get them and tell them we need a meeting.

"Oh, and Shug, that was the last time you ever speak to me like that without me ripping your fuckin' head off, got it?"

I decided it best that I say nothing, so I got up, nodded to him then went looking for the guys. They were standing at the bar already drinking and it wasn't even half-eight in the morning.

"Guys, Indie wants us in the back room for a meet ASAP," I told them.

I then ordered a drink for me and Indie. I just thought 'fuck it, a pint might be just what I need to take the edge off!'.

Brutis headed away and Rooster grabbed me by the arm.

"You okay, man?" he asked me, "You look a bit spaced out?"

"Nah, I'm just fucked off with Indie - he's doin' ma fuckin' nut in. I'll need to fill you in later, though, we better get back before he gets the hump again."

I lifted the beers and followed Rooster through. When we were all in, Rooster closed the door. I handed Indie a beer and he thanked me.

"Right, guys, this is the script," he began. "I've agreed with that Rocko cunt that I'll meet him at a factory unit at twelve today …"

As he told us, he threw a bit of paper with the address on the table.

"He's arranging for me to meet the guys he gets his gear from."

Brutis then piped up.

"You sure you can trust him, Indie?"

"Oh, yes, I fuckin' trust him alright …. about as far as I can throw the cunt!" he replied.

Indie went on,

"I've found out that he has a family and also a mother and father who are old and pretty frail. I told him that if he wasn't there at twelve then I'd waste his whole family. Just so he knew I meant business, I cut a bit of his ear lobe off …" he said, reaching into his pocket and throwing it on the table.

Indie, Brutis and Rooster then all burst out laughing and I felt inclined to join in, even though I didn't think it was in the least bit funny.

After they calmed down, Indie told Brutis that he should now take the lead and that he was going to round up the troops and let them know that they would be heading back up the road later in the day.

He then got up to head out. Before he got to the door, Brutis asked him when he was planning to leave? He told him that he'd wait until after the meeting, just in case there were any problems.

"Will you be joining us for the meet?" Rooster asked.

"Yep, I was planning to, unless you want me to stay put?" he told him.

"No, I think it would be much better if you headed it up with Brutis, man, so Rocko boy knows we mean business."

Brutis then told Indie he agreed with Rooster and I chucked my tuppence worth in as well, agreeing with both of them.

"Ok then, I'll come. We'll head back up the road afterwards," he told us as he made his way out.

I said to Brutis and Rooster that I needed to grab an hour's kip before we went as I was completely done in. They both nodded to me as I stood up and left the room. I then went looking for a couch to crash on. The lounge was pretty full, but I managed to grab a booth and lay down. I swear to God I thought I had just closed my eyes when I felt Rooster giving a bit of a shake.

"Come on, ya dozy cunt, shake a leg, it's quarter-to-twelve. We're all getting ready to head," he moaned at me.

I sat up, told him I would be ready in a couple of minutes and to stop moaning at me like a fuckin' wumman. The bastard then grabbed me around the neck and rubbed his knuckles on my head, laughing like a fuckin' hyena before splitting.

I gave my head a bit of a rub, thinking about how much of a cunt he could be sometimes, and tried as hard as I could to think of something that would piss him off as much as his rubbing shit pissed me. I headed outside, not really sure about what was happening. It looked like everybody was getting ready to go to the meeting.

I thought it would just be Indie, Brutis, Rooster and myself. I saw Brutis standing chatting with Indie and Gunner and asked him who was going to the meeting? Before he could answer, Indie piped up, telling me that we were all going because he wanted to make a show of strength for everyone to see and to let the locals know we'd arrived in big numbers.

"Surely we can't all go?" I suggested, then immediately wished I'd kept my fuckin' mouth shut.

Indie grabbed my arm and pulled me away from the group.

"Shug, why the fuck can't you just listen and do what's asked for once? Stop feeling the need to give your opinion all the time. Of course, we all won't be at the meeting - only you, Brutis and Rooster will be there. The rest of us will be hanging about, making sure none of Rocko's wee gang are planning anything, as long as that's okay with you of course?" he said really sarcastically.

"There's no need to take the pish, Indie. I only wanted to know what was going on," I told him.

"Yeah, I know, Shug, but there was no need for you to ask a stupid fuckin' question like that in front of everybody."

He then reminded me yet again, as if I was likely to forget,

"You're a fuckin' Officer now, so keep your fuckin' opinions between you and the rest of the other Officers. Always support each other in public. Sort out any shit in private. Got it?"

At that point, I just nodded. I knew where he was coming from and I knew, in my heart of hearts, that he was right.

Indie then, surprisingly, gave me a bit of a man / hug and whispered in my ear,

"You need to make sure everybody thinks you're in control, bud, even when you're not! That's the secret to being a good SAA."

He then patted me on the back and started blethering away with the guys again. Brutis and Rooster came over to me and told me where we were going and how they thought we should play it. I listened and offered my opinion, and after a few minutes, we were all agreed on how we wanted it to go down.

Chapter 20

We all got on our bikes and made our way onto the main road - it was a really weird feeling for me to be at the front of the pack. Brutis led then me and Rooster rode side by side with Indie behind us.

I had to keep telling myself that I was the SAA as I still couldn't take it in. I really wasn't sure if I'd be any good at it? Or more importantly to me, I wasn't sure if I really wanted it?

As I rode, I tried to plan a strategy in case we were greeted by a squad of Rocko's goons. After racking my brains a bit, all I could think of was just getting off our bikes and setting about them. I laughed a bit to myself thinking 'Some plan that, Shug! You must have learned that strategic battle plan from one of the great historic military leaders!'

Just then, Gunner, who'd been sitting behind Indie, drove to the front and indicated we should turn off to the right. He stopped his bike on the road, holding up the traffic, and as Brutis turned, he gave him a nod.

Freddie also passed us and led us down a lane on the left-hand side of the road which was very like the lane leading to our farm. Once he'd gestured for us to follow, he turned off onto what seemed like a small clearing in the middle of a field.

He then stopped, got off his bike and urged us all to do the same. I killed my engine and looked around. I wasn't sure what I expected, but it certainly wasn't this!

I began to get pretty nervous, feeling like we were trapped. I made a beeline for Freddie to find out why he hadn't warned us that we were stopping in such a vulnerable place.

Before I could vent my frustrations at him, he got amongst us and began telling us that the meeting place was off the main road, about a mile or so further up, and that where we were just now was a back way in. He finished up by looking at Brutis and saying,

"Not sure how you want to play this, Brutis, but if need be, we can surprise them by heading that way …" he told him, pointing to path between the trees. "We'll also get a good view of the industrial units from there …" he said, this time pointing to a clearing a bit further up. "It'll give us a chance to see if they've got a team waiting on you."

By this time, everyone had switched off their bikes and were either standing smoking or trying to see what was going on with us. Unbeknown to me, Gunner had already mentioned this road to Indie, and had suggested to Brutis that we'd be best served by going in this way. I was feeling pretty pissed thinking that someone might have had the decency to let me in on it.

"Well, Shug, how do you want to play it?" Brutis asked me, snapping me out of my huff.

"I reckon if you, me, Rooster and Indie head down the main road and let them think there are only four of us coming, we'll be able to gauge much better whether or not they think they can bully us or if they actually plan to make a deal. If the rest of the guys leave their bikes here and head around this way …" I said, pointing the same way Freddie had earlier, "then we'll be covered for all eventualities and if it does go tits up you can all wade in and help us out."

When I finished talking, I was waiting for someone to say something, but there seemed to be a really long pause which got me thinking straightaway that they all thought my plan was a pile of shite.

I could feel my heart starting to pound in my chest a bit as the silence continued.

It wasn't until Brutis said,

"Sounds like a winner to me, what do you reckon, Rooster?" and he replied,

"Yep, sounds like a plan." that I started to breathe normally again.

I then began talking.

"Freddie, Gunner, you lead the rest of the guys up to the corner. If you hear a bit of a commotion, you'll know to swarm the place."

After a few nods of approval, the four of us fired up our bikes and headed back out the way we had come in.

It's only at times like this, when you drive past the bikes, that you actually realise how many people there are in the Bats and how big they've become. On this occasion I was glad of the numbers we had because I'd had a really bad feeling about the whole thing, right from the start.

The four of us made our way back onto the main road and within a matter of minutes, we made another right turn, as Freddie had directed, which took us back off the main road again.

I looked around as we made our way up what could only be described as a small service road. However, when we turned the next corner, the road joined with another and it really opened up. I was pleasantly surprised when I saw that the surface had improved drastically.

There were a few factory-like buildings scattered around and some of them were a fair old size. I began to feel a little more relaxed now that I knew we'd be conducting or business in a fairly open and populated area. I was now pretty confident that there wouldn't be any trouble.

Brutis came to a halt in front of the factory Freddie had described to him and we all drew up behind him. I had a quick look around, trying to get my bearings. I was scanning the area to the right of us, which was covered in trees and bushes, trying my hardest to catch a glimpse of our guys, but I never did. I convinced myself that that was a good thing - or at least I hoped it was.

The unit was one of the smaller ones, but unlike the rest of them, it had no trading name advertised anywhere on it. I thought this was very odd because, if it was mine, I'd have stuck some signage on it to make sure it blended in. For me that would've been the best way to conceal it.

We were getting off our bikes just as Rocko came out to greet us. He made his way straight to Indie, telling him to go inside as the guys were waiting to meet him. Instead of doing as he was asked, Indie told Rocko to go back inside and let them know he wanted them to either open the large roller door or come outside and meet us.

"But, Indie, they don't want to meet in public. There are too many people around."

"Like I give a fuck about what they want, Rocko! I'm not going in there when I don't know what the fuck's behind that door. Do you think I'm a fuckin' idiot or something? Just get your fuckin' arse back in there and pass the message on or the deals off and you know exactly what that means for you!"

Rocko then began to plead with Indie, and just as he started talking, a couple of guys in suits came out of the small door. At the same time, the large door started to go up. I looked at them as they walked

216

towards us and thought how odd they looked. One of them, I guessed, was around twenty-five-ish and the other just a little bit younger. They both had suits and ties on, with highly polished shoes.

The four of us were standing together when they approached us. They introduced themselves and offered a handshake to both Indie and Brutis. At this point, both Rooster and I were checking out the factory as the door began to open wider.

It looked like a bit of a junkyard inside, with bits of cars lying scattered around. Right in the middle there was a brand new, top of the range, silver Ford Cortina 1600 GTE. When the door was fully open, the sun shone on it and it reflected back, almost blinding us for a split second.

Rooster leaned in towards me and suggested that we were in the wrong game as there must be plenty money in drugs. We both had a bit of a snigger before concentrating on the matter in hand. After the introductions were over, the older of the two, who was doing all the talking, suggested that we go inside. Indie agreed, but only after getting the nod from both myself and Rooster.

As we made our way in, the younger of the two told Rocko that he was done, and to fuck off. It's funny how perceptions of people can alter depending on the situation. We all thought, when we arrived, that Rocko was a bit of a player. However, after the scrap with him in the house and seeing him being treated like a pussy by these two nuggets, we knew that he was just a fuckin' wimp. When Rocko was told to fuck off, I got one of those gut feelings you get when you know something isn't right.

I started to wonder if this was some kind of set-up? When I saw a guy pressing the button to close the large door, I told him to leave it open. He looked at the guys in the suits, waiting for their response. When they nodded, he stopped and made his way into a small office at the side of the door. There was a table in the corner with half a dozen chairs around it. Alex, the younger of the two, directed us towards it then suggested we sit.

We all sat, except Indie and Tommy, the older of the two. By this time, Tommy was getting into the eyeballing stuff with Indie.

I made a point of sitting in a position that allowed me to watch the door and keep an eye on the guy in the office at the same time. When we were all seated, Tommy began speaking, staring straight at Indie, he began,

"I'm told by Rocko that you're looking to take over his patch. Question: What makes you think we would want to do business with you?"

Indie smiled and gave a bit of a snigger before reverting back to the aggressive pose he'd adopted since we arrived, then replied,

"Well, it's dead simple. If you don't then we'll use our existing supplier and do it ourselves. Listen, I'm only here out of common courtesy. Make no mistake, we'll be doing this, either with or without you. It makes no fuckin' difference to me."

At first, I couldn't believe what the fuck I'd just heard. But then, when I thought about it, I knew it shouldn't have come as a surprise. Indie, in his wisdom, had always been a master of negotiation and, true to form, he never even offered them a crumb to hold on to.

After a minute or so of silence and a bit of a look and a nod between them, Tommy began speaking again. This time, though, he took a step forward until he was straight in front of Indie.

"Firstly, I'm not impressed by your fuckin' attitude and also, just so you know, I don't do business with cunts who try to intimidate me. So, either you wind your fuckin' neck in or there's no deal going down today!"

Then it was Indie's turn to take a step even closer - he was now right in Tommy's face.

"Well, neither the fuck do I! In case your memory is as shit as your dress sense, let me remind you that it was your fuckin' monkey Rocko that tried to blooter my guys with baseball bats first. So don't give me any of your 'I don't do intimidation' pish - this is all on you. So stop wasting my fuckin' time and tell me, are we dealing or not?"

As I watched the two of them, I noticed that Tommy was looking a bit more uncomfortable than Indie, but he still stood his ground. He then, to my surprise, took a step back before speaking again,

"Okay, maybe you're right. I probably should take the hit with Rocko. But let me make it very clear, this is the last time I'll be threatened by you or any of your fuckin' gang, got it?" he told Indie.

Indie's reply was again no more than I expected.

"Listen, if I was threatening you, you'd already be in hospital or on the way to the fuckin' morgue. So I hope you're very clear on how we do business," he told him.

He then came back with a bit of a softer approach.

"Look, I have no wish to get involved in any aggro with you - or with any other cunt for that matter. I just want you to be clear that I won't be pissed about or shat on by anybody.

"I only want to strike up a deal with you because I'm told you're the main guy who can provide me with what I need. I would expect our arrangement to be tight and that we conduct our business in private. Oh, and another thing, we agree to chase that fuckin' prick Rocko - he's about as much use as a trap door in a fuckin' crane."

Indie then held his hand out and asked Tommy if they had a deal? Tommy shook his hand, telling him they had. Tommy then suggested that they go into the office to discuss terms and, thankfully, Indie agreed.

Chapter 21

The guy who was in the office opened the door for them then stood outside. Alex and Brutis followed them in which left Rooster and me standing about looking like a couple of spare pricks at a whores wedding.

Rooster offered me a smoke and we made our way outside, standing in a position where we could see the office. He then gestured to the guy standing outside the office, offering him a smoke.

The guy came over, took the cigarette from Rooster and thanked him. He lit up then introduced himself to us as Si and we told him who we were.

"So what's the deal with your guys then?" Rooster asked him.

"What do you mean?" he replied.

"Well, I'm guessing their pretty big players about here and I just wondered what the script was with them? You know what type of guys they are and what else they're into."

Si then replied, telling us that they were the only players in the area as they'd cleared out all the competition a couple of years before.

"They're quite happy to let Rocko think he's still a player and get his hands dirty on their behalf. They've also dealt with Gunner and Freddie before, they've moved plenty stuff for them in the past. They heard that you guys had come into town and cleared out all the bike gangs and knew you'd eventually want to meet so they arranged for Rocko to give you a bit of a scrap, to see what kind of resistance you'd put up."

I interrupted him at that point.

"Hang on a bit there, Si, we were led to believe that Rocko was there because of his Mrs, not anything to do with you guys?"

"After the incident with his Mrs, Rocko came straight to Tommy and Alex looking for help. He was told to round up some guys and take out as many of you as he could, and well, you know the rest."

Rooster then spoke quite aggressively,

"Are you telling me that this whole fuckin' thing was set up by that pair of cunts in there …?" pointing to the office.

Si replied very calmly,

"Yep, that's exactly what I'm saying. They wanted to know if you'd be worth doing business with. They knew if Rocko could take you out then meeting with you would be a waste of time."

"Tell you what, Si! They better not share that with Indie. He'll go off his fuckin' nut and, by the way, that's something you really don't want to see," Rooster suggested.

"You know what, Rooster, they won't give a fuck about him or anyone else for that matter. I bet you that's the first thing they'll tell him. I don't know anything about your guy, but the two of them can go to town. They're both black belts in some new Karate or Kung-fu shit - you know, that fuckin' Bruce Lee stuff."

"Not really sure about any of that shite. Seen it on TV right enough, but never met any cunt that can do it properly," Rooster told him.

"Well, I've seen them in action a fair bit and they've never even looked like losing. They once wasted eight guys between them, and they never even unbuttoned their jackets. I know for a fact that there's not a single cunt around here who would even attempt to take them on."

Rooster then told him what he thought.

"I hear where you're coming from, Si, but they won't have come across anyone like Indie before, that's a fuckin' certainty. If what you're saying is true, I reckon that it might be a bit of an interesting one."

As we continued to chat away, I made sure I kept one eye on the office.

The more he told us about them, the more I thought they were cut from the same cloth as Provo, Stiff and Indie. We'd been standing chatting for about fifteen minutes before they all came out of the office.

Looking at them, as they walked towards me, I thought that they all seemed to be happy enough with whatever it was they had concocted. We shook hands with Si, said our goodbyes, then made our way to our bikes. Indie and Brutis did the same.

We never spoke a word until we were back at the pub. We arrived seconds before the rest of the guys and when Indie got off his bike, he just said to Rooster and me to get the other Officers and meet him in the back room. I looked at Rooster and he shrugged his shoulders.

"They don't look very happy now, do you think the meeting bombed?" I asked him.

"Shug, you know Indie. He never looks fuckin' happy does he!"

"Good point, Rooster. Well presented," I told him, sniggering a bit to myself.

Next thing, DD's standing beside me, wanting to know what the script was and when I told him I didn't know anything, he was well miffed. I'm sure he didn't believe a word I said. Thankfully, I didn't need to

223

stand and debate it with him as Gunner, Freddie and Ludo were right behind him.

I told them Indie and Brutis were waiting for us then turned and headed inside.

"Thanks for nothing, Shug," I heard him calling, but I never let bug.

Rooster got a hold of Cowboy and Flick then we all went into the back room and took our seats. Indie then started to explain what had happened at the meeting.

"Right, guys, I've spoken with 'Hoddit & Doddit' and here's what we've come up with: For the next three months, we'll buy from them and distribute ourselves. The Rocko boy and his fuckin' cronies are now out of the picture, so I strongly suggest we pay them back for their visit at the first opportunity, just to remind them that we're not to be messed with.

"Brutis, I'll leave that in your capable hands. Gunner, you and Freddie will do the pickups and be in charge of the distribution during this time.

"We'll get together and review it just before the three months are up to make sure it's working for us. We also agreed that we'll provide any muscle they need and do the bouncing at their clubs. Instead of getting paid for this, I've told them we'll take it off the price of the gear - that'll make us more money in the long run.

"Just so you know, I don't trust them one fuckin' bit, but I think we need to deal with them initially to see how it plays out. I've told them that we'll review how it's working then meet with them to decide if we're going to continue with our arrangement."

"How did that go down with them?" Gunner asked him.

"Like a big, huge, fuckin' lead balloon," he told him, laughing like anything. "Don't think they were best pleased about it, but that's not my problem. They know, if push comes to shove, that there's no way they can take us out. So, as far as I'm concerned, it's in their best interests to deal with us not the other way around."

Just listening to Indie talk, I knew he wouldn't think twice about taking them out if they didn't play ball. I also knew, thinking back to what Si told us, that his mob would be thinking exactly the same.

Indie then stood up and told us he was leaving as he needed to get back up the road and attend to business up there. We all followed him out and watched as him and the rest of the Central guys headed off.

I stood in the car park, looking around at who was left, and wondered if there would be enough of us to cope if anything kicked off? As the bikes disappeared off into the distance, we all turned and headed back into the pub.

I asked Brutis if I could have a word with him in private. He nodded then led me back into the room we were in earlier. I explained to him about my job, moving into the nurses' home and the need to go back up the road so I could hand my flat back to the council. He asked how long I needed, and I told him a couple of days would be enough.

"When do you start, Shug?"

"Monday," I told him.

"Look, Shug, why don't you get your shit together and head off now? There won't be much happening here for the next couple of days anyway and we can catch up on Monday when you finish your shift?"

I told him that was great. Thanked him for being so understanding then went and got my gear together. Before I left, I had a bit of a blether with Rooster,

Cowboy and Flick and filled them in about what I was up to. I really wanted to ask Rooster about Julie and why he wanted to talk to me about her, but there was no way I could ask him in front of Cowboy and Flick without them taking the pish.

Rooster, again, for the umpteenth time, asked me to reconsider giving up my flat and tried to talk me out of taking the job. I cut him short, told him I'd made up my mind then jumped on my bike. I made my way out of the car park and onto the main road. As I rode, I started to feel really good. My side was no longer giving me any jip, the shit with Tommy and Alex was sorted, Rocko was no longer going to be a threat, and I had four days to myself before I started work.

I really enjoyed the ride back up the road. The sun was shining and although it was a bit cold it felt fresh rather than chilly. I turned into my street and drew up outside my flat, parked the bike then headed up the stairs.

I was opening my door when someone came out of Mark's flat. I turned to see who it was and was surprised to see a rather plump middle-aged lady standing there.

"Hi, my name's Morag. I've just moved in. Are you my neighbour?"

I kind of looked her up and down, feeling very confused, and wondering what the fuck she was doing in Mark's flat?

I went to ask her what the fuck was going on, but before I could say anything, three kids, I guessed between about three and seven, came running out from behind her, making all sorts of noise and pushing each other about.

"Eh, hi, I'm Shug. But I don't know what you're doing in there? That's Mark's flat, he's my neighbour."

She then looked at me, as curiously as I had looked at her, then said,

"Who's Mark?"

"Mark's the guy who lives here, or so I thought," I told her.

"Don't know anything about him. I was given the keys yesterday so I'm guessing he must have moved out?"

I just offered a wry smile then turned back to my door and went inside. I closed the door behind me and could still hear her little fuckin' brats, shouting at each other on the landing, and thought to myself 'thank fuck I'm leaving!'.

I went into the kitchen, filled the kettle then sat on the sofa. I wondered how long it would take to pack and what I would need to do with the shite I wasn't taking. I made a coffee, lit up a smoke and closed my eyes. I was thinking about the move when I remembered I was supposed to meet the warden the next day to get a look at my room in the nurses' home.

I wondered about the big items like my beds and sofa and stuff and wasn't really sure if I needed to dump them? I reckoned the best thing to do was just to leave it all. I thought about when I'd moved in and how I would have coped without my mum's stuff and the stuff I got from Malky's parents.

My view was that if the person who got the flat didn't have much then at least it would give them something to start off with. I wasn't sure if the council would be okay with that, but I wasn't really giving a flying fuck - I had no intention of leaving a forwarding address anyway.

The rest of the night was nice and quiet, I didn't really do much and, thankfully, I never saw anyone. I'd made a conscious decision to stay clear of the farm so none of the guys knew I was here. I felt a couple of days on my own would do me the world of good.

Next morning, I was up bright and early and ready to go. I was dying to see my room in the nurses' home and wondered if I'd be on the same floor as anyone I knew?

On the way there, the traffic was really thin on the ground which was good for me as I was eager to get there as quickly as I could. As I rode, I thought about the warden and what a crabbit cunt she was. I was feeling pretty edgy about meeting her again after our previous encounters and was much relieved when it was a different warden who greeted me.

I told her who I was, and she introduced herself to me. We shook hands then she picked up my keys, locked the door of her office then told me to follow her.

She took me up to the third floor and opened the room. She went in and I followed closely behind her. She turned around, handed me the key and told me to keep hold of it until I was done. She then left, telling me she had to go and show some other people their rooms.

I closed the door behind her and the first thing I did was open the window. The room had a bit of a stale smell about it, like it had been empty for a while. It seemed to be completely void of any fresh air. I pushed the window up as far as it would go and stuck my head out. I took in a large breath of air and surveyed the view. I could see hills in the distance, lots of trees and, surprisingly, not a road in sight.

I looked down and could see the hospital football pitch and the car park where my bike was sitting, nestled between two cars, it was almost a mirror image of the view from Julie's room. I turned my attention back to the room. Looking around it, I saw that it had a sink, wardrobe, chest of drawers, single bed, small table and a chair.

I started to wonder what the fuck I was doing, giving up my flat and moving almost fifty miles away to live in this little shithole, three floors up and bang in the middle of a corridor?

I sat on the bed and continued to look out the window. I could hear lots of noise coming from the car park and plenty of laughing and joking. I decided to move over to the chair and sat down so I could get a better view of what was going on.

There were a few more cars than when I last looked out, with people getting stuff out of their boots. It looked like there was a good few people moving in and 'Mummy, Daddy and all the family' were jollying around, helping them flit.

For some reason, I always felt kind of funny when I saw things like this, it actually made me feel that I'd been cheated out of the whole family thing – I'd even go as far as to say I was jealous of all their get togethers.

I moved back to my bed, not really wanting to watch anymore. I lay down, diverting my attention away from outside, and reverted back to focus on my own situation. Here I was, sitting alone in an empty room, without any family in the world and no really close friends.

It made me think, that compared to all the other people moving in, I was probably the only one who was really lonely, but instead of wallowing in it, as I usually did, I decided to give myself a shake and focus on the positives.

I was looking at a new start, a chance to re-invent myself, a bit of time to distance myself from the Bats and I aimed to make a real go of it. I headed back down the three flights of stairs, two steps at a time, shoved the key into the warden's letterbox as instructed, went outside, jumped on my bike and headed for home.

It was another beautiful day and the sun was shining, I had a smile on my face and a feeling of joy that I hadn't experienced for a long, long time.

Chapter 22

I hardly slept as I wrestled with the idea of giving up my flat and still wondered if I was doing the right thing?

Next morning, I was up and dressed by 7 a.m. and raring to go. I had already packed my stuff, for all it was worth, and was sitting nursing a cup of tea.

I wanted to leave there and then, but knew if I had that I'd need to hang about in the hospital car park for ages as the warden wouldn't give me my keys a minute before 10 a.m. I decided to leave at 9 a.m.

As the hand approached the magical hour, I lifted the clock from the mantelpiece and stuffed it into my bag.

I stood in the hallway, taking one last look around the place, and afforded myself a bit of a smile. I was thinking of all the memories I had gathered in such a short space of time. I'd lived there less than three years, but it'd been such an eventful time in my life that it felt more like ten.

I grabbed my holdall, put on my backpack and went downstairs. I strapped the holdall onto the seat then went back up to the flat for the very last time. I checked that I'd picked up everything I needed, slipped the keys into an envelope and stuffed it into my pocket.

I left the flat, drove into town and dropped the keys into the letterbox at the council offices. I wasn't really sure what I was supposed to do with them, but my rent was paid up, so I put a note in with the keys explaining that I was moving away and no longer needed the flat.

As I turned onto the main road, I looked up at the sky. It was another lovely day and it made the ride to the hospital a joy. I was feeling pretty carefree and totally relaxed. I arrived at the nurses' home on my bike with all my worldly goods split between a large holdall and a rucksack.

There was a football match going on and I stood for a bit, watching the players running around. The people standing at the side of the park were pretty animated and making a fair bit of noise. I smiled a bit to myself and tried to remember the last time I'd played?

I worked it back and realised it must have been more than four years since I last kicked a football and nearly five since I played in a team. I continued to watch the game for a bit and guessed that the players must be playing at a fairly low level as the standard was awful.

I laughed a bit, thinking that maybe I could get back into it here - I didn't think I could be any worse than the one's I was watching! I decided I'd had enough of the game and made my way into the nurses' home. I checked my watch just before I went in, it was five-to-ten. I wondered if they'd keep me standing outside their office like a lemon for five minutes or if they would just give me the keys?

Thankfully, it was the nice warden on duty and she gave me them straightaway, reminding me that she was called Mary. I thanked her and told her my name again.

As soon as she heard it, I could see a look of fear crossing her face.

"Is everything okay, Mary?" I asked, to which she just nodded.

I knew right away that the other fat cow had made me out to be some kind of ogre.

"Listen, Mary, don't believe all you've heard about me. Your colleague and I got off to a bad start. Hopefully, she'll come around once she sees I'm not a bad spud."

I then smiled, said goodbye and made my way upstairs to my room. I dumped my bags on the bed and decided I should pop into town for some provisions before I got settled. I emptied the contents of my rucksack onto the bed and put it back on before making my way downstairs.

I got to the front door just as a girl was coming in with a box full of stuff. I held the door open for her and she smiled then thanked me.

"Hi, I'm Sharon," she said as she passed me.

"Shug," was all I said to her, nodding my head in her direction.

"You've just moved in as well, haven't you?"

"Yes, I have," I told her.

"Thought that. I saw you with your bags. Cool bike, by the way. Maybe you can give me a ride on it someday?" she said smiling.

"Maybe I can. Just let me know when you're free and I'll give you as many rides as you want," I said, pretty much tongue in cheek, wanting to gauge her response.

I noticed that she went a bit red which made me smile.

"Maybe we'll meet up later then, Shug?" she said, laughing as she gave me the once over with her eyes.

"I'm sure we will, I look forward to it," I told her.

She laughed again, blew me a kiss then made her way towards the staircase.

I watched her for a bit before heading out. I wondered if she would look back? And, low and behold, just before she got to the top stair, she did.

233

I knew she would, I said to myself, then it was my turn to blow her a kiss. I went outside, shaking my head and laughing away to myself. As I made my way to my bike, all I could think was what a lovely arse and pair of tits she had.

Any of the people outside looking at me might have thought I was a patient by the way I was walking about with a stupid smile on my face and giggling under my breath.

I saw Sharon's parents giving me a bit of a stare, so I looked back at them and gave them a nod, but they never responded. I was still giggling away to myself and thinking 'You have absolutely no fuckin' idea what I want to do to your daughter!', which made me laugh out loud.

There were quite a few people in the car park. I assumed it was more people who were moving in, getting help from parents and friends. They were all standing about, exchanging pleasantries. When they saw me making my way towards them, I'm sure they all hoped I was visiting rather than staying. Just for devilment, I got on my bike, fired it up and revved the arse out of it until no-one could hear anything else.

I rolled it back out from between the cars and kept the revs high until I was almost out of sight. Looking back in my mirror, I could see the car park full of people looking at me with disdain and disapproval which again brought a smile to my face.

I went to a mini-supermarket just down the road, and filled my bag with what I thought I'd need for a couple of days. On the way back, I spotted two bikes heading towards me and thought I recognised one of them. As they got closer, I realised it was Ludo. He also clocked it was me and indicated to draw in. I did the same and switched off my bike. I got off and made my way towards them.

"How's things, Ludo?" I asked him, shaking his hand.

I then noticed it was Spooky, one of the new Prospects, who was with him and we shook as well.

"Wondered where you'd got to, Shug. Brutis told us you had a bit of business to attend to. Anything I can help you with, man, you just let me know, okay?"

"Cheers, Ludo, everything's cool, mate. But thanks for that. I'll bear it in mind."

"How's the side? You back to full fitness yet?" he asked.

"Just about," I told him, "Not getting much pain from it now, thank fuck," which brought a laugh from them both.

"Tell you what, Shug, none of us will forget our first run as a Bat in a hurry, that's for sure. You know I still can't fuckin' believe you got stabbed by one of our own fuckin' Prospects!" he said, continuing to laugh.

"Ha ha, I know. I still can't believe it myself. Anytime I moaned about it, Rooster would tell me that if I'd seen it from where he was, I would've laughed like fuck as well. I keep telling him the next time there's a scrap that I'll give him one in the side and see how long he laughs for."

"One good thing came out of it, though, Shug. The Prospect has decided 'No more drink and drugs before a scrap', so that's something!"

"Ach well, it was just one of those things, I suppose. Thank fuck it ended up just being superficial. Tell you what, though, I didn't know that at the time. For a minute, I actually thought I might be a goner -

especially when I saw the amount of blood spewing out.

"When I looked up and saw the cunt standing over the top of me, knife in hand, I thought I was getting it again. Then I recognised the daft fucker and asked him what the fuck he was playing at!

"The last thing I remembered was him kneeling down beside me, being all apologetic, and telling me how sorry he was. Next thing, I'm in the clubhouse with Rooster standing over me. Man, it was so fuckin' surreal. Aye, I can laugh about it now, but I certainly didn't see the funny side of it at the time," I told him.

We chewed the cud for another five minutes or so then I told him I needed to head off and would catch him at the meeting Indie had arranged for the start of the week. By the time I got back to the nurses' home, most of the parents and visitors were away and the football match had finished.

I parked up and made my way to my room. Inside the nurses' home there was a real buzz about the place, lots of people in the corridors and most of the room doors were open.

Everyone was introducing themselves and trying to get to know each other. I did my best to avoid it all and get to my room as quickly as possible. I'd just got in and closed the door when there was a knock on it. All I could think was 'why don't you fuck off and give me a bit of peace!'. I took off my rucksack and laid it on the bed, went to the door, took a deep breath and told myself 'Shug, smile and be polite' then opened it.

"Fuck, it's you, Lisa. What do you want?"

"That's nice, Shug. I've come to see how you're doing and the first thing you do is abuse me."

"Sorry, Lisa, I didn't mean that. Come on in," I told her.

As I closed the door, I apologised again.

"Sorry, Lisa, I thought it was going to be one of the new people wanting to talk to me and I really couldn't be arsed."

Lisa lifted my holdall from the bed, put it on the floor then sat down. I turned the chair around to face her and sat on it before asking her how she was doing?

"I'm great, Shug. Long weekend off, not back until Tuesday backshift, so if you're up for a wee party tonight, count me in."

"No offence, Lisa, but I'm starting my new job in the morning. The last thing I need is to turn up like a burst baw - not sure that would go down too well."

"Ah, well, maybe next weekend then?" she suggested.

"Now that sounds much more like a plan," I told her. "How's Julie, by the way?" I enquired, wondering if she would tell me anything.

"You know what, Shug? I can read you like a fuckin' book! I knew that would be the first thing you'd ask! I reckon that must've been all of thirty seconds before you blurted it out."

"Well, you know I care for her, Lisa, and I really need to know how she's doing?" I told her.

"I spoke with her the other day. She'd been in at one of her counselling sessions and we went for a coffee. She told me all about the carry-on at her house and a lot of shit about her dad."

"Did she mention anything about Rooster or me?"

"Yes, Shug. She spoke about the two of you a fair bit. She actually said she needed to talk to you and was hoping to pop up and see you after your first shift tomorrow."

"Did she say why she wanted to see me?"

"Eh, well, she kind of told me, but it's not my place to say. You really need to talk to her about it yourself."

"For fuck's sake, Lisa, just tell me. I'll end up going off my fuckin' nut here - wondering what's going on with her?"

At that point, she got up and left without saying another word. I think I might have been a little too full on for her. I followed her into the corridor and tried to apologise. I shouted for her to come back, but she never even turned around.

I watched until she went into her room and closed the door. It was only then that I noticed a few people in the corridor who seemed to be watching our goings on, so I ripped into them.

"What the fuck are you all looking at, ya shower of nosey bastards? I take it you've nothing better to do than watch what other people are up to. Well, you can fuck off back into your scabbie little fuckin' rooms now, the shows over!"

And with that, I went back into my room and slammed the door.

I lay down on my bed and thought about what Lisa had said. I knew that the reason she didn't want to say anything was because she knew Julie and Rooster were back together and expected that I might throw a wobbly. Well, she was right of course, because I'd just made a pure cunt of myself, not only in front of her, but in front of everybody else on the third floor, and that was without even knowing any of the facts for certain.

I wondered what I would've been like if she'd actually told me the truth about them? Sometimes I wonder what the fuck goes on inside that fuckin' tin-pot of mine I call a brain. I decided I needed to calm down a bit then I would go along and apologise to her. I was now convinced that Julie and Rooster were an item again and that I really needed to get over it.

I had a bit of a wash, grabbed the four cans of beer I'd bought, then made my way along the corridor to Lisa's room. I knocked gently on the door.

When she shouted, "Who is it?"

I replied, "Room Service, mam."

She knew it was me and opened the door, smiling a bit.

"Hi, Lisa, do you still fancy that drink?" I asked her, lifting up the cans and smiling back.

She closed the door, let off her security chain then opened it wide, gesturing for me to enter.

"Look, Shug…" she began talking, but I asked her not to say anything else until I'd spoken.

"Lisa, please let me talk for a minute. You don't have to say anything. I'm just off the phone with Rooster," I lied. "He's told me about them giving it another go so I've wished them all the best. Now, how's about us having a beer and not mentioning either of them for the rest of the night? How does that sound?"

"Sound's great to me, Shug, I'm sorry I couldn't tell you. Julie made me swear to her that I wouldn't breathe a word to you. She wanted to tell you herself tomorrow."

Although I felt like I was dying inside, I played along with her and said to her,

"Look, Lisa, it's fine. I would've been more disappointed in you if you'd betrayed a friends trust," I lied to her again. "Loyalty is really important and I'm glad she has a friend she can trust. Anyway, that's enough about them. What's the latest gossip here?" I asked her, changing the subject.

239

"Not much actually, Shug. It's been pretty quiet here. Let me think now, oh, yes, Elsie has lost three stones in weight and is looking great. And you know what? She attributes it all to you! She said you gave her a major confidence boost and she's now become much more outgoing. Calum has got engaged and is well chuffed with himself. I've met a few of the new people and they all seem okay. We've organised a get-together this Friday night in the common room.

"It's for all the newbies and you'll have to be there, you being one of them and all that. I can't really think of anything else so it's your turn now, Shug. Tell me what's been happening with you?"

"Fuck, Lisa, I wouldn't know where to start. Let's just say the last couple of weeks have been pretty eventful! Okay. The short version: I nearly killed one of my Brothers, he had to get the kiss of life from a copper in the jail or he'd be dead right now. I was stabbed in the side by one of our Prospects during a scrap. We managed to get Julie's dad lifted by the cops. I've been promoted to the SAA in the Bats. There was some other shit as well, but I don't want to bore the tits off you, so I think that's about enough to be going on with," I told her.

I was waiting for her to say something, but she just sat there, staring at me with her mouth wide open. I snapped my fingers a couple of times in front of her face which seemed to do the trick.

"Holy shit, Shug. Please tell me you're on a wind-up? You really can't be serious... can you? I knew about Julie's dad, but the rest of the stuff: the fighting, you being in jail and nearly killing your mate, how can that be possible? Tell you what, Shug! You seriously need to get out of that motorcycle gang, not be promoted higher up it. Honest, you really need to do it or you're going to be dead soon."

I put my beer down and took a hold of her hand as I could see she was really anxious.

"Relax, Lisa, it's fine. Nothing else is going to happen. It's just been a rough couple of weeks, everything's sorted now," I lied to her, for the umpteenth time. "I know we agreed not to talk about Julie, but I just wondered how she was getting on after all the shit with her father and how her counselling is going?"

"You're some man, Shug. You're like a dog with a bone."

"I know, Lisa, but I really care about her and I just want to know if she's well, that's all."

"Okay, okay, I'll tell you, Shug. You have to promise me that you won't go and see her or tell her I told you anything. Come on, swear."

I looked at her again and this time it was more a look of fear she was displaying, as opposed to the shock which was etched on her face at my earlier revelations. I really never had much time for that 'swearing to God' pish, or praying to a higher being or whatever the fuck people prayed to, but if it meant Lisa would tell me about Julie, I was happy to swear to whatever the fuck she wanted me to.

"Okay, Lisa, you win. Right hand up to God, I swear I'll never tell a living soul - especially not Julie."

"Right, okay, that's good. Here goes," she said before taking a deep breath.

"She's actually doing really great. She's much more like her old self. The counsellor has told her he's happy to sign her off to return to work in the next couple of weeks if she continues to improve the way

241

she's doing. He suggested to her that a holiday with her mother, somewhere away from here, would also help with her recovery. I'm not sure Julie thinks that's a good idea. However, she played along and told him that they'd spoken about it and that they were planning to go somewhere at the end of this week.

"Julie reckons she'll be ready to get back to work within the next two weeks, but I'm not sure if that's her being a bit optimistic or if she'll actually be ready - only time will tell. Anyway, that's enough of the serious stuff, Shug. Pass me that other beer!" she said, now smiling at me.

I wanted to know so much more about Julie, but I thought it best to leave it just now. Hopefully, she'd come in to see me the next day, like Lisa had told me. I handed her a can then cracked open the last one, raising it in the air.

"To Calum, to Elsie, to my new job and to you, Lisa, let's hope tomorrow's a new start for us all," I proclaimed, before lowering my can and taking a drink.

Lisa then raised hers.

"To Shug and his new job, to Julie – who'll hopefully be re-joining us soon, to Calum and his fiancée and to the awesome parties we're going to have over the next few months - If they're anything like the last one we had when you were here then I can't wait for the next one. Cheers, Shug!" she said, giggling a bit.

We both 'dunked' our cans together and started laughing. I told her she wasn't right in the head. She returned the compliment by telling me to watch myself at work the next day in case one of the Doctors signed me in as a patient.

After a bit more laughing and some non-sensible conversation, I told Lisa I was going to hit the sack.

"You can stay here tonight, Shug, if you want? My bed's big enough for two, as you well know," she suggested.

But I was having none of it.

"As great as it sounds, Lisa, I really need to get a full night's sleep. I want to be fresh for tomorrow and I know for a fact if I stay here with you, I'll be lucky if I catch a couple of hours."

I got up, gave her a cuddle then headed back to my room. When I got in, I looked at the clock and realised it was only ten-to-nine. I sat on my bed, stripped off, then got under the covers.

I closed my eyes and got into my favourite position, expecting to fall asleep straight away. Instead of conking out, I ended up trying to remember the last time I'd been in bed before nine p.m? That, however, was only the catalyst to trigger off other thoughts like: Julie, The Bats, Rooster, my new job and a shit load of other things to boot.

Needless to say, I hardly slept a wink the whole night. When my alarm went off, I swear I thought I'd only just fallen asleep. I got up, gave myself a bit of a slunge down at the sink then realised I really needed a shower. I grabbed my shampoo and towel before making my way to the bathroom, wearing only my scants.

After the shower, I got changed and headed down to the dining room for some breakfast. I had a quick look around before making my way to an empty table. I was surprised at first that I didn't recognise anybody, but in hindsight, I suppose 8:15 a.m. is an odd time for people to breakfast if they work shifts.

I ate my breakfast in silence then dumped my tray into the rack provided. I went outside and walked towards the main admin block. I noticed the big clock outside the main building above the entrance door. Shit, it was only eight-thirty and I didn't start 'til nine. The last thing I wanted to do was sit in the reception, listening to that little arsehole Larry being rude to everyone.

I clocked a bench beside another building, overlooking the football pitch, so I sat on it and lit up a smoke. I decided I didn't want to be there until five-to-nine and having a smoke would help me calm the old nerves.

I sat watching the clock as it moved closer and closer to five-to-nine. I took one last draw before pinging my butt onto the grass. I sorted my tie and gave myself a bit of a brush down to remove any lingering traces of ash. 'Okay, Shug' I told myself 'let's do this!'.

I made my way along the road and into the reception and low and behold, who's the first person I see? It's Larry the prick. However, this time, he had a female with him in the 'goldfish bowl'.

I had a quick scan of the room - I was the only one there. I remembered Mrs. Boardman telling me there were four people, including myself, starting today. I gave the glass partition a tap as I wanted to know if the other three had been in or if I was first? I then waited for one of them to slide it open.

That little prick Larry never even turned around. He just shouted for me to take a seat and that someone would come for me. I could easily have slapped the cheeky, ignorant little slime ball, but instead, I sat calmly down and began to think about how I was going to give him a doing away from work. I'd only been sitting for about five minutes when Mrs. Boardman came in to collect me.

"Hi, Ochil, nice to see you. Would you like to come along to my office ...?" she asked, pointing towards the corridor.

I stood up and gave her a smile before following her. When we entered her office, she told me to sit on the chair beside the desk.

As I sat down, I noticed a file with my name on it, on the top of a bundle of paperwork. Mrs. Boardman sat behind her desk and asked me how I was feeling? I told her I was doing great and that I was a little nervous about starting as I didn't know the first thing about mental illness.

"Don't worry, Ochil, you'll be fine." she said, trying to reassure me, "Everyone feels like that on their first day. I bet you, by the end of your first week, you'll think you've been here forever."

"I hope so," I told her. "Once I know what I'm doing, I'm sure I'll be fine."

"That's what I like to hear, Ochil, a good positive attitude. Right, I need to go through the formal bit with you first, after which I'll organise a tour of the hospital for you. Then we'll get you into the ward to meet the people you're going to work with. You're going to be in 'Tunnel' ward. Are you okay with that?" she asked.

'See! There it is again' I thought. She just asked me like I had a choice. What did she expect me to say 'Nah, fuck it! Just take me straight to the ward, I can't be arsed with the rest of it'. So, I nodded and smiled at her, gesturing that I was happy with what she had planned.

"Good, let's get cracking then. The quicker we get the paperwork out of the way, the quicker we can get you to the ward."

We started going through it. Every time she handed me a form, she told me to read it then sign it. By the time we'd finished, I felt like I'd signed my name a hundred times.

All the way through the process, she was continually telling me all sorts of different facts, but I never really picked up on any of it. I kept thinking to myself 'Why in fuck's name do I need to fill in all this shit? What a waste of fuckin' time and energy!'.

She handed me yet another piece of paper. Thankfully, she told me that it was the last.

"Bet you're glad that's us done?" she suggested.

I wasn't sure what to say. All I could think was 'Thank fuck', so I just smiled again. Mrs. Boardman then stood up and walked towards the door. She lifted her coat from the hook and started to put it on.

"You're very quiet, Ochil, are you okay?" she asked.

"Yes, I'm good, thanks. Just trying to take everything in," I lied.

"I know most of it will have gone right over your head, but don't worry, I'm sure you'll pick it all up very quickly."

"I hope so," was all I could muster as a reply.

I was beginning to think that I'd made a big mistake coming here and wondered perhaps if I should've taken Rooster's advice and stayed well clear?

"Come on, Ochil," she told me as she walked out, buttoning up her coat.

I followed her to the door and went outside. We then entered a sort of passageway between two buildings. There was an open entrance at either side which was big enough to drive two lorries through, side by side.

The roof was made of glass and the span between the buildings was connected by metal framing. For all intent and purpose, it looked like a massive greenhouse roof.

"I'll take you across to the stores later …" she said, pointing to the building opposite, "and we'll get you sorted with your uniform. First, I'll introduce you to one of the Staff nurses who'll give you a tour of the grounds and explain where everything is. After that, he'll bring you back to my office and we'll have some lunch. Okay?"

"Yes, that's great, thanks," I replied.

She then took me to a large building, behind the arcade we were in. She explained that this was the building where I'd be working, and that there were two wards downstairs, the acute and non-acute admission wards. She gave me a quick explanation on the fundamental differences between both wards which again went straight over my head.

All I could remember was that the acute ward was locked and had the maddest patients in it. We entered the non-acute ward and she took me straight into the office to meet the Charge nurse. I was pretty shocked when she introduced me to him. I was looking at a man who wouldn't have been out of place in the Bats. When he stood to shake my hand, I noticed he was taller than me, with a full beard and hair nearly as long as mine.

As I shook his hand, Mrs. Boardman introduced us.

"Ochil, this is Billy Chatterson. He's the Charge nurse here and also the Union Representative. Billy, this is Ochil Kinnaird, but everyone calls him Shug."

He released his hand then sat back down.

"Will you be joining the Union?" he asked me, as he fumbled about in his desk drawer.

Fuck, I had no idea about joining the Union. I didn't really know too much about it. I was aware of the problems the miners had in the past - with stories about families and friends fighting because some were in the Union and others weren't, but I only knew about it from the TV and the papers so I kind of put it back into his court.

"Not sure, never been in one. But if you think I need to then I will."

He handed me an application form and said,

"Fill this in and bring it back to me. I'll give you more information on it then."

I took the form from him, folded it up, then stuffed it in my inside pocket and thanked him for giving me it.

He then asked me if I played football?

'Fuck', I thought, what a really strange thing to ask me, especially in the middle of my tour.

"I used to, but not anymore," I told him.

Then, because of my curiosity, I asked him why he wanted to know. Before he got a chance to reply, Mrs. Boardman told me that Billy ran the hospital football team and was always on the lookout for new players.

"Training is Wednesday nights at six. If you're interested, we meet at the changing rooms around a quarter-to-six, okay?"

I just nodded and thanked him for letting me know. Mrs. Boardman then asked him if it was still okay for Peter to give me the grand tour?

"Yep, he's making beds in the Annex, just give him a shout," he told her.

She then thanked him and as we left the office he shouted,

"Remember, Wednesday nights! And bring me back that form when you've filled it in!"

I never said anything, and we left, making our way into the Annex.

Mrs. Boardman then laughed a bit as she spoke about Billy. Telling me he was 'some man' and commented that it was better to have him as a friend than an enemy. Again, I never said anything, I just gave her a nod.

When we went into the Annex, there was a guy and a girl making a bed. When they spotted us, they both stopped. Mrs. Boardman introduced me to them and told me the guy was Peter and the girl was a student nurse called Becky.

Peter offered his hand for me to shake and told me it was nice to meet me. Becky gave me a cuddle and said it was great to see me again. I told her I was glad to see someone I knew.

"I take it you two know each other then?" Mrs. Boardman asked.

"Yes. Shug's a friend of Julie's. We've met a few times when he's been visiting her."

"That's good to know, Becky. Why don't you give Ochil the grand tour then - seeing as you know each other?" she then suggested.

"Yes. No problem, Mrs. Boardman. I'll just go grab my coat."

"Okay, Ochil. I'll leave you with Becky. When you're done, come back to my office and we'll have lunch."

"Yep, will do, Mrs. Boardman," I told her.

She smiled, nodded to us, said goodbye then left. I was standing with Peter, waiting for Becky to come back, and it was one of those awkward silences - when you feel the need to say something but aren't really sure what.

"So where do you come from then, Peter? Are you local?" I asked him.

"No, I come from up north, but I'm living in the nurses' home just now. I've just qualified as a staff nurse and I'm not really sure whether or not I should move back up the road or stay put?"

Again, I wasn't really sure how to answer that, but, thankfully, I didn't need to as Becky arrived back.

"Ready for the grand tour then, Shug?" she asked.

"Sure am, Becky, just lead the way."

I then turned to Peter and said,

"Nice to meet you, Peter. I'm in the nurses' home as well. Maybe we can grab a beer sometime?"

"Yep, sounds good, Shug. Just let me know when you're free."

"Will do, Peter, catch you later," I told him then headed out with Becky.

We went out into the corridor and Becky pointed up to the staircase which was adjacent to the ward.

"There are two long-term wards up there. One male, one female. They're for patients who have conditions that mean they are unable to function well in 'normal' society but are no danger to themselves or others. Do you want to go up and meet the staff?"

"Only if I have to, Becky. I'm not sure about the whole grand tour stuff. I'll forget it all by the time we're done anyway. Is there somewhere we could grab a coffee and you could just tell me a few things you think Mrs. Boardman might ask me?"

"If that's what you want, Shug, it works for me. I remember when I got my tour. It was the full class and it took forever. By the time we were done, I was about losing the will to live. C'mon, I'll take you to the Hub, that's where most of the patients spend their day. You'll probably learn more about the hospital sitting there with a coffee for half an hour than you would going in and out the wards anyway."

We walked past the main building and made our way towards the central block which was about halfway between the main admin block and the nurses' home.

Becky stopped just before we were about to enter and said,

"If any of the patients ask you for anything, like money or cigarettes, you need to tell them no. The majority of them have been here a long time and are great at spinning you a story or two, to make you feel sorry for them. When we go in, you grab a seat and I'll get the coffees."

We went up the five stairs and into the building. It was huge. The hall was bigger than the whole of my flat. On the right was a set of double doors with a sign above them saying: 'The Hub'. On the left there was another set of double doors which led to the Gym hall.

Looking through the windows in the Gym hall doors, I could see another set of doors. It looked like they led into another room at the very back. Directly in front of me was another set of doors. There was a sign on them saying: 'Private - Staff Only'. There was no way to see what lay behind them as there were no windows.

We entered the Hub and all I could think was 'Fuck's sake, I've just entered the village of the dammed'. I'd never seen anything like it. There were people walking about talking to themselves. Others were shouting at nobody in particular and everyone seemed to be trying to mootch something from somebody else.

I spotted a table with a couple of free chairs and made a beeline for it. I hardly got my arse in the chair before I was surrounded by people asking for cigarettes and shit - I guessed it was very easy for the patients to spot a newbie.

I told them all that I didn't smoke, that I had no money with me and the nurse I was with was buying ME a coffee. One of them asked me what ward I was in and when I told them I was in Tunnel Ward, they all took a bit of a step back. I quickly realised that they thought I was a patient. When I tried to explain that I was a nurse, they all just nodded and started to disperse.

Becky then arrived back with the coffees, placing them on the table, and asked the patients who were still lingering about to take a hike, which seemed to do the trick.

"Well? What were they saying?" Becky asked.

I couldn't really be arsed going into all the exact details, so I just told her that they were all on the cadge.

I changed the subject back to the matter in hand.

"Okay, Becky. Tell me what I should and shouldn't know about the hospital and give me the low down on who's who?"

She gave me a bit of a rundown on the wards, the patients I needed to look out for, the staff she thought were good eggs and the one's she thought were arseholes.

During our conversation there was a stream of patients coming up to us asking for a variety of things.

Becky dismissed them all as politely as she could, but also made it very clear to them there was no chance of them getting anything from us.

We'd been sitting chatting for about half an hour before the subject of Julie came up. I'd been dying to ask if she had any updates but made sure I never mentioned her. Becky asked me when I'd last seen Julie and I knew that was my road in.

"It's been a bit of a while. I haven't seen her since all the shit with her father went down."

"That was terrible, wasn't it! I couldn't believe it when I heard. I met her father a few times and he seemed like a nice man, just shows you, though! You never really know anyone.

"The thing I don't understand is why Julie or her mum, didn't tell someone about him?" she quizzed.

I decided the time was right to go for it so I fired in a couple of questions just to see what her response would be.

"I know. I can't understand that either, Becky, especially Julie. I always thought her to be really strong willed. When did you last see her?" I asked, "How's she coping?"

"Lisa and I went to visit her a few days after the incident, and we spent a good couple of hours with her. It was nice. She was on her own and we had a right good natter."

Fuck. I couldn't believe it. I felt the rage starting to bubble up inside me. All I could think was what a cow Lisa was. Why the fuck did she not tell me about the visit? The way she spoke to me about it had implied that they'd only had a brief chat.

"Her father's been given a restraining order. He can't go near either of them or he'll get arrested and put in jail. But, wait 'til you hear this, her mother is

253

visiting him in a supervised centre with the view of them getting back together!"

"Tell me you're shitting me, Becky? Surely to fuck she's got more brains than that? What a stupid cow! What's Julie saying about that?"

"She's well raging, but her mother won't listen. Julie's told her that if her father ever comes back to the house then she's off for good. You can imagine what the atmosphere is like in that house just now!"

I sensed this was a good time to find out what Julie's plans were.

"So is Julie planning to come back to work in the near future?" I asked her.

"Yes, she wants back as soon as the Doc will let her. I think she's dying to move back here so she can put some distance between her and her mother for a bit."

I happened to look up at the clock and noticed it was nearly time for lunch.

"Fuck, Becky, we'd better get back. I'm supposed to be having lunch with Mrs. Boardman."

"Shit, sorry, Shug, I didn't realise that was the time. We'd better get you back before they send a search party out for us."

We headed out of the Hub. As we walked towards the main building, Becky gave me another few pointers about the different hospital facilities and where they were located. At least, when I went back to Mrs. Boardman, I'd have something I could tell her.

I thanked Becky for the info and told her I'd pop in and see her later. She gave me a bit of a smile then headed back to her ward. I watched for a minute as she left and thought to myself what a lovely arse she had. I then went back into the admin block and knocked on the office door.

"Come in," Mrs. Boardman shouted.

I went in and noticed she was on the phone. I did that thing we all do, where I pointed to the door and suggested in mime, that I would leave and come back later - as if I was playing fuckin' charades or something.

Then, using her free hand, she mimed that I should shut the door, sit down and be quiet until she was finished her call. I did as she requested, following her hand signals, which, for some strange reason, I understood perfectly well.

I sat down and started thinking about the hand signalling and how fuckin' stupid it was - but we both knew exactly what each other had meant by it. I almost burst out laughing as I thought a bit more about it and had a job restraining myself in order to keep quiet. Mrs. Boardman was looking like she was ready to do the same.

She ended her call, put the phone down and we both burst out laughing at the same time. The funny thing was neither of us felt the need to explain why we were laughing and only stopped when there was a knock at the door.

Mrs. Boardman cleared her throat and shouted,

"Come in!"

The door opened and a girl, about my age, came in with a tray which was covered with a dishtowel.

"Just leave it on the table," she told the girl, who eagerly obliged.

After she placed the tray down, Mrs. Boardman thanked her. She turned around towards the door and as she was leaving, she gave me a bit of a smile, so I returned the compliment.

When she left, Mrs. Boardman then said,

"I see you've got a bit of a roaming eye for the girls there, Ochil!"

"Why would you say that?" I asked her.

"Well, I saw you watch Becky as she wiggled her way back to the ward. Then I noticed you give Samantha a cheeky little smile just now."

I had no idea what to say in reply. I could feel my face reddening so just smiled a bit and said nothing.

She then got up and made her way to the table, lifted the dishtowel from the tray and brought it over to me.

"Help yourself, Ochil," she told me, "I think they've given us enough here to feed a small army."

Again, I never said anything, just lifted a plate and began filling it. While I was selecting my food, I couldn't help but notice Mrs. Boardman's ample chest, which seemed to be trying to burst out of her bra.

I actually wondered how someone as thin as her managed to end up with such a large pair of knockers? I'm sure she knew I was looking at her tits and I swear that she'd undone another button since I'd seen her last.

I finished filling my plate and told her I had enough.

Out of the blue she said to me,

"Are you sure there isn't anything else here that you fancy, Ochil?"

Well, talk about shock. Fuck me! I was sure she was coming on to me and I didn't have a clue what to do about it.

"No. I'm fine, thanks. I've got all I need here."

'All I need here' - who the fuck would say that? – 'You're such a fuckin' dooshbag, Shug!' I thought to myself.

"Are you sure you don't want a sweet?" she then asked.

"No thanks. I'm fine with what I have here," I told her.

'Come on, Shug, time for the old reality check' I told myself. She was asking about a fuckin' sweet ya prick, not a fuck.

She turned away and put the tray down on the table then lifted a plate and started putting some food on it for herself. I decided that the 'come on' thing was all in my head and that I was just being a dick. I offered myself a wry smile and started munching my way through the food on my plate.

I watched as she lifted the food from the tray. I swear she was bending over way more than she needed to. That started my mind racing again. I started to wonder how old she was and if she was a dirty cow or just a tease?

I thought briefly about the old chicks in the caravan that Malky and I had shafted and the chick from the beach that I'd fucked in her house. I reckoned the three of them had been roughly the same age. Looking at Mrs. Boardman, I reckoned she was at least ten years older than them.

The next thing, she dropped a bit of food on the floor and said,

"Shit!" which I'm sure she said just to make sure I looked up.

She turned around until her arse was facing me then bent over to pick it up. With one hand on the table, she spread her legs a bit then bent over from the waist.

Now, anyone else would definitely have bent their knees, which convinced me that she was gagging for it. I watched as she reached for the food on the floor.

257

As she bent over, her knee-length skirt started to rise. By the time she grasped the food on the floor, her skirt had risen significantly.

I could see she had a little pair of white knickers on, underneath her black tights. She placed the food back on the table before lifting her plate. She then turned towards me and said,

"Ochil, are you sure there's nothing else you fancy?"

I couldn't believe it. I was starting to get a bit of a semi by this time so decided, fuck it, let's test the water here and see where it takes me.

"Is there any chance of a blowjob for dessert then?" I asked, staring straight at her.

I could tell right away that it was the last thing she expected me to say and she looked a bit taken aback by it.

"Ochil Kinnaird! I'm a married woman. What makes you think for one minute that I'd want to do such thing for you?" she replied, in a very stern, but quietly spoken voice.

'Oh, well, here we go, looks like I've read it all wrong again' I thought to myself.

She then spoke again.

"I'm waiting, Ochil!"

Again, I thought 'fuck it, tell it how I see it', I've already fucked up big time anyway, so I had fuck all else to lose.

"Look, Mrs. Boardman, you made reference to me looking at Becky's arse then about me smiling at the bird with the tray. Then you bend over, flashing your tits at me with an extra button undone. Not content with that, you then flash tomorrows washing at me after throwing a bit of food on the floor. Twice you asked if there was anything else that I fancied! If that's not a come on, then I'd love to know what is? From where I'm sitting, it seems like you're gagging for it. And, by the way, I think for your age, you're a pretty horny looking chick."

I then stood, expecting to get my marching orders, but I couldn't resist finishing my rant. Still keeping eye contact with her I began,

"Look, if I'm wrong then please accept my apology and I'll head off. However, if I'm right, you need to tell me where we can go, so I can give you the fuck of your life."

As I watched her, I got the impression that she was stunned. It seemed like an age before she said anything – I, for sure, wasn't going to say another word, but I did want to hear her reply before I bolted. She moved from the table to the front of her desk. She sat on the edge of it, placed her hands on it either side of her body and crossed her legs at her ankles. Her head was lowered, and I couldn't see much of her face because of her hair.

"Well, Ochil, I'll say this for you, you've got some balls! You come in here, accuse me of flirting with you then tell me you want to give me the ride of my life! I take it you do actually remember I'm a Senior Nursing Officer at this Hospital. The accusations you're making here are nothing short of scandalous, malicious even!"

At that point, I tried to interrupt her, but she told me to be quiet until she finished. She stood up and walked over 'til she was standing straight in front of me.

"Right Ochil, here's what you're going to do now: You're going to go back to your room and I'm going to contact the ward and tell them you won't be going there this afternoon."

259

Again, I tried to butt in as I wanted to tell her she didn't need to sack me as I'd just head off. But, again, she told me to shut up. Fuck, it was like getting a row from my mother - she wouldn't let me get a word in edge ways.

"Right. What's going to happen now is I'm going to do the handover to the backshift SNO. It'll take about half an hour. When I'm finished, I'll come along to your room and you can give me the 'fuck of my life' like you promised earlier," she then grabbed my dick with her hand, squeezed it, then said, "and it better be worth it! Who knows, if it is, then maybe you'll even get that blowjob you wanted! Now go on, get out, I have a report to write."

I kind of stood for a minute, trying to take in what had just happened. I must have been daydreaming a bit because the next thing I know she's lifted the phone, pressed a few buttons then she's snapping her fingers at me, telling me to get out.

As I made my way out, I met a man who was going into the office. I held the door open for him and we both nodded. I guessed he must've been the backshift guy that Mrs. Boardman spoke about. I made my way outside and began walking towards the nurses' home, trying to work out how the fuck I'd ended up in this position: one minute, I think I'm facing the sack and the next, I'm heading to my room to wait on a married woman - who was old enough to be my fuckin' mother, who I'd just promised the ride of her fuckin' life!

I went into the nurses' home and made my way up the stairs only to be greeted by Lisa and Calum.

"Oh, Shug, the very man. It's Elsie's birthday today and we're all heading to the pub after she finishes her early-shift. Make sure you come down when you finish. She'll be delighted to see you."

"Yep, no probs, I'll be there," I told her.

Calum then asked what I was doing in the nurses' home when I should be working?

"Hope this isn't you skiving on your first day?" he said, laughing.

"No. If only. I'm just picking up some stuff they want photocopied. That's all," I lied to him. "I'll catch you at the pub the back of tea-time," I told them, then made my way towards my room.

I went in, shut the door and stood leaning against it for a minute, while trying to catch my breath. 'Fuck, Shug! What are you doing, man?' I asked myself. I haven't even done a full shift and I'm already planning to fuck a Senior Nursing officer. I went over to the window and opened it to let some fresh air in.

When I looked down, I saw Mrs. Boardman making her way towards the front door. I pulled my head back in and slumped on my bed. I still kind of thought she was taking the piss and that she wouldn't turn up. But fuck, here she was, on her way and soon to be in my room.

The next thing there was a knock at the door, and I jumped from my bed to open it as quickly as I could. I'm not really sure why I was panicking. After all, it was her that was cheating, not me. I really shouldn't have been giving a fuck about it as it could well end up with me getting a bit of leverage out of it.

She walked in and I had a quick glance, both ways, up and down the corridor, just to check no one had seen her. I closed the door. By the time I turned around, she already had her jacket and shoes off.

"You don't waste much time, Mrs. Boardman. Not even going to buy me a drink first?" I said, trying to be funny, but it went straight over her head.

"That's because I don't have much time," she told me, "So come on. Get your kit off and let me see what you've got."

I took off my jacket, kicked my shoes off and started to unbutton my shirt. By this time, she was down to her bra and pants and was unbuckling my belt. She put her other hand behind my head and drew our lips together.

We began kissing as she fumbled about trying to get my trousers off. I quickly unclipped her bra. Eventually, I removed my own trousers then lifted her by her arse. She wrapped her legs around me as we shuffled to the bed.

I laid her down on the bed, removed my pants then proceeded to remove hers as well. I decided I was going to lick her out first, so I lowered my head and gently pulled her legs apart. She lifted my head until I was looking at her.

"No, Ochil, I want you to fuck me first," she told me, but I thought 'fuck that!'.

"Listen. You may be my boss out there, but in here, I'll decide what's best, okay?" then I moved my head back between her legs.

Within a matter of seconds, she was pulling at my head again, but this time it was for me to get my tongue in deeper. I stuck a couple of fingers up her and tickled her arse with my thumb and it really got her going.

She was panting really heavily now and bucking like anything. She actually had a bit of my pillow in her mouth to muffle her screaming. I decided that I had enough of licking her pussy and told her to stand up, that I wanted to fuck her on the chair. I think, at that point, I could've told her I wanted to fuck her in the middle of the football pitch, and she would've gladly obliged. We kissed a bit as we stood then I told her to bend over the chair.

"Whoa, hang on a minute, Shug. The window's open - someone could see or hear us if we do it here," she suggested.

"I know, how cool's that? Don't you think that makes it all the more exciting?" I asked her.

I then put my hand back on her pussy and began to rub her clit which seemed to do it for her. I then got her to lean over the chair and grab hold of the arms as I entered her from behind.

As she moaned and wriggled, I closed my eyes and began to imagine I was fucking Julie. The last time Julie and I had a session we did it over the chair and we both loved it, which was why I decided I wanted to do it like this with Mrs. B. I'd hardly got into my stride when she started bucking for all she was worth, telling me to go harder as she was coming again.

"Come on, Shug. Harder, faster, fuck me, fuck me hard!"

So much for her worrying about someone seeing or hearing us!

She was now making enough noise for people as far away as the canteen to hear her. She stood up and made her way back to the bed, telling me she hadn't come like that in years. I actually had to help her as she was very unsteady on her feet, her legs were like jelly.

She lay down on the bed, still panting a bit, then asked me if I'd come? I lay down beside her and pointed to my erection and said, "What do you think?"

"I take it that's a 'no' then?" she said, smiling. "Well, I did promise you a blowjob so let's see if we can sort you out!"

She slid down the bed a bit and took my dick in her mouth.

I wasn't sure what to expect, but I never thought for a minute that she'd treat it like a fuckin' ice cream cone. Fuck, I couldn't believe it. She grabbed the base and started licking my knob like it was a fuckin' lollipop or something. I wasn't sure what to do. Should I tell her she hadn't a fuckin' clue or just let her get on with it? One thing was for sure, it was never going to make me shoot my load.

She kept looking up at me every time she ran her tongue up my knob. I think she was waiting for me to tell her how good it was, but there was no fuckin' chance of that. I gently got hold of her head and said to her she had to stick my knob right in her mouth. Fuck, you'd have thought I'd asked her to cut off her own tits or something. The look she gave me would have melted a fuckin' iceberg.

"Just try it. I'm sure you'll like it. In fact, turn around and I'll lick you out at the same time," I told her.

She never said a word but turned her body around until her legs were facing me. I lifted her on top of me then parted her legs until her pussy was directly in front of my face. I started teasing her a bit, licking her clit and sticking my fingers in both her minge and her arse - this had her wriggling and bucking a fair bit.

Fuck knows what she was doing to me. I couldn't feel a fuckin' thing. I pulled my mouth from her pussy and said to her if she wasn't going to suck my knob then she could at least wank me off. She said she didn't want to suck me while I was playing with her as she was scared she'd bite it off.

Talk about a passion killer. I burst out laughing then said to her,

"You really don't have much experience in the old sex department, do you?"

She never replied.

I shook my head a bit then put my tongue and fingers back inside her. Almost immediately, she was bucking away and forcing her pussy towards me.

I then felt her rubbing me off and thought 'Thank fuck, at last I was going to get something out of it'. I teased her some more with my tongue and pushed my fingers deeper inside her, making her buck harder and faster, she was moaning loudly as she wanked me off like there was no tomorrow.

I actually had to stop her as I thought she was going to pull it off. Just as I moved her hand away, she let out a scream, which gave me the fright of my fuckin' life. She then rolled off me and grabbed her pussy with both hands, as if she was squeezing the water out a fuckin' sponge, then pulled her knees up almost to her chest. I sat up and looked at her. Her eyes were closed, and she looked like she was biting her lip.

I put my hand on the side of her face and asked if she was alright. She just nodded and I could see tears rolling down her cheeks. I lay back down beside her and cuddled her, which made her straighten her legs. After a couple of minutes, she removed her hands from her pussy and cuddled into me.

I asked her again if she was okay? This time, she burst out crying and held on to me really tightly. I thought it best not to say anymore, just let her get out of her system whatever it was that she was upset about. If she wanted to tell me she would, after she stopped sobbing. After a few minutes, she sat up, dried her eyes a bit then started to give me the story of her life.

'Fuck, here we go again' I thought to myself. 'That's all I need. Another fuckin' bunny boiler!'. I was starting to think that I must have a fuckin' neon sign above my head saying, 'All female neurotics – please report here'. She started rabbiting on about how she married her childhood sweetheart at seventeen. How she'd never cheated on him and all sorts of other shit about her life and her kids. Then came the guilt trip bit and, at that point, I'd had enough.

I stood up, took my cigarettes out of my jeans then lit one up and offered it to her. She refused so I started smoking it myself and sat on the chair facing the window.

As I looked out, sort of staring into space, I started to wonder what the fuck I was doing? Fuck, I hadn't even started in the ward and already I was up to my neck in it!

Out of the corner of my eye, I noticed she was getting dressed. I wasn't sure if I should say something to her, but she spoke first, asking me if I'd keep what had just happened to myself.

Fuck's sake. Like I was going to go about bragging that I'd shagged an old bint, eh ... like I'd want any cunt to know that! I reassured her that I would keep it between us, and she thanked me like I'd just done her some kind of favour or something.

Once she was dressed, she walked towards the door as if to leave. I told her to wait and I'd check to see if anyone was about. I thought it would be better if I checked the corridor first. I grabbed a towel, wrapped it around my waist then went to open the door. Before

I turned the handle, she put her hand on my arm and asked me to wait a minute.

I thought 'Oh, well, here we go!'.

Then she started.

"Ochil, I need to tell you something, but I'm not really sure how you'll take it."

I told her not to worry about it, just to spit it out.

"Remember I told you that you would be working in Tunnel ward? Well, you need to know before you start that it's my husband who's the charge nurse in there."

'Holy fuck! Did she just say what I thought she said? No, surely tae fuck I must've misheard her' I thought to myself.

I was totally dumb-fuckin'-founded. I looked at her in total disbelief. I couldn't believe my fuckin' ears.

"Whoa, whoa, just hold it a fuckin' minute. Please tell me you're having a fuckin' laugh here? You came up here and shagged me knowing that I'd be working with your husband every fuckin' day? Un-fuckin'-believable. Well, that takes the fuckin' biscuit. I'll tell you what, Mrs. B.? I thought I was fucked up, but you! You take 'fucked up' to a whole new level. You really are totally fucked up, aren't you?"

I turned away from the door and walked back to the window. She followed me, trying to apologise, but I was having none of it. She put her hand on my arm again and tried to speak, but I told her to let me go and get out.

She tried to protest but I told her to shut the fuck up and fuck off. I then said something along the lines of 'You should be in the hospital, not fuckin' running it' or some shit like that.

"Ochil, I know I've made this whole situation really awkward for you, but I want to thank you for

267

agreeing not to say anything to my husband. I really appreciate it. I'm really sorry that I've put you in this position. I'll try to move you to a different ward as soon as I can. Sorry, Ochil, goodbye," and with that she left.

I never said anything else. I thought I'd probably said enough. When I heard the door closing, all I could think was 'What a fuckin' cow' and, just to put the tin lid on it, the sex was fuckin' shite.

Chapter 23

'Good old Shug', I thought, 'you certainly know how to keep making a cunt of it, that's for sure!'.

Next thing, there's a bang on the door. I reckoned it was Mrs. B back because she'd forgotten something.

I was still feeling pretty pissed with her and when I opened the door I said, "What now?" only to realise it was Lisa standing at the door. She barged passed me into my room. The first thing she said was, "Nice towel, Shug. All your clothes in the wash, are they?" followed by a bit of giggle.

"Very funny, Lisa, what the fuck do you want?" I asked her.

"Oh, that's nice, Shug. I pop in to see you and you have a go at me. What's eating you?" she asked.

"Look, I'm sorry, Lisa. I didn't mean to whinge at you. I've had a shit day and I'm just getting ready to go for a shower."

"It's okay, Shug. I forgive you," she said, laughing a bit. "Right, I came to tell you something, but that can wait. What I really, really want to know now is, what the fuck Mrs. Boardman was doing in your room in the middle of the afternoon and you wearing only a towel?"

"For your information, Lisa, she was along here to see someone else and decided to hand in my new uniform, if that's okay with you?" I lied through my teeth.

I watched Lisa as she scanned the room. I guessed that she was looking for my uniform. However, I knew there was no way she'd see it as it didn't exist, so I tried to distract her and asked her again why she was here.

"Oh, yes, two things, Shug. Firstly, I wanted to let you know that we're all heading down to the pub now, and secondly, I've just spoken with Julie and she told me she's been signed off, fit to return to work, and will be starting back on Monday. Now my question to you is this: did you just fuck Mrs. Boardman? Come on, Shug, please tell me you did?"

"Fuck's sake, Lisa. At least give me a bit of credit. Why in fuck's name would I want to shag an old bint like that when this place is hoatching with fanny my own age? You really do have a warped sense of humour," I lied to her, hoping she would take the bait.

Before she got a chance to say anything else, I changed the subject.

"That's great news about Julie," I told her. "Do you know if she'll be coming back to stay here?"

"Yep, she's coming back on Friday so she can have the weekend to settle back in. She told me that she'll only be doing three days for the first few weeks, then once her counsellor assesses how she's done, they'll talk about her returning on a full-time basis."

I was curious how she managed to get Julie's call if she was out with Calum so I asked her about it and she told me that one of the girls had taken a phone message from Julie and passed it on to her when she'd come back.

I wondered if she'd been to see her or perhaps Julie was here, and she didn't want to tell me? Whatever it was, I just knew something wasn't right, but thought I'd wait until she'd got a few over her neck before I pursued it.

She then jumped onto the bed, lay back, grabbed hold of her tits, then sarcastically said,

"C'mon, Shug, shower or shag? What's it going to be?"

I just laughed, told her she was fuckin' mental, shook my head then made my way to the shower.

I gave myself a good scrub down first. Then stood under the shower for a bit, hoping the water would rinse away all the shit that was floating about in my head, but I think it actually made it worse.

The thing I couldn't empty out was the one thing I didn't really want to think about, 'Julie', and her decision to return to work so soon. I wondered if she would be talking to me or if it would be a strange silence? What about Rooster, were they still an item?

I turned the shower off and gave myself a bit of a shake, got out, kind of dried myself then made my way back to the room. I was surprised to still see Lisa there as I thought she would've split.

"You still here? Not got a home to go to?" I asked her, smiling.

She leapt up from the bed and stood in front of me, looked me straight in the eye, then pulled my towel away, leaving me bollock naked. She then cupped my balls with her hand. She gently gave them a squeeze then asked,

"What do you think, Shug? One for the road?"

Fuck! After the afternoon I'd had, that was the last thing I wanted to do so I blew her off.

"Eh, don't fuckin' think so, Lisa. I'm heading to the pub. However, I may well be tempted on the way back if you're still up for it?" I suggested then started to get dressed.

"Maybe it won't be on offer later, Shug! Did you think about that?"

"Ah, well, I guess I'm just going to need to take that chance then," I told her, smiling.

I finished getting dressed, stuck on my boots and told her I was good to go. We bundled out and made

271

our way along the corridor, down the stairs and out the door. It still felt a bit weird living in the same place I worked. I never imagined that there were places like this.

I always thought of work and home as two completely separate entities. Here I was, not only eating, sleeping and shitting in my place of work, but also fucking the boss.

I must've been laughing out loud a bit as Lisa gave me a dunt, wanting to know what I was finding so funny? I just told her I was daydreaming a bit.

"Do you think Julie and Rooster will make a go of it this time, Lisa?" I asked her.

"Yep, I reckon they will. Why? Has Rooster said something different to you like?" she quizzed me.

"No, he hasn't. I just wondered what her take was on it, that's all."

"Oh, right. Well, she did tell me on the phone that he was at hers last night and things were good so I'm guessing they're still into each other."

"Good for them," I said, lying through my teeth, "they deserve a break, don't you think?"

"Absolutely, couldn't agree more," she replied, putting her arm through mine.

"Come on, Shug. Let's just forget about them for a while and have a bit of a laugh."

I thought about it for a minute and said,

"You know what, Lisa! You're right! Let's get a good few beers down our neck and see how it goes."

"Okay, sounds great, Shug, count me in. Oh, and by the way, you're on the bell!" she told me, laughing away to herself.

When we arrived at the pub, I was a bit surprised just how busy it was for a Monday afternoon.

Straight away, I noticed the table we were going to be sitting at was easily the liveliest one in the place. The door had hardly closed behind us when Elsie clocked our arrival and straightaway made a beeline for me.

"Shug! It's great to see you. Thanks so much for coming," she roared, as she cuddled and kissed me.

She then whispered in my ear,

"Shug, I can't thank you enough for what you've done for me. You've changed my life so much and all for the better. I have a steady boyfriend now, a social group, a couple of really close friends and it's all because of you."

I felt really embarrassed listening to her paying me so many compliments and tried my best to play it down.

"Look, Elsie, all that stuff you just said has got fuck all to do with me. Think about it, it's you who took the leap of faith. It's you who found your way into a new social circle and it's you who got yourself a boyfriend. I just happened to be there on the night you were ready to take that step."

She then interrupted me and said,

"Shug, I don't care what you say. As far as I'm concerned, you're my hero and always will be," then planted a big smacker right on my lips. "C'mon, Shug, come and meet my boyfriend," she told me, as she dragged me over to the table.

I looked at Lisa and shrugged my shoulders. Lisa then shook her head and said,

"Okay, Shug, guess I should go to the bar for the drinks then!"

I just smiled and nodded as I was pulled along by Elsie until we reached the table. Elsie opened her arm out in the direction of one of the guys and said,

273

"Shug meet ...", I interrupted her, leaned over the table, stuck my hand out and said, "Peter," who then stood up and shook my hand.

"Is your name not Ochil?" he asked me.

"Yep, but everybody calls me Shug," I told him as he sat back down.

"How come you know each other then?" Elsie asked.

"Oh, I remember Peter from the last time I was in jail. He'd been arrested for shagging a minor and got three months," I told her for a laugh, just to see how she would react.

The minute I said it, I could have bit my fuckin' tongue out. She picked up a pint from the table, threw it over him and called him a 'fuckin pervert'. Tell you what, I certainly wasn't ready for that! I thought she'd clock that it was a joke, but oh, how wrong was I. It took me almost ten minutes to get her to calm down and, thankfully, she eventually saw the funny side of it.

Peter went to the toilet to get cleaned up. Thankfully, by the time he came back, she was full of apologies and they kissed and made up. I thought it best to apologise as well and later on we had a right good laugh about it.

We spent the next few hours celebrating Elsie's birthday, but by 10 p.m. we all decided it was time to head back as most people were working early-shift the next day. On the way back up to our rooms, Lisa reminded me that she was back-shift and suggested a nightcap at hers.

I tried like a bear to get out of it, but she wasn't taking incoming calls, so we ended up back at hers, had another couple of beers, then one thing led to another and we ended up shagging before we fell asleep.

The next morning, I was up and away without her even noticing. I grabbed a bit of breckie before heading to see Mrs. Boardman. As I walked towards the main building, I was trying hard to get the picture of her, bent over my chair, well out of my head.

I tried to focus on being professional, which, by the way, was taking some doing. I bypassed the Reception and went straight to her office, knocked on the door and waited. I then heard a man's voice telling me to come in. I opened the door and Mrs. Boardman was standing in the middle of the room with a bloke.

"Ochil, I want you to meet Gordon, my husband. Gordon, Ochil."

We then shook hands and gave each other a bit of a look up and down, as you do.

"Shelly says she thinks you're going to make an excellent nurse. I hope you can live up to her expectations!" he told me.

"I'll certainly do my best," I replied, then realised that I never even knew her first name.

Fuck! I knew she had a mole on her right arse cheek, but not that Shelly was her first name!

I had to work really hard to keep a straight face as I waited for his reply,

"That's all anyone can do, Ochil," he told me.

Mrs. Boardman then asked me if I could give her five minutes as she needed to speak with Gordon. She then raised her hand, pointing towards the door. I knew that was my cue to make myself scarce, so I smiled then made my way out of her office.

There was a chair directly outside her door and I planked my arse on it. It looked out of place, as if it had been abandoned by someone. I began to wonder

275

about Mrs. Boardman and tried to figure out how she could be so calm, introducing me to her husband and shit, after what we had been up to the previous day? Within a matter of minutes, Gordon came out and told me I had to go back in.

"Ochil, Mrs. Boardman is going to get you sorted with a uniform then she'll bring you to the ward, okay?"

I just nodded, smiled and said thanks. You know, I really hate it when people are telling you to do something but add 'okay?' onto the end of the sentence, inferring that you actually have a fuckin' choice. Again, I thought, what am I going to say? 'Fuck you! I don't want her to do that. I'll just come to the ward with you ...', would his reaction be 'Yeah, that's okay, that'll work for me' ? Aye, like fuck it would, he'd blow a fuckin' gasket.

Anyway, I got up and went back into the room. Mrs. B was sitting behind her desk and asked me to close the door, which I did.

"Thanks again for not saying anything, Ochil. I'm sorry about the position I've put you in," she told me, almost repeating what she said to me the day before.

"Look, Mrs. Boardman, you don't need to keep apologising. Everything's cool. No-one will ever hear anything about it from me," I told her, before trying to lighten the mood. "Anyway, the sex was fuckin' great, don't you think?" I said, lying through my teeth yet again. "You certainly know how to get a guy going, I'll say that for you!" I whispered.

Whispering back, she said, "Okay, Shug, cut the crap. I know I didn't do much for you but let me tell you, I was blown away with it. I never knew sex could be so good. I can't remember the last time I had so many orgasms at one time!"

276

"I think you're just feeling like that because you've been doing the same thing with the same person for so long. It's nothing to do with me."

I looked at her and her face was scarlet.

"I'm sorry, Ochil, I don't know why I'm telling you all this. Please, let's just focus on the matter in hand and put all that stuff behind us, okay?"

See! There's the old 'okay?' thing again. Did I have a choice? Did I fuck!

She cleared her throat then started again, this time on a completely different topic. It was like she'd flicked a fuckin' switch that put her into work mode and expected that I could do the same. I think I've only got the one mode: what you see is what you get, and her sudden change made me feel a little uncomfortable - even though I wasn't sure why.

She stood up and said,

"Come on, Ochil, let's go to the stores and get your uniform sorted out."

We left the building through the back door then crossed the Arcade until we entered the building opposite.

Mrs. Boardman introduced me to the lady behind the counter.

"Hi, Mrs. Uist, this is Ochil Kinnaird, the gentleman I spoke to you about. We're just here to pick up his uniforms."

Mrs. Uist was a very old lady - there was no way she should still have been working. I reckoned she was eighty if she was a day.

She looked at me like I was a real inconvenience to her and grunted in my direction before disappearing through to the back of the store. Within minutes, she reappeared with a couple of uniforms wrapped in polythene. She ripped open one of the packs, handed me a pair of trousers and a jacket, and told me to try them on.

I lifted them from her and asked where I should go to change? She gave me a bit of a cold stare then said,

"Son, you don't have anything I've never seen at least twice before. Just try them on there and stop moaning - unless you've got something to hide?" she moaned.

I never replied. All I wanted to do was rip into her. I thought she was a really crabbit, ignorant old cunt and it took me all my time to bite my tongue. I removed my cut-off, jacket and jeans then tried on the uniform. It looked more like a suit than a uniform and it fitted me fine. I went to take it off, but Mrs. Boardman told me just to keep it on.

She then turned to Mrs. Uist and told her she wanted two white shirts and two clip-on ties for me. Mrs. Uist started to speak, telling Mrs. Boardman that I wasn't supposed to get shirts, but she interrupted her, and with a very stern raised voice said,

"Get me two sixteen-and-a-half-inch collar shirts and two ties, now!"

That was enough for the old witch. She turned and high-tailed it through the back store for a second time, whilst mumbling away to herself. It was then that I realised Mrs. Boardman had a side to her that I hadn't seen before and I quite liked it - she could certainly call a spade a spade when required.

I looked at her and gave her a bit of a smile and in turn she shook her head and rolled her eyes, suggesting Mrs. Uist was not her favourite person. While the auld yin was through the back, I went to put my steelies back on. Mrs. Boardman asked me what I was doing?

"Eh, putting my boots back on, why?"

"You can't put them back on. They're no use for working on the wards. You'll need a good, comfortable pair of black shoes. What size are you?"

"I'm a ten," I told her, then asked if it would be okay to pop down to the village at lunch time to get myself a decent pair?

"That won't be necessary, Ochil. I'll get you a pair from here. Mrs Uist!" she shouted on the old bat, who seemed to be taking forever to get the shirts.

"Yes," she replied, "What is it?"

"I want you to bring a pair of black shoes, size ten, the soft leather ones, for Ochil to try on."

"Okay, just give me a minute," she roared back.

We stood in silence for the next couple of minutes. I watched Mrs. Boardman, who was continually checking her watch and seemed to be getting more agitated with every second.

I think she was just about to shout on Mrs. Uist to get a move on when she appeared with the shoes and a shirt in one hand and a freshly ironed shirt in the other. She dumped the shoes and shirt on the counter and handed me the pressed one.

"Couldn't have you walking around with a creased shirt on your first day, now could we!" she told me, before turning to Mrs. Boardman. "Anything else?" she asked her.

"No thanks. That's fine. We've got all we need for now and I appreciate you ironing the shirt for him."

Mrs. Uist nodded in the general direction of Mrs. Boardman before disappearing through the back of the store.

By this time, I'd removed my t-shirt and jumper and was trying the shirt on.

"Perfect," she told me, looking me up and down. "Now try the shoes on …" she said, pointing to a chair behind me.

I took the shoebox from her, sat down, opened it up, threaded the new laces up then tried them on. I got up and walked about for a few seconds then sat back down.

"They're a perfect fit as well," I told her.

"Good, here's a bag. Stick your stuff in it and I'll put it behind the counter. We can pick it up later when we're done," she suggested.

I really didn't fancy leaving my leathers and my cut-off with some old fuckin' neurotic. Chances were she would throw it out or try and wash it or something.

"Sorry, Mrs. Boardman, if it's okay with you, I'd be much happier if I could leave my stuff in your office?"

"You don't have to worry, Ochil. It'll be safe here. No-one will touch it, I'll make sure of that," she told me, before shouting on Mrs. Uist again.

She appeared back at the counter looking like someone who'd lost a fiver and found a pound.

"Yes?" was again all she said.

Mrs. Boardman then lifted my bag onto the counter.

"Please put this somewhere no-one will touch it and I'll be back shortly to collect it, okay?"

Mrs. Uist replied again with a one-word answer, "Okay," then lifted it and carried it through the back.

Mrs. Boardman then picked up one of the ties, slipped it from the packet and clipped it onto my collar.

"There you go, Ochil. That's you ready to start. How does it feel to be suited and booted?" she asked me.

"To be honest, Mrs. Boardman it feels really weird. I could count on one hand how many times I've had a suit on. I don't know if I'm really comfortable with it," I told her.

"Nonsense, Ochil, you look great. You'll have all the young nurses swooning at you," she told me laughing.

We headed outside and made our way to the ward. The closer we got, the more I was shitting myself. I was sure I'd made a big mistake and almost convinced myself I should leave before I even went in. Mrs. Boardman unlocked the door. As we entered, she was greeted by an old man. He thanked her for opening the door and proceeded to make his way out.

"Come on, Mr. Hyslop, your wife is waiting for you inside. Let me give you a hand and we'll go and see her."

He then turned around. She clasped his arm, handed me her keys and told me to lock the door. By the time I had it locked, he was standing beside me again, asking me to open the door. I told him that he was better off where he was as it was raining outside. He thanked me and told me he would go out later when it had stopped.

I had no idea why I'd said that - it was the first thing that came into my head. I handed Mrs. Boardman back her keys and she said,

"Well done, Ochil. See! I told you you'd be a natural. Come on and I'll introduce you to the staff."

The distance from the door to the office must only have been about thirty yards, but during the small walk, I was approached by about a dozen patients.

Some with weird requests, some wanting to know who I was and others telling me I was all sort of things - from Hitler to Jesus!

We went into the small office and Gordon told me to take a seat. Mrs. Boardman then excused herself. She said she'd catch up with me at the end of the week to see how I'd got on.

When she left the office, Gordon got up and told me to follow him, which I did. He took me out of the ward through another door and into an area belonging to another ward which had six beds.

There was a small partitioned space which was half glass with no roof. It had a door and a window facing into the ward. Gordon told me it was the staff tearoom. I recognised it as the place I'd met Peter and Becky in the previous day.

Gordon told me that the staff used the room for short breaks and the window allowed them to see what was happening in the ward - in case there were any incidents.

Gordon made me a cup of tea and told me that I should enjoy it as he never made tea for anyone. He suggested that I'd be the one who'd be expected to make the tea for the rest of the guys on my shift.

I never said anything, but I was thinking to myself, 'Like that'll fuckin' happen!'. He then asked me to give him a bit of background. I was very careful with what I said and told him the things I thought would keep him happy, but never delved into any of the real stuff that I was involved in.

I thought, if I'd told him even a quarter of the shit I'd experienced, he would've had me in one of the beds as quick as a flash. He gave me a quick rundown on all the patients and tried to explain a bit about their illnesses - in the hope that I'd understand the reasons why they behaved the way they did. I never took in a single fucking thing. I just kept thinking 'What the fuck am I doing here?'

We finished our tea and he told me it was time for the patient's breakfast. He explained that they had to leave the ward and go into the dining room with patients from the other wards. This required all the staff to be in attendance. I asked him what I should do? He told me just to observe and try to pick up some of the patients names. I followed him out of the ward, and he stood in the corridor beside the dining room door. I presumed he did this to stop anyone from trying to leave. The rest of the staff headed for the dining room, keeping an eye on the patients as they went.

In the dining room, I noticed that it was divided into four areas, each ward had their own space. It was self-service, but only one ward at a time was allowed at the serving counter. I thought it a bit strange that they were all segregated, but after only a few minutes, I realised why. One of the patients from another ward tried to attack one of the patients in my ward and had to be restrained then removed by several nurses.

I was told later that the reason for the attack was that our patient resembled the brother of the patient who'd attacked him. The patient claimed that his brother had stolen all his money and put him in the hospital. All the nurses just took this in their stride, but I really struggled to get my head around it.

I couldn't understand how someone could be that deluded: that they really believed what they were thinking and doing was real, when it clearly wasn't? What a major eye-opener it was for me. This was something I'd never seen before and, hand on heart, I didn't actually believe was possible. But when you see it with your own eyes, it completely changes your perception - it forces you to think that much harder about how it can happen. After breakfast was over and everyone was ushered back into their wards, it was medicine time. By fuck, what a palaver that was!

Some of the patients took their medicine and screamed at the staff for not giving them enough. Others had to be physically restrained then given an injection because they refused to take it orally.

After the medicine round was done, it was time for the staff breakfast. There were four staff plus Gordon and myself on duty. That meant we had to do it in two sets of three's. I went with Gordon and one of the staff nurses for first break.

I hadn't brought anything to eat, thinking I'd only get a lunch break. Having already eaten breakfast before I started, I really wasn't ready for anything anyway. When I went into the tearoom, the staff nurse had already made tea and there was a plate of sausage and bacon rolls sitting in the middle of the table.

Gordon introduced me to the staff nurse, telling me he was called Russell Greer, then introduced me as Ochil, but when we shook hands, I told him to call me Shug.

"Strange choice of nickname that! How did that come about?" he asked me.

I told him I wasn't sure, but that I'd been called Shug for as long as I could remember.

He asked me some more questions, but I really couldn't be arsed going into any great detail about anything, so I fed him just enough to satisfy him. I couldn't believe that everyone wanted to know your business - it was like twenty fuckin' questions everywhere I went.

He then started to tell me all about himself, what he was up to, who he knew, and shit like that. I had no fuckin' interest in any of it so I just munched on my roll and never said a word.

The two of them started chatting away about what was needing done: who would be doing what, etc. I was still a bit zoned out until I heard my name being mentioned then the old ears pricked up.

"Sorry, what was that?" I asked.

Gordon then repeated it for me.

"I was just telling Russell that I want him to take you under his wing and show you the ropes."

"That's great. Thanks very much," I told him, but I didn't really mean it.

I'd hardly spent five minutes in Russell's company and he was already getting on my fuckin' nerves. He then piped up with a stupid grin on his fuckin' face,

"You can relax now, Shug. You're in good hands. I'll have you whipped into shape in no time."

I just smiled and nodded, but inside I was thinking to myself, 'If I have to spend the whole fuckin' day with this cunt, I might end up killing him before my shift ends!'.

Gordon stood up and told us we should get back into the ward and let the others have their break. He handed me the tray with the dirty dishes and asked Russell to show me where to wash them.

We went back into the ward and I followed Russell into a room that he explained was the 'Clinical room'. He told me that it was like a kind of treatment room, but also housed the medication. I put the tray of dirty dishes down on the bunker and started to fill the sink with hot water. Russell said that after I'd washed and dried them, I would need to take them back into the tearoom for the other guys.

I stood there washing the dishes, thinking to myself that if this is the type of thing I needed to do every day then I wouldn't be here long. I wasn't really sure what to expect from the job, but the last thing I thought I'd be doing was running around after everybody's arse like a fuckin' servant.

He then told me that this room must be kept locked at all times and that no patients were ever allowed in without a nurse being present. Just then, Gordon came in and handed me a key.

"Shug, this key opens all the entry and exit doors in the whole building. Make sure you keep it safe. If any of the patients ask you to open a door, always check with one of us before you do anything. I'm sure you'll pick up very quickly who has and hasn't got parole – and, for fuck's sake, don't lose it."

I took the key from him and immediately pushed it into my pocket.

When Gordon left, I asked Russell what the parole thing was all about and he told me it was a patient status term, which still meant fuck all to me.

"Listen, take the dishes through the back then come into the office. I'll give you some info about the different type of parole the patients have."

I locked the 'Clinical room' then took the dishes back to the tearoom. When I went in, the three guys who were there all introduced themselves, but by the time I got back to the office, I'd forgotten all their names. I spent the next hour or so listening to Russell prattle on about parole, special nursing, the different sections patients were under, and a run down on all of the patients. By the time he was finished, my brain was mush.

I had to laugh when he told me at the end of his spiel that I should now be much better prepared to deal with the patients because of the information he'd given me.

I had no fuckin' idea what to say to him. All I could think was 'What a sleverin' bastard, all full of his own fuckin' importance', but, thankfully, I didn't need to say anything as Gordon came back into the office and started chatting with him.

The next thing we knew, there was a crashing sound followed by a lot of screaming and shouting coming from the ward. Gordon and Russell ran out towards a couple of patients who were fighting with each other. The rest of the staff got there first and by the time we arrived, the patients had been split up and were being restrained.

I helped a couple of the staff get one of the patients back to their bed. We bodily carried him up the ward as he struggled and kicked, trying to get free.

When we dumped him on the bed, one of the nurses pulled the curtains around as we tried our best to keep hold of him. He was lying face down, still screaming like a banshee and kicking away. The nurse who'd shut over the curtains told us to keep hold of him and he would prepare an injection with a sedative in it.

This seemed to agitate the patient even more. He started calling us all the names under the sun and was wriggling about like a snake in heat. The other nurse put his hand on the back of the patient's neck and told him to 'Shut the fuck up' and this just agitated him even more.

Somehow, the patient got free and managed to punch the nurse right on the nose. The fuckin' idiot nurse then released his hand off the patient's neck and just stood there, holding his nose. This left me trying to restrain the patient on my own.

287

By this time, he was on his knees and swinging punches at me. I tried to put his arm up his back in a 'police hold', but the cunt elbowed me in the side of the head which made me lose my grip. I tried to grab hold of him, but he grabbed hold of my neck first with both hands, and started squeezing as hard as he could.

Well, for me, that was the last fuckin' straw. I hooked him a good one on the side of the face, but he didn't even flinch and kept squeezing at my neck. I kneed him right in the stones and cracked him another beauty, this time right in the eye, and he fell back onto the bed.

Just as all this was taking place, unbeknown to me, the nurse who'd gone to get the injection, opened the curtains and saw me weighing into the patient. I grabbed the patient and turned him over onto his front then lay across him to make sure he couldn't move. The nurse with the bloody nose then grabbed the patient's trousers and scants, pulling them down to his knees.

I wondered what the fuck he was doing as I had no idea that they fired the injection into his arse - I wondered for a minute if the cunt was a pedo? The other nurse then stuck the needle into the patient's arse, emptied the syringe then pulled his trousers back up.

"Okay, Shug, turn him onto his back," he told me.

By this time, there was no fight left in the patient. When I turned him over, I couldn't believe the state of his face. It was covered in blood, his eye was already swollen and looked like it was starting to close up. His nose was also well burst open. The two nurses looked at each other then at me, but I ignored them and kept hold of the patient. The dude with the syringe told the other one that he'd go and get stuff to clean the patient then disappeared behind the curtains.

The patient was no longer struggling with me but was shouting that he'd get me the sack for attacking him and demanding to see a Doctor immediately. I leaned over and whispered in his ear, telling him that if he didn't shut up, I would give him a proper tanking. That seemed to work as he settled down a bit. I looked at the nurse with the burst nose and asked him if he was okay?

He looked really nervous, but never said anything, just nodded a bit. The other nurse then came back in and this time had Gordon with him. Gordon looked at the patient's face then at the both of us.

He asked if we were okay and I told him I was. The other cunt never said a word, he just shrugged his shoulders. The patient then told Gordon that he wanted him to call the police as he wanted me done for assault. Gordon sat on the bed beside him and started wiping the blood from his face with cotton wool and stuff. Every time he wiped a bit, the patient let out a squeal.

The other two then disappeared and I was left listening to the conversation between Gordon and the patient. The patient was still adamant that he wanted me charged. Gordon started speaking to him really quietly and explained that if that was what he wanted then the police would certainly be called.

He then advised him that he would also be charged: One count of wilful damage to property - he had thrown a chair through the window and three counts of assault: One for the patient he'd been fighting with and Two for assaulting the nurses who'd intervened. The patient then told him to forget it because he didn't want to end up back in the state hospital. By the time
289

he was cleaned up, he'd started to drift off to sleep - I assumed the sedative was now taking effect.

Gordon asked me to stay put and that he'd come back after he disposed of all the stuff he'd used to clean the patient's puss. I sat on the chair and watched as he fell asleep. I couldn't believe the state of his face and guessed I was going to be in some serious shit for it.

Gordon came back about five minutes later with a different nurse and told him to swap places with me. When I stood up, he asked me to follow him into the 'Clinical room', which I did. When we were both in, he closed the door and put the snib down. He then pointed to a seat, suggesting I should sit.

He sat down as well then told me he needed me to explain exactly what had happened and how the patient had ended up in the state he was in. I told him the truth, exactly how it happened, and waited in silence for his reply.

"You do know it's a serious offence to attack a patient who's sectioned under the mental health act, don't you?"

I thought to myself, 'Who gives a flying fuck about the mental health act! The bastard tried to strangle me, so he got what he deserved'.

"So what about all that pish you told him earlier then?" I asked him but started ranting away again before he had a chance to reply. "Just so you're clear, Gordon, I couldn't give a rat's arse about sections, or who he is, or who anybody is for that matter. Any cunt who tries to strangle me will be getting a fuckin' licking and that includes you, by the way," I told him, then wondered why I'd put the last bit in.

"Okay, Shug, I hear what you're saying. Thanks for your honesty. Unfortunately, this isn't the street, with two normal people having a square go. This is a psychiatric ward - it's full of people with mental health issues. Most are detained under section because they are either a danger to themselves or others.

"They are in here, sheltered from normal society, with us providing support and care for them in the hope we can improve their quality of life. Maybe even get them to a stage that, one day, they could be able to function at a level which is within the parameters of what we'd call normal living.

"What you've done today, albeit under extreme provocation, is completely and utterly unacceptable. It goes way beyond the level of restraint allowed by the authorities and you'll have to be held accountable for your actions."

He then started to tell me about the process that was going to follow, but I'd heard enough. I interrupted him, telling him that I didn't give two fucks about any of it and I would save him any bother by quitting.

"Look, I wasn't really sure about it when I got the job," I told him, "but Mrs. Boardman convinced me I'd enjoy it and that I'd be good at it. Well, you can tell her from me that she was wrong."

I then stood up, handed him my key and went to lift the snib on the door. He asked me to sit down for a minute before I left. I sat back down waiting to see what he was going to say and, fuck me, he didn't mince his words.

"Okay, Shug, here's how it is: this incident will have to be reported to Senior Management, who in turn will contact the police. Also, an independent Doctor will be asked to assess the patient's injuries.

"We'll all have to give statements and it'll be up to the police if any charges will be brought against you.

You may well be arrested and detained until the case is resolved.

"You're telling me that you want to quit, and I hear what you're saying, unfortunately, it's not quite as simple as that. I have to suspend you, pending enquiry, you'll not be able to return to work until the conclusion of that enquiry.

"I'll make it very clear in my report that you were severely provoked and that you felt your life was in danger, which is why you lashed out. I'll also make sure I document that this was your first day, that you hadn't even completed your induction training. Therefore, you had no idea how to handle an aggressive incident such as this."

I took a minute to digest what he'd said then asked him if he'd been involved in anything like this before, and if so, how had it played out?

"Over the years, I've been involved in a few incidents where people have maybe used a bit more force than they should have whilst restraining patients. The outcome of all the cases have been verbal or written warnings, but to be honest, this is the first time I've dealt with an incident where a nurse has actually beaten up a patient so I've no idea what the outcome will be."

"Fuck's sake, I hardly beat him up! But I know where you're coming from," I told him. "So what now then? Do I just go back to the nurses' home and sit it out?"

"Yes, that's what I think you need to do. If I can offer you a bit of advice: keep a low profile and don't discuss this with anyone."

I don't know why, but I thanked him before he let me back out of the ward. I got outside and went to unclip my tie, only to realise it was gone. I'd probably lost it in the scuffle. I opened my top button, took in a large breath of air then exhaled slowly.

'Fuck, Shug, here we go again!' I thought, 'it never rains but it fuckin' pours!'.

I remembered that I'd left my leathers and cut-off in the stores and knew I needed to get them now - in case it was shut later. I went around the side door and avoided the admin block completely. I had visions of the pigs being in there already, talking about what had happened, the last thing I wanted was to bump into any of them.

I went in, got my stuff then made my way around the back of the building again. I walked as quickly as I could to the back gate, around the back of the central block and into the nurses' home. It was a bit of long road for a shortcut, but I knew if I went that way that I wouldn't bump into anybody - I was so glad when I made it back to my room without needing to speak to anyone.

When I got in, I looked at my neck in the mirror and realised that it was all scratched and bruised. I wondered if I should get a photo of it so I could show the cops. If they came after me, as I expected they would, having a photo of the marks would be good evidence for my defence.

I then realized that I didn't know anyone with a camera and even if I did, I couldn't tell them why I wanted it. I decided the best thing to do would be to jump on my bike and go for a bit of a blast. I got changed, grabbed my helmet and headed out. I fired up my bike and made my way towards the back gate.

I stopped at the entrance before drawing out onto the road. As I did, I saw a cop car coming in, I guessed that they were there to discuss the incident. I knew that they could've been there for umpteen reasons, but when paranoia gets a hold of you, you can't see beyond your own nose. I decided I would head down to the pub and see if any of the guys were there?

I really wanted to talk to Rooster or Cowboy about what had happened and thought that they were bound to know someone who had a camera.

As I rode, I could feel my head beginning to clear a bit. By the time I arrived at the pub, I was much less agitated. There was a fair sprinkling of bikes in the car park and, thankfully, I saw Rooster and Cowboy's amongst them.

When I went in, I saw there was a bit of a pow-wow going on. About a dozen guys were huddled around a table, some sitting, some standing.

Brutis must've heard me coming in, as he lifted his head,

"Well, hello, Shug. You're here at last! About time too, we've been trying to get a hold of you for ages."

"I was at work, man, you knew that," I reminded him. "Anyway, what's going on here? Looks like you're all planning and scheming and definitely up to no good."

I said hello to everyone and sort of muscled my way in amongst the group, grabbing a spare chair. I nodded to Rooster as I sat, and he nodded back. He must've noticed my neck as he leaned over and lifted my chin.

"What the fuck happened to you, Shug? Something we need to know about?" he asked.

"Nah, it's cool, just a work thing. I'll fill you in later," I told him, but that wasn't good enough for him or anybody else for that matter.

The next thing I know, it's twenty fuckin' questions again, everybody wanting to know who did it? What happened? And all the other shit people ask when they think you've been in a fight. Whatever they were doing before I came in had now moved down the pecking order. Everyone was demanding me to tell them what had happened.

After I told them, I was looking around at a bunch of people who looked totally dumbstruck. I don't think anyone could believe it. Rooster then gawked at me, giving me the big serious eyes and stern face look.

"Shug, that's bad news, man. I think you're in deep, deep, shit there, mate. If I was you, I'd think about maybe moving up north for a bit, until this thing passes. I'm sure Indie would be more than happy to sort that out for you. Tell you what, bud! You certainly don't want to get sent down for this type of shit. It sounds like you could be a bit fucked.

"If you get yourself up there, there's no chance the pigs will get a hold of you and it would give you a bit of breathing space to decide what to do," he suggested, which brought a series of ayes and yes' from around the room.

At that point, I wondered what the fuck was going on inside some of their heads, especially Rooster's?

"Are you all fuckin' mental? I'm going no-fuckin-where. As far as I'm concerned, I was defending myself. The cunt would've killed me if I hadn't scudded him!"

Brutis, who, as usual, was very quiet, then spoke up,

"Listen, Shug, I'm with you on this. I think you could have a bit of a case to get him charged you know, I'm pretty sure even fuckin' loonies need to abide by the law. First thing we need to do is get some cunt who has a polaroid camera and take some pictures of your neck."

295

Freddie then piped up saying he had one at home and told us he'd head off and pick it up right away.

Brutis then continued,

"I'll give Indie a bell, Shug. Get him to have a word with his solicitor dude. He's bound to know what you should do. Right, let's finish up here first, then I'll phone him."

I had no idea what was happening but was very quickly brought up to speed.

"Carry on, Rooster," Brutis told him.

"Right, as I was saying, tomorrow morning, Gunner and I will be picking up the gear. When we get back, I want you all here so we can get it moved quickly.

"Remember what I said, I want you all in groups of four - you all know who's with who. DD, you, me, Cowboy, Flick and Gunner will be going to see our friend Rocko. It seems he's still giving it large and I want to waste him and his cronies again, this time in public.

"I know they're going to be at their local tomorrow night to watch a football match on TV. We'll pay them a visit then."

"What about me, Rooster? Can I come with you? I could really do with letting off some steam," I asked.

But before he had a chance to answer, Brutis interrupted,

"No, Shug. You either stay here or head back to the hospital. Once I've spoken with Indie, we'll decide what's best."

I told him that I could really do with firing a rake of drink down my throat and crashing out, so I made my way to the bar and ordered a couple of bottles. I went into the booth in the corner, hoping I'd be left alone for a bit.

Some chance of that!

Within five minutes, I was joined by Rooster, Cowboy and Flick - all wanting to know how I was! We analysed the situation to death and I eventually had to tell them I wanted to hear no more about it. I then changed the subject and asked Rooster how he was getting on with Julie?

That was enough for Cowboy and Flick. They both stood up at the same time, with Cowboy moaning,

"Come on, Flick, let's split, I can't bear any of this 'Mills & Boon' pish again."

They both laughed as they headed to the bar. I watched and smiled a bit when I saw them shaking their heads. They obviously knew we were going to bore the tits off them.

I looked at Rooster, waiting on his reply to my question, but he just stared at me.

"Well?" I asked.

"Well what?" was his reply.

"Fuck's sake, Rooster. It's not mastermind. I only wanted to know how you and Julie were doing?"

"Not sure, Shug." he began, "We're taking it very slowly, she's still not a hundred percent so I don't want to do anything to upset her. I've seen her a few times and we're working through all our shit, a bit at a time, but I think we'll get there. I've told her that she's my main priority now, that I'll always put her first, which has made her well happy."

"Do you think you'll be able to do that now you're a VP?" I quizzed.

"Well, I'll just need to find a way, Shug. I'm committed to the relationship and even if it means I have to take some time out then that's what I'll need to do."

I couldn't believe what I was hearing. He had already committed to the Bats and blew her off. Fuck! She'd even aborted his kid because he wouldn't put her first - now this, what a fuckin' turnaround!

"Fuck me, Rooster! You aren't half making some commitment here," I told him, thinking out loud. "How the fuck do you think that'll go down with Indie and Brutis? Don't you think they'll blow a gasket if you tell them you want some time out?"

"To be honest, Shug, I'm not sure how it would go down, but I'm not going to worry about it. I want to be with Julie long-term and I've decided I'm not going to let anything get in the way of it."

"So I take it that means you'll be settling here then?" I asked him.

"Well, I suppose so, Shug, but I really haven't thought that far ahead."

"Will you be moving into hers or will she be moving back to the nurses' home?"

"Fuck me, Shug! Listen to yourself, man! You're like a fuckin' interrogator. I've told you we're taking it slow so there's no plan to do anything yet, okay?"

I thought I'd better stop with the questions as he was getting ratty with me. The only thing I really needed to know was if she was moving back into the nurses' home, but I couldn't get him to discuss it. I wondered about asking him when she planned to go back to work, to see if it matched with what Lisa had told me, but knew he'd freak, so I left it.

Just then, Brutis came back and sat down. I was kind of glad about it as it reduced the tension that was building between me and Rooster.

Chapter 24

"Shug, I've just talked with Indie and he's spoken to his brief. What he's said is that you should go back to the hospital, speak to whoever is in charge and ask them what the next step in the process is, now that you're suspended.

"When you find that out you've to give him a call back and he'll advise you from there," he said, handing me a bit of paper with his number on it.

I thanked him then told them I was going to grab another beer. I asked them if they wanted one, but they both declined.

I stood beside Cowboy and Flick while I waited to get served and they were ripping into me about Julie and Rooster, telling me we'd turned into a pair of soppy bastards.

After a bit of craic, the three of us headed back to the table with our drinks. By this time, Brutis had disappeared, leaving Rooster on his todd. When we joined him, Cowboy and Flick continued relentlessly with their smartarse comments, directing them at both Rooster and me, but we both started to give as good as we were getting and from there it turned into a great wee night. We were joined by DD, Ludo, Freddie and the Prospect, Winker.

I knew I'd be heading back to the hospital in the morning, so I didn't want to get too pished, just in case I needed to see somebody about the incident. I suggested that I needed to crash, and they all started ripping the pish. DD said that if I left first then they'd have no option but to tie me up outside, bollock naked, and leave me there 'til morning.

It seemed everyone was in agreement, so I thought it best to have another beer. I'm not sure how it came about, but somewhere along the line, it was decided that whoever wanted to leave first or fell asleep first would be the one getting tied up.

It was around 3 a.m. when Rooster nudged me, nodding his head in the direction of Flick. I was so drunk that I had no idea why he was doing it. I stared at him through my half-shut eyes until he lifted his hands up, placing them both on the left side of his cheek and tilting his head to the side, mimicking sleep.

I then remembered the forfeit and nudged DD to let him know that Flick was sleeping. He was already aware and had sent Winker to go and get some big cable ties from his bike. By the time Winker came back, we were all ready to strip Flick. We were tiptoeing around him and giggling like a bunch of fuckin' schoolgirls.

We then grabbed him, stripped him, tied his wrist and ankles, then lifted him, making our way out to the first lamppost we could find. From what I remember, it ended up a bit of a damp squib. Flick was almost unconscious and not really aware of what was happening to him.

By the time we'd him tied to the post, we were all ready to crash as well. I walked down to the house on my own. The rest of the guys decided to sit beside Flick and have a smoke, waiting to see if he'd wake up. I thought it best to go first as that way I'd have more chance of getting a bed. However, as it turned out, I had to make do with the sofa as all the beds were taken.

I was wakened the next morning by Gunner and Rooster shouting at everyone, telling them to move their arses as they'd be back to get them in half an hour. I sat up and swung my legs onto the floor and reached for the smokes in my jacket. Rooster asked me how I was doing, and I told him I was rough as fuck. I asked him what time it was, and he told me it was half-seven.

"Fuck, Rooster! No wonder I'm rough! What the fuck are you doing wakening me at this fuckin' time in the morning?"

"We've got a busy day ahead of us and so have you, so get your arse into gear and get ready to go back up to the hospital. I'll see you when I get back," he told me, before grabbing my head and rubbing it with his knuckles - the bastard!

I told him to fuck off, but he just laughed as he and Gunner disappeared out of sight, through to the kitchen, then out the back door. I sat back, closed my eyes, smoked my cigarette and tried to think about what we'd done the night before. By now, people were starting to mill around and there was a bit of a buzz going on.

Fuck! Then I remembered about Flick and thought that the cunts may have left him tied to the fuckin' lamppost! I jumped up and headed back to where we'd left him the night before. When I saw he wasn't there, at first, I thought 'thank fuck', but then I wondered where he was? I made my way back to the house, wishing to fuck I'd asked Rooster about it earlier, but I really wasn't that 'compos mentis' then.

When I went in, I was asking everybody if they'd seen Flick, but most just shrugged their shoulders or mumbled a "no" under their breath. I then spied DD and Cowboy crashed out on the floor in the back room and gave their feet a bit of a kick, which got me a 'Fuck off!' from both of them.

I knelt down between them and asked them where the fuck Flick was? They both answered, almost in unison, that he was tied to the pole outside the pub. I gave them a bit of a shake, trying to get them to come too, which didn't really go down well with either of them, but I wasn't giving a fuck about them.

"I've just been out to see and there's no cunt there. So where the fuck is he?" I asked them both.

Cowboy sat up a bit, rubbing his head as he came too.

"I think maybe we let him go before we came back here?"

"Okay, so if you did let him go … where the fuck's he now?" I wanted him to tell me.

"For fuck's sake, Shug! Wind your fuckin' neck in, man! I've only just opened my eyes, gimme a fuckin' minute!"

"That's okay for you, Cowboy, but what about your best mate? You don't even know if something's happened to him. He could've been lifted, for all you know. Can you even remember if you gave him his clothes back?"

"Shug, you need to shut the fuck up. You're doin' ma fuckin' head in. Just let me get ma shit together and we'll go and look for him, okay?"

He then got up, shook his head at me, then went to the loo.

"What?" I asked him, holding my hands out in front of me.

"Two fuckin' minutes, Shug! Just give me two fuckin' minutes, okay?" he roared at me just before slamming the toilet door.

I then turned my attention to DD who looked like he'd fallen back asleep. I gave him another kick on the feet.

Without even looking he said,

"Shug, fuck off! I won't tell you again!" he roared at me, which really pissed me off, so I hit him another kick, this time a bit harder which made him jump a bit.

He stood up and took a couple of steps towards me.

"I fuckin' told you not to do that again - apologise or we're boxing!"

I was in no mood for any of his pish, so I head-butted him on the nose. As he staggered back, I lunged for him, hitting him a couple of times before we both fell. When we landed on the floor, it couldn't have been better for me as he had hit the chair on the way down. I was right on to him as he lay on his back. I got on top of him and grabbed his throat. I looked right at him and said,

"Well, DD, your call! Are we square or do you want to keep going?"

He held his hands out at his sides and told me he was done. I removed my hand from his throat, stood up and offered out my hand to help him up, which he took. When I pulled him up, I went to apologise for hitting him. I wanted to explain why I was so pissed, but the bastard hooked me, dropping me to the floor.

"That's us fuckin' square now, Shug. If you ever fuckin' do that to me again, you'll be fuckin' sorry," he told me, before holding his hand out to help me up.

I wasn't really sure that I wanted to take it any further, but there were a few people watching and I'd just been made SAA, so I really didn't have a choice.

I ignored his hand and lifted myself to my feet. He just stood in front of me like he was the 'big man', which really pissed me off. I made a lunge at him, which seemed to surprise him, and again, I got a couple of good digs in. When we fell to the floor again, it was almost like a repeat of the first time except, instead of grabbing his throat, I started punching the fuck out of his face.

He was pretty much done after a few minutes of this and was no longer putting up any resistance. The next thing I know, Cowboy's got a hold of me and is dragging me off him.

"Fuckin' leave me, Cowboy! I gave the cunt a chance and the bastard hooked me," I roared at him.

He then stood in front of me, still holding me pretty tightly.

"Shug, he's done. Enough's enough. Come on, man, whatever the fuck's going on, I think you've proved your point," he told me.

"Okay, okay, I'm fine," I told him, then pushed past him making my way to the door.

Before I left, I leaned over DD and said to him,

"Just so you know, this isn't fuckin' over until I get a fuckin' apology!" then gave him a bit of a kick before walking away.

I went outside, making my way up the street towards the pub. I was fuckin' raging about what had just happened and was still none the wiser as to what had happened to Flick? I heard a shout behind me and turned around to see who it was. Cowboy had followed me out and was asking me to wait up. I stopped but told him if he wanted to talk about the fight then he was wasting his breath. I waited 'til he caught up with me then started walking again.

"What do you want, Cowboy?" I asked him.

"Fuck, Shug! Slow down a bit, man! I just want to talk. I've remembered what happened with Flick. He's safe. We put him back in the pub when we decided to it was time to split. We noticed that he was well out of it so me, DD, Freddie, Ludo and Winker huckled him back in, chucked him into one of the booths then threw his clothes on top of him."

"I fuckin' hope so. The last thing we need is someone calling the pigs and having them sniffing about here."

We got to the pub door and Cowboy grabbed my arm,

"Shug, listen, man I know you're under pressure with the hospital stuff and the shit that went on with Julie and Rooster, but you need to get your head straight. You're our SAA, man. That means people are looking at you and following your lead. You can't just go about knocking fuck out of people, even if they deserve it."

"Listen, Cowboy, you weren't there. You didn't see the cunt goading me. Just ask anybody who saw it and they'll tell you what happened. That's the second time he's tried it - fuck's sake, I nearly killed the cunt the last time as I knew he didn't mean it when he gave me all his apology shit. The bastard only did it 'cause Indie made him. You heard what I said to him and I meant it. I'm sick to death of the prick. He's lucky I never fuckin' stabbed him, 'cause let me tell you, I fucking thought about it."

With that, I walked in and had a look for Flick and found him exactly the way Cowboy described. He was still out for the count, but just seeing he was safe made me less tense. I never saw Brutis when I went in, but he shouted for me and Cowboy to join him in the back room, which we did.

The first thing he asked me was how I got the bruise on the side of my face. I told him exactly what had happened. He shook his head and told Cowboy to go and get DD. When Cowboy left, he told me he was going to bump DD down to Prospect and let him know he was lucky that's all that was happening to him.

Normally, I would have protested about something like that and come up with a hundred reasons why we shouldn't do it. But this time, I wanted to know why that was all we were going to do to him?

"Are you sure that's all he deserves?" I asked him.

"Why? Don't you think that's enough like?" he replied.

"Well, the thing is, Brutis, that's the second time the cunt's had a go at me and if it happens again, I'll end up doing time for the bastard!"

"You telling me you want him out, Shug?"

"I don't know, man, am not sure. It's just that he's a loose cannon and I know it's going to happen again. He just can't fuckin' help himself and I don't know if the club needs that?"

"Oky, Shug, so tell me, what you want me to do?"

"Well, I think that we knock him back down to Prospect like you said, but we should also make it really hard for him to get his Colours back. Maybe we should treat him like shit until he learns some respect?"

"Okay, I'm good with that," he agreed.

Just then, Cowboy came back with DD in tow. Brutis told them to come in and for Cowboy to sit. DD went to sit down beside him, but Brutis said,

"Not you, cunt, I never told you to sit!"

DD then stood back up and gave Brutis a bit of a stare.

"Right, take your cut-off off," he told him.

DD then asked him why and Brutis said,

"Because I'm fuckin' telling you to and you don't need to know any more than that. What you do need to do for a fuckin' change, though, is listen to what your fuckin' told. Now get it off!"

Brutis stood up and walked towards him, waited until he'd removed his cut-off then took it from him. He went back to his seat, put the cut-off on the table, and asked me for my knife, which I gave him. He then started to rip the top rocker off. When DD realised what he was doing, he said,

"Whoa, man, what the fuck are you doin?"

Fuck! I thought Brutis was going to explode. He growled at him saying,

"How many fuckin' times have I to tell you to shut the fuck up?"

You would think that he would have learned and shut his mouth like he was told, but, oh no, not DD.

"Brutis, why are you removing my Colours, man?"

Well, that just about put the tin fuckin' lid on it for Brutis and he roared,

"Fuck's sake, how fuckin' stupid are you? Any more of your shite and It'll be you're fuckin' tongue I'm cutting out!"

He then stood up, stuck my knife into the table then made a breenge for DD, planting a seriously hard dig right on his jaw, which completely floored him. Cowboy moved to help him up, but Brutis roared at him,

"Just leave the bastard where he is!" which prompted Cowboy to sit back down.

Brutis then returned to his seat and carried on removing the top rocker and said,

"Why the fuck can he just not fuckin' listen?"

By the time he,d finished removing all the Colours, except the bottom rocker, DD had picked himself up. He was standing with his hands on the table, looking really groggy.

Brutis took one look at him and said,

"Sit …" pointing to the chair with the knife.

DD pulled it out and sat down. Brutis then picked up the cut-off and threw it at him. DD looked at it then lifted his head saying,

"I don't understand," while looking totally bemused.

"Well, let me spell it out for you," Brutis began. "You are now a fuckin' Prospect again and will be until I tell you different. You're lucky Shug vouched for you. Let me tell you, if he hadn't you'd be OUT and on your way to either the hospital or the fuckin' morgue."

I was now starting to get a bit confused myself, I wasn't really sure why he'd told him that I'd vouched for him when I was the one who wanted to put the boot in. I thought about asking him, but knew it wasn't the time or place.

"I want to offer you a piece of advice, DD," he told him. "You better start putting your fuckin' brain into gear before your gub or you'll end up in some real serious shit. Now put your fuckin' cut-off on and stand up."

DD did as he was told, saying nothing for a change. Once he was sorted, Brutis asked him if he had anything he wanted to say? DD then cleared his throat and began,

"I just want to apologise to you all for my behaviour. I know I've been bang out of order and, Shug, I just want you to know I'm really sorry for having a go at you - it won't happen again, that's a promise, Brutis. I'll do everything that's asked of me in the hope you'll give me back my Colours when you think I deserve them."

Brutis then stood up and said,

"Prospect, when you've learned to respect this club and the Officers in it then maybe we'll talk again. Now, I want you to go and get the rest of the Officers and tell them to come in here. When you've notified them, go to the bar and get us all a drink."

All DD said was "Okay," then left.

"Right, Cowboy, you're on 'Guru duty' with that cunt. I want you to make it as shitty as you can for him over the next month, then we'll see how he's doing. You ok with that, Shug?"

"Yep, that's good for me," I told him.

The next thing, the door opens, and the rest of the Officers piled in. I had a good look at Freddie and knew he wasn't best pleased - I wondered if he'd say anything to Brutis?

Once everyone was sitting, Brutis started by reminding us that what is discussed around the Officer's table stayed at the table. After he looked around and got a sufficient number of nods, he declared the meeting open.

He said, before he told us anything, he wanted to go around the room and get updates on anything we thought would be relevant. He must've clocked that Freddie was pissed because, straightaway, he said,

"Right, Freddie, best we start with you. You seem to have something on your mind?"

Freddie didn't beat about the bush, he went straight for it.

"I want to know how the fuck you can just decide to boot DD down to Prospect without it going to a vote?

"I was led to believe that decisions like that were made around this table, not just by you when it came up your humph?"

Fuck me! I thought Brutis was going to go mental.

All eyes were on him, waiting on his reply. Instead of losing it, he leaned back in his chair and let out a big sigh.

"Do you really think that's what I did, Freddie?" he asked him very calmly, which seemed to rub off on Freddie, as the next thing he said was much less aggressive.

"Well? What else could it be? One minute, he's on a 'Full patch' and the next, he's bumped to Prospect. We're all Officers and we only find out about it when he comes to get us! I think if you're going to do that, it should at least be discussed here first!"

"You know what, Freddie? You raise a good point. Yes, normally I'd look for input from all of you, but not in this instance. In my opinion, what DD did was serious enough for me to boot him out and make sure he got a proper send-off.

"If it hadn't been for Shug then he'd be lying at our feet right now, so I think he's lucky that I only stripped him back to Prospect. I'll not have anybody disrespect an Officer, end of. When the meeting is finished, you should go and ask him why I did it? Come back to me and tell me if you think I was unfair with him then.

"Oh, and by the way, just for the record, as President, I don't need the approval of anybody to make a decision like that if I think it's in the best interests of the club.

"That's not how I operate, though. I want us to run this chapter together and the best way to do that is to have a meeting every week to discuss anything we feel needs acted upon."

We then had a bit of a chit-chat about what had happened over the last week or so. When we started chatting amongst ourselves, Brutis decided there was nothing of interest left to say so closed the meeting.

"Okay, guys, that'll do for today. Right, listen up! Rooster, Gunner, you'd best head off and pick up the stuff. Freddie, you go and have a word with DD. Cowboy, Flick, Ludo, you get the guys ready to roll. Shug, you hang back, I need a word."

I watched as the guys all left the room and wondered what the fuck he wanted to talk to me about?

It's funny how you always get that sinking feeling in these situations - you convince yourself that you must be in some kind of bother. It wouldn't matter if you knew a hundred percent that you hadn't done anything wrong, there was still that element of doubt because you were the only one asked to stay behind.

When the last person went out and the door closed, I asked Brutis what was up?

"Nothing's up, Shug. I just wanted to update you about the thing at your work. I spoke with Indie again and he told me that his brief did a bit of research into cases like yours and, well, eh, there's no easy way to tell you this …. but it seems you might be totally fucked!"

I stood up, feeling a bit shell-shocked and paced about a bit before speaking,

"How the fuck can that be? I was only defending myself! Surely to fuck I'm not supposed to just stand there and let him knock fuck out of me? Fuck's sake, man! He'd already floored one nurse and I wasn't about to let him do the fuckin' same to me!

"What did he say actually? Did he give you any reason why he thinks that?" I asked, wanting him to explain it to me.

311

"Sit down, Shug, and let me tell you what I know …" he said, almost whispering.

I sat back down, but I was still feeling well agitated.

"Okay, shoot! Tell me the script?"

"From what Indie has told me, it seems that when you start working in a loony bin, you've got to sign a contract of employment. Within the terms of that contract, there's a section that covers violent incidents. The long and short of it is, you should only use minimum force while restraining patients.

"If it's deemed that anyone uses excess force, it not only becomes a disciplinary matter, but also a police matter. According to the brief, it's highly unlikely that you'll end up with a favourable outcome."

I interrupted him, asking if he knew what that meant for me? He said the brief had told Indie that the most likely outcome would be me getting the sack and also getting charged by the police.

"He said he wasn't sure what the punishment would be, but if he was a betting man, then his money would be on a custodial sentence," he explained.

I stood up and started pacing around the room again, this time kicking a couple of chairs as I went. I could hear myself shouting,

"Agghh! Fuck! Fuck! Fuck!" then continued my rant. "Why the fuck didn't I listen to Rooster? He told me it was a stupid fuckin' idea to take the job. But, oh no, not me, I told him I knew better. Well, it doesn't fuckin' seem like it now!" I roared out loud. "Did he say what kind of stretch I could expect?"

"What he said was that there was very little precedent to follow. All the previous cases had specifics attached to them, making it impossible to judge them collectively. His best guess was you could get anything from eighteen months to eight years - depending on the severity of the incident."

Fuck! I nearly passed out. I stopped pacing and sat down.

"Eight years! Eight fuckin' years! Fuck me! I've done ten times worse than that and got fuck all jail time for it. Eight fuckin' years for defending myself! Surely tae fuck he's got that wrong? Tell me he's made a mistake, Brutis, that can't be right!"

"Shug, you need to settle, man. You're going to end up giving yourself a fuckin' heart attack! Listen to what I'm saying here! He never said you would get eight years! He was only giving you the worst case scenario. From what you've told us, he doesn't think you'll get anything like that."

I reckoned, at that point, Brutis was adding his own little bit to try and calm me down. I was so wound up, though, that I was having none of it.

"So why the fuck would he say that then? He must be thinking it's a possibility, or he wouldn't even have fuckin' mentioned it!" I challenged him.

"Shug, come on, man. You really need to get a fuckin' grip and calm the fuck down. Listen to what I'm saying here! He's said that if you need him, he's happy to represent you. Indie's said he'll pick up the tab."

"Him fuckin' represent me! Oh, let me see now? Would you want the cunt who told you that you could get eight fuckin' years to represent you? I don't fuckin' think so! I'll end up getting eighty fucking years if I let that cunt look after me! You tell him from me that he can go fuck himself!" I roared at him.

I think that was enough for Brutis. His tone and demeanour changed as he raised his voice,

"Shug, shut the fuck up right now. I've heard enough of your pish. Listen to me and don't say another fuckin' word until I tell you, okay?

"He says you need to go back to the hospital, speak to your boss and your Union rep then call Indie to let him know what they're saying. My advice, for what it's worth, is that you get back up the road and do it ASAP."

I got up, still feeling shell-shocked and left without saying anything else. All I could think was 'How the fuck will I survive inside for eight fuckin' years?'. The number eight was firmly planted at the front of my brain. I could hardly remember anything else about our conversation.

I walked straight outside and got on my bike. I fired it up and started to negotiate my way out the car park. I was just about to leave when Rooster and Gunner turned in.

"Where are you off to, man?" Rooster quizzed me.

"I need to head back to work," I told him.

"Why? What's up?" he asked.

"Sorry, man, I need to split. Speak to Brutis, he'll fill you in."

I didn't think I'd be able to tell him about it without bubbling like a wean. I gave him a nod, drew out and blasted away.

I don't know why, but I drove all the way there like a fuckin' idiot, taking chance after chance. I was almost daring someone to crash into me. I must've been flashed and tooted at a hundred times, but I just ignored the lot of them. When I finally arrived at the hospital, I made my way down to the back entrance. I drew into the side of the road and got off. I needed to try and clear my head before going in. I had no idea if the police would be waiting to see me, or if I'd be able to get a chance to speak to Mrs. Boardman? In fact, I wasn't even sure if she'd want to see me?

I wondered about going to see the Union rep? I knew I hadn't joined, but I did tell him I was planning too - I think it was 'Sod's law' that I never got the chance to sign up before this shit happened. I dismissed the Union support as an option as I really didn't think they'd be able to help me.

I lit up a smoke and sat on the dyke facing the entrance. I looked into the hospital and felt the tears running down my cheeks.

'This was supposed to be my fresh start! My chance to get my life back on track! A chance to distance myself a bit from the Bats! An opportunity to become integrated into what most people would consider a 'normal' way of life! Well, look where the fuck that's got me!' I thought to myself.

I made up my mind the best thing would be to go back to my room, ditch my Colours then head to Mrs. Boardman's office. I finished my smoke, plan intact, got back on my bike and headed to the nurses' home. I parked up, went in and ran straight up the stairs.

Chapter 25

I opened my room door, went in and quickly closed it behind me. I was so glad no-one had seen me. There was an envelope lying on the floor - it looked like it had been shoved under the door. I picked it up, sat on the chair and looked at it for a minute.

It was addressed to Mr. Kinnaird, so I assumed it was some kind of formal letter relating to the incident. I ripped it open, unfolded it and began to read....

Dear Mr. Kinnaird,

I would be grateful if you could contact me the minute you receive this letter. I would like to discuss the incident which took place in Tunnel ward involving yourself and one of the residents.

If you wish, you can bring a Union steward or representative of your choice along with you.

I have provided my direct dial phone number below. You can contact me at any time on this number, or alternately you can attend in person at the reception and ask the telephonist to call me.

I look forward to hearing from you.

Yours sincerely,

Marge McTear

Marge McTear
Director of Nursing
Tel: 0141-4960352

I looked at the date, it was two days old. She must have written it five fuckin' minutes after the shit had hit the fan. To say I was shocked about receiving the letter was putting it mildly. I never expected this. I thought the ball would be in my court until I decided to speak to them. Now I began to realise just how serious this was. I knew I really needed to get some advice from someone who knew how this all worked.

Although I had dismissed it earlier, I now thought my best move would be to go and see the Union rep. I ditched my Colours, put on a jumper then began to make my way to his ward.

Just as I approached the admin block, I saw Mrs. Boardman at her office window, she was gesturing for me to go in. I wasn't sure if I should but thought I'd better as she looked a bit agitated. Before I entered, I decided that if anyone else was with her, I wouldn't say anything, I would just make my excuses and leave.

I turned the corner, moving towards her office, and saw her standing at the door. She was gesturing for me to hurry up, which I did. When I entered, I noticed her checking both ends of the corridor before closing the door.

"Sit down, Ochil, and don't say a word. We don't really have long. I'm sure you know that I shouldn't be speaking to you right now, but I want to share something with you. The patient you had the altercation with has now been transferred back to the State Hospital - this is the sixth incident in as many weeks where he's been involved in assaults on members of staff.

"You really need to have Union backing for your case, so I hope you don't mind, I've spoken to Billy on your behalf and he's agreed to help you put your case forward."

317

She then took my hands in hers, gave them a bit of a squeeze and told me everything would be fine.

"Ochil, don't look so worried. it'll work out, you'll see! With a history like his, I'm pretty confident nothing will come of it."

I wanted to ask her how she could be so confident, but she lifted her finger to her mouth suggesting I say nothing. I told her I needed to talk to her about the letter I was given and handed it to her. She smiled and handed it back to me.

"I know about the letter, Ochil. It's so she can make an appointment to see you and explain the process. Don't call her until you've spoken to Billy."

She then went to the door, opened it and checked there was no one in the corridor before telling me to leave. Before I left, I thanked her for her help and then we exchanged smiles and nods. I went straight into Billy's ward, made my way to his office and knocked on his door.

"Come in," he shouted.

When I opened the door, he pointed to one of the chairs and said,

"Sit."

Before I got a chance to say anything he spoke again,

"I don't have much time to discuss the shit you're in just now, but I want to go over a few things with you. We'll need half an hour or so to look at it. I finish at 4 p.m. today. What if I meet you at the pub around 5 p.m., is that okay for you?"

"Yes, that's great, thanks," I agreed.

"Okay, I'll see you then," he told me as he stood up.

I held out my hand and thanked him for his help. As he shook, he said,

"Don't thank me yet. Wait until we've got you cleared."

I left the ward and made my way back to the nurses' home. I felt so relieved that I had someone in my corner. I wasn't counting my chickens or anything, but at least now I had a bit of hope.

The walk back to the nurses' home was so much better than the walk I'd made to the ward, that's for sure. I felt much more relieved now. I couldn't begin to describe how great it made me feel. As usual, I took it to the extreme. I was now really confident that it wouldn't even go as far as the police. I thought that I may even keep my job, although I wasn't sure if I really wanted it after my disastrous first day?

I entered the hall and noticed the warden coming out of her office. As she locked the door, I knew she was leaving for the day, so I held the front door open for her. As she walked towards me, I said,

"Good afternoon, Warden," offering her a smile, "I hope you have a wonderful evening."

She never said a word to me, but did give me a really strange look, which made me laugh.

"See you tomorrow!" I told her as I closed the door.

All of a sudden, I had a spring in my step and skipped up the stairs two at a time. I then made my way along the corridor into my room and closed the door.

I looked at the clock and saw it was ten-to-four. I just had enough time to grab a shower and make my way to the pub. I decided to have a smoke first, so I opened the window, sat on the chair and lit up. I began thinking about the last three or four days and wondered, yet again, how it was possible for so many things to happen to one person in such a short space of time?

I was just sitting kind of daydreaming and I heard a knock at the door. When I opened it, I was really surprised to see who it was.

"Mrs. Boardman, please come in," I told her as she hurried past me.

I closed the door behind her then asked her if she was alright.

"I'm fine, Ochil. What about you? Did you manage to see Billy?" she asked.

"Yes. We spoke earlier, but he didn't have time to talk at length about it, so I'm meeting him in the pub at five o'clock."

She sat down on the bed and let out a huge sigh of relief, which confused me.

"Are you sure you're okay? You look a bit troubled, Mrs. Boardman?"

"Yes, honest, Ochil, I'm fine, thanks. I'm just stressing a bit about the situation you're in and the fact I put you straight into the acute admission ward. This whole sorry situation that you find yourself in, it's all down to me. I should never have put you in that position in the first place. It was a very foolish thing to do and I just came to apologise and let you know I'll do everything in my power to make sure nothing comes of the charges against you."

She then stood up, smoothed out her skirt with both hands, then walked towards the door. I was finding it hard to work out her logic. I was sure she'd placed lots of new-starts in that ward over the years. But then again, I bet none of them had blootered a patient on their first day.

"Hang on a minute, Mrs. Boardman," I told her, "You really need to stop beating yourself up about this. The whole thing is down to me. I hit him and I take the wrap, simple as that. You could've put me in any ward and the same thing could've happened. It wasn't about where I was put, it was more about me being a square peg in a round hole. I'm not cut out for this shit and I should never have applied for the job in the first place.

"Hopefully I can get off with this and clear my name after which I'll be resigning. I thought this job would've been a chance for me to make a change, but I realise now that I've been too fucked up for too long for that to happen."

She started to protest about my response, but I pulled her towards me and gave her a cuddle, telling her not to say any more. I thanked her for her concern and apologised for putting her under all this pressure.

I told her not to worry, that I'd be fine and that in her heart of hearts she knew it was for the best that I go. She kept trying to speak, but I wouldn't let her.

"Look, Mrs. Boardman, I'm sorry, but I need to go. I've got Billy to see at five," I reminded her, then ushered her out before she had a chance to say anything else.

I closed the door, got my towel and shit then gave myself a few minutes, until I reckoned she'd be gone, then headed for the showers.

When I opened the door, I was glad to see she was away. I had visions of her still standing outside waiting on me, wanting to repeat our earlier conversation.

I showered quickly then went back to my room to get changed. I decided to put my originals and my cut-off on. I thought 'What the fuck! I'm done with the hospital anyway'.

I looked at the clock and it was five-to-five. I knew it took a good fifteen minutes to walk to the pub, so I decided I'd take my bike. I picked up my helmet and made my way out. It was starting to feel a bit cold and I knew the winter weather was well on its way.

I kicked it into life and revved the arse out of it before riding off. I arrived at the pub two minutes later and found Billy standing at the bar. I ordered us both a beer. He suggested we grab a table so we could chat in private.

The pub was pretty empty, so we had our choice of seats. Billy pointed to the table which was furthest away from all the others and we made our way over to it. The minute we sat, he handed me a piece of paper and a pen asking, no, telling me to sign it.

"What's this for?" I asked him.

"It's you're Union membership, back dated to the day you started."

"How can you do that?" I asked him.

"Because, my old son, we have a witness who'll testify she saw you sign it when you were being shown around my ward."

I knew right away who the witness would be.

"Mrs Boardman, I take it."

"Exactly, and who better than a senior nursing officer as your witness!" he said, smiling away.

I signed it and handed it back to him. He checked it was right then put it back into his inside jacket pocket. I then lifted my letter out and handed it to him.

"What should I do about this?" I said, pointing to it.

He took a minute to read it then said,

"Just phone her and tell her you've received it. She'll ask you to make an appointment to see her and you then tell her you need to consult with your Union rep first and I'll take it from there," he told me handing it back. "Right, I need you to tell me exactly what happened, then we'll decide if it DID, got it?"

I nodded and laughed a bit then went through the story, telling him every detail I could remember. He was taking some notes as I spoke and I wasn't sure if he was listening at times, but I carried on anyway.

When I told him that was everything, he asked me to give him a minute. I picked up my glass, finished my beer then told him that I was going to the bar. He never even acknowledged me, he just kept writing away on his notepad. I stood at the bar waiting to be served when the bar manager approached me. He sat on the stool next to me and asked if he could have a chat.

"Yep, go for it," I told him.

So he began, "I have a bit of a problem and I was hoping you and your mates could help me out."

"Okay. Tell me the problem and I'll tell you if we can help?"

He cleared his throat and had a bit of a cough before speaking,

"It's about a function that we have on next Saturday night. Just to give you a bit of background: There are two local football teams here, one is a Catholic team and the other a Protestant. I've always remained neutral, by the way, so I could get everybody's business. Someone booked the hall a good few weeks ago, but I've only found out recently who it was for. It's the Captain of one of the teams as he's having his 'Stag Night'. I know he's in the Orange Lodge so all his pals from there will be invited too. I've now been told on the Q.T. that the other team are planning to be in here as well and that they're going to set about the 'Stag's' group. The bouncers I

323

normally use have told me they'll not be working it because they live locally and don't want to take sides.

"I was hoping your guys would do it for me - just name your price and it's yours. I really can't afford to pay a lot, but whatever it costs, I'll give you - it's bound to be much less than if they smash up my pub."

"Yes, we can do that. You'll need to let me think about the cost, though. One condition, though," I told him, "If we do this, we get the gig every week."

"Perfect. I was hoping you would say that."

The barmaid then placed the drinks in front of me and asked for the money. The Bar manager told her that all my drinks were free from now on.

"I'll come and see you in the next couple of days and sort out the arrangements, okay?" I said as I picked up my drinks.

"Thanks very much, I really appreciate it. I'm on every day, right up 'til next Saturday. So anytime that suits you, is good for me," he told me.

I went back to the table and noticed Billy had stopped scribbling and was now watching me. I put the glasses down and he said to me,

"What did that little fuckwit want?"

"Nothing much," I told him "He just had a bit of business for me."

The minute I said it, I burst out laughing. There I was, saying it myself! Even though it used to frustrate the hell out of me when that was the reply I'd get if I asked what was going on.

"Right, back to the matter in hand, tomorrow, I'll speak to Marge McTear, find out when your hearing's going to be. I'll try and suss out what she's thinking about in terms of disciplinary action and we'll take it from there."

"Will she tell you what my punishment is likely to be if I'm found guilty?" I asked.

"Shug, you ARE guilty - that's not in question here. The evidence against you is overwhelming. We're not going in to argue that you're innocent. We're arguing mitigating circumstances and extreme provocation."

"So what the fuck does that mean in layman's terms?"

"What that means, Shug, is that yes, you did do what they said, but it wasn't pre-meditated or with malicious intent. This is how we'll play it: I'll tell the panel you'd just started. You had no idea what to expect. You saw him attack another nurse before attempting to strangle you.

"You had no idea about restraint techniques, and you feared for your life. I'll drag up the patient's recent history of violence and the fact that he had to be returned to the State Hospital due to the severity of his underlying condition. How does that sound?" he asked.

I told him I thought it was excellent and that I was feeling much less worried about it now that we'd met and spoken about it. He said he was glad and that it was my round so I made my way back to the bar. We spent another hour or so chatting, and I got to know a fair bit about him. It sounded like he had the management in his back pocket and that in itself filled me with a fair bit of confidence.

Billy then said that he had to go, and I thanked him for what he was doing for me. He smiled, shook my hand and said he'd be in touch in the next couple of days. I sat back down and looked out the window. It was pouring with rain so I decided I would stay put and have a bite to eat - in the hope that it would go off.

325

I went to the bar, ordered some food and another pint then went back to the table. I started thinking about our conversation and I was definitely feeling much better about my whole situation. I was also well chuffed about picking up a bit of work for us in the pub. I ate my meal, had another drink then headed back up the road.

It was still a bit wet, but I guessed it wasn't going to get any better.

When I got back, there was no-one about and I began to wonder if everyone was avoiding me? It seemed a bit strange that I'd walked about the hospital, was in and out the nurses' home three times and in the pub for ages and never saw a single soul I knew.

I got back into my room and dismissed the idea as me getting paranoid again. I removed my jacket and boots then lay down on my bed. I don't know if I was just tired or totally drained, but I conked out and never stirred until 8 a.m. the following morning.

I went down to the dining room, grabbed myself a cup of tea and couple of rolls and took them back to my room. It was another bleak day with the rain now being joined by a strong wind. I'd thought about heading back down to see the guys but decided to wait and see if the weather improved.

I munched my rolls, lit up a smoke and spent the next half hour cuddling my tea and staring out the window at nothing in particular. I picked up the letter and read it again. I wasn't sure if I should call Marge McTear about it or if I should just go to her office? I decided to take Billy's advice and call her. I didn't want to walk along in the pissing rain to be told to come back later. I went down to the payphone and rang the number on the letter. A secretary answered.

"Mrs McTear's office, how can I be of assistance?"

"Can I speak to Mrs McTear please?" I asked her.

"Who's calling?"

"Tell her it's Ochil Kinnaird."

"Will she know what it's in connection with?" she asked.

"Yes. Tell her it's about the letter she sent me."

"One moment, sir, I'll put you through," she told me, before putting me on hold.

Next thing, it's her on the line.

"Ochil, this is Marge McTear here. I was hoping we could meet at your earliest convenience. Are you free later today?" she wanted to know.

"Eh, yes, I am," I told her, "Do I need to bring my Union rep with me?"

There seemed to be a bit of a long silence before she answered, I guess she thought I'd be going on my own.

"Only if you feel it necessary," she told me.

"Okay, I'll contact him and get back to you," I said, before putting the phone down.

I then phoned Billy and told him the script.

"Right, I'll take it from here, Shug. I'll see if I can put her off for a couple of days. Phone me back in an hour and I'll let you know when we're meeting."

"Okay, will do," I said before hanging up.

I decided to head into the dining room and grab another cup of tea. I met a few people on the way, but no-one I really knew that well. I sat at the window and watched as the rain battered off it. I was miles away when someone put their arms around me and kissed me on the cheek. I looked around and saw it was Elsie. I stood up and gave her a hug.

"Mind if I join you, Shug?" she asked.

"Of course not, I'd be delighted …" I told her, pointing to the chair opposite me.

I thought it would be refreshing to get some conversation that didn't involve all my fuckin' woes.

"So how've you been, Elsie?" I asked her.

"Forget about me, Shug! What's been going on with you? The whole hospital's talking about it!"

Fuck! It hadn't even crossed my mind that anyone else would know about it or even care. I should have known you couldn't keep something like this quiet.

"Okay, Elsie. You tell me what you've heard, and I'll let you know if it's right," I suggested.

"Well! Rumour has it that you attacked a patient and beat the living shit out of him because he threw his dinner at you and he is now in a critical condition at the Royal. Apparently, you were taken to jail and are now out on bail waiting to go to court."

Fuck! I burst out laughing. I couldn't believe what she'd told me. Instead of laughing too, she went all serious on me.

"Shug! You really shouldn't be sitting here laughing. You're in real trouble, don't you need to get a lawyer or something?"

"Elsie, Elsie, Elsie. What a lot of fuckin' shite you've been fed, hen. There's hardly a grain of truth in the whole fuckin' story. I can't believe how quickly a story can get out here and how it's distorted every time it's passed on."

I then told her the real story and she actually seemed disappointed.

"Sorry it's not as dramatic as your version, Elsie, but it is the truth."

"Shug, I don't mean to be disappointed, eh, what I actually mean is I'm so glad my version is rubbish. I was really worried about you. I thought you'd be going to jail or something. It's not disappointment you see on my face, it's relief," she said, as she leaned over the table and squeezed my hands.

We chatted for a bit about her and what she was up to and she told me all about her new boyfriend.

After a good half hour or so of listening, I excused myself, telling her I needed to go to the phone.

"I'm back-shift, I should get going too," she told me, "Come on, Shug, you can walk me to the door."

She put her arm through mine and continued to talk all the way up the corridor.

I was never so relieved to say goodbye to someone as I was with Elsie at that point. I loved her to bits, but I thought my ears were going to bleed - such was the verbal battering she gave them.

I waved her away then picked up the phone. I got straight through to Billy and he told me we wouldn't be meeting with Mrs. McTear until Monday afternoon which gave me three and a half days. I went back to my room and wondered what I should do? I guessed I really should've gone back down the road to see what was happening there. However, I also knew Julie was supposed to be coming back the following day. Well, that was according to Lisa anyway.

I thought I would rather catch up with her first and see if she was talking to me. I decided to stick a note under Lisa's door for her to give me a knock. Hopefully, she could tell me if Julie was moving back this weekend or not? If she told me Julie wasn't coming, then I'd spend the night in my room and head back down the road in the morning.

I scribbled the note to Lisa and shoved it under her door. As I walked back to my room, I heard her calling on me. It never even dawned on me to check if she was in – I'd just assumed she wasn't.

She was standing with my note in her hand, waving for me to go to her. I walked back towards her room. When I went in, I got the shock of my life.

Julie was sitting on the bed. When she saw me she smiled - I was lost for words seeing her sitting there as it was the last thing I was expecting. I smiled back and asked her how she was. She never said a thing, just stood up and gave me a long hug, squeezing really tightly.

I can't tell you how much I needed that - it was such a long time since we'd cuddled. It brought out all the feelings that I'd been trying so hard to keep suppressed. I felt like I was going to cry. For some reason, I'd turned into an emotional wreck.

Lisa then interrupted our moment saying,

"Right, you two, that's enough. Any longer and you'll need to get a room!"

When we parted, I could see Julie had tears in her eyes as well. We tried to apologise to each other at the same time, which made us both smile. We then asked each other how we were doing, again at the same time, then both burst out laughing again.

Julie sat back down on the bed and I sat on the chair. Lisa grabbed three bottles of beer from her fridge, handed us one each, then sat on the bed beside Julie. I never took my eyes off Julie and she was the same with me - we were transfixed on each other.

Lisa then let rip.

"For fuck's sake, will you two snap out of it or I'll need to send you both to your own rooms!"

We then broke our gaze and I asked her how she was feeling? She told me she was good and felt like she was almost back to her old self.

For the next hour or so the three of us caught up with what we'd been up to. The conversation mainly focused on me and the incident with the patient.

Every time I changed the conversation, it somehow managed to roll straight back to me. I asked Julie about Rooster and her? She told me she was seeing him again, but that they were taking things a day at a time. I, of course, thought that meant they weren't serious, and it gave me a bit of hope. I wondered if that meant there was still a chance for us? Then she dropped the bombshell.

Lisa asked her if Rooster was coming up to see her? Julie told her that she'd fobbed him off until next weekend to give her time to get sorted with work.

"Do you think it'll work this time around, Julie?" Lisa asked her.

Then she said it,

"I don't know, Lisa. But I'll tell you this … if it doesn't, I'll never have another boyfriend as long as I live."

Fuck! That was like a severe boot in the nuts. I nearly burst out crying. How I managed to hold it together was nobody's business.

"That's a bit extreme, is it not?" Lisa suggested.

"It may sound like that to you, but Rooster is probably the most compatible partner I could have. So if it doesn't work with him then I've no interest in trying to make it work with anybody else."

Fuck! There it was right there, boot number two, right in the knackers. That was enough for me. I finished my drink, made my excuses, gave them both a cuddle then went back to my room. I closed the door and stood with my back to it, standing in the dark, staring at the window. I still couldn't understand why I felt so crushed about Julie.

Yes, I thought I loved her, but fuck! I thought I loved Angel, Fiona and Lorraine too! I wasn't long in getting over all of them, so why the fuck was I like this about Julie?

I thought the best thing to do was to forget all about it. I grabbed the bottle of vodka off the unit, skinned up a joint, opened the window and did my best to get smashed.

I must've been successful as when I opened my eyes, it was daylight. I squinted around to look at the clock - it was twenty-to-eleven.

I tried to orientate myself and get my bearings. I looked at the floor. The vodka bottle was more than half empty. There were three half-smoked spliffs in the ashtray and my head hurt like fuck. Knowing I'd achieved my goal didn't make me feel good in any way, shape or form.

I stood up and could feel myself wobbling a bit and had to take a minute before continuing. I decided the best thing was a shower, some food then another kip. 'Okay, Shug! That's the plan for today. Let's do it!' I told myself. I showered first. Surprisingly, I felt all the better for it. When I went back into my room, I noticed a note on the floor. I picked it up and opened it.

It was from Julie. She wanted to meet me for a chat and wondered if I'd be up for it? I instantly smiled and started thinking to myself that there may be a chance for me yet.

Could it be back on again I wondered to myself? If that was the case, I was determined that I wouldn't blow it by being over enthusiastic. I needed to be as casual and relaxed about it as I possibly could. I made a note on her bit of paper, saying I'd be happy to talk.

I quickly got dressed and went along and gave her door a knock. As I thought, there was no answer. I fired it under her door then went down to the dining room for some scran. I got some stuff and headed back. I thought it best to eat it in my room, in case I missed Julie. I finished eating and farted about the room for a bit until I was bored shitless. I stuck my jacket on and headed out. I thought I'd go for a couple of beers and get a carry-out on the way back. I hoped that Julie was maybe out with Lisa and that they'd hit the pub at some point.

When I got there, I had a quick scan of the room. I noticed a couple of people I knew, but no Julie. I ordered a couple of beers and made my way to a table where I could see who was coming in and out the door.

I sat down and began to drink. It was then that I realised I still had a bit of a hangover. I actually felt like I was chewing the beer on the way down AND it tasted like shit. However, by the time I worked my way through the first one, normal service was resumed.

I spotted the bar manager coming in. He too was scanning the room. The minute he saw I was there, he came right over to my table.

"I heard what happened with you at work. Will you still be able to come with your guys next Saturday?"

Fuck! Talk about self-interest! He couldn't give a fuck about me or my problems - all the cunt cared about was that we would still be able to look after his precious fuckin' pub!

Rather than get into it with him, I reassured him we'd be there. He then thanked me and asked if I had paid for my drinks, I told him I had. He then excused himself and went to have a chat with the bar staff.

Five minutes later, the barmaid who served me came over with two pints and apologised for taking my money.

I thanked her and told her not to worry about it. We agreed that he was a prick, which left her smiling all the way back to the bar. I'd been in the bar for a couple of hours and had spoken with a few people who worked in the hospital, but I was getting fed up with everybody asking me the same questions, so I decided to split.

When I got outside, it was chucking it down again, so it was 'quick march' all the way to the garage for the carry-out, then again all the way back to my room. When I got in, I had to strip-off as I was soaked through to the skin. I wrapped a towel around myself and went for a shower to see if I could get a bit of a heat back into my body. I got back to my room and noticed another note on the floor.

Fuck! I was out all of five minutes and typical, I'd missed her. I picked it up and it read:

Shug,
Can you please pop round to my room after 8 p.m. I don't want Lisa to know you're coming. She's heading home for a party tonight and is getting picked up at 7:30 p.m. She thinks if we get together alone then something will happen. I've told her that's nonsense, but she didn't believe me anyway.
Hopefully, see you tonight,
Julie

I didn't know what to think? On the one hand she wanted to be with me, and on the other, she thought it 'nonsense that something could happen'. I felt like she was sending a mixed message and had no idea what to do about it. I looked at the clock. I had a couple of hours before I went around there. I lifted my jeans off the radiator, stuck them back on, put on a clean t-shirt then sat down and opened a beer. I started to think about my relationship with Rooster and how long we'd been friends. I smiled, thinking about all the scrapes we'd got ourselves into and the way we always had each other's back. I knew how much he wanted the relationship to work and what he was prepared to do to make sure of it.

I started to feel really bad about having the feelings I had for Julie but didn't know how I could make them go away.

I began to think about the stuff we'd done behind his back and it made me feel physically sick. That was when I decided that nothing else was ever going to happen with me and Julie. I looked at the clock and thought 'Fuck it!', it was only ten-past-seven, but I decided to go to her room anyway.

Chapter 26

I grabbed my jacket, as it had my smokes in it, lifted some beers then went and knocked on her door. Lisa opened it and asked me what I was doing? I walked past her, told her it was none of her fuckin' business and that she could relax as there was no way anything else was ever going to happen between me and Julie.

She looked straight at me for a bit then said,

"You know what, Shug? I believe you, I really do."

She then gave me a kiss on the cheek and said her goodbyes.

When she got to the door, she turned around and said,

"Oh, Julie, I'm not sure if I'll be back tonight. Depends if I get a better offer or not, if you know what I mean," then left.

We both smiled as we listened to her laughing all the way along the corridor.

I offered Julie a can, took one myself then sat on the bed beside her. I made sure I was far enough away from her that we weren't touching. I really didn't want to tempt fate.

"Did you mean that, Shug?" she asked.

"Mean what?"

"You know! What you said about nothing going to happen between us!"

"Yep, I did, Julie. As much as I'd like something to happen, I won't go behind Rooster's back again. I feel bad enough about everything that's happened, and he really does love you. I hope you know that."

"I do, Shug, and I'm glad to hear you say that. I really want to give this the best shot I can," she told me, before leaning over and giving me a cuddle.

I gave her a little hug as well and it was really strange. For the first time it felt like I was cuddling a sister or a friend, not somebody I was looking to poke. I smiled and raised my can high up in the air,

"To Rooster, to Julie and their future together," I exclaimed.

Julie followed suit with her can then we both burst out laughing.

We spent the next couple of hours drinking, laughing and telling each other 'Rooster stories'. Julie started closing her eyes so I suggested it was time for me to split, but Julie wouldn't have any of it. She stood up, took her housecoat off, got under the covers then pleaded with me,

"Please, Shug, please cuddle me until I go to sleep, then you can go."

I felt a bit nervous doing it, but she went on and on, so I agreed.

"Okay, Julie. You win," I told her, "But just until you go to sleep, then I'm off," I told her.

I took off my t-shirt, got into bed and cuddled in. We were both sleeping when we heard the door being banged. I looked at Julie and raised my finger to my mouth in the hope she'd be quiet.

She nodded to me to let me know she understood so I got up, put my t-shirt back on and went to the door, thinking it was Lisa back. Just before I opened it, it was rapped again. This time, however, it was accompanied by a voice we both recognised straight away.

"Julie! Open the fuckin' door, I need to talk to you!"

'Shit' I thought to myself, it was Rooster and he sounded well pissed.

"Julie! Open the fuckin' door, I know you're in there. I've just been to Shug's room and he's not there. I know neither of you are working and his bike is outside so I'm guessing he's in there with you. For fuck's sake, Julie, just open the fuckin' door before I boot the fucker in."

I wasn't sure what the fuck to do? The last thing I wanted was him to catch us together - especially as nothing was going on.

Julie jumped up and was putting her housecoat back on and trying to sort her hair. I went to the window and opened it to see if there was a way I could climb out without him seeing me, but there was no chance of doing it without risking my neck.

I sat back on the bed, shrugged my shoulders and suggested she let him in. Julie was now organised and made her way to the door. I moved onto the chair thinking it would look much better than me sitting on her bed.

Julie was just a moment too late in getting to it. She had almost touched the handle as Rooster booted the door in. Julie jumped back and let out a scream.

I never moved off the chair. I just turned my head towards him and said, sarcastically,

"Hello, Rooster, nice to see you too! Why don't you just boot the fuckin' door in instead of waiting for someone to open it?"

As you can imagine my sarcasm didn't go down to well with him.

"Shug, shut the fuck up!" he roared at me at which point, I just held my hands up and shrugged.

Someone came to the door to see what was up. Rooster looked at her and told her 'To get tae fuck!' which she did pretty sharpish. He then turned his attention to Julie.

"Okay, Julie, I'm only going to ask you once: Are you fucking him?"

I stood up at that point, to try and interrupt him. But, without taking his eyes off Julie, he pointed in my direction and said,

"Shug, shut the fuck up! Sit on your fuckin' arse and don't say another fuckin' word! I'll get to you in a minute!"

I just thought 'Fuck it, he's going to go off his chump anyway' so I just sat back down, lit up a smoke and continued listening to him have a go at Julie.

"Well, Julie? I'm waiting …"

"Oh, you're waiting. Well, bully for you! Fuck you, Rooster! I don't believe you! You've just kicked my fuckin' door in! What the fuck are you all about? You certainly know how to make a girl feel loved, that's for sure! At least I know now how much you trust me. You know what, Rooster? I'm done. I've had enough. Why don't you just fuck off right now and never come back!"

I couldn't believe what I'd just heard. Julie didn't half let rip at him and it seemed like he'd frozen. He just stared at her for what seemed like an age, without doing or saying anything. Julie then pushed him backwards towards the door. Rooster grabbed hold of her as if to cuddle her, but she wriggled until she was free of him.

As she took a step back and repeated what she'd told him earlier, he responded by asking her again if she was shagging me. She told him that she wasn't, but even if she was, it was none of his concern.

"For your information, Shug stayed here last night. We had a few beers and we were both pretty drunk. We ended up sleeping together on top of my bed, but we were both fully clothed.

339

"I'll tell you what! If I knew you were going to come here all guns blazing, I would have shagged him just to piss you off! I want you to leave now before someone calls the police."

Rooster was still looking a bit stunned. I couldn't blame him after what she'd told him. I decided it was time I intervened and got Rooster away - just in case someone had called the cops.

I stood up, put my hand on his shoulder and said,

"C'mon, man, we need to split, the last thing either of us needs is to get lifted again."

He then turned his attention to me, looking like he was staring right through me. He lifted my arm from his shoulder and asked me if I'd been shagging Julie?

"Fuck's sake, Rooster! You know I wouldn't do that to you, man. We're Brothers, for fuck's sake." "Look, nothing happened last night, that's a promise. It's how she told you it was. We had a few drinks then we crashed out and that was it. Fuck's sake, man, we were sleeping on top of the covers and we were both fully clothed."

He moved a bit closer to me, looking straight into my eyes he said,

"You better not be lying to me, Shug! If I find out you are - I'll kill the fuckin' pair o'yies!"

Before I could reply, Julie stood between us and told Rooster he should go. Rooster wasn't for moving. I got hold of Julie, asked her to be quiet then sort of pushed her to the side of us. I put my arm around Rooster and tried to get him to come out with me, but he told me to let him go or he would burst me.

By this time, I'd had enough, and I let him have it with both barrels.

"You know what, Rooster? I'm actually trying to do you a fuckin' favour here, but you're acting like a fuckin' dick, so you can please yourself what you do. But see me, I'm off."

I walked past him, picked up my jacket and headed towards the doorway. Fuck knows why, but he grabbed my hair from behind and pushed me on the floor.

"You're going nowhere until I get some fuckin' answers …" he said, leaning over me, pointing his finger right in my face.

"You've had all the fuckin' answers you're getting. We've told you everything. I can't help it if you're fuckin' paranoid, that's your shit and you need to deal with it," I roared at him, as I made my way back up onto my feet.

"I'm leaving now, Rooster, so either get out of my fuckin' way or I'll fuckin' move you!" I told him.

"Well, that's just what you'll need to fuckin' do then," he said, squaring up to me.

All I could think was 'Fuck! Here we go again!'. The last thing I wanted to do was have yet another scrap with him, so I just said,

"Aye, whatever, Rooster," then went to walk out.

True to his word, he grabbed me and started laying into me. Julie tried to come between us, screaming for us to stop. By the time she did that, we'd smacked each other a few times and were getting right into it.

One of my punches accidentally caught Julie a bit on the side of her face and she looked like she was going to fall. I got hold of her to try and lay her down.

Stupidly, I thought that Rooster would stop until I had Julie out of harm's way - how wrong was I! He continued to lay into me and I'm sure he even caught Julie with one as well.

We both fell to the ground. I landed on the broken door and Julie landed partly on me and partly on my jacket. Rooster then bent down to lift Julie away so he could get at me. I managed to grab him by the hair and pull him down on top of us.

I caught him on the side of the face with a punch which didn't seem to affect him in any way. Then, all of a sudden, my lights went out. I wasn't sure if he'd punched, kneed or head butted me, but I was out cold.

Next thing I know, I'm being lifted off the floor in handcuffs by a couple of policemen. I looked around and saw Julie, with a cover around her, being comforted by a policewoman.

Rooster was lying motionless on the floor and a couple of ambulancemen were at his side. He was covered in blood and when I looked at myself, I realised I was the same

As I began to get my bearings a bit, I asked the cops what the fuck was going on and why the fuck was I handcuffed? Only to be told that I'd stabbed Rooster and that he was in a bad way.

As they marched me out, I protested my innocence, but they never said another word. All the doors were open along the corridor and most of the people were watching me being hauled away.

As I got close to them, they all lowered their heads or looked away. I had considered most of them to be friends, but seeing them now, behaving like this, it made me realise that they were only work colleagues.

As I was dragged along the corridor and down the stairs, I continued to protest my innocence, but my pleas fell on deaf ears. I was quickly horsed into the back of the police van.

The officers sat in the back of the van with me, one of them gave the bulkhead a slap and I was whisked away. I tried to talk to the officers and get them to tell me what had happened?

342

Neither of them said a word for the whole journey. I sat with my eyes closed and tried to replay the events of the night. Every time I did it, I always stopped at the same bit – I'd grabbed Rooster, pulled him down, then - bang - nothing after that until I was being huckled by the cops.

We arrived at the station and I was put straight into a cell. They made me take my belt and boots off and empty my pockets. I had carried a knife for a long time, and I had a pocket inside my cut-off where I kept it. It was only when I went to lift it out that I realised it was missing. I asked the police if one of them had taken it off me already but was told it was recovered from the scene and that it was now evidence.

I had no idea what they were on about so I asked again and was told that Rooster had been stabbed in the chest with my knife and that I'd be interviewed about it in due course. They lifted my stuff then left.

As one of the officers was locking the cell door, I asked him if Julie had been hurt? He told me she also had a stab wound, but that it was only superficial. I tried to ask him another couple of questions, but he just ignored me, turned the key in the cell door, pulled it out then disappeared.

Chapter 27

I couldn't believe it! Both Rooster and Julie stabbed with my knife and me without any clue as to how it happened and no-one telling me how either of them were doing!

I did my best to rack my brains for some answers, but continually came up with zilch. I'd been in the cell for about an hour when two officers and a plain clothes dude came in. I was told to stand up, which I did. They handcuffed me again and marched me out and into an interview room.

One of the officers pulled out a chair and gestured for me to sit, which I did. Both the officers stood behind me and the guy in the plain clothes sat opposite me.

He told me he'd be recording the interview and that he'd be joined by one of his colleagues before we started. I asked him if he could tell me how Rooster and Julie were doing?

All he said was that they were both taken to hospital and that his colleague was on his way back and he'd maybe be able to update me when he arrived.

Just as he'd finished telling me this, another plain clothes dude opened the door and asked the guy to step outside. They were outside for about ten minutes before finally coming back in.

They both sat down, and the guy who'd been in earlier told me he was going to start the interview. He asked me if I wanted a lawyer before we started. I asked him why he thought I needed a lawyer for being involved in a bit of a stupid scrap?

He told me that it was because I was going to be charged with murder - the murder of Rooster!

I genuinely thought he was taking the piss and trying to scare me. I burst out laughing and said,

"Aye, guid yin, very fuckin' funny. Why don't you pull the other one, it plays jingle bells." then continued to laugh away to myself.

The other guy then told me to shut the fuck up and listen to him very carefully which I did. He then began,

> *'Ochil Kinnaird, I am charging you with the murder of William Foster. You do not have to say anything, but it may harm your defence if you do not mention when questioned something which you later rely on in court. Anything you do say may be given in evidence. You have the right to legal representation, if you cannot afford a lawyer then one will be provided for you, do you understand?'*

At that point, I was taking nothing else in, nothing at all. All I could hear was blah, blah, blah. Except the words, 'Ochil Kinnaird, you are charged with the murder of William Foster', I just couldn't believe they were saying that to me.

One of the officers behind me gave me a bit of a dunt which brought me back from my thoughts.

"Do you understand your rights?" he asked me.

I just nodded.

"Do you understand the charges?"

Again, I nodded.

"Do you have your own lawyer, or do you require us to provide you with one?"

Again, I just nodded, then they got up, told me they would contact a lawyer then left, telling the uniformed officers to take me back to the cells.

They removed my handcuffs and dumped me back in the cell without a word being spoken. I lay down on the bed and tried to comprehend what had just happened. All I could think was how is it possible that Rooster was dead and how could I have killed him when I was knocked out?

The only thing I could come up with was - Julie. Julie must have done it, but that just seemed a bit too farfetched. 'She couldn't do something like that!' I thought to myself.

I must have dozed off. The next thing I know, two officers are in the cell, handcuffing me again and marching me back into the interview room.

There was a man already in there, sitting where I'd been earlier. He was an older man, grey haired with thick black round spectacles, the one's like the kids get from the National Health Service.

He had a reddish complexion and could've done with shedding a few pounds. The officer told me to sit down then left the room. The guy introduced himself as Mr. Ferry and told me he'd been appointed as my lawyer. He had a briefcase on the floor which was overflowing with paperwork and a couple of files lay on the table. He lifted a blank notepad and pulled a pen out from his inside jacket pocket.

He looked over his glasses at me and began speaking,

"You're Ochil Kinnaird. Is that correct?"

"Yes," was all I said before he started again.

"Well I think you've got yourself in a bit of a pickle here!" he announced.

"You don't fuckin' say," I replied angrily.

"No need to be aggressive, I'm just here to try and help you, my apologies if I've upset you," he said, which made me feel a bit guilty for having a go at him.

"I'm sorry too," I told him, "perhaps we could start again?" I suggested and thankfully he agreed.

"Okay. Here's what I know so far: You were found in a room with two others - covered in blood. You and the other male were both unconscious. He had blood pouring out of his chest and you have a knife in your hand. The other person, a girl, was conscious. She had been stabbed in the arm and was sitting sobbing in the corner of the room, almost delirious. Is there anything you can add to or discount from what I've just told you?" he asked.

I thought for a minute and again tried to replay everything in my mind. I just kept getting to the same bit over and over again then - bang - nothing.

I told him exactly what I'd remembered, right up to the point I was knocked out. As I spoke, he was furiously scribbling in his notepad. When I stopped talking, he lifted his head and said,

"Please don't tell me that's all you've got!"

"Afraid so, there's nothing else," I told him.

"Oh, that's not so good. What about the girl? Could she have done it, or at least seen what happened?" he asked.

I didn't really know what to say. Initially, I didn't think Julie would be capable of murder, but then I thought about it for a bit and wondered if maybe she would be?

My rationale behind it was, anyone who had the bottle to try and take their own life could quite easily take someone else's.

I then replied,

"I'm not sure, man, if I could talk to her then maybe I could suss her out, but I guess that's out of the question?"

"I'm sorry to tell you this, but you won't be seeing anyone until the trial. I can try to get you bail, but the chances of them agreeing to it are very very slim."

"What about you?" I asked him "Can't you speak to her? Get her to tell you what she remembers?"

"I won't be allowed anywhere near her until the preliminary hearing and neither will you. Look, I'm not sure how you feel about this, but you're going to have to give it some serious thought. The only way that I can prove your innocence is by implicating the girl. You need to understand that there were only three of you there and one's dead. It's either you or her."

I think that was the point where it really sunk in that Rooster was actually dead and that I was responsible for his murder.

The lawyer wanted to go to the preliminary hearing and tell the Judge that I was innocent, and Julie was the culprit, argue my case in front of a jury. I certainly didn't want to go to jail, but equally, I didn't want to see Julie getting sent down either. I asked him if there were any other options open to me and he said the only other option was to make a manslaughter plea, claiming self-defence.

I asked him what that entailed in terms of jail time. He explained, that if he could get the jury to agree the plea of manslaughter, I could get as little as four years. With good behaviour, I could be out in just over three. I then asked him what the sentence would be if I was found guilty of murder?

He told me he thought it would be between eight and twelve years. Fuck! Just hearing that sent a shiver right through my whole body. I knew there was no chance that Julie could do that amount of time inside, and to be honest, I didn't really think I could do it either.

He told me that I should sleep on it and that he would come back and see me the following day around 10 a.m. to get my decision. When he left, I was dumped back in my cell and I lay down on the bed thinking about what he'd said. 'Sleep on it. fuckin' sleep on it' I told myself. Like that was going to happen – I was never going to sleep with all this shit going on in my head! I just kept thinking 'If only I could get a chance to speak to Julie, just five minutes, then I could decide what I was going to do.'

Chapter 28

It was the longest night of my life. I never got a wink of sleep as I continually wrestled with the ramifications of any decision that I made.

I finally decided the best option for me was the four years, behave myself and out in three. It would allow me to avoid a 'head to head' with Julie and take away the worry of a long sentence.

Mr. Ferry was true to his word and arrived at ten. Again, I was put into the interview room with him. He cut straight to the chase.

"Well? Have you decided what you want to do then?" he said as he got a notepad from his briefcase.

"Yep, I think my best option would be to plead self-defence and hope for a shorter sentence. What do you think?"

"What I think isn't really important. It's what the Jury thinks that's important. If you're sure, then it's now my job to find a way to make it happen. I'll need to do a bit of digging over the next couple of days and see if I can pick up anything about what the girl has told the police."

I interrupted him,

"Can you please stop calling her 'the girl'? Her name is Julie," I asked him.

"Oh, okay. Sorry. Julie it is then," he told me, as he continued explaining what came next in terms of the court stuff.

He then asked for some background information about myself and also wanted to know what my relationship was with both Rooster and Julie.

As I started to give him a brief history of myself and explain the depth of the relationship I had with the two of them, I could see he was starting to look quite uncomfortable.

He then interrupted me and asked,

"Do you think that this Julie girl is going to testify that you committed the murder?"

I had to think about what he said for a minute before replying, then told him I had absolutely no idea what she would say.

"My best guess is that she'll tell the truth, whatever that may be. If I did kill him, I'm pretty sure she will say so in court."

He then lifted his notepad and put it back in his briefcase. He stuck his pen in his pocket, stood up and as he passed me, he whispered that he was going to find out who Julie's lawyer was and see what she's saying before he submitted my plea.

I was then dumped back in my cell and the officer who un-handcuffed me told me that a few people had been trying to get in to see me, but they were all told I wasn't allowed any visitors.

Later on that day, I was taken back into the interview room by the two detectives who told me that they just wanted to have an informal chat. They started off by telling me that Julie was currently unable to give a statement as she'd been hospitalised.

I asked them what was up? Why was she in hospital if her wounds were only superficial? They told me it was nothing to do with her physical state and that she was in a psychiatric ward because of her poor mental health.

When they told me, I wasn't really that surprised, considering her history. I think it would have been more of a shock if she hadn't needed some kind of treatment.

"How is she?" I asked the detective who was doing all the talking.

He just told me that she was under sedation and that he couldn't discuss it with me.

"Okay, so why am I here then?" I asked him.

"Well, we just want to run something by you to see if you can help us with it," he told me.

"Okay, what do you want?" I asked thinking they maybe wanted some background on us.

"Well, I think we could maybe do each other a favour here. I need some info you have and you need a reduced sentence. What about you telling me what you know and I speak to the prosecutor about some leniency?"

Straightaway, I knew that they'd want info on the Bats, but they could talk all fuckin' day if they liked and they'd still get fuck all from me. But, having nothing else to do, I was quite happy to play along and see what was on offer.

"Okay, come on then, let's hear it! What is it that I have that you want?" I asked him.

"Well, we know you're a 'Full Patch' Member of the Black Bats bike gang. We believe you're not only a Member, but an Officer. We're hoping you could help us out with an ongoing investigation. What we're hoping you could tell us about was a situation that took place a couple of weeks ago relating to the..."

I stopped him right there.

"Look, don't waste your breath. I won't be playing your stupid fuckin' games and I won't be telling you fuck all, so you can take that and ram it right up your shite pipe!"

They both then stood up - looking well peeved. One of them tutted at me and said,

"Oh, dear. What a fuckin' numpty you are!"

Then, without another word, they left and that was me dumped back in the cells again.

I don't know what had happened in the interview room as one minute I was going to play along, the next, when they mentioned the Bats, I freaked. I started to think that I really wasn't right in the head and that maybe I should be in beside Julie!

That night, the lawyer came back and told me we were going straight to trial and that it was starting the following day. He said he would meet me at the court and that he'd pursue the 'manslaughter / death by misadventure' plea, if that's what I wanted? I told him to do what the fuck he liked as I was past caring. I had lost the two most important people in the world to me and I was done. I had no fight left and no interest in pleading for a smaller sentence.

The next morning, they came in with a suit for me to wear. After I'd changed, I was put into a large van and driven to court. I was placed in the dock with an officer at either side of me. We all stood when the Judge came in and once he'd sat, we all followed suit. I saw a few of the guys in the gallery and some of them exchanged nods with me.

My trial started with an opening statement from the Crown Prosecutor. He described things from my past, painting a pretty horrendous picture of me as a person. He finished by declaring that I should be charged with murder and punished to the full extent of the law.

My lawyer then opened by challenging the Crown's statement. He told the court all about my sad and difficult upbringing, labouring the point about the loss of my mum. He also added in the details surrounding the tragic deaths of Malky and Max and how I'd had to cope with it all - he really laid it on thick for the Jury.

He then went on to talk about how Rooster and I had been very close friends for a number of years and explained that the killing was a complete accident.

He then told them that he'd make them realise that this was in no way a premeditated murder, but a tragic case of death by misadventure and sited a plea of self-defence on my behalf.

The trial lasted three days, with the lawyers batting stuff backwards and forwards, then the Judge spoke directly to the jury,

"Ladies and Gentlemen of the Jury, you have heard the facts as presented to you by Council and I urge you to take into consideration all the factors laid out in front of you before reaching your decision. You will now retire to the chambers and I will await your return."

With that, the speaker guy in court said, "All rise!" and everyone stood up until the Judge left the court room.

I was huckled out of the court by two officers then back downstairs, un-handcuffed and horsed back in the holding cell. I had no idea how long I was going to be there and was pretty pissed that no one was allowed to visit.

I'd prepared myself for a manslaughter charge and was pretty sure I was going to jail - it was just a matter of how long for. My lawyer was pretty confident that the Jury would accept my plea of self-defence.

He even thought I would have got away without any jail time if I hadn't been carrying a knife. He said I should prepare myself for a two to four years stretch which, with good behavior, could be halved.

I'd been in the holding cell for two days going off my nut before I was eventually called. I'd seen others come and go and no-one had appeared to have been

354

held as long as me. The policemen came and opened the cell, telling me the Judge was ready for me.

They handcuffed me again then led me back to the courtroom. When I entered, the jury was already there, and the gallery was packed. I saw some of the guys and, again, we exchanged nods. I saw Julie and her mother at the front of the public area, but she had her head bowed and never lifted it once.

I was ushered back into the dock then the speaker dude shouted,

"All rise for the right honourable Judge McCarroll, presiding over case 119: The Crown verses Kinnaird."

The Judge then entered. After he sat his fat fuckin' arse on his fucking throne, the dude then asked us all to be seated.

"Chairman of the Jury, please stand," the Judge ordered.

A guy at the very end of the front row stood up.

"Chairman of the Jury, have you reached a verdict?" the Judge asked.

"Yes, your honour, we have," he replied.

"Is your verdict unanimous?" he then asked him.

"Yes, your honour, it is."

He nodded to the dude that was doing the 'stand up and sit down' shit.

He went over to the Juror, took the piece of paper he had in his hand then gave it to the Judge. He looked at it, handed it back to him and watched as he returned it back to the Juror. The Judge then spoke to the Juror again.

"Do you find the defendant guilty or not guilty?"

"Guilty, your honour," he replied.

I thought I was going to burst out crying but managed to hold the tears back. The Judge then spoke to him again,

355

"Do you find the defendant guilty of murder or manslaughter?"

"Murder in the first degree, your honour."

Holy fuck! I nearly shat my pants! I couldn't believe what I'd just heard. I looked directly at my lawyer who looked back and shrugged his shoulders. He then looked away.

I had no idea why, but I started shaking uncontrollably. I could also feel the tears running down my cheeks. I lifted my head and looked at Julie trying to get a bit of eye contact, but again, she never lifted her head.

I was aware that there was now a fair bit of noise reverberating around the courtroom as everyone shared their opinions with each other. The Judge then slammed down his gavel. The minute he did it, the place fell silent.

He then prepared to deliver my sentence. He coughed a bit, cleared his throat, then began,

"I have considered the facts and the guilty verdict delivered by the jury. Ochil Kinnaird, I sentence you to twelve years for the murder of William Foster. You will not be eligible for parole until you have served nine years."

At that point, the noise level rose again. He then banged down his gavel again a couple of times and shouted 'silence' until there was no more sound. He then looked at me and said,

"Officers, take him down."

I couldn't believe it. All the way through the courtcase, my lawyer continually told me I'd get no more than four years. 'Four fuckin' years' he kept saying. 'Don't worry, Shug, four years is your max'.

Well, how wrong was he? Twelve fuckin' years. Nine before I could apply for parole!

As the officers lifted me, I felt like I was unable to walk. They almost had to support me all the way back to the holding cell. I was numb. I couldn't think of anything other than my sentence as they walked me back.

I kept repeating in my head over and over again: Twelve years! Twelve fucking years!

The officers opened the cell door, removed my handcuffs and motioned for me to enter, which I did. One of them locked the door and told me I'd be there until the end of court after which I'd be taken to the jail where I'd be serving my sentence.

I sat down on the bed, still numb, and thought back to the night of the incident.

I still couldn't believe it - Rooster dead! Me jailed! And all because of a stupid fuckin' fight over a half daft fuckin' lassie! I kept thinking if only she hadn't tried to break it up then Rooster would still be alive and I'd be free. I played it over and over again and knew in my heart of hearts that it was her that had stabbed him with my knife.

As I sat looking out of the very small window above the bed, I began to wonder if I should have grassed her up? Thinking back to the trial, she'd never looked at me once. Even when she was giving her evidence, she never afforded me any eye contact whatsoever.

Would I have reacted differently if I'd known Julie was going to put the blame on me? Perhaps. If I'd known I'd end up getting twelve years, would I have blamed her? Who knows? Maybe I would have! Anyway, it was all academic now.

What I did know was that for the next twelve years of my life, I'd be locked up with the death of my best friend on my conscience - every single fuckin' day.

This was not the first time I'd had to endure a feeling of great loss, but I guessed this time I'd have plenty time to think about it. I wondered, at that point, is this it? Is it really over? Does my life end here? Well, who knows! Only time will tell!

Perhaps, if I survive my sentence and get an early release, I might even write a book or two about it all…

Unfortunately, when doing my time, I 'racked up' another three years, over and above my original sentence, for committing a series of misdemeanours.

They also denied me parole on three separate occasions.

I ended up serving a total of 15 years in prison.

I was eventually released in August 2000 and I now live a solitary life at an undisclosed location in Scotland.

I continue to ride a bike, but I have no contact whatsoever with 'The Black Bats' - or any other motorcycle organisation.

Was I Guilty? I still have no idea…

The End

Printed in Great Britain
by Amazon

38887958R00202